The Conviction

Charity Mae

Contents

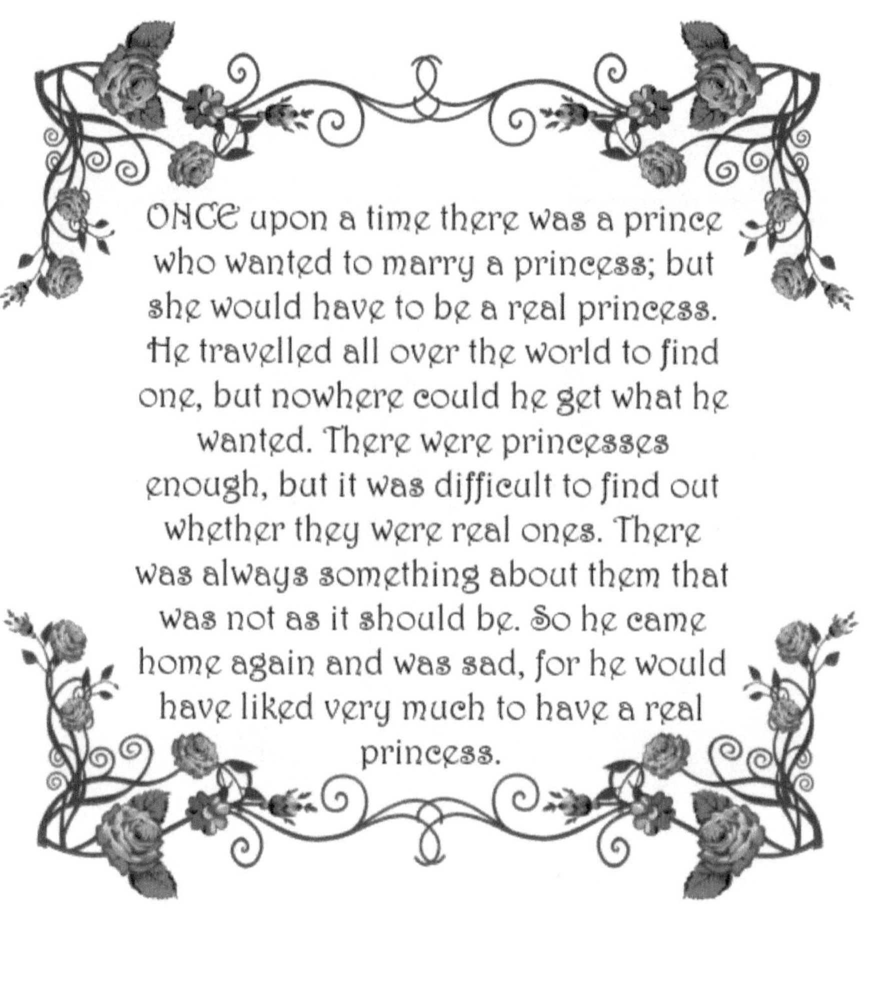

ONCE upon a time there was a prince who wanted to marry a princess; but she would have to be a real princess. He travelled all over the world to find one, but nowhere could he get what he wanted. There were princesses enough, but it was difficult to find out whether they were real ones. There was always something about them that was not as it should be. So he came home again and was sad, for he would have liked very much to have a real princess.

Map of Purerah

Chapter 1

My desires and direction in life have flipped completely upside down. My life now depends on winning a game I never wanted to play. It is still surreal that I've turned my back on all I'd believed in just a few short months to come to this point.

Black ocean waves crash on the cliffs just beyond my balcony as I bounce between pacing my room, falling into nightmare-filled sleep or sitting by the ledge, watching the storm. I've struggled with chronic insomnia since I was a child, but that has little to do with my inability to sleep tonight, not with all I have on my mind. Not to mention how late it was when Damian finally left me last night — or this morning — to try to sleep.

Last night changed everything. I didn't let the rebels in. I'd told my father, leader of the Custod rebellion, to get out. He'd listened but with a warning I'd see the dreaded truth of the prophecy. A prophecy that said if Prince Gavril married, our kingdom would fall. Something he'd neglected to tell me when he beguiled me into The Enthronement to be his spy, so he could break into the palace and assassinate the royal family.

Once, I agreed with him. The royals started this five-hundred-year war by over-taxing the people and never letting up, but after I'd met them, lived with them, seen their side, I have doubts. Doubts that led me to reject the leaders chosen by the three factions: Potentate, Loyalist, and Custod. I'd betrayed my Custod commission and family. But where would that leave me?

I await the guard coming to bring me in to be questioned by the royal family for last night's events. Could I prove my innocence without revealing my past and being tried for treason?

I jump as my bedroom door opens. My maids enter the room to get me ready. I was numb to the sunrise, not realizing that meant they'd come in soon. Vivian, my head maid, looks around and realizes I'm not in bed before my second maid, Flur, does. Flur's gray eyes are wide in worry as they dart about the room, searching for me; Vivian's dark eyes are calm. They scan the room and spot me without too much trouble.

Softly, Vivian taps Flur's arm to point me out. I force a smile for them as Flur gives me a gentle smile. Guilt settles into my stomach. My maids have been angels through everything. They don't deserve this. Even when my third maid, Ro, was kidnapped by rebels, Vivian and Flur stood by me and looked after me with as much care as ever. I could never repay them.

I wonder how much they have heard about last night as I slip off the balcony rail and walk back into my room. Do they know I was found armed in front of the royal family's safe room, or did they only hear that I'd fought the rebels instead of going into the Chosen Ladies' safe room as I should?

They don't let on their thoughts as my angelic maids help me get ready for the day. Flur is most gentle with me, giving me a sympathetic smile, brushing her light blonde hair from her face as she works. Vivian comforts me by exuding confidence, such a contrast to Flur. She works as if sure that I'm already queen. She looks confident too, her dark hair smoothed back without a hair out of place as always. To her, it's just another day at the palace.

I let them dress me, not questioning what they dress me in. My team is the best. Damian Lexus, my attendant, and these amazing women are the reason I've made it to the top twenty-five in the Enthronement. I'd not shine half so well without them.

I wince when they touch my right shoulder. Sage, the prince's Custod guard, held me a bit too tightly last night when he found me in the throne room. Vivian frowns angrily as Flur apologies, noticing the bruise.

My maids are just about finished when the door opens once more, and my attendant strides into the room.

"Good morning, my lady," he greets me with his formal tone. How does he not look tired? He'd been up late with me trying to calm me down before I tried to sleep, but he looks as perfect and put together as ever. His straight, black hair is pulled into a ponytail at the base of his neck and tied with a claret red ribbon that goes well with his matching suit jacket, black waistcoat and trousers, and dark cravat; all of which offset his emerald eyes. "You look beautiful." He smiles softly at me. Though he looks young, he feels more like my father with how he smiles at me in understanding and pride. "Are you ready, my lady?"

I swallow and nod, slipping into the shoes Vivian placed down for me, before finally finding my voice. "As I'm going to be."

Damian smiles and offers his arm like a proper gentleman. "I shall escort you if you like."

"Thank you." I could use his support, even if it feels like I am being led to the gallows.

The splendid halls of the palace feel too bright to me. Though it's early, the seashell white, sand gold, and Purerahian blue themes are naturally bright, like the beach that lies outside. It contrasts my dark mood painfully. I always thought the castle was dark and foreboding before I came. Instead, it's bright and light. But with where I might be going, it should be dark like a storm.

I numbly follow Damian's gentle guidance down the main staircase to the entrance hall. My heart tightens to see its splendor. The narrow hallway to the right, lined with meeting room doors and the main entrance, is mostly in shadow, but the grand glass dome that lights the room is as beautiful as ever, soaking in and reflecting the first rays of morning light. Damian leads me left, towards the oval center that holds the doors to the throne room, and via the grand staircases curving on either side, the ballroom.

But Damian does not take me to the throne room as I feared. He leads me to the left of this oval and to a door that's about halfway down its stunning curvature. This door doesn't lead to the throne room, but to a hall that goes across the length of the dome with a door on the other end, two on the right side, and three on the left.

Damian takes me to the first door and stops, releasing my arm. "I've been told they want to talk to you alone first, but I swear to you, Kascia, as I did the other night, I will do everything in my power to help you. Remember, you have done nothing wrong. I won't let them punish you for it," he says, trying to meet my eyes.

I nod, trying to play the brave princess, but inside, I'm struggling to hold it all together. Apart from lying about why I joined the Enthronement, I have done nothing wrong. I changed my mind and did my best to protect the royal family, even keeping the king's lung condition a secret when I accidentally found out. I just have to tell the truth yet avoid saying anything incriminating, like my father is the leader of the Custod rebellion or that I'd been engaged to the son of the Loyalist rebellion leader. Maybe this wasn't so simple.

"I just have to remember to be the princess they want." A true princess doesn't need more than the truth, so neither do I. I can prove a true princess and win this and not be beheaded, right?

Damian smiles at me. "Exactly." His smile gives me more confidence.

I take a deep breath and square my shoulders. "I'm ready." The authoritative tone I manage impresses even me.

Damian beams to hear it. "Best of luck, my lady." He opens the door for me. "Not that you need it."

I pull my shoulders back and step inside.

The queen's frantic pacing catches my eye first. She paces along the opposite wall from me. The room is a long rectangle with an oval table in the center. The short side on my left has a hearth while the other side looks to simply be paintings. In the middle of the room, the queen paces, elegant m even in her agitation. Her mane of royal coils bounces off her shoulders with volume I couldn't dream of having. The train of her dress follows her as she paces in a regal glide. The gold and green of her gown contrast her dark warm skin beautifully.

The king sits at the head of the oval in a chair just a step down from a throne. He is a stark contrast to his wife; relaxed, sitting cross-legged, brushing something off his knee as if this is just any other day. He's handsome in a very different way with a charming smile that makes his eyes crinkle at the corners; his gray hair that clings to the slightest hint of brown it once had.

In the far-right corner, Sage, the prince's personal Custod guard, leans on the wall, arms and ankles crossed. He would have blended into the shadows with his dark clothes and cloak, but his deep green eyes which study me with mistrust and his pale skin gives him away. I swallow as I glance at his wrists where I know the mark of his assassin class waits to attack me at any provocation.

Prince Gavril paces the short side of the room, but unlike his mother, his pace is not elegant or anxious. His is like that of a caged tiger: irritated, contained, and ready to spring to action. The corner of my mouth twitches as I watch him: a handsome combination of his parents, skin like chocolate, amber eyes like sunrise, warm smile like his father, but the grace of his mother; two opposites making a positive no one had expected.

I take all this in within a second of stepping into the room. The smell of dark wood and books fill my nose. Prince Gavril's eyes immediately snap to mine and lock as the door closes behind me. He turns away before I can read into his expression, returning to his pacing. Does he think I'm the traitor his guard believes me to be? Or does he still think I'm the girl who should win the Enthronement and be his queen?

My eyes go to the prince's chest. He's not as put together as he normally is. His parents are dressed perfectly as always, but the prince's waistcoat isn't fully buttoned, the loose sections rising up and down with his agitated breath. I've seen him on and over the edge of exasperation more times than I can count. If this is a formal interrogation as I feared, the prince is underdressed for it. His jacket is missing. His curly hair is an agitated mess. I discover why as he runs his fingers through it in an attempt to vent off his temper.

I look back at the king and queen, giving them a proper curtsy. "You called for me, your majesties?" I ask with the proper tone. My voice is oddly quieted in the carpet and decoration of the room. Out of the corner of my eye, I notice Gavril freeze.

“Yes, Lady Kascia,” the queen says, hurrying to her seat beside her husband and taking his hand. The familiar longing rises in me as I watch their tender exchange.

The king doesn’t tense like his wife. He leans back in his seat, squeezing her hand with assurance. Is that a good sign? The king is a bit of a goofball, making him hard to read in these situations. None of them are wearing their crowns; perhaps this means this can’t a full trial.

“Yes, now we’ve all had a chance to get our heads, we can discuss what happened last night like the gentlemen and ladies we are.” The king gives me his playful smile. I wish he’d be serious for a moment! My life hangs in the balance, and his lighthearted nature makes it hard for me to know where I stand.

“You explained after the last incident how you know how to fight. We accepted that your father trained you to defend yourself on the rough streets.” The king frowns at the reminder of the state of his kingdom. “But you can understand our concern when you’re found holding a blade at the safe room door during an attack.”

“I was startled,” I say meekly. “I was helping to drive the rebels away. I didn’t know where the safe room was, so when I heard the creak of the opening door, it frightened me. I meant you and your family no harm, I promise.” I’d also been just about ready to drop my sword in tears as I’d just thrown my family ring at my father and told him I never wanted to see it again.

“You expect us to believe that?” The queen asks, her voice more scared than accusatory.

“It is the truth,” I state simply. “Do you have any reason to doubt me?” I meet her brown eyes, so close to her son’s, but lacking the golden tones I have come to admire in his.

“Lady Kascia,” the queen chides, “you were standing with a sword drawn on our guard.” That was not true. I’d not pointed it at Sage more than a second. I was going to drop it long before he jumped at my throat to pin me to the wall. “Is that not suspect?”

I fight the hurt that rises at her tone. I know she’s a nervous woman, but I thought I’d earned more trust than that. “I did not draw on your guard,” I say evenly. “Is my silence not enough? I’ve not told your secret to anyone. If I was a rebel, would I keep that secret? You know my father is displeased with my position here. Does that all mean nothing now?”

“She has a point,” the king says to his wife. It sounds like they are playing out an interrupted argument.

“You knew about the attack.” Sage’s voice cuts across the royals’ in a low growl. He pushes himself off the wall and quickly starts to circle me like a predatory cat. "Yet you said nothing until they were inside.”

Honest, be honest. I take deep breaths, trying not to let him intimidate me. "I explained that to you last night. I didn't think they'd try when I said I'd not help them. You already suspected me. I feared if I said anything you'd have me thrown out."

"You said 'he' last night," Sage presses. "Who? You spoke like you knew who it was."

I bow my head. "I know what I said."

"What did you mean?" Sage asks slowly.

I can't confess he's my father. Sage will have me hanged before I could take a breath. I glance at his vambraces. If I even got that far.

"I have friends who sympathize with the rebel cause. They asked me to let them in. They didn't put names on the letter. I just meant 'he' in a general sense."

"But it was a team job. There were Loyalists and Custods in the palace last night. You only mentioned Custods."

"I… I know some who are Loyalist sympathizers too. You must understand. I'm a prima actress by trade. It's quite common for people in that art to be quite rebellious in nature. I know those two factions don't always get along, but they try. I suppose last night they felt the chance to get in was worth uniting over."

But how did they get in without help? They never had before, and I didn't help them. There had been other attacks that got in since the Enthronement started, and none had been me. Was another girl letting them in? I had little idea who, but that seems the only way it was possible.

"So, you know who but not names?" Sage's tone is full of disbelief. "You expect me to buy that?"

"I have guesses. I don't know for certain who. You must understand, most sympathize with one rebellion or another but take no action. How can I say someone I know is a sympathizer but don't know if they've actually done wrong? I'd be accusing with no evidence."

"But you said 'he'. I'm not asking for all of them. I'm asking who that 'he' is."

"Only a guess." I can't give them my father's name. But there is someone else I could give them. The other "he" who betrayed me: Jake, my ex-fiancé who until last night hadn't realized I'd abandoned him. Was that fair to a man who'd been so good to me and treated me like I was already his princess — other than telling me to do whatever it took to kill his enemy, including sleeping with him.

I am angry with Jake. He'd broken me with how he'd pushed me into this, but to give him up like this? Most of all, when I feel guilty that I couldn't even admit to his face how I hated him for what he'd done to me?

"If it's just one person, we'll find him innocent or guilty easily enough," Sage replies. "Or does this 'he' matter more to you?"

The prince and I meet eyes. We can't help it. We both know what Sage means. He's challenging me. Prince Gavril knows I have an ex at home I am trying to get over. It was how I explained why I was so unhappy when I came here. Sage suspects this 'he' is the boy I once loved.

Sage set me a test. Who matters more? I have to prove it: Jake or Gavril. Though I already made my choice, having come down to this moment makes it all the more real, and so much worse.

"Jake..." I whisper as my lip shakes; my eyes drop to the floor. It is like denouncing who I had been, denying everything about my life before I came here: the good, the bad, everything in that world, and who I'd been. I have to become the princess they want and reject the life I had before. In giving up Jake's name, I give up all I had been. If I am forced to go home now, I'll be worse than dead. The Loyalists will never forgive me for this no matter how my father tries to defend me. I gave up their choice for king.

"What?" Sage encourages me to speak up.

I shut my eyes against the flood of tears, glaring up at him. He heard me. I know he did. He wants the others to hear it from me. "Jake," I spit bitterly at him.

"Last name?"

I pause. "I-I don't know." The realization is a blow. I was going to marry him, and I don't know his last name? He knew mine, but I'd never asked his. What kind of relationship had we been in? I was sure it was real, loved him, loved how he loved me. I was sure all would be perfect. Did he even know my fake surname?

What would Jake say in reverse? An image of him being grilled just like I am by his father and fellow Loyalists comes to mind, Jake whispering my name as the traitor as I had his. His face filled with pain and shame like mine is. My best friend and love is now the enemy I had to betray, and he me. What had I let my life become?

"So, what were you doing in the throne room last night?" The queen cuts into my thoughts.

"I-I wanted to make up for not being wise enough to warn you of their possible attempt," I reply, rambling a little as I struggle to take in this new revelation.

"How were you armed if not by rebels?" The queen asks. Why is she so set on me being a danger? Sage relaxed at my confession; why wouldn't she?

As if on cue, Damian steps into the room with the calmness of a summer morning. I hadn't heard him open the door. It was like he morphed out of the shadows.

"That was my doing," he says as he strides forward, commanding the room like it's his stage. "I gave it to her," he says, meeting Sage's glare with a confident smile. "I hope I didn't come in too soon."

"Not at all, we were just about to send for you," the king waves it off. "Please go on."

"The guards were leading her to one of the safe rooms, but when I saw her desire to help, I had her lead me to the throne room to head off the main attack," Damian says.

"Why?" The queen's brows draw together as she looks at Damian, clearly unable to understand. I can't blame her for not taking him at face value. He is my attendant after all.

"Because one should never shirk help, no matter where it comes from," Damian says. "I knew she was capable, and she knew the minds of her former friends far better than I. I knew in that moment, forcing her to hide would only hinder our side and aid our enemy. Besides, nowhere does it say that a lady cannot fight. If there is a problem with that, I suggest you take it up with Cedrick." He gives the queen a knowing smile.

The queen sighs and nods. "Alright, I cannot fault you for having friends who aren't in perfect alignment when I suppose there are not many out there to be had." But fear is still clearly in her eyes. Is that woman ever not afraid? I suppose it can't be easy with her people wanting her head and losing so many children, but can't she have some faith?

Though it persuades the queen, Sage narrows his eyes at Damian. "That explains some things, but not everything. There is still something you're hiding."

I shake my head. "That's what happened."

"It is, indeed." Damian nods. "Though I'm afraid, I bear some fault in this matter." He bows his head in humility, and I can see a little hint of guilt in his eyes. "For you see, I knew about the attack as well." His head remains bowed as his eyes snap up to meet the king's.

"Yet you didn't mention it? Even to—" The king stops at a look from his wife.

I frown. To who?

"He knows. But I told no one else." Damian says, raising his head. "You know he doesn't like to get involved."

"I see. In that case, how does that make it your fault?" The king asks while the queen looks horrified he is so bold. *How was it bold?* I think I catch Gavril rolling his eyes, but it's hard to tell with his pacing.

"Well... to be bluntly honest, I noticed over a month ago she was getting letters that were upsetting her and asked her about them. She opened up to me then about her friends and what they were pressuring her to do. I offered her my support and encouragement to stand by her answer of telling them 'no'. I even offered advice on how to speak their language, so they'd be more willing to accept her answer. But I failed to advise her to give you warning. The thought didn't even occur to me that she or I should do something more about it. And for that, I am sorry to you and her." He nods to the king and queen then looks at me with his dark green eyes filled with his apology.

I force a small smile. I suppose that would have been good advice, even if he'd had to talk me into it. I still fear that if they learn who my father is, I'm as good as dead.

"That likely would have been a better course of action," the queen says, still frowning but not really at me or Damian, more like she is struggling to understand.

"Of course, your majesty." Damian nods to her in perfect politeness. "I apologize I didn't consider the matter with more severity. Rest assured it will not happen again. And if you have any doubts about my character, I suggest you take that up with my brother." He gives the royal couple a look if he is daring them to do it before his eyes shift and land on Sage.

Sage narrows his eyes a little but doesn't comment. He gives Damian a sharp, quick nod of understanding then he looks at the king and queen, bowing his head to them. "In the end, it is your choice to make," he says. "But someone has been letting the rebels in."

"I agree." Damian's eyes move back to the king and queen. "Someone has. Who that might be, I don't know enough to say. But trust me as I say this, Kascia is not a threat to you or anyone in this room. She has been honest in her account. I believe she not only cares deeply for your son but for you as well, Your Majesties. She does not want any of you to come to harm. I swear my life, power, and name upon it."

There's a pause in which I can't look at any of them, afraid of their reactions.

"Well said." The king nods, looking down as he thinks it over, making that face he does when he's thinking about something that confuses him with his brows coming together and his lips pursing just a little as if his whole face is pinching in the middle as he tries to think it out. "And it is true she's given us reason to be trusted. We have the others to interview." He looks up and nods at me. "I believe that wraps up our questioning, Lady Kascia," he smiles. "We are asking the girls to keep to their rooms until further notice. We'll have your meal brought up to you."

I curtsy, hiding my swallow as I did. "Thank you, Your Majesties."

"Thank you, Lady Kascia. For your time and loyalty," the king says, his voice comforting and warm.

I give a weak smile back. Both he and Gavril have this odd ability to soothe me. But it only helps a little when I feel guilty for not being honest about that being the only reason I came here. Though it's not why I stay.

As I turn to go, I meet eyes with Prince Gavril. His eyes are filled with pain, confusion, and longing. He's standing still as we meet eyes. Does he believe me? Does he think I am lying? Or is he unsure how he feels about Jake? Did he figure out he was the ex I came here to avoid? Is he angry for it?

"Sir Damian, if you wouldn't mind making sure she gets back to her room safely," the king asks.

Damian bows to him. "It would be my pleasure, your majesty." He offers me his arm. I take it with a weak smile, forcing my eyes away from the prince.

Chapter 2

"You did well," says Damian as he escorts me to my room.

"Thanks. Best I can do." But Damian knows the truth. He helped me sneak out once to try to get answers from my father only to have him turn me away, so I'd not get caught.

"And you did it beautifully. The king believes you," Damian says as he takes my arm and starts to lead me back. "And honestly. They already have reasons why they should trust you. After all, you've not told anyone about the king's condition."

"But that's not enough for Sage, and… it's not everything."

"Well, as we have already discussed, Sage was bred as an assassin," he reminds me as he fiddles with his cane, "and they learn very quickly you can't trust anything. Assassins are methodical and calculating. They take in everything, so they know how to take down their target. So, he is still taking in everything, and he can't let go of anything. In his line of work, letting your guard down or the slightest miscalculation could mean death. Or in this case, the death of his protectee, which I'm sure is one of the few friends he's been able to have. And he can't let that happen."

I swallow and look around. Seeing we're alone, I dare ask, "So what happens if he finds he's right?"

"That you came here under orders from your father?" Damian arches a brow. "Well, it depends on how willing he is to listen. And I imagine he'd listen more if he hears it from you, rather than finding out some other way. But if he is willing, best-case scenario… he understands you've had a change of heart and stops watching you so closely. He might even try to stop rebels like your father from trying to get to you. Worst-case scenario, he doesn't listen and exposes you to the royal family. They may or may not remove you from the Enthronement, but as you have committed no crime, I doubt they'll do worse than that."

My heart sinks. So, I can't confess without being thrown to the wolves. My only choice is to keep playing this game with Sage. A worse thought comes to me.

"And if I win and they find out after it's all over?"

"Then I think they'll be in for one hell of a shock." Damian smiles.

"Yes, but then what?"

"Well, if you win, that means you are a true princess, former rebel or not. Personally, I think Sage will be annoyed no one listened because he was right, but he wouldn't do anything because he was also wrong."

But won't they feel betrayed? I wish I could tell them, but I know why I can't. Besides, what does this all mean for me as a Custod? I broke protocol.

Damian turns to me. "Kascia, Sage may have been right when you came here, but that is in the past. I know your heart has changed, and that makes you just as worthy to be here as any other girl here."

"It's going to take getting used to, not seeing myself that way." I said no. I drove Father out. I gave them Jake's name. I was no longer on the fence. I made my choice. There was no going back.

I spend the rest of the day in my room with an anxious knot in my stomach. I'd made it this far. But what does that mean? The way Gavril looked at me... what does he believe? And a better question, what do I believe?

My maids try to be bright and cheery as they serve me breakfast, but all I have are questions. I still do not know why things in the kingdom are so bad when it's clear the royal family aren't the kind to hoard money. Yes, the castle is fine with a good staff, but from what I know, they are paid average if not below average; though of course, they have room and board. The castle is stunning and beautiful, but is it new?

The castle has stood at least five hundred years if it is not older. If I can't answer that question for myself, how will I ever answer it to my father or my former friends? I am certain the royal family doesn't want the kingdom in such a state, but it was. Why? And why hadn't they fixed it?

And the worse question: what was this about a prophecy?

When I'd driven my father from the palace, he said we couldn't allow the prince to marry because the Merlin prophesied that if he did the kingdom would fall. Was it true?

I have doubts. Why did my father never tell me until the moment he needed to talk me into helping him assassinate the royals? And even more worrying, how could such a prophecy be true? Gavril is not the spoiled rat we had all thought him to be. He clearly wants to do right by his people. How could his coming into power mean the downfall of the kingdom?

My maids can tell their attempts to cheer me up aren't working. They suggest I use some of the open space in the room to do some of my dance routines or even practice my vocals. I force a smile and claim I'm too tired, but honestly, it hurts too much. I'd had to give those up when I came here too. As much as I loved the life I'd had as the star prima actress of the royal theater, and how much I'd liked keeping up my skills while here, I denounced those as much as the rest of what my life had been. And enjoying those things only reminds me of all I was forced to denounce. I do my best to hide the tears from my eyes as the guilt bubbles in my stomach. Losing it hurt more than anything.

"Kascia, you can at least work on some of your favorite pieces in here. No one is going to judge, and even if I think it, I'll keep quiet," Damian teases warmly.

I look away, playing with the end of a blanket on my bed. "It's not that."

Damian tries to meet my eyes, "Then what is it?"

I frown. "I told them."

"What?"

"I gave them Jake's name. I had to or..."

"Or you feel you'd have disappointed Gavril," Damian deduces. I nod. "What does that have to do with your music?"

"I gave him up. I gave up all I was. I had to. There wasn't another choice. I chose him over Jake a long time ago. Even if that still aches," I keep playing with my blanket, pulling it up and long, "I can't be what I was anymore. If I have to give up dancing to prove it, I'll do it. It just," I swallow, "hurts."

"I see. Even the good things?" he asks gently.

I nod, looking away and hugging myself. "I feel so guilty. I know it was the right choice, but I still feel guilty. It's not like it was all bad." I can't be the Custod I trained to be, the actress. Who even am I anymore?

"Then don't let the good go," Damian says simply. "Kascia, I understand you want to prove to Sage and the royal family you mean no harm, but denying your past in how it built you into who you are, good most of all, won't help anyone."

"So, I go back on what I said?" I ask.

"No, just because you gave them Jake's name does not mean you have to throw out the good parts of your past. Your talents, passions, and I would suspect your mother from what you've told me, can still be part of your life. Even your father if he gets over his pride. Your friends weren't all active rebels, were they?"

"I don't think so." But the truth is exactly what I told the royal family. I don't really know. I'd never seen a co-worker do anything. I'd only been in one raid myself where I did all I could to make sure no one got hurt. I wasn't a help that day. I try not to think about it.

"Then you can keep them as well. Don't deny the good just because there was so much bad. It's like uprooting a tree when all you have to do is prune the bad limbs. You don't have to start over from nothing. You can keep the good things. Besides, it would be a shame to never hear my night angel sing again." Damian gives me a small smile.

I manage to return it. I look at my hands. "He was all I had. Do you know what that's like?"

"My dear Kascia, more than you could ever know," Damian gives me a sad smile of understanding. He knows. I see it in his eyes.

I take a deep breath. "They were my world. I gave them everything. Now I've turned them both over and betrayed them."

"Remember why. It will help," he encourages me.

"For a family and life I might not even get? How can I win when I'm a liar?"

"You are perfectly honest in your intent now. It doesn't matter what you were, only what you are. Trust me." He meets my eyes firmly then glances to the floor. "I once allowed the past to ruin my present and future for far too long." He meets my eyes again with earnesty shining in his own. "It's not worth all the good you'll miss out on. Trust me, I know. I did. It took far too much pain to get me back to a good place. Don't make my mistake, Kasica. And don't lose faith yet. This game is only just beginning."

"But... I'm not a true princess. I'm... his infiltrator." I frown.

"Were. You threw that mantle aside." Damian reminds me.

"But that's what I am."

"No. What you were."

"Then what am I now?" I argue.

"Whatever you choose to be. But as now, to the prince, you are the voice of the people. To your maids, you're a woman of valor and a beacon for a brighter future. You have a vast array of talents, Kascia. Your people adore you. You can be what they need you to be. But that choice is up to you."

"So I'm nothing?" I blink back more of the tears I've been fighting.

"Of course not. You just are at the point of transformation. A butterfly may feel like nothing awaiting the moment it emerges from its cocoon. But that moment comes sooner or later. Only you decide what kind of butterfly you'll be. Don't let your past, present, or anyone else make that choice for you."

"I don't know how to choose." I never was allowed to choose. "I'm a Custod. We don't get that choice."

"Yes," Damian nods his head a little, "that can complicate things, but that doesn't change what I've said. A Custod's duty is to protect the people, is it not? Then how better than doing what you've been doing."

"But I can't win, then what?"

"Do you really believe you can't win?" Damian gives me a look. "Then why try?"

I think that over. "I want it too badly not to try." That realization floods me with horror and peace at once. I want it. I want to do what I had never wanted before. I don't want to be princess, but I want to protect the people

I love, so I want the position. I never wanted to join this game, but I joined. Now, leaving this palace terrifies me. "I don't know what I am anymore. I wish I knew what I wanted."

"You have plenty of time. The holiday is coming quickly and that brings its own kind of magic," Damian encourages. "Don't lose heart, Kascia. Not until the end. If you want it, don't give up. I made that mistake, and I will do all I can to stop you from facing that fate."

I nod, feeling a bit better as I fiddle with my fingers.

Damian smiles sadly and softly sings a line from one of my favorite shows. "Angel of music, hide no longer."

That brings tears of relief, and I can't help but laugh and hug him. "Thanks, Damian."

"Anytime," Damian says as he strokes my hair soothingly like my father once did. "You'll find your wings, night angel. Just hold fast."

I nod as I try to decide how to choose what I'll be instead of having it forced on me like I always have. "They aren't what we all thought they were. Yet the kingdom is still hardly surviving. Why?"

Damian lets out a heavy sigh. "Well, such questions are complicated, and I don't presume to parade myself as an expert by any means, but wars are expensive and complicated. Perhaps therein lies the answer to your question."

I bite my lips. "And the prophecy?"

"You mean as your father mentioned it?" He arches a brow. "As I said before, prophecies, real or not, are often misunderstood. So I suppose the real question is, how much do you trust the source?"

That is the problem. I trust him with my whole heart and yet none of it. I thought him my source for all truth only to learn his version is just that, his version. How much reality is in it, I cannot be sure.

"Is there a way to find out?"

"There are always ways to find truth, but how is up to you to pursue. Just know that could make some people nervous." Damian studies me over his work with a look he often gives me, but I'm never quite sure what it means. "But I will support you in your choice in either way, my lady."

I bite the inside of my lip as I think. Either way, I am not going to get answers in here. I have to wait. But I do have access to the royal library. Perhaps that and a more careful study of the news articles could provide some answers.

I have to wait two days to get into the library, so I do my best to keep spirits up. Damian was right, after trying to enjoy some of my calming activities and a good night's sleep, I am ready to find the parts of myself I need to hold onto. I'm able to do some dance exercises but am a bit too nervous to do vocal warm-ups around my maids who likely have never heard how funny-sounding they can be. It's all I can do to keep busy until they finally tell us we'll have our old range of the castle the following day.

My plan is to get into the library and see what I can dig up about my questions. I may have no questions about the royal family's character, but I have plenty about what is going on in this kingdom that I love. As a Custod, I know I shouldn't feel attached to any one kingdom, but Purerah is mine, and the people I have seen suffering my whole life feel like my own. I'd come here out of duty to them. I couldn't skate by knowing the royal family is doing their best. I need to know why it isn't enough.

I'm more than ready to return to normal when the next morning dawns. This visit will also give me a chance to see if they found which of the other girls let the rebels in. That troubles me just as much as it being me. How could I as a plant not spot another plant? I have to assume it's a Loyalist who is letting them in. I was the Custod plant, and the Potentate rebellion wasn't organized enough for such infiltration.

The first sign things are not going back to completely normal is how my maids dress me. They don't put me into a day dress, but something that resembles a uniform. A white puff-sleeved button-up, Purerahian blue waistcoat with Purerahian yellow details, knee-length skirt, stockings, and heels. They put my hair into a braided chignon bun, looking cute and elegant but keeping most of it out of my face save for the elegant sweep of my side fringe.

When I get down to the dining hall for breakfast, I notice I'm not the only one in a uniform. Not all of us are wearing identical ones, but the button-up, waistcoat, pleated knee-length skirt, stockings, and heels are consistent.

It's odd to see all of us together again. It has only been a few days, but it feels like a lifetime. I am one of the last to arrive. There were twenty-one of us left at the Harvest ball. My eyes rake over the table and notice there are only twenty place settings at the Chosen's table. That means one girl was out. Had they found the spy?

A squeal of delight cuts off my wondering, and a timid tackle of a hug wraps around my side. I look to see Lilly hugging me tightly.

Lilly is the youngest Chosen at just eighteen. She looks like she's hardly fifteen: small, pale with stunning, straight black hair that is twisted into a nice bun held in with long hair pins. Her hazel eyes look up at me in concern. "What were you thinking?" She asks in her soft voice.

My brows draw together, and I begin to open my mouth to ask when Bella joins us. "We all heard what you did that night." She smiles, folding her arms. "How weren't you eliminated?" Bella asks, admiration in her voice.

"Defending the royal family is treason now?" Princess Zelda smiles sweetly as she joins our huddle.

"Besides, if they thought she was the danger, they wouldn't have interviewed all of us," Jonquil says in a bored drawl. Her dark eyes snap up from her tea that she's been sitting in front of, fiddling with the teabag. "Yet we're all still here."

"Of course, they interviewed everyone. It was only fair and proper," Princess Zelda says.

"Even the born princesses?" Jonquil asks in interest; the steam from her cup makes her dark honey skin look ashy, making it even harder to read her expression.

"Yes, even us," Princess Rose says in irritation as she passes us.

"Of course they did," Zelda says more patiently. "With so many rebel attacks lately, and more getting into the palace than ever, they have to talk to everyone. At this point, they can't rule out espionage, even if the motive is lacking."

"And in all reality, just because they may not be typical rebels doesn't mean they don't have real grievances," I say. "Which makes a foreign nation just as likely to want to use them as a tool than anyone else." The second I say it I wonder if I should have. I don't want to look like what I was. But... It's true.

"I'd not thought of that." Lilly frowns in distress.

"That's why it's wise to check everyone, most of all with the stakes so high," Zelda says. "Prince Gavril is the only heir to the throne."

"But why would any of us let them in?" Lilly's frown increases.

"We're the citizens who have been taxed so heavily they can hardly get by all their lives," Lark reminds her. "Which means any one of us could have a reason."

"But that's what we came here to escape," Florence argues. "Who would be mad enough to jeopardize that?"

"For some, they may feel it's their duty," I say with a frown. I know that feeling. I was very nearly the one who did.

"Duty to attack a royal family who only tried to help us?" Jonquil frowns. "Twisted duty," she huffs derisively.

I notice Lilly starts fiddling with one of her cuffs. She's rubbing it so hard it could start to fray at any moment. I glance around to be sure no one else noticed before I gently pull her hand away. "We should sit down. The royal family appears to be waiting."

That breaks up our circle as we hurry to our places. Thankfully, even with the missing girl, Lilly is still next to me. Azalea, Chosen number thirteen, is on my right. Jonquil sits on Lilly's other side.

Once all twenty of us are settled into our seats, the king stands to address us. My stomach tightens. I glance at Prince Gavril, but he's as relaxed as ever, looking at his food as if wondering if it is worth the energy to eat.

"Thank you for your patience with the security measures, ladies." The king smiles around at all of us. "It takes some acclimatizing after such an impactful attack. You also may have noticed we are short one lady. Princess Neeraja requested to return home after the last attack. We have realized the final twenty."

Only twenty? It sounds so large and yet so small after we started with fifty girls.

"And it is that coveted number that brings us to a change in the schedule of our dear Chosen Daughters of Purerah." The king nods at us. "Starting this morning, after breakfast, you will meet in the Ladies' Chamber for royalty lessons. They will extend until the lunch hour, after which you are free to enjoy the palace as you have before; the library, conservatory, and dance hall are all free to you as well as the Ladies' Chamber to play games. Unless of course, you are lucky enough to have a date."

The king winks at his son who gives him a pained grimace as he fakes trying to be excited. A few other girls and I cover our mouths to hide giggles. "If you have other questions about what you are permitted and not permitted to do, I'd check with security, your guard, or other guards. Thank you again for all you've sacrificed, ladies. I know this cannot be easy on you." He has no idea.

I jump as the king pauses to cough into his handkerchief. I'm the only one who does. Since I saw his lung attack, for lack of a better name for it, any sign of his weak lungs startles me. I know it's unlikely he'll have another one, but I'm still anxious.

"And while I have your attention, I wanted to get a poll. I was wondering if you ladies would like to—"

Prince Gavril does something I never thought I'd see him do. He grabs his father's coat and yanks him down into his seat. I cover my mouth to smother my laughter as the king looks at his son innocently. The queen rolls her eyes as the two men exchange a rapid whispered conversation. Did I hear the prince say something about not setting up another event for him to ogle at?

We hold a quick devotion and start to eat. The girls are as chatty as ever, despite the events. My mind is too lost in my own thoughts to talk much. So now I only have a half-day to study, but at least royalty lessons could only help my chances in this game as well as perhaps explain some of what is going on.

Lost in thought, I lose track of how many other girls have finished eating and I suddenly realize I'm among the last to finish. I hastily take my last few bites as the others excitedly head off to royalty lessons. I can't help but notice the prince isn't exactly done either.

Unsure if I want to be alone with him, I shove down the rest of my food to hurry out. I'm not fast enough. The prince catches up to me in the hall.

"Are you nervous?" He teases warmly.

I try to ignore my annoyance. After all that's happened, the first thing he says to me is joking?

"What for?" he asks. "You're a natural. You'll be the prize of her collection in no time. I should know. I've had to take lessons from her and your royalty teacher since I was young."

"Really?" I frown.

The prince nods. "You have nothing to worry about. Even with the other born princesses there, you'll be the star." He's making me more nervous, not more relaxed. "You already walk, talk, sit, stand and look like a princess. They don't have to work on you."

"Please stop," I beg.

"I'm serious. I still have occasional 'refresher' lessons with her now and then. I know what she's like; you'll be fine, Lady Kascia."

We stop at the top of the stairs where we'll part ways, and he kisses my hand. "I'll see you at lunch." He gives me a smile. There's meaning to it, assurance we will talk soon; it soothes me a little. His hand tightens on mine a short second before he pulls away.

I pause, watching him go, my hand still hovering where he left it. Why does he do that? I shake myself out of my confusion and turn to the Ladies' Chamber.

I nod my thanks to the guard as she opens the door for me. I walk inside and jump at the delighted cry that splits the air.

"There!" It cries as I look around in bewilderment, wondering what I'd done wrong. "That's what I'm talking about, ladies. Perfect poise, confidence, and it's natural! Not at all forced or artificial."

I finally spot the speaker. She blends into the Chosen girls so well, no wonder I had trouble spotting her. She's wearing a similar but not identical uniform. She wears stockings and heels, but her knee-length skirt is straight, and she wears a blazer jacket over her waistcoat and button-up shirt. Her suit is royal purple. She looks like she could be the queen's younger sister. Her coiled hair is pulled into a beautiful ponytail that hangs over her right shoulder. Her skin tone is almost a perfect match for the queen, but her features are warmer and her smile much larger than any I'd seen on the queen.

The woman walks over to me with the grace of a queen and the confidence of a conqueror. She walks around me and gives me a quick nod of approval. "Not only can she walk the walk, but she can look the look. Her uniform is unique and perfect for her. What kingdom are you from, sweetie?" She asks me.

"Purerah," I reply with a question in my tone.

"You're not a born princess?" She asks, her tone going up in surprise.

"No, my lady." I shake my head.

"Hmm, indeed." She doesn't comment, but I see judgment in her eyes, but not for me. I wonder who she's judging.

I didn't think my uniform was that unique. Sure, I used white and the two royal colors, but many girls went for Purerahian blue or yellow. Zelda has gone with more white, and Princess Rose with light purples and lavenders.

"Is that all twenty?" The lady asks.

Kamala, Chosen number eighteen, opens her mouth to answer, but Hawi, Chosen number twenty-four, stops her with a look. I'm sure she was about to say 'no' to throw off the teacher. I wish Hawi would let her; maybe she'd be eliminated. The fewer of us the better. And they weren't known to be the nicest girls. They even made fun of each other in ways that were less than friendly.

The lady looks over her clipboard before she tucks it against her side and left arm, pen set in her other hand as she looks us over.

"Greetings," the lady says as if it's a call to do something rather than a welcome to us. I notice the girls are in a line of who is top of the Chosen list and quickly get into place.

The lady starts at the head of the line, with the four born princesses. Princess Rose curtsies properly to the lady. "Princess Rose of Emilimoh, Lady Keva." She greets her with perfect poise, ever the perfect appearance of a princess with her cacao skin, stunning coils, and posture above reproach.

"Adequate," the lady says, giving her a nod, making a note on her board, then moving on to the next girl in line.

"Princess Amapola of Spearim, your ladyship," Princess Amapola, dressed in red and black, with hints of yellow – her nation's colors – says and curtsies as well. The light reflects on her jet black hair.

"Don't bow your head so much and look down at the guest, Amapola. It is not becoming the power of a princess to be abased or so lordly," the lady corrects before moving on, making another note on her board. Amapola gives her an indignant look as she moves on.

"Princess Laurina of Bruag, your ladyship." Princess Laurina curtsies like the others, bending at the waist, so it's more bow-like. Her fall-like colors match her bright red hair and make her look bright and cheerful, fitting the harvest time.

"Try not to sound so brash, and you don't need to bow and curtsy. Pick one," says the lady with yet another note on her board as she steps forward to the last born princess.

"Princess Zelda of Hyvil, your ladyship. It is a pleasure to meet you." Zelda curtsies with a meekness that makes her feel gentle and powerful. Her blonde hair and striking green eyes make her one of the more unique princesses, but it is her slightly pointed ears that are the most distinctive.

"Nice personal touch. Careful not to bow your head so much, darling. You're a queen-in-waiting; no need to be shy," says the lady with a mark. I presume she'll do that every time. She steps up to the first non-born princess in line.

"Lady Bella of Purerah, your ladyship." Bella's dark blue eyes shine with welcome as she greets her brightly with a warm and excited curtsy. Her red and gold uniform is easily one of the most beautiful. It goes well with her black hair and fits her frame perfectly. I wonder if she designed it herself. If I am not the best dressed, I would think it would be her.

"Your curtsy is too low, and no need to make such a fuss of your skirts, dear," says the lady as she moves on, hardly giving Bella a look. I see the flash of hurt come over Bella's eyes. I wonder if it's because she's not a born princess.

A slight smirk crosses Dahlia's face, dazzling against her dark skin just before the lady turns her attention to her. Dahlia cruises formally. "Lady Dahlia, also of Purerah." She sounds almost smug to me.

"Not so much in the knees, and don't sound so self-important. The rest of you are all Purerahian," says the lady with a bored air as she makes another tick on the clipboard or she's making a quick note. I can't tell which. Dahlia purses her lips as the lady moves on.

"Jonquil, lady of Purerah." Jonquil curtsies perfectly with a gentle bow of her head. Her coiled hair is struggling to stay neat as she bows her head, but she looks prettier and warmer than Dahlia, even if their overall appearance is similar.

To my surprise, the lady says nothing to her, bowing her head back, but she still makes a mark that is almost certainly just a tick. Jonquil beams in pleasure as she moves on.

Lilly is next, standing next to me. I can feel her shiver even though I can't see it, and she's not touching me as she curtsies with her skirts. "L-Lady Lilly of Purerah, ma-am," she says sweetly with a cute but shy smile.

"Sweet girl, you've done nothing wrong. No need to be nervous. Be confident in your name. You're a lady with a proud name. No need to stammer," Lady Keva corrects with a warm smile and comforting touch on Lilly's shoulder. It makes me smile and Lilly relax.

The lady makes a note on her board before she steps up to me. I give her a curtsy. "I'm Lady Kascia of Purerah, your ladyship. Thank you for your time." It is how I always thanked patrons of our theater (not that we had many).

"Hmm, 'thank you' is a good touch." She nods to me before moving on, but there's something judgmental about her walk that makes me review what she said, looking for the hidden insult. But I can't find it.

I notice Dahlia and Forsythia giving me death glares. Why? Then I realize the lady did not make any mark for me. Is that why? Is it good or bad? Does it mean I was the only one who didn't pass?

See, look how good I am at this, I mock Gavril in my mind, annoyed.

I'm so distracted by my thoughts, I miss what the lady says to Azalea, though she's softly flushing when I bring my attention back to the room.

Ericka gives the lady the most stereotypically perfect curtsy I have ever seen. "Welcome Lady Keva. I am Lady Ericka of Roseple."

"Hmm, why did you choose to name yourself by city rather than nation?" the lady asks with a cocked brow.

Ericka's dazzling smile makes her blue eyes sparkle and her curly blonde hair come alive in happiness. "It's my proper greeting, your ladyship. I'm the mayor's daughter."

"I see." The lady makes another note and moves on without further comment.

"Lady Forsythia of Purerah, your ladyship," Forsythia bows her head as she curtsies. "Pleased to meet you." She smiles her sweet smile which always makes me feel sick. It makes her narrow eyes narrow further, but something about it feels calculating. Like she is trying to trick everyone who sees that smile, and she is sure she can do it.

"Less in the waist, but pretty good," says the lady with another note. It's amazing how she steps forward as she makes each note each time, a perfect rhythmic pattern.

"Lady Isla of Purerah, your ladyship," Isla says meekly with a timid curtsy, her dark hair dropping over her shoulder as she does so. Her warm brown eyes closing, but it is graceful too.

"It's a curtsy, not a prayer, my dear," the lady says. "No need to be so timid. You are a beautiful lady. Own it, girl. Your face should not perfectly face the floor. The hands in front of you are fine, but don't use prayer positions for them. It can make you look weak. And you are anything but weak, my girl." She gives Isla that same warm smile she gave Lilly before she makes her mark and takes a step.

"I'm Lady Kamala, your ladyship." Kamala curtsies.

"Slower, slower!" cries the lady. "You look like you'll slam your head into the floor. No need to smash those pretty features." She actually pushes Kalama's shoulders back before she steps forward with her normal mark. Why didn't she mark me?

"Lady Marigold, Miss Keva." Marigold bows her head to her with the smallest of bobs, making her beautiful mane of hair bounce.

"You are a lady, as am I; such as, use proper titles like one," the lady's tone carries a hint of offense, and the glare she gives Marigold shows the same. She makes her note with a bit more force as she steps forward to the next girl.

"Lady Nicholl of Purerah, your ladyship; thank you for your direction." She gives the lady a formal curtsy.

"Don't copycat just to look good," says the lady, "and don't be so rote. You're a person. Let that show in your etiquette." She makes another mark.

Hawi is beaming like the midday sun as she curtsies to the lady. "Lady Hawi, I'm so happy you're here to instruct us. I can't wait."

"It's a greeting, short and sweet is appropriate. Save the rest for later." The lady makes her tick and moves on.

"Lady Lark, your ladyship." Lark gives her a stunning curtsy, tilting her head at a strange diagonal.

"Straight on with your head. I'm not even sure what that movement is supposed to be, dear," the lady says, makes her note, then presses onward. Lark purses her lips when she passes too.

"Lady Elice, your ladyship. Happy you're here." Elice gives her a curtsy that borderlines a bow. I often wonder why she is here. She comes across as a girl who hates the formalities of being a princess and resists doing them, yet she joined a contest to become princess.

"A lady curtsies, sweetheart; they don't bow," the lady corrects with another tick.

The worry about what each tick means is starting to creep into my stomach.

"Lady Florence, your ladyship." Florence gives her a quiet, polite, and proper curtsy, or so I thought, but as always, the lady had something to say.

"More pride, sweetheart, you are not a servant; you're a lady," the lady corrects, makes a final tick then turns to look at the line again.

"Well, I see we have our work cut out for us," she says. "I have notes on what to work on for almost all of you."

Instantly, all eyes go to me. I keep my face composed while I feel a flush creek up my cheeks.

"As I said, I am Lady Keva. I am going to instruct you in the art of etiquette for a lady and princess as you progress." She starts to walk. "And from today I can see there is a lot of work to do on walks and greetings, and I'm sure, yet further instruction. I will teach you for an hour and a half; you'll get a half an hour break, then you'll have your lessons with Lady Hydrengia until lunch."

"What will she teach us?" Elice asks curiously.

"You ask for your turn to ask a question, Lady Elice. I like your confidence, but the key to being a proper lady is confidence mixed with humility. Don't tear yourself down, and do not let others force themselves above you," Lady Keva says. "She will teach you the skills you'll need to handle the politics of ladyship, history, culture, political sciences as well as politics."

"There's a difference?" Hawi gapes.

"Please, ask for your turn." Lady Keva gives her a look. "Remember humility and confidence. Respect others as you respect yourself, and so you better respect both. But yes, there is a difference, but that is for Lady Hydrengia to cover later."

Lady Keva's smile softens. "Ladies, please understand, I'm not here to make you feel like you're not enough. I'm here to teach you that you are enough and how to show it to yourselves and the world. Inside each and every one of you is a queen. Whether you become Purerah's queen or queen of your home nation, or not royalty at all, it does not matter. There is a queen inside of each of you. And you alone can find that confidence and peace that comes from understanding it and how to let that out to others and yourselves. I correct because you're better than that. Don't forget it."

She frowns a little. "Though many of you may need a word with your attendants on color choices."

"Excuse me?" splutters Ericka. Then she flushes, "Pardon, Lady Keva, I just..."

"Indeed, the born-princesses have gone for their home colors, which actually suits each of you well," Lady Keva nods her heads to them, making them smile, "but many of you tried to copy it a bit too much. Lady Dahlia, that dark blue is not complementing your skin tone well at all. I'd think lighter colors. For you, yellows or greens would do wonders."

We all look at Dahlia nervously. She's incredibly competitive. Would she argue it? She clearly does it to try to look more like she should represent the kingdom or because I wear a lot of blue and others try to copy me as I'm seen as the frontrunner.

Dahlia surprises us though. She just bows her head as if in thanks but doesn't speak. Likely wise. Who knows how she would have snapped?

"Lady Elice, reds would suit your pale skin and dark hair nicely, far more than this lighter blue you've gone for," Lady Keva goes on. "In fact, I see far more blue than any other color. Lady Forsythia and Lady Ericka have done lovely work with their purple and pink respectively, matching them well."

My stomach knots as Lady Keva beckons me forward. "Lady Kascia, however, has gone for blue, but this suits her. The Purerahian blue and yellow just happen to fit her tones. The yellow contrasts her brown hair and helps her blue eyes pop. Only go for blue if it suits you.

"And make sure the fit is good too." Lady Keva calls Bella forward. "Lady Bella's outfit is a wonderful example. Wear things that fit you and don't worry too much about what else is in fashion if it does not suit you. She's taken advantage of her shape and outlined it nicely with her waistcoat. Your attendants are good at their tasks," she compliments.

"I make them." Bella flushes.

"A lovely talent and hobby," Lady Keva praises. "You may return to the line," she says to Bella then turns to me. "Lady Kascia, if you wouldn't mind walking along the line for me."

I can't stop the pink rising to my cheeks this time and do as she asks, trying not to think about it, but it's hard as she points out what I'm doing right. "Shoulders back, think tall by pushing against the floor, step firmly in your stride but not forcefully. Not too quickly but not too slow for a casual walk. She keeps her heels in line. She could run in them if she needed to because she has the control and confidence in her balance. That carries over into her curtsy."

She stops me as I reach her, and we curtsy to one another. My face is all pink by now and moving towards red. Ericka looks ready to smash something as she glares at me in envy. Forsythia's lips are pursed and pushed to one side as she studies me, preparing to learn and outdo me. Dahlia's eyes are narrowed hard as she tries to see how her curtsy was wrong.

Or so I thought. "Pardon Lady Keva," she says, "but Lady Kascia is not doing it perfectly."

"Oh really?" The challenge in Lady Keva's voice is obvious.

"No disrespect, your ladyship, but she puts weight on her right foot."

"Which is proper, it helps keep your body straight and not bend forward," Lady Keva says.

"I thought you didn't put weight on it," Lilly frowns.

"There is one version where you don't, but a princess will rarely use it as it is a dance step, only in that dance will you use it," she explains. I smile. I did it many times in ballet.

"When?" Lilly asks.

Lady Keva looks at her list then laughs, "Ah perfect! Lady Kascia, you are the dancer, yes?" I nod. "Will you show them?"

I sigh and shut my eyes to pretend it's just the end of a show as I turn and give them a proper reverence. My right foot points out to my side, behind my left foot. Then, with the back of my toes sliding on the floor, I keep my weight on the front foot and bend down, keeping the rest of my body upright.

"Exactly," Lady Keva praises, "there is also the plié," she nods at me to do it, so I do as she goes on, "which is often used when greeting someone of lesser rank from another kingdom, or when heavily pregnant, as it helps keep your balance. It's hard to tell if you plié or curtsy in a long skirt which is always worn by a lady when expecting." She gives us a playful wink, making a few of us giggle.

"But Lady Kascia's example shows exactly what I'm talking about. She is comfortable and confident in her body, but also knows her place and does not pride herself above or below it. It results in these movements being natural. The notes I have made for all of you will remind me which end you need to work on, confidence or humility. And in each piece of etiquette we learn, I will focus on that aspect for you. Win this or not, you will come out a stronger lady and person for it. Now we've gotten the concept," she claps her hands then smiles delightedly at us, "let's begin." She sounds suddenly excited and bubbly.

"We'll start with walks. Queens, I want you to star walk," and she explains how star walks work. I used these in theater exercises before. You walk to the first point you see, turn, then do it again. Then you can move about a room without pacing, and it helps work on character or stylized walks more easily.

We do those for a while then go over the elements of a curtsy, reverence, and plié in practice. Turnout is a struggle for many. Lady Keva even makes me explain turnout to the girls by showing them some of my turnout exercises. The envy in the room is mounting.

When the break finally comes, the room shows its cliques. The "elite", as they call themselves: Ericka, Forsythia, and Dahlia, all go to a table set with tea and sit so no one else dares join them. The other girls just move away from me, glaring at me. All but my friends: Lilly, Bella, Azalea, Jonquil, Isla, and Zelda. Though Isla mostly sits in quiet.

Girls chat with me happily, wondering if getting dance lessons from me would help them. Their joking makes me feel a bit better, but now I'm nervous for the second half of lessons. We all are.

But those lessons aren't as bad. We're all seated, by number once again, in school desks with the built-in tables like we used before when we learned the proper way to eat around the royal family.

The teacher, Lady Hydrengia, walks over. I hadn't noticed she'd been sitting at the back of the room reading until she stood up. She wears browns and blacks and is very tall with her hair pulled into a bun. The way she looks down at us reminds me of an owl looking down from a tower roof.

"I am Lady Hydrengia, and I will be teaching you the truly important skills of royalty," she says. "The ability to understand the political struggle, use it to your advantage, and understand history and cultures to give you insight into how to diffuse tense situations. I will make you more than idols of your people, but powers in the world to be reckoned with."

The silence that fell in the room makes me think a few girls just had to fight not to wet themselves in fear of that idea. Being a princess is supposed to be fun, not a duty, and not someone to be feared for political power. But that is the truth of it. You don't get the beautiful parts without the dirty work too.

"Let's start with economics then," Lady Hydrengia says and turns to the whiteboard she'd pulled up and starts explaining basic economics. I'm bored at first until I realize, as dull as it sounds, these lessons might be my best key in finding answers to how decent people let the kingdom become as it has.

Chapter 3

After lunch, I immediately go into the practice hall to dance. It is a stress relief and a way to help me focus on studying later. It also allows me to avoid the gaggle of jealous girls in the Ladies' Chamber.

I don't suspect anyone else wants my attention today. So, when I'm getting close to the end of my routine for the day and there's a knock on the door, I figure someone else just wants the space.

"Give me a minute," I call back.

The door opens a little. I sigh and turn to tell them to wait when I freeze.

Prince Gavril gives me a sheepish smile. "Sorry, I figured you weren't indecent or anything, and I can hardly hear you through that door."

"Oh." I wish I had something better to say as I bow my head as I should for the prince.

Gavril frowns. "You know you don't have to do that; you never have before."

"I have so."

"Around others, not just us." Gavril's still frowning a little as he looks me over. "I've never seen you in your dance gear before. It's... simple."

"What did you expect?" I ask with amusement.

"Well, at least a practice tutu or something."

"I don't own a tutu. They all belong to the theater," I reply, suddenly realizing how improper such dress is, at least for a princess, in such a setting.

I wore my style of dance gear: leggings that fit snugly to my form, a tight-fitting dance shirt tucked into the leggings with a low scoop in front and back with three fourth sleeves. I have my chestnut brown hair pinned up with my fringe swooping across my forehead but pinned into the bun at the back of my head. I'd taken off my shrug and left it by my bag that protects my pointe shoes when I am not wearing them.

"I never thought of that. I forget how little you had before you came," he apologizes, looking me over.

I clear my throat and look away. I suddenly wish the color of my dance gear didn't compliment me so well, the Purerahian blue and yellow that makes me shine. Damian sometimes is too good at his job.

"I didn't miss out much," I reply stiffly.

"Sorry, I don't mean to be condescending. I just mean to be understanding," he apologizes again.

"Did you need something?" He doesn't use the dance room. The girls have free reign of it.

"I was told this was the best place to find you. Apparently, it's the only time anyone knows exactly where to find you." Gavril smiles at me shyly.

"I suppose that's true," I agree, hugging myself. We hadn't spoken alone like this since the ball.

"I'm sorry. I didn't mean to make you uncomfortable. Don't people see you dressed like this all the time?"

"Yes, I just... it's not very ladylike, is it?" I say, avoiding the main problem.

"Why not? Your dress fits what you're doing. My being here doesn't change that," Gavril says. "I wanted to talk, is all. Should I wait?"

"It's alright. You're right. I used to be dressed like this for most of the day. It's just not what I'm used to with you." I let my arms drop and turn to work on packing up.

"No, they've made everything between us formal," Gavril agrees. I hear his shoes tap against the floor as he comes closer. "But that can't last forever."

"What about the tour of the ship?" I ask.

"That's one small example," he says. "Do you not want to talk to me?"

I think that over. Did I want to? I want to know what's happening, but I'm scared of what that might be. What does he think of me after seeing a hint of my true colors?

"I won't force you." The disappointment in his voice reminds me of one of the most frightening things in this twisted game. Jake forcing me into this game shattered my heart after falling so hard for him. What if I do the same to Gavril? That idea frightens me more than anything.

"I'm afraid of how it ends," I confess, still not looking at him as I pack my bag, but I can't hide forever.

"Why?"

"I'm scared of what you're thinking," I say, turning to face him as a million thoughts rush through my mind about what he'd said that night before the attack and the pain in his eyes as I turned away from him in what I felt sure was the last time.

"What do you think I feel?" A hint of fear enters his concerned eyes.

"I don't know." And that is terrifying.

He watches me for a long moment, trying to read me. He's so observant, so careful, so intelligent. He'll read it all on my face like he read what the rebels are like by the signs they leave behind.

"What are you afraid I'm thinking?" he asks. "That I take back what I said, or I don't?"

I take a deep breath. Which is worse? He told me at the ball that if he chose, the game would have ended that very night. I knew he meant that would be with me as the winner. Which is worse? That he still wants me to win more than anything, giving me the power to crush him, or that he has figured out what I am and hates me? "I don't know."

"The person whose name you gave, it was him, wasn't it?" he asks gently.

I know which 'him' he means. Gavril knows I came here to avoid an ex who broke my heart. I think about how much Jake telling me to sleep with the enemy shattered me. I didn't know who Gavril was when I admitted that part of the story to him. But it made Gavril extra gentle with me, constantly worrying about hurting me over my still sore heart. He does not know Jake's name or how exactly he broke my heart, but he knew I still have feelings for him, or he fears I do. He'd offered to let me go home to him if I really wanted, but even then, I knew there was no going back to Jake. I'd never trust him again.

I look down, unable to meet Gavril's face.

"Did you really choose me over him?" Gavril asks gently. I don't know how to reply, so I don't. "Kascia." There is so much compassion and tenderness in his voice, I manage to meet his gaze. "Please, I want to understand."

"Do you think Sage is right? That I'm just a spy out to get you?" I ask dismally.

"No," Gavril shakes his head, "I think you just gave up the man you'd poured your heart and soul into for who knows how long to prove you were serious about wanting to be here."

My lip quivers, and I fight to stop it, making it worse. I bite it to keep it still. He nailed exactly what I'd done. I love and hate how he does that.

Gavril is still studying me with those stunning amber eyes, filled with concern for me. "But was it to stay here in the game, or did you really choose me over him? We both know that's what Sage dared you to do. Did you do it just to prove him wrong, or did you mean it?"

"Is there a difference?" I ask.

"Kascia, do you want to be here to escape, or do you want to be here?"

"Does it really matter?"

"Yes, because you are not bound to be there or here," Gavril says. "I will make sure you're safe even if you want to escape this castle and never look back."

"I thought you would have chosen me," I reply dully.

"Kascia, that has little to do with the answer to that question."

"It does!" I snap back. "Because it tells me how you feel about me."

"Does it?" Gavril challenges. "What shows my dedication more? Not caring if you want to stay with me for your own want or your own safety, or trying to see what you want and letting you choose it, no matter what it is? Do you want to stay in the game and play it, or are you trying not to go home to the rebels you just rejected?"

"What?" But he said he wanted me to win. Did he change his mind?

"You gave up your old world for this. I know what giving us his name means, Kascia. Do you want to stay here because you have nowhere else to go, or do you really want to be here?" he asks again.

"I already proved I chose you. Why does it matter?" I ask.

Gavril groans in frustration. "Because I want to make sure you're happy. Do you want to be here, or do I need to be sure you're safe?"

"I don't understand."

"You never do." Gavril shakes his head and paces a little. I pray he doesn't lose his temper. He does so easily; it's frightening when he does. I'd seen him dent wood. "I offer to set you free, and it confuses you every time. I'll do whatever is best for you, Kascia. No matter what it does to me. So, are you fighting to stay in this game to protect yourself, or do you want to be here?"

"Gavril, you can't change any of it anyway. So why does it matter? I proved I chose you over them."

"When they might hurt you if you went home?" Gavril cocks a brow at me. "My parents might be stupid about that, but I'm not. I know you betrayed them the other night. Not only did you not let them in, you fought them off. You left me to do that and protect me. I'm not blind, Kascia. I'm not stupid, and I'm not a child, despite how my parents and court behave. Your desire to stay could, and honestly either way partially is, motivated by the need to protect yourself. I imagine they're not pleased with you."

Gavril pauses his pacing, thinking a moment, and turns to me. "And no matter what you want, I will do whatever it takes to protect you. I may not have power in my kingdom, but at least outside the castle walls, my name means something for those who have no idea I have no power. You're a talented actress I hear, and your voice is second to none, my lady. Other kingdoms do as we do in using entertainment to raise funds for the kingdom. You are a highly valuable commodity in that sense alone. If you don't want to be here but need to be kept safe, I can ensure you go somewhere safe where you can use your talents to support yourself and be safe. I can't promise your family can follow, but if I have to sell my soul to make it happen, it will happen, Lady Kascia.

"So, what is it? Do you want to be here, or shall I make arrangements?"

"You don't get to dismiss us," I remind him. They told us he could when we were chosen, but we've learned that was more a formality than reality.

"I can a few. And I haven't used one yet," he says, "and I will let you have one if you want it."

I blink at him. "So, you are taking it back?"

His eyes bore into mine. "Does it matter? I don't get to choose. You're just one of twenty, aren't you?"

He is throwing the last thing I said to him at the ball back at me. Words I knew hurt him, but that he had to remember. His desire for me is dangerous for his heart and sanity in this game. He shouldn't get attached to me or any one of the twenty of us. It hurts having it thrown back at me like that.

"I don't want to hurt you."

"And I'll do whatever it takes to protect you. So, what is it? Do you want to stay, or shall I make it happen?"

"Don't dismiss me," I beg in a hurt squeak. I have to stay. I can't leave my people like that. I can't give up on my mother and father like that. I can't give up on him though I am unsure I can win. If I do, I'm going to trick their tests. I'm no true princess, but perhaps I can pass their tests anyway.

"Do you really want to stay?" Gavril is closer than I realized. He'd stepped forward as I'd fought to keep control of my tears and begged to stay. "Damian will assist me in this, I'm sure. He's very talented too. He'll be able to help you get into a splendid position. Between us, you'll have better than you could have dreamed."

"No, I won't." I hate myself for saying it. Because the best I could dream is here with him. I hate him for reminding me of it. I tense in anger and push him away. "Why are you doing this to yourself?" I demand.

Gavril frowns. "I don't understand."

"You can't choose, so why are you doing so?" I ask.

"Because I don't choose," he shoots back at me. "I can't control any of this. I know that far better than you. None of this has been my choice. I get no choice in any of it. The closest I've gotten is giving you the offer I'm giving you now. You chose me over that... that..." he fights for the world, "possible rebel," he settles on. "I can return that favor. Do you want to stay or to be safe?"

"I can't give up on them," I say. "I can't give up on my family." I can't give up on him.

Gavril huffs sharply through his nose in frustration. "So you stay here for them?"

"Yes..." I swallow, "...and no."

Gavril groans and runs his fingers through his hair with both hands, messing up his hair sharply as he paces a bit before he lets his hands drop. "You drive me insane, you know that?" He rounds on me. "I can't get a straight answer out of you on any of this. Do you have any idea what you do to me?"

"Then don't let me!" I don't want to do any of this to him.

"I don't get to choose," he snarls at me. He's so strong, so enraged, out of control, and yet, perfectly composed. I admire it and want to watch it. My heart beats in desire for that to be mine. But it can't be. Not now. Perhaps not ever, but if I leave, I'll never know. I'm not ready to give up that chance yet. Why do I want him so suddenly at this moment when he's losing his temper with me? "Perhaps you don't quite fully understand what that means, Lady Kascia. It means I don't choose any of this, any of it. So please, what do you want?"

I study him, lip shaking again as I fight for a balance to honestly protect myself and protect him. "I don't know. I don't want to leave. I know that."

"Even with it being dangerous? I might not be able to help you if you are suddenly eliminated," Gavril warns me.

"I know," I nod.

Gavril shakes his head. "Can I not get a pure answer?"

"I told you I wasn't fully honest with you," I say, my heart breaking. He said I was the most honest with him. But that isn't true.

"I never said you were. I said you were the most honest with me," Gavril replies, "and yes, that is part of why I feel the way I do when it comes to you. It's not the only thing, but it's part of the complicated web this has become."

"What answer do you want? Do you want to get rid of me?" I ask. Maybe that is it. He wants me but knows he cannot choose me, so it is better to lose me now rather than later. I can respect that. "If so, please, just eliminate me and leave me to my own devices. It would be kinder."

I will break to lose the chance with him, but if it prevents me from shattering him like I had been, I'd be alright. As alright as I can be after having Jake shatter me and then Gavril, but I'd been broken once. It would make little difference.

Gavril sighs heavily. "Kascia, despite what you may think, the Harvest didn't change much for me. I am not taking back what I said. I still mean it now. But do you want that? You came here when you didn't want to but feared going home. I know that has only grown worse. I still can't just choose you. I cannot end this game as much as I wish it. I'll free you of all of it right now. You left me that night, not the other way around."

"I did it to protect you," I say quietly.

"I know. But you also reminded me of why I matter more, and it had nothing to do with how you felt. Just the fact I'm the only heir to the throne, and the last of my family line. Not for any other reasons. If that's as deep as it goes and you are done being used as a beat-up piece in the game, I'll let you step out."

But that is not the only thing I was protecting him from. "Sage is right," I squeak. "I'm dangerous."

"I know."

"Do you?" I look back up at him. Does he know that I am more likely to shatter him than any rebel infiltrator could?

Gavril meets my eyes and nods firmly. "I know."

"Yet you still want me here?"

"Yes."

"Then why offer?"

Gavril gives me a sad smile. "Why would I release the pigeon I've cared for so? My songbird?"

That strikes me. I know what he means. He's referencing an ancient story that speaks about a girl who looked after a wounded bird, nursing it to health. She grew to love it, and her heart broke to let it free, but she chose to let her heart break and let it go. She never saw the bird again, but the prince who had been cursed to be the bird returned to her, explained everything, and offered her anything she wanted. All she wanted was her beloved bird to return. He wanted to stay, so they married and lived happily ever after.

He's calling me his songbird. He's letting me go not because he wants me to go. But because he cares about me more than his own heart. This is why I am dangerous. This is what I feared doing to him. I don't want the power to shatter him like I had been shattered.

"I don't want to hurt you," I say.

"Neither of us gets that choice. Remember? I don't get to choose," Gavril says.

"Oh." My voice breaks. He means in a lot more than this game. He means in anything: his feelings, his life, the direction his kingdom takes. Not even to choose to be able to protect his heart by not falling for one of us, for me.

"So, what will it be?" he asks me.

"I don't want to go," I say firmly.

"Are you ready to accept what might happen?"

"No," I give him a weak smile, "I don't get to choose."

Gavril returns the weak smile. "Me either."

I frown. "You aren't going to ask about that night?"

"You told us. I believe you. No more to be said." But his eyes tell me he knows, just like Sage, there's more. But he, unlike Sage, doesn't care. He trusts me anyway.

I am in so much trouble.

Chapter 4

I try to hide my mixed emotions when I get to my room to change. Damian isn't fooled, but he politely doesn't ask. Once I'm dressed, I head for the library to start my studying, but my heart isn't as in it as I'd hoped. I am uncertain how this study will help me anymore. What I felt sure of suddenly felt just as inconstant as everything else.

I'm halfway there when a voice I recognize greets me. I turn to see it's the grand duke. I'd met him at the welcome ball where he'd pretended to be the prince. I was glad to learn he wasn't because, to my annoyance, he just felt pushy as he tried to charm us the whole night.

He is tall and handsome, had royal dark skin, fine beard, and thick curling hair brushed back from his face and down to the base of his neck. But he doesn't feel right to me as odd as it sounds. Most of all when he really is good looking.

His deep brown eyes sparkle at the sight of me as he greets me, "Lady Kascia, it's been far too long."

Yet not long enough. "It has been. I'm sorry, you never actually told me your name." I try to be polite, but I just want away from him. I give him a warm smile, but my feet turn away from him, longing to leap for an exit.

"Grand Duke Aldgrone," he introduces himself with a proper bow to me. "I've tried to keep my distance until now. I am happy to see you doing so well. I knew you'd do well in the Enthronement." How? He hardly knows me. "I have heard you've finally started learning about the ins and outs of noble life," he says brightly. "How are you liking it?"

"Oh fine," I say, wishing he'd go away. Why does he make me so uncomfortable?

"Good. I'm sure Lady Hydrengia is doing a good job preparing you for court life," the grand duke smiles. "We're all looking forward to it. Now it's down to twenty, we have our collection of girls who will qualify for court positions. I'm delighted you're one of them." He studies me a moment with his large eyes and smiles a little, making his perfectly trimmed beard lighten. I'm sure someone would find him charming, but I don't feel comfortable with him. "Though we'll get to meet you at the Christmas

Dinner, some will want a head start. I could hardly wait. Have you noticed the court is more interested?"

"No, in fact, you're the only non-royal member of the court I've spoken to," I admit.

"Ah, so I'm quicker than they are," he laughs as if it's a big joke. "I see." He tosses his over-gown behind him, drawing my eyes to his clothing. He's dressed finer than I have ever seen any member of the royal family on a casual day. "I'm honored to spot you first then. You certainly will be a gem in any court position you receive," he says, studying me again.

I want to cross my arms as if to defend myself from his gaze. He's awakening a rare part of me that can get combative. It's not like his eyes are lingering on somewhere they shouldn't or anything, but I don't like how he studies me as if evaluating me for something, something I'd rather not think about.

"Actually, the prince spotted me first," I say.

The grand duke laughs, "That is true. He does have a good eye for talent and beauty." He gives me another look-over. I wish he'd stop. "And I've seen how stunning you are. I've heard you are quite the talented singer. I see how well you dance at the balls. I hope next time you'll save one for me."

Oh my vene, is he flirting? Is that why I feel uneasy around him? Is he allowed to do that? Legally, I'm the prince's alone, right? I was told I'd be in trouble if I was found with anyone else, hadn't I? Had that been in the rules or just implied?

"I'm still a Chosen," I remind him, hoping that protects me.

"Doesn't mean you can't dance with other people. The prince won't mind," he smiles.

Godwin, the prince's valet, had. He'd helped me avoid the grand duke at the Harvest ball. Did that mean Gavril felt the same?

"And not everyone gets to win." The grand duke smiles warmly again. Yet it doesn't make me feel warm. His smile makes goosebumps rise on my arms as if cold. "I'm just being friendly. I may get the honor of working with you shortly. In fact," he steps closer to me, "if you wanted some insider help navigating the court, I'd be happy to be your contact."

I step back as surreptitiously as I can, hoping he doesn't notice, but I don't want him that close. I don't like what he's implying. He's trying to make a deal, to put me in his pocket no matter what court position I receive. I hadn't realized that even if I wasn't princess I'd deal with such politics. Had he tried this on the other girls too?

"I have an excellent teacher, as you said yourself, Your Grace," I reply. "I think I'll handle the court just fine when it's time."

The grand duke frowns and opens his mouth but pauses as his eyes land on something over my shoulder.

I turn to see someone else I know from the Harvest Ball, the reporter I'd mistakenly overheard talking to Godwin about the refugees up north.

The reporter smiles a huge smile at the two of us. The grand duke takes that as a cue to leave. He bows low to me, taking my hand and kissing it before I can try to object. "Thank you, my lady," he says quickly.

I yank my hand free before he straightens up and hastily leaves as the reporter joins me, still beaming like a cat who caught a juicy mouse. He's lightly tanned with short blond hair that looks like the wind blew it straight up and away from his face. His narrow but light brown eyes turn to me after watching the grand duke go.

"He seems to like you," he says.

"We only met properly just now," I reply. "I'm sorry, I don't think we've properly met either."

"Fabian." He offers me his hand. I take it, surprised someone didn't bow to me for once. It's rather nice. "So, you've only just met?"

"I've met him before, but not properly," I reply.

"Hmm, interesting," he says, mischief in his eyes.

But I don't care. I have been dying to ask him about the rebels up north, to learn which rebellion drove thousands from their homes, what the war is really like. My father told me, but I don't feel like I can believe what he says anymore. I'm dying to have what I believe confirmed, to have faith in my own thoughts again.

"I hear you've spent a lot of time up north," I say.

"Where did you hear that?" he asks with a slight frown.

I open my mouth when Godwin's voice cuts in. "Cousin, what are you doing?" It's Godwin, sounding nervous yet friendly as he joins us.

Am I on some courtier superhighway or something?

Now I see them together, I can see the relation. Godwin is more freckled than his cousin, but their hair is the same shade of blond, though Godwin's borders on brown depending on the light, and though Godwin's face is narrower, I can see how similar the two are in other aspects. Though Godwin dresses better, making the servant's blue and yellow uniform uniquely his own. Damian would be impressed.

"What? No one said I can't say hello," Fabian says defensively.

"Yes, we did."

"Nope. The court is allowed to speak to them now." Fabian grins like he got a good bite of the mouse he caught.

"Oh, for Merlin's sake," Godwin sighs. "I'm not sure that counts, Fabian. The lady has other things to do; you go and bother the court like you're supposed to." He sends Fabian off.

Fabian chuckles and gives me an apologetic smile as he leaves. I open my mouth to stop him, but I don't have another choice. How could I undo Godwin's dismissal?

"Sorry about him. He's court born, but being a scandalous reporter is his real passion," Godwin says to me. "I'd recommend you be careful with what you say to him. Why was he even bothering you?"

"He saw me talking to the grand duke," I say.

"What? What did he say?"

"Fabian or the grand duke?"

"Both." Godwin looks a bit alarmed. "Were you two alone?"

"Yes, I was on my way to the library, and I ran into the grand duke. It wasn't planned. We've never properly met before."

"Please tell me you didn't say that to Fabian." Godwin frowns.

"He asked if we'd met before, I admitted we'd not met properly." I frown too. "Godwin, what—"

"I'm sorry to interrupt and run, but I have to play defense." Godwin sighs exhaustedly. "Enjoy the library, my lady." He gives me a quick bow and runs off, cursing his cousin under his breath.

I frown, unsure what that was all about as I make my way to the library, heart sinking in disappointment. I'd been dying to ask Fabian how bad the rebel attacks really were. I'd spent my whole life thinking we were the saviors only to fear we might be the actual problem.

But that's what this afternoon is for. I'm going to find answers about that prophecy my father spoke about and perhaps the truth about this war.

Unsure where to start, I look for a librarian, but I can't find one or any sign of a self-directory. I spend most of the afternoon learning the lay of the library.

Zelda comes in after a while and smiles at me. "Looking for something?"

"History," I smile, "and where old news reports are kept."

Zelda shows me where they are, conveniently side by side. The books neatly sit on a shelf while the old reports are kept in organized file drawers marked with their dates. The paper they're printed on is thicker than traditional papers. I suppose that's how they get them to last so long, some kind of enchanted paper to make it last longer for archives.

"If you're looking for the kind of books that might help us with lessons, they're over here," Zelda says helpfully. "I ordered my own copies after I asked Gavril if we might need them later."

I frown. We hadn't been given homework yet. Not only did that mean we might have homework, but Zelda had talked to Gavril in-depth about it recently enough for her to buy her own copies.

"Is that not what you were looking for?" Zelda notices my frown.

I quickly cover up. "I was hoping to learn more about the royal family from five-hundred years ago."

"Ah, family history then." Zelda smiles and shows me where that's kept, on the other side of the archives. "Sounds fun! Mind if I join in?"

I shake my head. It would be fun to have someone to study with and her insight might be helpful.

The princess orders tea and treats brought up, and we spend the last few hours before dinner looking through a general book on the royal family history, lying on our stomachs in front of the fire as we flip through the pages, laughing at the anecdotes we find.

Zelda was right about it being fun. There are stories about the royal family ages ago with plenty of odd cousins, crazy uncles, and weird aunts, but once you reached the family of the time of the war, the anecdotes became sparse, far between, shorter with far less detail, like a funny story about a birthday or funny misstep in court.

I find basic family history and impressions. I pause at the rulers who'd started the war. I admire one of King Hysoppin with his queen, Queen Amara standing beside their daughter Princess Cecilia, dressed in a stunning wedding dress, next to her new husband Prince Jerome of Athadina. On the prince's other side are Princess Cecilia's brothers, Prince Alder and Prince Christopher. Standing between the two princes is Prince Alder's wife Princess Sarah.

They all look happy and content in this impression. They all remind me of Queen Dalilly, all with impressive coils, the king and crown prince sporting impressively trimmed beards. You can tell who married into the family because Prince Jerome was not as dark-skinned as the Purerahian family. But they all look happy. Prince Christopher has a glint in his eye that tells me he was up to no good. Was he the problem?

But just like the sparse antidotes, the impressions get rare and far between. Prince Christopher died only a year after that impression was taken, but apart from the births of Prince Alder and Princess Sarah's children and the passing of King Hysoppin and Queen Amara, which happened only about six months or so after Prince Christopher died, there is little to note in the family history portion.

I try the news clippings, but I have little luck. I read a report about the torching of the Burned District with an impression of what the area looked like before it was burned. It was beautiful. Grand buildings stood tall and stately with copper roofs, (or at least they all look like blue copper), elegant seashell white mixing with the sandstone we have today, and the Governance Building was larger and more beautiful with a clock tower with the imaginal display below that.

The second impression shows the damage just after the attack happened. It makes my stomach twist. It is like witnessing an accident where you want to look away but can't. The tower is completely gone, the roofs of every building demolished, black smog obscuring everything, filling huge gouges in the buildings, streets, and wreckage.

The article I found is a reflection on the events a year after it happened. I try to find the report that would have come out after it, but the file folder that should hold it is empty. And not just for that day, if I read the history reference right, but the whole two weeks after it happened. Was this just bad archiving with no librarian on hand? Had someone checked it out? Or was it missing on purpose?

That only makes me more suspicious, but the only way to find out more might be to ask Gavril, and I'm not sure now is the best time for that. I'll start with what I have.

I spend a week researching after lessons every day. But for all my efforts, I am not learning anything new. I follow the history books and use the news reports to dig deeper as I follow the timeline, but it is not much help to me in learning more about what caused this if the royal family is not corrupt.

After a week of dead ends, I am cautiously optimistic more time in the library on rest day will provide answers. I do my dance and music training in the morning, then plan a whole day in the library. I can't sit still that long though, so I take breaks to walk around the castle to help me focus.

On this walk, I notice boxes are slowly filling the hallways, packing boxes. When I go to my room to prepare for lunch, Damian answers my question saying the palace is getting ready to prepare for the holiday once December arrives. I suppose a castle this large takes a long time to prepare for the season.

After lunch, Zelda joins me in the library. The angel staff surprise us with popping corn as a treat. They are too good to us. I don't remember how Zelda and I ended up in a mock fight, but we're laughing and throwing bits of popcorn at each other in front of the fire.

"Well, it looks like I'm missing a party," the prince's voice cuts into our laughter.

Princess Zelda flushes like she's been caught and sits up quickly.

I just adjust to smile up at him. Gavril is smiling at us, hands in his pockets. Sage looks bored, but as I study him, I think it's just his way of hiding his real reaction.

"A messy one," I agree.

"I don't have to clean up, do I?" Gavril asks. I shake my head.

"Sorry, I didn't mean to mess up your library." Zelda is flushing.

Gavril shrugs. "Enjoy it, I don't mind. Looks like fun. Don't let me ruin it."

"What are you doing up here?" Sage asks.

"It's only the second floor. It's not up," Zelda corrects him. I laugh.

"It's up," Sage states. "What are you doing in here?"

"You said 'in' instead of 'up'," Zelda says as if saying "I win". Sage rolls his eyes.

"Reading," I state.

"About?"

"Mostly the royal family." Zelda picks up her book and shows it to Sage.

Sage's brows draw together, and he looks right at me. "Why?"

"Why not?" I smile.

Gavril tilts his head and takes the book and looks it over. "Lovely, looking for blackmail?" he asks.

I shake my head. "No, not really searching. Just curious."

"Why?" Sage is glaring at me again. How can he think my research into the royal family is a plot? But maybe that's the point. If he doesn't know why, he's nervous.

"If I'm to help rule this land, it's nice to know where we came from," I say.

"Sage, can it really be that bad if she knows history?" Gavril raises a brow.

"Perhaps," Sage says.

Zelda laughs. "You are so weird. What are we going to do? Find out the first king was a pirate and riot in the street with the others?"

"I haven't the faintest idea," Sage says.

I shake my head. "Me either."

"Perhaps you better choose other research materials." I can hear the veiled threat.

Oh, for heaven's sake! What horrible thing can I do with the knowledge of the royal family?

Zelda frowns. "Or what?" she challenges.

Sage just looks at her. I don't think he has an idea how to back up that threat. I sigh. Zelda frowns deeper. "What's wrong with it?"

"I'm worried about why," Sage says.

"Why not me?" Zelda defends.

"Because you're a nerd. You just like to know things," Sage says.

Zelda's head pulls back a bit. I giggle. Well, if that wasn't a "shots fired" moment, I don't know what is. "And that's so bad?" Zelda asks.

"I didn't say it was," Sage states.

"But you meant it to be," Zelda retorts. "Sit down."

I hide my giggle behind my hand as Gavril chuckles and allows Zelda to shove Sage into a chair to give him a solid telling off about why being a nerd isn't so bad.

Gavril comes over to sit next to me, cross-legged on the floor. He picks up the book Zelda dropped. "So really, what are you doing?"

I shrug. "I figure if I understand your family better, perhaps I can be better at stopping all this, win the Enthronement or not."

Gavril nods a little, scanning the family tree on the page he was looking at. "Me too," he sighs. "Though I have read these. Doesn't tell you what they were thinking, does it?"

"No." I shake my head. "But maybe seeing when the thinking changed may help."

"Maybe," Gavril agrees.

"I thought with all I'm learning about diplomacy and the like that maybe historical context would be helpful," I say, hoping that story does not make Gavril suspect something is odd too.

Gavril nods once more. "Sounds like a good plan." He puts the book down. "So, is this what you girls have been doing?"

"What have you been doing?" I ask.

"Normal." He shrugs. "Lessons, staying fit, dates."

I pretend the last one doesn't sting. He'd not asked me out since before the ball.

"Anything exciting?" I ask.

"You know I can't tell." Gavril smiles sadly.

What other girls has he kissed now? Dahlia keeps a board with a list of who has done what with the prince, but I don't trust it to be accurate. My count isn't. Gavril and his father found it one night and "corrected it" while adding Sage, the king, and queen to the board as a joke. But as far as I know, they aren't updating it. It is all hearsay.

"I know, sorry." I give him a weak smile.

"But you seem to be having more fun than me." Gavril looks at the popcorn bowl.

"Maybe." I shrug. "Dating is fun."

"Not when your kingdom depends on it," Gavril replies.

I frown. Every now and then, Gavril says something like that. As if the outcome of this competition is more than just him finding a true princess. Like the fate of his whole life and kingdom rests upon it. But why? It is important, sure, but the way he says it makes me feel he means more by it. I am hoping my research into the past, and hopefully, the prophecy gives me a hint.

A light goes off in my mind. I'd not looked at a single paper or record from the time Gavril was born. If the prophecy was about him, it likely was given around the time of his birth, right? The announcement of the queen expecting him or when he was presented or something.

I quickly pull my mind to the moment, so the prince can't follow my train of thought.

"It's still just about finding you a partner," I remind him. "The war won't fall apart just because you pick a companion not as brilliant as another."

Gavril sighs frustratedly but does not elaborate. Am I onto something? Instead of replying, the prince tosses a bit of the popping corn into his mouth. "More butter next time," he advises as he gets up.

I smile a bit. "Harder to throw." I toss a bit up at him. It somehow lands in his hair.

Gavril laughs and tosses it back at me. Then his eyes light up, and he looks at the bowl then at Sage. I grin and nod him on. "Do it," I whisper.

Gavril grins and picks up the bowl. I keep nodding him on. Zelda sounds like she's almost done anyway.

Gavril walks up behind Sage, waits until Zelda sees him and dumps the bowl out just as Zelda starts to laugh. Sage jumps up, shaking the snacks out of his hair and glares at Gavril then at me. "You're a bad influence," he says.

"How do you know it wasn't my idea?" Gavril grins.

"I'm sure it was. She just didn't stop you," Sage says.

"You pick on me; I'll let him pick on you." I smile.

Sage growls and throws some of the popcorn at me in irritation.

"How rude," Zelda says and throws a handful at Sage.

That makes the prince's eyes light up, and he throws some at her. In about four seconds, we start an all-out popcorn fight. We have made a royal mess by the time we suddenly realize we have to rush to be ready for dinner.

I dash into my bedroom with popcorn still clinging to my hair and maybe even my clothes.

Damian looks over from his work with a smirk and arches his brow. "I see the studying went well."

I blush. "Yeah, the prince came in, and Sage demanded to know why I was interested in the royal family. Zelda got offended, and it ended in a popcorn fight," I admit as poor Flur helps pick popcorn from my hair.

Damian chuckles. "I see." He looks to Flur. "We may want to use perfume tonight. Unless you like smelling like popcorn." He smiles at me.

I laugh. He has a great point. Vivian helps do my hair once Flur is done picking popcorn out and gets a ready dress for me. They help me change as quickly as they can before they give me a light layer of perfume before I rush down to dinner.

Zelda is still giggling. I am glad Damian thought of the perfume. I can smell the popcorn on Zelda. I pretend I don't. We look over at Gavril and cover our mouths. His mother leans in to smell him and asks why he smells of popcorn. Sage glares at us. Zelda beams back. I'm glad she's willing to mess with him. It's nice to have someone defend me.

Chapter 5

Though I am feeling better the next time Zelda and I are sitting in the library, it's clear she's worried about something. But honestly, I'm not much in the mood, so I'd rather not talk much about it. This only makes Zelda worry more.

"We could talk outside," she suggests.

I give her a sideways look over my book. "Like we could get permission to go outside."

"I have ways." Zelda smiles.

"Like what?" I have a feeling I know what she's going to say.

"I... just do," she finally lets out.

"Like?"

"Well, you ask the king first." She's still hedging, but there's a lingering smile on her face too.

"Only you could get him to agree to that. How do you get him to do that?" I'd love that power. Might be able to escape whatever punishment my father has in mind no matter what.

Zelda sighs and shrugs, making some of her blonde hair fall over her shoulder, making her oddly pointed ears easier to see. "The king likes me. We corresponded for years before I finally came out here."

I do recall Zelda saying something about being the first, but she hadn't given me a lot of detail. Was she the first one asked? But then why is she only number six, most of all when that is the lowest of the born princesses? You'd think the king's favorite would at least get number two behind his wife's first pick.

"So you were his first choice?" I ask.

"I don't know if I'd go that far, but he likes me." Zelda's cheeks turn slightly more pink.

"You're his favorite." I smirk. It is no secret to the rest of us.

"After your talk with them, everyone thinks he likes you," Zelda teases warmly. "Though some like to say it's because he'd like you to win for... other reasons."

I frown. "It doesn't help the way he jokes." Do I dare confess I once honestly thought I may have to guard myself from him as much as Gavril? Zelda is smart. She'd put it together if I said too much.

Zelda giggles. "No, and you seem to not mind teasing him back about liking to watch us."

"I'm an actress. I always put on a show," I sigh in mock drama and toss my braid over my shoulder, making us both giggle.

"And he loves a show," Zelda agrees.

"So why aren't you higher up?" I ask. "In the number system, I mean."

"Well, everyone knows Rose is the queen's first choice." Zelda rolls her eyes.

"If you're the king's choice then why aren't you at least number two?"

"There are a few reasons, I think." Zelda's demeanor changes the way it does when she's talking more officially. She sits slightly more erect, and her voice goes softer and more formal. Though the warmth and familiarity about her posture towards me and her expression doesn't change. "The fact that the king and queen argue the point is likely a large part of why. The king isn't stupid and knows to keep his wife happy. So perhaps letting his choice have a lower number meant nothing to him as, in the end, those numbers mean almost nothing. It's just the order you were picked to be in the Enthronement in. Which is a bit ironic as all six princesses were going to be a part of it from the start no matter what.

"The other part is relations with the other nations. Those other nations are more likely to retaliate if their princess isn't higher on the list. I am not so easily offended and neither is my family. And even if we were, from that far away, it would be more foolish for us to retaliate in any way. Which I think is perhaps how the queen argued it when really she just wanted her choice boosted."

I roll my eyes. "I'll never understand it."

"Me either." Zelda frowns; her eyes growing sad. "It's a cultural difference between Hyvil and the old world I'll never understand. It's the same formality that made her want to throw you out for defending yourself." I shudder at the memory of killing someone. "Sorry," Zelda apologizes quickly. "But you understand what I mean. I couldn't believe she found it wrong. I... where I'm from — and I looked it up, even here the Potentate code agrees — princesses are encouraged, and it's seen as proper for a princess to learn to defend herself, even violently if needed. Her reaction boggles my mind."

"Guess that puts us both lower on her list." I force a smile.

"Well, the tests are what matters." Zelda shakes her head.

"But... they are the ones who decide if we pass a test or not." I point out.

"If it was just their choice, I think this would have ended long before you or I ever got here." Zelda looks around to ensure we're alone. "I doubt you've seen, but there is clearly more than just their choice going on in this game. I don't know what. I thought perhaps it was the desire to have Gavril have a choice, but when they added so many common girls... well... I don't know."

I study Zelda carefully, wondering if she might actually know what I've been trying to find. "What else could it be?" I ask.

"Frankly, Kascia, I have no idea." Zelda settles back into her armchair with a slightly morose expression. "But as I mentioned, the king and I were in correspondence for years before I finally came. And I didn't come for the Enthronement. You could say the Enthronement came because of me."

Zelda sees my shocked and confused expression and elaborates. "I agreed to come before any other girls were coming. I was here two weeks before they even started planning to bring the other princesses here. As we were close enough in age, I suppose the king thought I'd be a good match for Gavril. I never spoke to Gavril though, not until I arrived.

"It was fun at first. I was having a great time learning about the old world and this country, and Gavril was a lot of fun to be around. They threw a little party after two weeks in which Gavril confessed his parents had told him, he either had to say it was me he wanted or they were going to invite the other princesses. He admitted he didn't know his feelings yet.

"And I'm glad he didn't. I wasn't sure either, and for Hyvia's sake, we'd hardly known each other two weeks. I was thankful for his honesty and not putting the pressure on me. You know how his mother is. If Gavril said it was me, she'd expect marriage no matter what I said. But I... I sometimes wonder if maybe I should have gone home." She slouches into her chair slightly, turning the page of her book, looking at the new page but clearly not seeing it.

"Why didn't you?" I ask gently, studying her face carefully.

"I didn't want to just turn around after two weeks," she says defensively. "And... Well, honestly it was mostly Gavril. I could tell he'd not had anyone stick around or do something just for him, you know what I mean?"

"Far too well," I grumble.

It makes Zelda smile. "And I didn't want to leave him without a friend. I don't know if this will grow into more. I will admit he's a great friend, and I'm fond of him, but I don't know if... if it's ready for more." She sighs once more. "But I knew he needed someone to stand up for him, and at the time, it was the most natural thing to do. And I cannot say it's been bad." She smiles at me. "I've had some great times. It's just..."

Her expression changes into a quiet thoughtfulness again. I give her a moment before I press. "It's just what?"

"It's like there is something else they are looking for." Zelda's green eyes meet mine. "You know what I mean? Gavril doesn't choose. Half the time, he gets no say in who passes a test or not. Yet his parents don't seem to be testing just for what they want. It's like they are measuring us up to some perfect princess measurement found in some book somewhere or something. I haven't a clue where they are getting their measurement from, but I'll admit after the queen's near panic in the safe room, I'm nervous even if I or someone like Rose can pass.

"I have no doubt Rose is a proper princess, and I have full faith I've been raised properly and but can even we measure against this strange ruler they're using? And where are they getting it? It all seems so strange. It's not about who the prince likes, what his parents think — not alone anyway — something is odd. I'll be a goddess if I know what."

"Makes two of us." I sigh sadly. I was hoping she knew what I didn't.

"Anyway, that's why the king is more accommodating to me. I think he's been fond of me for a while, and honestly, I feel he's the only one here who really knows me. We quite literally were pen pals for years." I laugh at the word choice. "Even if it was clear he was inquiring after a bride for his son." Zelda smiles too. "If not... the favorite for him might be you."

"Stop it." I roll my eyes.

"But on that note, I don't think you're on Sir Sage's." Zelda frowns. So that's what she was worried about. She must have noticed how Sage's eye on me has grown even closer since the attack. "The way he got all defensive about you looking at old records. What exactly is going on there?"

"Nothing." I shrug.

"Sure it is." Zelda raises a brow at me.

"Alright," I laugh. "He... doesn't like me. That's all. He doesn't trust me."

"But why? He has no reason or right to study you so closely. Perhaps if it was just after the incident at the Harvest, but it's far more than that, isn't it?"

I debate trying to cover it up, but Zelda's eyes are intent and full of honest concern for me, I can't bear to lie. "We didn't get off on the right foot," I confess, playing with a corner of the book I was still holding.

"How exactly?"

It's my turn to check we're alone. "Promise not to tell or get angry or jealous."

"I was here two weeks before everyone else. What kind of leg up could you have I'd be envious of?" Zelda teases.

I laugh. Of course, she wouldn't. I explain how Gavril and I first met in the garden. I was clueless about who he really was, and though we'd bonded, I'd also yelled at him demanding how he could stand working corrupt royals which made Sage nervous. "And he's thought me trouble ever since," I finish. "And what I did at the Harvest didn't help."

"But you aren't letting them in; you were there all night," Zelda says. "You couldn't have let them in. There's no need to be so rude." The anger on Zelda's face reminds me of some of the girls in the theater reactions when they heard their boyfriend hurt their friend's feelings. I can't help but smile. Zelda shows her Custod heritage with how protective she was.

"He's an assassin by trade," I remind her. "I doubt they care if their tactics are dirty or not."

Zelda purses her lips. "It's still not right."

I shrug. "I'm just going to have to toughen up. If I have any hope of winning, it's my only shot." I look down at my hands. "I wonder if it's better to just give up."

"No, why would that be better? Honestly, you're easily one of the best choices they could make." Zelda frowns.

"Because I'm good in Lady Keva's lessons?" I challenge. "You are Lady Hydrengia's favorite."

"That has nothing to do with it," Zelda insists. "You ask questions that show you don't know the royal world, and that's all. There's nothing wrong with asking the teacher if that was a wise choice. Though admittedly, I'm not sure Lady Hydrengia would survive actually working in court."

"She'd do better than me." I think of my meeting with the grand duke and how bad I am at coping with the other girls' envy. I'd avoided all non-required interactions with them.

"You've not tried," Zelda comforts. "I think you'd do well. You handle the drama of the girls well enough. It's not that different."

"I doubt that. It's royal court."

"You'd think so, but it's not different at all. You just deal with ladies and gentlemen acting like toddlers all wanting their way," Zelda says.

"I ran into the grand duke and did a horrible job," I say.

"Oh?" Zelda frowns. "Did he offer you help learning the lay of the land?"

"Yeah, how did you know?" I frown.

"He did the same to me. I laughed at him. I'm a royal. There's no need for me to worry about that." Zelda waves it off. "He was just hoping we'd owe him a favor."

"I said no for the same reason," I agree.

"Then you handled him well."

"I felt uncomfortable the whole time."

"Normal."

We both laugh.

"But really," Zelda smiles at me, "you would be a wonderful pick. If you're talking about fitting your kingdom, no one is better, not even me." She looks out over the waves, towards her home.

"Do you want to go home?" I frown.

"Not exactly," Zelda sighs. "I'm sure I could do a lot of good here too. It's Gavril I'm unsure of."

"That would make it hard," I agree. "Politics and romance."

"A miserable combination that all royals deal with. Sadly, our love lives are part of the politics, like it or not." Zelda smiles at me.

"Which just makes this harder knowing that I don't fit the politics, so I'll likely just let Gavril down like Sage fears."

"I don't know if the king would let that happen." Zelda smiles. "I think he cares about what his son feels. I get the impression Gavril is afraid to just choose most anything. He was with me only two weeks and couldn't decide. Not that I complain. I don't think I was ready to say yes either. I might have been upset with his presumption if I didn't know the truth.

"But I wasn't ready to give up then yet. Not only had I spent more time on the ship than here, but I felt like there could be an us. I felt he deserved the chance and what we wanted. That night, I saw a chance we could work out."

"Saw?" I frown.

"Well," Zelda sighs and gives a half shrug, "I suppose it still can. I have an obligation to him and my people to see this through, but I can't help but wonder if it's best for him, me, or our kingdoms. I know mine will be fine. My sisters would rule well. If not, I'll go home and take that throne as I always knew I would." She sounds sad as she looks put over the waves again.

"Do you not want to rule your home kingdom?" I ask.

"Oh no, it's not that at all." She smiles at me. "I wouldn't want to go home right away though. I'm fine returning to my duty. I came here open to either option, but there are things here I'd... I'd miss. I suppose with home being so far, I'd not have to go back right away if I lost. If I'm here long enough, perhaps I'll be lucky enough to get a wedding invitation." She gives me a look.

I turn pink.

"What?" She smiles. "You got the first kiss for a reason." Her smile grows.

"Maybe," I sigh, "but there are still twenty girls here, four of them born princesses. A king and queen who have other picks, and a guard who wants to see me hanged," I summarize. "And no one wants me to win but me."

"That's not true," Zelda says. "I do."

"What?" My face falls.

"If it's not me," Zelda adds hastily, but I didn't miss that she had to add it.

"Do you not want to win?" I ask.

She sighs heavily. "I don't know," she admits. "I'm still trying to figure that out." She smiles. "But I also bet he wants you to win."

"I don't know if that's true. And I don't think I want him to. What if I can't win for him? What will happen to him if he picks anyone and they don't win?"

Zelda shrugs. "I don't know. I sometimes wonder if I should have just said no to take one less girl out of the equation for him, but would that really help? Perhaps letting him do his best to pick will help. Let the poor boy choose something. He's not even seen a play or been in public. I mean, he's been outside, but they clear the streets and shops. They let me see the town with them, but they drove out all the other shoppers and the streets for security. He can at least have one risk in his life, right?"

"I suppose. I just don't know if I could handle ruining him like that," I say.

"It wouldn't be your fault. Would be his parents' fault. I see no reason he shouldn't get to decide," Zelda says. "But it's clear they will do this until there is only one winner. So he won't even get a say at the top five or three. I guess that's why he's guarded. Except with you. You seem to break that wall down."

"Yell at him. That should do it," I say dully. I still feel sure that's all it is. I was the girl who does not treat him like a prince. That has to make me attractive.

Zelda laughs. "You're joking."

"No, when we first met I rather yelled at him."

"I doubt that's the only reason he likes you," Zelda says. "Some girls who were eliminated yelled at him too. I heard a rumor that Violet slapped him."

"No," I gasp.

"Yes, twice," Zelda says. "Sage was so shocked then amused he wasn't fast enough to stop her."

"That's rude." I frown. I can't imagine how that would have hurt. "Is that why she was eliminated?"

"I heard it was after she was eliminated. He was telling her she lost, and she slapped him," Zelda says.

My face flushes with heated anger. How could Sage let her do that? Gavril would be... I remember something from our first few dates. Gavril was uneasy about having dates with me. Was that why? He thought I might be one who'd slap him if he had to tell me I was out?

Zelda and I had both gone quiet after her comment. After the silence lingers a while, Zelda speaks, "What if we were the last ones standing?"

I look up at her. "Do you think that's likely?"

"I don't know. I was just thinking," she pauses again. "If it did, I'd choose you."

"What?"

"I mean it, I would pick you. You know your people far better than I ever could. You understand this war and the whys far better than me." She shrugs. "If they are looking for the best political match, the obvious choice would be you."

"Not when they fear I'm a spy," I object.

"That just means you know them well," she argues. "And I think you match Gavril better too. You get him to open up in ways I haven't."

"No, I haven't." I don't buy that for a moment.

"Do you really not know that?" Zelda gives me a look. "You told me you got the first kiss. And that is proof."

"It's nothing. I got him in the mood. I was lucky." I look away. If Zelda had seen the king's breathing attack and helped, she'd have been kissed in the conservatory, not me.

"Kascia, do you really think you aren't a good choice?" Zelda asks.

"I'm not the worst." Dahlia and Ericka would be far worse. "But they want the best, and I'm not the best. You have knowledge of how to run a kingdom. That would help Gavril be more confident. He needs that more than anything. He can do it; he just has to believe it."

"You're right. And we're equal on that. I've not gotten him to believe it either. I don't think he'd be more confident. I think he'd rely on it," Zelda says.

"Let's just hope it doesn't come down to that," I say.

"Let's hope it never gets that narrow with Ericka."

We both laugh.

"Gavril might throw up. He doesn't say it, but the jokes he makes give me the impression he doesn't like her much."

"He hates her dog," Zelda jokes, making us both laugh.

Chapter 6

On the first workday, Lady Keva changes up our routine in her lessons. "We're going to have a day to get impressions," she informs us. "In a few days, we'll have an impressionist come by and take you into a session one by one. They also will be talking to some members of the staff and getting information from your original applications to write small features on you to accompany the impressions. This is standard work for a royal. Often, royals will have to give appearances to the press to keep them happy."

"Or to distract them when they are trying to make a small problem bigger than it is," Lady Hydrengia says.

"So, we'll be helping you prepare," Lady Keva says, ignoring Lady Hydrengia's comment. I get the impression that Lady Keva doesn't often agree with Lady Hydrengia. "And you will work with your attendants to plan out your outfits and where you'd like to take the impressions as you will get to pick."

The lessons are all about handling the press. Lady Keva has been teaching us about how to handle impression collections, how to politely wait our turn, accept direction from the impressionist, and how to politely say no to a request we don't like. Lady Hydrengia has been teaching us how to handle awkward press questions by deflecting them. I think I'll be good at that one without help.

I wonder what kind of look Damian will choose for me. But when I ask him, his answer almost scares me. "Actually, I was thinking about that, and it made me realize that I have been so focused on making you look good, I neglected to consult with you at all. That is unfair of me, and I want to do better in the future, so I want you to take the lead on the decision-making for the photograph. After all, this is about you, and it should reflect that and the person you've become. So, for this first case, I want you to tell me what you want, and I shall do it," he says.

"Oh." But I honestly really have never minded. I also wonder why he called it a "photograph", but it feels foolish to ask, so I return to the main point. "It's alright. I don't mind at all. I like what you make."

"I know you do." Damian smiles a little. "But that isn't the point. I haven't consulted with you for anything since the talent show. And I feel that I have thrown my image onto you, and that isn't right. So, I want it to be your choice. That doesn't mean you'll have to dictate everything, but a queen should decide how she wants to be seen by others. That is why I think you should choose."

I bite my lips. He has every point there, but that doesn't mean I exactly like that. I am just fine letting him direct. "I don't even know where to start."

"Well, I do have a few ideas drawn up. Would you like to take a look at them?" Damian asks.

I swallow and nod. Might as well. I start flipping through the pages. Damian has amazing taste. I see a few of the ones he's already designed as well as plenty of new ones. Where does he find the time to design these? I see many I like, but which would be best for the impression?

A strange thought comes to me. If I won this, would it be my official portrait? I swallow hard.

I could do that starry dress again. It did stun the prince and the others. But that does not feel like the right look for the princess or queen of Purerah. What would the lady who served her people and stood for them to other kingdoms look like? What does my version of her look like?

Then I spot it. A dress that's perfect for a ballgown but also hales back to my ballet roots.

It's floor-length, white, flowing, and decorated with little yellow flowers. The dress matches, but I have a better idea.

"Damian, what about this with the national blue instead of the white?" I ask.

Damian looks and tilts his head. "I think that would be lovely." He looks at me and smiles. "Any other changes?"

I look it over and shake my head. "I think the rest is perfect."

"And for hair?" Vivian asks.

"Um..."

"I have suggestions." Vivian smiles.

She shows me a few ideas, and I like the one with my hair mostly down with just a bit pulled back and more of the small white flowers done throughout my hair. It reminds me of the style one of the girls wore to the Harvest masquerade as an opera star. "Yellow Edelweiss." I smile.

"Oh, even better!" Vivian cries. Damian beams.

Then I have to decide where. I figure I can look at what other royal portraits have done. I go back to the library and bring up a few of the books I have been reading that would have impressions to help me pick a place.

I sit on the floor to flip through the pages, pausing at an official portrait of King Hysoppin and Queen Amaya. It's a sweet impression. The king sits on his throne hand in hand with his queen. I can see a bit of our queen in both of them. The king has a friendly smile. This had to be early in his reign. They both are younger in this portrait. It's not too different from my impression of the current royal family. They don't look or feel evil.

Flur finishes her work and rather than asking Damian if he has anything else for her, she comes over to help me look. I smile my thanks and look back at the impression.

"Aw, this is a sweet one." Flur spots the wedding impression I'd seen in my research. "I can see Gavril in the prince's smile." She indicates Prince Christopher with the mischievous smile.

"I didn't notice." I smile, but she's right. I turn the page without really thinking.

"Oh, Lady Kascia, you should do this," Flur suddenly gasps.

I look down. I'd flipped more pages than I meant to. The impression is of a young princess standing in a gazebo near the ocean. The lighting and background of the ocean is spectacular. Her long flowing dress waves down like the waving water crashing against the beach behind her in a splash perfectly caught by the impressionor. The color choice is stunning too, using a nice lilac to contrast her dark skin with national blue highlights.

"With your hair and dress, this would be perfect," Flur praises.

The princess in the impression looks so much like Queen Dalilly, Gavril's mother. I glance at the label on the impression to see who it is. "Who is this?" I ask.

"Princess Cyrisa," Flur replies.

I frown. I know that name. I review the family history in my mind and recall. "Shouldn't she be Gavril's aunt?"

Vivian beams at my use of the prince's first name as she replies over her work, "Yes."

"But…" I begin to ask, but Vivian fills in as Flur's face turns red.

"Rebels get on the grounds," Vivian says darkly.

I knew the rebels had caused her and her family and loved ones a lot of grief over the years. I do not blame her for her anger. It reminds me of the night Ro was taken. I don't really have much to say. I wish I could say I was surprised, but after all I'd seen I believed it.

"How is your fiancé?" I ask Flur. I'd been so busy with the Harvest and life, I'd forgotten.

"Recovering well, but slowly." Flur smiles her thanks. "Don't worry. When we feel he's well enough for the wedding day, I'll warn you."

"Warn or invite?" I say in mock offense. We all laugh.

I close the book, not wanting to think more about these depressing thoughts. "Well, I suppose if we want that sight, I'll have to get permission."

"Ask your guard; she can help arrange it," Vivian suggests as she starts to wrap up their work for the night.

Lila, my head guard, one of the Custod ones I believe, says she can make it work. I also apologize for mostly ignoring her. She guards my door during lockdown days and ensures my safety, but she does such a good job being out of the way I often forget about her. She laughs and assures me that means she's doing her job well. I'm still embarrassed.

With that done and with my staff ready for their task, I figure there's no reason to stick around and go back to the library to return the books and look up the more recent news reports.

Zelda is already there, doing her own studies and greets me with a small wave. I notice a pile of reports sitting beside Zelda at the desk and sit to look them over and make sure she doesn't already have the ones I need.

I've only just started to comb through them when Isla walks into the library.

"Hello Isla. Not sure I've ever seen you in here. What brings you here?" Zelda asks cheerfully.

"I just wanted out of the Ladies' Chamber. It's as tense as piano wires in there, and I'm not much for being in the conservatory alone."

"Really? I thought it was just them all being envious of me." I smile.

Isla laughs. "No, the 'elite' are getting more tense. Hawi, Kamala, and Marigold are louder and ruder to one another than ever. And the rest are struggling to prove their worth by being better in lessons or comparing styles to one another. It drives me crazy. Though Azalea is still trying to get the girls to get along."

"She's always been the mom." I smile. I rather miss seeing it. Maybe Zelda and I should get over ourselves and try to study in there with the others again. "Don't Jonquil, Azalea, Bella, and Lilly play games anymore?"

"Oh, they do, and I sit with them sometimes, but it's hard to think over all the noise," Isla says. "The born princesses aren't in there often anymore either. I think Rose and Amapola take turns spending time in each other's rooms, and Laurina gets permission to be with her dragon."

"Lucky." I sigh. "Think I'd be safe to join in the games again?" I do miss the girls sometimes.

"We could find other places to go," Isla suggests. "Maybe do what Princess Rose and Amapola do and take turns in our rooms."

I like that idea. "We should ask after dinner."

"That would be lovely," Isla agrees. "But how have you been? I've been worried. You have been avoiding the Ladies' Chamber. I feared as much."

"I am getting sick enough of being glared at in lessons," I confess. "The envy is choking."

"They're getting over it," Isla assures me, "and you have a talent. No reason to shy away from it."

"Now you sound like Lady Keva."

We all laugh.

"'Flaunt it, my queens'," Zelda quotes what Lady Keva tells us when we aren't confident enough.

We all laugh again. We all take our turns mimicking Lady Keva's elegant yet vibrant manner.

"You're really good at that," Isla laughs hard as I demonstrate how she tries to make us feel powerful.

"Thanks, I am an actress." I grin.

"Yes, we should do our stretches together. We said we would," she reminds me.

"Oh yeah, we should," I agree. We hadn't since we'd finished exchanging talents with each others two months ago. "I always take over the room after lunch. You should join me sometimes."

"I'll sketch you," Zelda says, and we laugh again.

"I agree," Isla says. "Your routines would be good to get me into shape." She smiles at me.

"You're more flexible than me. You're an acrobat."

"I wasn't a contortionist." She laughs. "I did aerial."

"Doesn't mean you aren't stronger than me," I say.

"Well, I saw you perform. You are far better than me either way," Isla says. "And I don't mind at all. I'd rather watch than perform."

"Really?" I can hardly believe that. I'd rather perform than watch any day.

She nods. "Oh yes, even my own craft. I loved doing it because I loved to watch it. Being born into this line of work, it was the only one I wanted to do."

I smile. "That I understand." I feel the same in many ways.

"And I'd love to watch your shows," Zelda hints.

"Lovely plan. In the meantime, how about we get the others together for a game?" Isla suggests. "We can use my room."

It has been a while, and I glance at Zelda. She loves the idea.

We spend the rest of the day with Isla, Lilly, Jonquil (though Jonquil mostly just watches over her newspaper), Azalea, and Bella. We play Tamer Battles, a game with different creature cards that you used to battle one another. I'm not very good, but most of us aren't, so it's just fun. Zelda shows off some of her unique Hyvian cards.

It's rather comforting to sit with Lilly on one side of me and Bella on the other. I feel light with Lilly grabbing me nervously as it looks like me or one of them will lose or Bella squealing and hugging me when I or she win a round with Lilly hiding her face at every twist, good or bad.

We left the bedroom door open to help it not get too stuffy in the room. It feels wonderful to be there with all of them. It reminds me of why I originally told my father no. It was to protect these girls, my new friends, my Enthronement troupe. And in this moment, it was all worth it.

I'm too distracted to notice for a good while, we have an audience. The prince watches one of our rounds with a soft smile on his face. I only realize it when we start to pack up to get ready for dinner, and he slips away with Sage close behind. I don't say anything though. It actually makes me feel nervous. Why was he just watching without a word?

But I have more pressing matters to worry about as the day of the impression shoot arrives. I've done these for advertising performances before, but this is different. They have us do our impression captures in reverse Chosen order, so I'm likely going later in the day. My staff proves how impressive they are yet again, and the ensemble is ready the night before, with fitted gown and everything.

At breakfast, the girls are too busy worrying about how they'll look to shoot me angry looks. The prince wishes us all good luck by saying, "Be your most stunning selves, my pigeons."

"If you insist," Ericka teases him as she leaves the room at about the same time as him.

"Of course, my sweet albatross." He kisses her hand, making her beam at him then smirk over her shoulder at us.

My heart can't help but sink. Albatross? She gets a sweet name like that while the rest of us are pigeons?

"Not got your own name yet?" Forsythia taunts me as we leave the dining hall.

"You do?" I shoot back for self-preservation as I struggle to hide my sinking heart. I thought Gavril didn't care for Ericka much, so why did she get the nickname?

"Of course," Forsythia smirks at me. Then she calls out to Gavril as he makes his way up the main staircase. "Enjoy your lessons, my dear prince!"

Gavril stops and turns. He gives a small smile as he sees who spoke and gives her a small wave. "Enjoy your dress up, dear fox."

Fox? He called her fox? That only makes me feel worse as I turn away to get ready.

I hear Damian snicker to himself. I give Damian a look. Even if he finds the names funny, it still means something to Gavril. Meanwhile, he told me I'd get picked, yet he has no sweet name for me. Closest is the title he'd made up for me for my introduction at the presenting interview: starlight princess. Everyone had gotten their own special title that day though; it didn't make me special.

I try not to dwell on it too much as my maids prepare me for my turn. We're ready in plenty of time, leaving me with more than enough time to feel anxious until a servant finally calls me out.

When we arrive on the beach, a familiar face is beaming at me. "Hello Kascia," Adam, the impressionist who took my first Enthronement impression, greets me, "did you get the impressions I sent you?"

"Yes, thank you they were amazing." I'd gotten them the day after the Harvest, but I'd been distracted. I'd hardly even noticed him at the ball, but I had noticed he'd made sure to be in the impression they sent me of my little "fan club".

"My pleasure." Adam grins delightedly at me. "Anything for my princess." I flush, but he ignores it. "Are you ready, my lady?"

"Yes, thank you."

"Will be beautiful. Let's get to it. I'm glad we waited until now. The lightning is perfect." Adam beams. "Makes you that much more stunning." I blush again. He laughs in delight. He offers his hand and leads me into the gazebo.

He has me sit against the railing and drape my skirt just right. He steps back to check the angle then comes forward to adjust a few things.

"Perfect," he says after three or four rounds of this. "Now chin up." I go through the normal check I was taught as an actress, helping me get into the best angle. "Oh yes! Keep that pretty smile. Good." Adam holds up the impressionor. "Stunning, now breathe. Make it real," he says.

"What does that mean?" I laugh then I hear the snap.

I flush. Oh, I hope that turns out.

Adam laughs. "It means be in motion, natural," he says. "Think of it as I'm getting stills of you doing a show, just move around, act it out, dance a bit, you know what I mean?"

I swallow and nod. I think so.

"Here, I'll check that one really quick." He pulls the example from the impressionor and shakes it to help speed up its development. Then he checks it and smiles. He puts it into his binder. "Perfect."

He adjusts something on his impressionor. He takes my image and runs it through the device. It spits out two more images that he starts to shake. "Copies," he explains as he shakes them out. "I love the touch with the ballet shoes," he compliments as I change them out for my sandals.

"Thanks. My attendant told me to, so I thought that would help make it unique," I say.

"It worked." Adam nods. He pauses. "I have a bit before the next girl. Want to check out the beach?"

"Are we allowed?" I ask.

"Sure. Just say I'm getting more impressions." Adam smiles.

"I thought you were asked to get just the one." I let him lead me out of the gazebo.

"I'll take it out of pocket." He smiles.

I shrug. I'd not mind getting to see the waves up close. I'd not felt the sea in months. I'm surprised how much I miss it.

"Here, play in the surf," Adam directs.

"In this?" Damian worked hard on this. The square sweetheart neckline lined with yellow flowers looks perfect on me. The skirt flows like water, feeling like a dream to dance in, I'm sure.

"It's the palace. They can wash it," Adam chuckles. "Oh, I know, dance in the surf." He beams. I laugh at the idea. "Come on, I can make money for myself just fine. I'll cover it. Give it a go." He holds up his impressionor. I must admit it sounds like fun. "Please," he begs playfully.

Well, since he asked so nicely. I take off my sandals, glad the skirt is just a bit off the floor, naturally making it easier to keep it out of the water and sand as I push myself up on tiptoe, not that it works too well when as my feet sink into the sand, but it helps enough to make letting my feet enjoy the waves not as frightening.

"There you go. Give me a spin," Adam says. I can hear him clicking away. He must have changed it to delayed development. I laugh at him as I do as asked.

My skirt flies around in a beautiful arch, fine as any ballet costume I'd ever worn if not better. I can see the yellow flowers around the hem shine in the sun's last light. The effect is really beautiful.

Adam snaps a lot of impressions before turning to clean up his gear. "They all miss you and send their love," he says after a while. "Though Alsmeria's friend, the dark guy, hasn't come around for a while, but he said he sends his love too."

I can't stop the heat that rises to my cheeks. He means Jake.

"I always forget his name, Jack, Jake, something like that." Adam clears his throat again. "But the rest all send their love. Your mother most of all. Oh, I almost forgot," he says as he straightens up with his gear on his back. "Your mother asked to let you know she's sorry she's not written in a while but when things change, she will. She was insistent."

Does that mean at least she hasn't given up on me? A small light of hope goes off in my chest. "Thanks Adam." And I mean it.

"Of course." He manages a small smile.

"Don't flirt with the girls, Adam," a voice cuts in that makes me start. "That's the prince's job. Wait until they're not taken."

I look over to see Fabian trotting over. He's grinning at Adam then at me. "Sorry if he's rude."

"He's not the rude one," I reply.

"Ouch, I deserve that," Fabian laughs. "I am going to be making up a small, little piece about each girl to go with the impressions. Not a full article just yet, but a little piece. I was hoping to ask you a few questions."

"He's asked everyone," Adam tells me.

"I was busy with the last girl when you ditched me. Just wanted to be alone with this one?" Fabian teases him.

"We needed the light for the outdoor shoot. If I waited until now, the light would have been gone," Adam defends.

"Well, I'm here now," Fabian beams at me. "I have been looking forward to speaking with you again."

"What did you want to ask me?" I ask, holding back the millions of questions I want to ask him. If I learned anything from our last meeting, it is to be careful. Godwin thinks he's trouble, and for now, I'll go with Godwin's instinct. He did try to keep this man away from me.

"Only two questions," Adam reminds him as he plays with his equipment, pretending he isn't done putting it away. Is he protecting me? I don't need it.

I lock eyes on Fabian. I can play his game. Adam's defensiveness after Godwin's makes me feel oddly competitive, like I have to prove myself. "Ask all you want."

Fabian's eyes light up. "Ah yes, the girl in green."

I frown, unsure what he was talking about. When was I ever the girl in green? I wear mostly blues. It's why the other girls sport the color.

"What was the reasoning behind the choice of green that day?" he asks me.

"I'm sorry, I'm not sure what you're..." I say slowly as I try to think.

"During the Presenting Ceremony," Fabian says, "most girls wore the royal colors, but you chose green. What was the thought process?"

"You should have asked my attendant and maids that when they were interviewed. They chose it."

"You didn't have any part in that?" Fabian asks.

"No, until recently, I let my staff handle all the choices for my look. I trust them," I say firmly.

"You trust your people?"

That is a trick question. I smile back, knowing I won. "I do."

"Ooo, no hesitation," Adam says. "And that was your two. Let's go, or we'll be even more late than we are."

"What makes you so confident?" Fabian asks me, pulling his arm free as Adam tries to lead him off.

"Because I've seen what people who are given what they need can do, good and bad. And all the people I've dealt with here have been better than any of my expectations."

Fabian whistles. "Lady in Green, may I..."

"Let's go," Adam insists.

"You can start without me." Fabian waves him off.

"You have others to interview, and we should finish before dinner," Adam insists.

"It's alright. He can ask one more then go. Fair?" I try to compromise. Adam looks at me nervously.

"Thank you." Fabian nods his head at me. "May I just say, you are a lovely change from the normal interviews I get in this city. Is the palace as wonderful as you expected?"

"More than you can know." I'd expected it all to be miserable. It is not. "It is far better than I expected."

"And by that you mean..."

"Okay, come on. Let's not keep Lady Lilly waiting." Adam grabs Fabian and drags him off.

I smile. Perhaps I could get answers out of him, but I'll have to be clever in a unique back and forth game.

Chapter 7

At breakfast the next morning, three girls' places are missing: Nicholl, Hawi, and Lark. We're down to seventeen girls. I wrack my brain to try to figure out what the test could have been. How did the impression shoot yesterday prove anyone a true princess or not? All I come up with is vanity, but how did that shoot prove that?

I'm not the only one looking worried. Most girls are looking around at one another, at the royal table, trying to figure out what had happened to eliminate three girls.

Lilly in particular looks nervous. She is wringing her hands until someone looks at her, and she starts to fiddle with her cuffs instead. I can't help but notice they look rather frayed as if she'd played with them a lot. It must be a nervous habit of hers. If it is, what is she so anxious about? At least this anxious. She'd seen this kind of thing happen before. Why was it more terrifying now?

"Are you alright?" I whisper to her when no one is looking.

My question clearly made it worse. She frantically rubs the fabric between her fingers before she puts on a perfectly calm smile, but not one that is at all comforting. It reminds me of how someone tries to hide something hurting them. "Of course. It's just... who could have known how to make sure they passed that test?" she asks in her soft voice.

"No idea, but are you sure?" My eyes go back to the cuff she's almost rubbed to threads.

"Certainly. Sorry." She stops playing with her cuffs and returns to her meal. "I am just surprised, that's all."

"Are you sure?"

"Perfectly." She smiles warmly up at me, much more like herself. "I'm still not used to this," she admits with a slight giggle.

"Is anyone?" I ask. I am sure she's not being perfectly honest, but I don't think she's faking. My concern had made her feel at least a tad better, so I let it drop.

But her question is the one buzzing in everyone's mind throughout our lessons. What were they testing for?

"It was for vanity," Damian confirms when I go to my room to change for dance practice. "A true princess is not vain. So according to my brother, I'd never pass." He grins.

"I knew it," I laugh. "So, you're out then. But how did that prove vanity or not?"

"The eliminated girls either hated themselves in all impressions and required too many retakes or were simply too demanding. Even how they prepared and what they demanded for the shoot was judged which is why I could not simply dictate to you what to do. Though to be perfectly honest, I think you were the better for it." He smiles with warm pride. "And on that note, unless you are completely opposed to the idea, you could have more input here on out."

I smile sheepishly. "I trust you. You know better than me. If I hate it, you know I'll say no."

"True. I was merely thinking you seemed to enjoy being involved in the process once you got into it."

"I enjoy your surprise miracles more." I smile. A lot more.

Damian chuckles. "Well, if you insist."

There's a knock at the door. Flur answers, and to my surprise, Adam walks in. He smiles and asks if I'm available. I nod to let him enter, and he gives me copies of impressions from the day before.

I gasp. I can't believe it's me. I look stunning. I suppose I'd thought myself that pretty in character before, but this isn't a character. This is really me. I flip through them, blushing. I love them and am embarrassed that I like looking at them so much.

Adam laughs in delight. "You are a pretty subject." He winks.

I chuckle and mutter my thanks, feeling a bit anxious. He, like Jashon, the cobbler who'd made my dance shoes most of my life, reminds me how many people want me to succeed here.

After Adam leaves, I pick up the other impressions he's given me, and sit on my bed, lost in my conflicted emotions.

I want to win for them and for me, but I fear failing and letting them down. It's why I get so nervous every time I feel Gavril get close. I'm more afraid of him setting his heart on me and breaking him when I fail.

I fight tears as I look over the impressions of my friends and fan club Adam sent me and the impressions from the Harvest ball before the attack happened. I do notice something odd. In the Harvest ones, I can't find an impression of Jonquil or Florence. Maybe I am missing them in the crowd. I smile sadly at Alsmeria's beaming face from the fan club impression as I put it down.

"Something wrong?" Damian invites me to vent. He's so good at that!

"I'm scared of disappointing them... breaking the prince," I admit, feeling a little healed with the confession. It is like how I could vent to dad before this nightmare. "I'm more scared of shattering him like Jake shattered me than anything."

Damian smiles gently. "I understand, but Kascia," he sits down on the end of my bed with compassion in his eyes, "you cannot control how he feels. Only Gavril can. He knows the consequences. To be frankly honest, choosing how he feels about you may be the only major decision he has made in his life. If you care for him too, then don't take that from him. Yes, there is a chance it may not last, and it may hurt in the end, but it is far better to live, love, and hurt than to live life full of restraint and fear. It is better to have loved and lost than to never love at all."

"Does he really control it though?" I recall all too well Gavril's pained bitterness as he struggled with that thought himself when he came into the practice room.

"The heart sometimes chooses when the head does not," Damian says. "However, I find the heart shows a truer form of what we'd choose in the depths of our souls. Though wisdom should be taken in consideration, it is the heart's job to love and feeling hurt is better than rejecting love because of the machinations of the mind. I have seen it time and time again, and I've done so myself at times."

"Really?" I look at him. I can't imagine him being foolish.

Damian chuckles. "Really. I have had many growing pains in my time. But the important thing is that I had them, and I grew from them. Gavril doesn't need one more person in his life sheltering him. He needs someone who will help him grow. Even if that growth is painful." He smiles sympathetically.

"That it has been," I agree, looking at the impression, my eyes trapped on Jake's smile.

Damian follows my eyes. "Do you want to win the prince?" he asks gently. I nod. Even if I'm still not fully free of Jake, I'm also certain I'll never go back. If I truly got to pick how this Enthronement will end, I know exactly how I'd make it go. But is that because I love the prince or because I want to survive?

"Then don't hold back. Remember, Gavril made the first move. This was his choice. And while he isn't allowed to decide who he marries, you can," Damian says, his tone stressing the urgency and importance of what he is saying.

"What?" I frown.

"If you are willing to fight for him. You're already in the top ten in the way of favor, so you don't have that far to go." Damian smiles. He notices I'm still looking at Jake in the impression. "But you're torn?"

"Not really. I wish sometimes I could go back to when he was mine, but it was always fake. I do feel guilty I didn't... he didn't even get a chance to try to win me back." It feels so good to admit that guilt.

"Well," Damian tilts his head and gives me an apologetic smile, "he's already had his chance. You said you basically dated your whole lives. It's doubtful your relationship could get much stronger than it was when you came here. And he forfeited any further relationship when he told you to agree to come here. But that's in the past, and I know that doesn't really seem fair to you." He smiles gently. "I suppose the only thing you can do is ask yourself, if Jake broke in here today, and asked you to go with him, would you want to go?"

"No," I say firmly, "even if that hurts a bit."

Damian nods his understanding. "Kascia, that boy made his choice. When he told you to sell yourself for his cause, he made the choice. And even if he didn't fully know what that choice was, he made it. That is not your fault. You bear no guilt in that. Standing up for yourself is your right, and what is all you did. There is no shame in that. I told my daughters the same."

It's so odd to think of Damian having daughters old enough to tell that to. "You're just saying that. What daughter?" I tease.

"Lady Kascia, do not deflect," he teases me a little. I do that without meaning so often. "But yes, I had several daughters, and I would tell them what I am telling you. He does not get to make that choice for you. He made his choice, Kascia. There is no need to feel guilty for not giving him a chance. He had it for over ten years with you."

I nod, closing my eyes and taking a deep breath. I'd just have to learn to accept that truth. Even if my heart still hurts, he did get his chance. In all reality, he broke it off, not me, in sending me here. "I'll try."

"I pray you do." Damian nods then smiles a little. "But I believe you dressed in your leotard for a reason?"

I chuckle, cheered up by the idea of a distraction and thank Damian the same way I had my father after one of these talks, kissing his cheek without thought and getting up to distract myself with one of my favorite things. Damian simply chuckles.

After that, I rush to the library, hoping to finally get some answers before any of the girls come to distract me, but I run into a problem. I have no idea how old the prince is.

It is kind of a joke among the girls because he refuses to admit his age. Most crown royals are engaged by sixteen and married by eighteen, and that likely is why Gavril is so embarrassed. But the oldest limit for the Enthronement is thirty, so I doubt he's older than that.

I try to pull up the family history reports to find it. I find the year and date, deciding not to mentally do the math to figure out his age. I'll let him confess that when he's ready.

But I'm disappointed. I read the article about the royal family announcing the queen was expecting, which they did only when she was halfway along, likely because she'd miscarried so many before that point. The only fact of note is when he was presented as the heir and voted on by the representatives, there was some kind of disturbance with rebels coming to protest, but it did not overrule the majority vote that elected him as the crown heir. But that's not odd or proof of anything. There isn't one word of a prophecy.

My disappointment in finding no answers leads me to neglecting research for a few weeks in which the girls are happy to play with me and boxes filled with holiday goodies fill the halls. The girls are all buzzing about it in the Ladies' Chamber.

Dahlia had shoved Lilly into one of the boxes, but to our surprise, when her hand went on the lid to hold herself up, it didn't slide open like it looked like it would. It was locked shut. The boxes are not only strong but secured to prevent someone getting into them without permission.

"What do they think we'll do with decorations?" Jonquil asks in an offended huff.

"I doubt it's us they're worried about," I reply quietly. I'd seen what the rebels do to everything in sight when they get in. I'm sure the toughness of the boxes is to try to repel the rebels.

"Why would rebels care?" Jonquil correctly guesses my thoughts as I make sure Lilly is okay. Thankfully she's unhurt and smiles at me shyly.

"Why did they wreck everything in sight?" I retort to Jonquil. "You've seen what they do."

"The Harvest attack wasn't so bad," Lilly says.

"That's because the Custod rebellion was involved," I say as I straighten up and walk with the rest of the girls into the Ladies' Chamber.

"What is that supposed to mean?" Jonquil demands. I shrink at her tone.

"That Custods are cleaner," Bella laughs, making the rest of us laugh too. "Really though, if it's the Loyalists who keep getting in, they make a mess, and the staff say the Harvest attack was Custod led."

"Just because real Custods are good at this sort of thing doesn't mean the wannabe rebels are," Jonquil huffs. "They are all just pretending to be real Custods. Everyone knows real Custods are Royalists. Look at Sage. He defends the prince with his life."

I bite my lips as the girls set about setting up a game. That's true. Father was assigned here to overthrow the current rulers. The Head Custod authorized it. Which meant it had to be Creator guided, but that doesn't make sense. Was the Head Custod just misguided too? Do I dare ask him? What would he do to me if he knew? Did Father tell him already? What would happen to me then? Am I even a Custod anymore or had I been disinherited?

The thought makes my skin go cold, and I want to run to my bedroom to hide the rapid beating of my heart. I'd lose the magic I had, the authority I had. I'd hear horrible stories of what happened to Custods who lose their magic. First, their ability to fight is taken away, and they can hardly defend themselves. Then fate seemed to always put them into a bad place. What if that ill fate lands on me?

A scream makes us all jump. Me most of all with my horrible thoughts. "Who did this?" Dahlia demands as she runs over to us, holding the board in her hands.

It's about three feet wide and two feet tall. The last time I'd seen it, it had a list of all the girls left in the Enthronement with "points" for how they were doing. Dahlia had spearheaded its creation and filled it in with hearsay. Not long after, Prince Gavril and his father found it and messed with the numbers, making it more accurate, unfortunately for me. They'd also added feminized names for the king, Godwin, and Sage as well as the queen. The queen's points are impressively high.

"I was going to add points for nicknames and found this!" Dahlia snarls at us, brandishing the board at us.

The old scores are gone. Instead, the words "Nippers' Board" are written across the top. All the girls remain as well as the royal family, Sage, and Godwin. The dating activity list is replaced with things like "feeding, petting, cuddling, and sleeping on lap".

"Who is Nippers?" Dahlia demands in a furious snarl, almost huffing and spitting.

"No idea." Jonquil is studying the board with interest. "Another trick from the royal family?"

"Maybe," Bella is laughing. "I hope so. He can be so clever when he wants to be. Is Nippers some kind of pet?"

"He's a stray cat that wanders the castle," I explain. "He's come into my room and bugged my attendant quite a few times. The prince has seen him at least once I know. Perhaps he did it." But the handwriting doesn't match.

"Nippers is a cat!" Dahlia shrieks. "You have to be joking!" she groans and slams the board onto a table. "Now how are we ever going to get it to work?"

"It looks accurate to me," Bella giggles.

The queen is still in the lead even on this board. The king has almost no points, and Sage has none at all. Then I noticed new names. "Damina" and "Gabriella". Feminine forms of Damian and Gavril no doubt.

"Who's Gabriella?" Lilly frowns.

"We never had one of those." Azalea frowns too.

Bella and I look at each other. We're trying not to laugh. Clearly, she figured it out too.

"We didn't have a Damina either," Marigold points out haughtily.

I nod at the others, we should go up to my room. I don't want to get stuck in another one of those fights. Bella follows which gets Azalea to come, but Jonquil has to stay and prove her point. Ericka is arguing why her spot is higher than Dahlia is recording as they try to fix the board, and Jonquil is contesting it.

"She'll come watch when she's done. She hardly plays anyway," says Azalea.

"Suppose not." I sigh as the rest of us go out into the hall.

I don't know why Ericka thinks she should be so high. Gavril has openly made jokes about her to me in private. She isn't one he's hoping will win.

The open-air in my room is a relief after the drama of the Ladies' Chamber. My maids left the balcony door open to air out the room as the afternoon gets warmer.

We settle on the other side of the room from where my staff work to lay out the game. "I can't believe how many girls have nicknames," Bella comments. "Enough that Dahlia wanted to add it."

"Apparently, Heather had a nickname, and when Dahlia heard that, she thought it was worth adding." Zelda rolls her eyes. "Like it matters."

"What did he call her?" Lilly frowns.

"Fish."

I am ashamed to admit I am one of the half of us that laughs. The way Zelda said it so straight faced made it sound less cute than it likely was.

"Do you think he's sad she's gone?" Lilly frowns.

"Who knows?" Zelda shrugs.

"Well, Ericka and Forsythia made sure we knew their nicknames." Bella rolls her eyes.

"Are they the only ones?" Lilly asks.

"No, there are a few," Zelda says.

"Like Rose," mutters Azalea.

I frown. "Why is that annoying?"

"He calls her 'swan'," Azalea says dismally.

"So?"

"Why? It's not like she was a swan at the Harvest. I was the one who wore that costume. Childish, I know, but kind of annoying when I don't have a sweet name."

"I don't either," I try to comfort. "So maybe it's not a big deal."

Isla and Lilly blush. I guess they have nicknames.

"I assume the names have meaning. He can't have gotten you and Rose mixed up. You don't look alike," Bella chuckles. "I get the others are just cute pet names mostly. Fish I'm sure was meant to be cute. She was a fisherman or something like that, and he likes the ocean."

"So that's why Kamala is Magpie?" Azalea frowns.

"Hmm, mostly birds," Bella observes. "Well, Florence is 'doll'," Bella points out.

"Well, we're all pigeons." Zelda tries to cheer Azalea up.

"Is a kit a bird?" Lilly frowns.

"Maybe." I frown and look at Zelda.

She shakes her head. "I've never heard of that. A kit is like a baby animal, right?"

"Yes," Damian says from his workbench without looking over.

We all stop and look over at him. Has he been listening this whole time? Of course, he has. I am used to it, but having everyone else be startled makes it more real.

"I'm not sure exactly what though. Is it for rabbits or is it mice?" Zelda asks.

Damian sighs and spins around in his seat. "Young mice are called pups or pinkies, due to their colouring after birth. But yes, a kit is another name for young rabbits. Or equally, it can be short for 'kitten', as in a baby cat. Both animals are small and adorable, but also fragile and flighty. No offense meant Lady Lilly, but I believe the prince means all parts of the term." He gives her a gentle smile.

Lilly flushes but more in pleasure than embarrassment. She covers her mouth to hide the smile. I smile too. It's not like Gavril is wrong. She is a nervous person, most of all around him. It's nice to see that his noticing makes Lilly happy. Gavril is really good at that. I swallow down my heartache.

"So do any of you have nicknames?" I dare ask as a distraction.

Azalea shakes her head dejectedly. Bella shrugs, but Isla flushes a sweet pink. "Nothing that special," she tries to downplay it. "He just calls me 'dove' sometimes, not that often. Normally to calm me down when I get nervous." I wonder if that's it. He uses a cute name to calm people. Ericka, that fit, but Forsythia?

"Do you understand the name?" Damian arches a brow at her.

"Not really. I thought he was trying to be cute. He does call us pigeons," Isla says.

"What does it mean?" Azalea asks with interest. Bella hits her arm with a chuckle.

"Which are you referring to?" Damian asks with a slight smile. "They have different meanings."

Azalea gaps. "Both!"

Damian bows his head in amusement. "Very well." He raises his eyes to meet ours. "When he calls you pigeon, it means he sees you as his responsibility. The name can also mean that you are young and attractive, which you all are. But I believe in his mind, he leans more to the former. You are his stewardship, and he is telling you that he will take care of you. As for dove, Lady Isla, I would not be one to count yourself out. The dove is a symbol of faith and purity. It also is often the symbol of peace and hope. In calling you a dove, he is recognizing your faithful devotion to The Father and likely that you are a peacemaker."

I beam at the pleased flush that climbs Isla's cheeks before she looks away, trying not to be too proud of herself.

"Guess he really thinks the names through." Bella frowns a little.

"Why so many birds though? Magpie is for Kamala," Azalea says. "Then, of course, 'albatross'."

"'Fox' isn't a bird," Bella chuckles.

"Guess not." Azalea sighs. "'Swan' is though."

"Ah yes. The swan," Damian chuckles. "Be glad you didn't get that one."

"Why?" Azalea frowns. "At least it makes sense for me."

"Does it though?" He tilts his head while leaning his head on his fist.

"Well... what does Rose do that makes her more of a swan?" Azalea asks.

Damian studies her for a moment with that narrow-eyed look he sometimes gives me. Then smiles. "If I tell you, I'll have to kill you." He grins.

"Oh ha-ha." Azalea rolls her eyes. I look around to see where Cedrick is awaiting his payment for a lost bet. A meow cuts the air, and Nippers, the little black cat, slinks out from under the desk.

"Hello Nippers, how long were you there?" I tease him as he comes over to get pets.

"Hey, I need points on the board," Bella jokes and lures that cat onto her lap.

Damian ignores the cat, chuckling and sitting up straight. "In all reality, I'm not sure I should. I wouldn't want to get the prince in trouble."

"Wait? How is it a bad thing?" Azalea frowns.

"Are some of them really not compliments?" I ask in shock.

"How could 'swan' be insulting? Maybe 'magpie', but 'swan' or his 'little bug'?" Bella asks.

"Oh, I almost forgot about hers." Azalea nods.

"Who is 'bug'?" I ask.

"Jonquil," Lilly says. That makes sense. Jonquil used to study them before she became a Chosen.

"There are two sides to every coin. But if I tell you, you all must swear not to tell anyone else," Damian says seriously.

"All our friends are here. Won't tell a soul," Azalea promises.

"Not even Jonquil?" Bella teases.

"Oh, well alright," Azalea promises. Zelda giggles.

"So long as you understand this conversation does not leave this room," Damian says firmly.

"Promise," Azalea says in interest. I smile.

"Not a word," Isla agrees.

Damian sighs and nods then looks at the floor. "Have any of you ever seen a real swan?"

"Not up close," Azalea admits, and the rest of us shake our heads.

"Well, they are graceful and beautiful to be sure, and they do mate for life, unlike most animals. However, they are also combative, aggressive, and vicious creatures that would bite your head off as soon as you get close to them." He glances up once he's finished.

"Oh," Azalea says awkwardly as Zelda tries to smother her laughter on a lounge pillow.

"So, as I said, you don't want to be a swan." Damian smiles.

"I thought 'bug' sounded bad." Azalea pushes a small smile. "But 'doll' is sweet enough."

Damian winces through a smile. "You would think so, wouldn't you?"

"I suppose so." Azaela frowns.

Personally, I'm not sure about any of them anymore.

"Guess doll could mean empty," Bella muses.

Damian nods. "Dolls are pretty. They are fashionable and always wear a smile. Most people enjoy dolls because they give them a sense of companionship when they have none. Dolls are always pleasant because they don't argue back. But the reverse is also true because they provide no amount of meaningful conversation. Their smiles are painted on, and therefore, fake when it comes down to it. In calling her a doll, the prince is saying she seems nice and lovely to look at, but he isn't sure she is real. Their interactions end up hollow because she is trying to be pleasing to him, instead of being herself."

"Is the prince just a jerk?" Azalea's question makes us all lose it laughing, not even Azalea can hold in a smile. "Are any of these names nice? It's 'bug', isn't it? That's the one nice one."

Damian chuckles. "No, she 'bugs' him."

"Oh. But then why be so open with the name? It has to be more than that." Azalea frowns once more. Why does all this bother her so much?

"Because he's putting up a facade, at least with her. Jonquil, I'll admit, is an interesting woman. Much like the bugs she studies, she can be fascinating to watch, and it's obvious why if you watch her day-to-day. Being called a bug could be he sees her as someone who is small and helpless, and therefore, in need of protection. But even the most seemingly helpless of creatures can be deadly in the wrong circumstances. In calling her "little bug", he may be indicating that while she may appear to be vulnerable and intriguing to watch, he is unsure if there is more to her than meets the eye."

"And that proves he's not a jerk how?" Bella is smiling, still more amused. "So getting a nickname means he doesn't like you and wants to hide it."

"Not always." Damian smiles in amusement of her assumption. "Dove wasn't bad, was it? And Kit, while it points out a few flaws, still means she's adorable." He gives Isla and Lilly each a smile.

"And 'bug' isn't too bad as some of the others." Bella agrees. "I mean, 'fox' or 'albatross' is better. I assume 'magpie' is because she's loud," she guesses. "But others are good too... I think."

But Damian chuckles yet again. "Some of them are, but it's true. Magpies are pretty to look at. I, myself, have often admired their colouration and beauty, but they are loud, obnoxious, and hard to be around because of it. However," he pauses for a moment, "I'd rather that than be an albatross."

"Why? They're beautiful." Isla frowns.

"They certainly are." Damian nods. "But I'd rather be a *swan* than an albatross."

"How could it be worse than being called rude and told you want to admire them from afar?" Bella asks in shocked fascination.

"The term among sailors is derogatory and given to one whom they see as a burden," Damian says with a slight frown. "And not a light one at that. In sailor terms, it literally means "my cross to bear". That term goes back to stories about the Protector who died on a cross. In giving her that nickname, the prince is essentially saying Lady Ericka is the heaviest burden he may have to carry to his death."

"Ouch!" Bella laughs.

Zelda is covering her mouth, and Isla looks embarrassed for the girls in question.

"So maybe we're safer without a nickname," Bella suggests to Azalea.

"Maybe." It only seems to have cheered Azalea up a little.

"Lady Azalea, you are not any less for not having one. If you don't have a special name, it is not because you are any lesser in his mind than those that do. Though I think I may have made my point that Prince Gavril does not give out names simply to be cute. They all have meaning, hidden under the surface, though not all of them are bad," he admits. "But the nicknames are the prince's way of expressing his feelings without revealing them. If you don't get one, it just may be that he does yet know how to express his feelings for you through a specific name that would do you justice."

"And now they don't have to be added to a board anyway. Unless Nippers can nickname you," Bella jokes, making us all laugh. Nippers purrs his agreement.

It does make the tension drop. Though I'm still smarting a bit over "fox". I don't know why that one bothers me. Perhaps it's because it means Gavril actually likes one of the snotty elite. At least the others he knew were trouble. Forsythia though, she somehow makes him see past it.

We joke about what other nicknames some of the girls might get as we play, cheering up Azalea for sure. Nippers' playfulness certainly helps. We all gather plenty of points.

Not all the girls are excited about the Nippers Board, but Bella and Lilly are really into getting points on the Nippers board. They even start setting up little treat stands to try to lure him into the Ladies' Chamber.

I watch as Bella sets one up as Marigold and Kamala argue loudly over why they'll out last the other. I'm just glad the smell of tuna doesn't permeate the room.

"With the numbers low, it must make it easier for him to take interest and not be overwhelmed," Marigold is saying in her typical loud voice that drives Lady Keva mad.

"Of course, why not?" Kalamala says. "The more interesting girls are left."

"You kidding? You're the ugliest of the lot," Marigold teases warmly. I've never understood how harsh insults like that are supposed to be friendly, but between Kamala and Marigold such teasing is normal. I am never sure if it is really teasing, but they do it to everyone, and they never take it personally that I can see. "He's just waiting for you to fail."

"He's just waiting for all of us to fail," Isla says in a quiet voice.

Finally, Ericka butts in trying to cut down the fighting. "He's just waiting for you *all* to fail," she says with an air that makes me imagine she was powdering her nose as she said it.

"Right, like you're at the top," Kamala sneers, and Marigold laughs rudely.

"Mostly because he already has a favorite," Forsythia boasts confidently.

"Not in this circle," Florence mutters bitterly over her book.

"Speak for yourself," Ericka huffs.

"Oh, don't deny it. It's obvious. If he picked, we'd all go home tonight." Florence sounds a bit angry.

"Ignore them," Zelda gets my attention. "I know they're loud but ignore it."

"They want to make us fight with each other like they do," says Azaela, shuffling the cards.

Dahlia huffs, "You mean they act like how it is, a competition."

"But not for the prince's affections," Princess Rose points out. "You silly common girls seem to forget that often. It's a test to find a true princess, not a true love."

Those words are like a dart to my heart. It's so sad, so empty. Gavril isn't getting help to find a lover, but a coworker with how Rose says it. This game isn't really for him but for the kingdom. It isn't called a love game; it is an enthronement. It is to put the right girl on the throne. Gavril is just the step between the two.

"So, fighting to be his favorite won't get you far." Princess Rose puts down her tea.

"But that will make it easier, right?" Lilly frowns.

"Maybe. It might make you better liked by the king," Rose says, making me think Gavril's choice of "swan" was perfect.

"But he gets some say, right?" Lilly says. "I mean, he has to live with her."

"Perhaps if the numbers get lower, but being royalty isn't like the shows," says Rose. "It's a job. It's a position. It's a duty to your people. Why do people fantasize about being royalty but not a Custod? It's no different. You marry into that role or are born into it. It's a different type of duty, but it's no different. Name one girl who dreams of being a Custod. But how many do dream about being a queen or princess? The girls who learn that lesson first are most likely to get into the top ten and earn more noble positions. That's what it's really about. If you intend to marry the prince, make sure to build that relationship, yes, but that's not how you win."

"But that's not bad," Jonquil says. "A ruler should find joy in the work." She smiles at Lilly. "Even if it might not always be fun, and you have to make sacrifices, it's a chance to help people in a way few others can. Think of the good you can do for this suffering kingdom."

"Only if you can silence the rebels," Princess Laurina mutters.

"At least someone is trying to help," bickers Jonquil.

"Really? By attacking innocent girls who want to help them?" Princess Laurina challenges.

"They just don't know we're trying to help. Can you blame them for being angry? I guess you've been a princess too long to know what it's like to be hungry and unsure where your next meal is coming from," Jonquil shoots back.

I can see the angry retort already forming on the princess's lips, so I cut in. "But it doesn't make them attacking the castle right. Mercy doesn't deny the action was wrong."

"Defending yourself is wrong?" Jonquil asks.

"Well... no." But I also can't really justify what they've done either. I also can't reference my Custod heritage to explain. If that even applies to me anymore.

"Only when you're being too pigheaded to see you're attacking the wrong problem," Princess Laurina says.

"Either way, we aren't going to solve it here arguing. And it won't make anyone happy," Azalea tries to help.

I wish I knew what to say. I'm never sure how to help when this comes up. I'm constantly unsure after I had my life long convictions ripped from me.

"Not like you can fix it," Princess Laurina says to Jonquil. "You aren't a favorite. You aren't high on the king or queen's list. Your only hope is to outlast ten others to get a rank of nobility that has a job of real meaning."

"She already has a high enough spot to get something helpful." Princess Amapola finally comes to my aid. "Even small jobs make a big difference. Even in a position like this."

I look between Jonquil and the others, wishing I knew what to do. My only hope moving forward to help is to try to win, but am I a good choice when I can't even help these girls calm down? I bite my lip as they go back and forth, and I just sit and watch, my heart sinking. The grand duke was more right than he realized. I can't even get my friends to stop fighting.

I decide if I can't end the fight, I don't want to deal with the noise. I get up and leave the room. I hear a meow and notice Nippers following me up the hall.

"What? Think I should have made them shut up?" I ask him. He sits at my feet and looks up at me with those amazingly blue eyes. "Or did you not like the noise either?" I smile and bend to pet him.

He meows in happiness and arches into my pets. I sigh. "You ever going to let someone own you?"

He meows a most certain "no" before he trots away, making me chuckle. I wonder if that won me points on the board and how many treats he stole without Lilly or Bella noticing.

At dinner, the girls are glaring daggers at one another. Forsythia is the only happy looking one, smirking as she eats as if she won the argument proving herself to be the favorite. Is it her? She is beautiful, and perhaps she does show a different side to Gavril, but she's a conniving little snake. I hate the idea of losing; I hate the idea of losing to her even more. Even her beauty is rather snake-like: stunning sharp eyes, pale skin, dark hair, and a playful little smile when she wants to. It would hurt to lose to anyone, but at least Bella or Jonquil would be a decent choice.

I take the last bite of my food, determined not to let Forsythia get to me. True or not, as Princess Rose said, it doesn't actually determine who's winning.

I pat my mouth with my napkin, about ready to push my chair out when a hand touches my shoulder. I jump and turn to see who it is, startled.

"Sorry, I thought you were about to scoot your chair out. Are you not done?" Gavril is standing there, a bit pink in the face. Lilly giggles behind her hand like the little traitor she is. The other princesses smile in more polite amusement.

"Oh no, I was done." I smile and move to push out my seat, but Gavril does it for me.

"I should have been more observant," he apologizes.

"Unless he just wanted an excuse to touch her." I could kill Lilly. Bella blushes deeper than me as Zelda tries to hide a giggle and shakes her head at Lilly.

Gavril grins as if caught. I wish it was proper to slap him. But I'd not dare in front of his mother. I can just imagine her freaking out, yelling at me to get out while coming over and dabbing the red mark on his face as if he were a toddler pouting over being hit. Maybe it would be worth giving him a little slap. He'd be as embarrassed as me at least.

Gavril pretends he didn't hear her though. "I was hoping to ask if you were free tonight." Of course we are, the guards make us keep to our rooms after dinner. He knows that. But at least he's polite in asking. "And don't worry, your all-knowing attendant was forewarned," he teases.

"He doesn't need to be," I tease back.

"If you say so." Gavril rolls his eyes. "But I'll come by in say half an hour?"

"I can be ready in fifteen," I state. I don't need that much time.

"Oh really? Poor maids rushing about." Gavril shakes his head. "I'll give them half an hour then."

He bows to me then to the other girls before leaving the room. I go to leave as well. I notice the girls at the other table whispering behind their hands. I just catch a bit of what Kamala says as I pass. "How long before she's caught snogging her attendant and is kicked out?"

I freeze in horror and anger. How dare she!? I turn, as if to give her a piece of my mind but snapping at her at the dinner table would get me in trouble. I will have time later in the Ladies' Chamber to get things straight.

I force myself to turn and leave. Besides... We all know I can't talk them into anything.

Azalea, Bella, and Lilly turn to the other table, giving Kamala death glares. Well, at least any girl who really knows me knows I'm not having an affair with my attendant. I am not the only girl who has a male attendant. Part of me wants to prove myself Gavril's favorite just to prove I'm not interested in Damian. He's like a father to me.

I'm almost out of view of the dining hall when I hear a crash. I turn to see Kamala had gotten up after me and fallen flat on her face. She is notorious for being clumsy in heels. She is a mess on the floor, skirts all but tossed over her head and tangled in her own petticoats. A guard has gone over to her to help her up.

Forsythia smirks as she passes me, looking at Kamala. "That's what happens when you're competitive with the wrong girl." She smiles at me dismissively. "And don't think for a moment they're still talking about you. After your stunt at the Harvest, you're not going to be a favorite when everyone knows you're letting the rebels in." She tosses her dark braid over her shoulder as she marches past me.

I really don't know what Gavril sees in her. But if she's saying she's taken my spot in Gavril's heart, she has something else coming she doesn't expect. Even if she's technically right.

Chapter 8

"This is stunning!" I declare to my staff as I twirl in the mirror. The dress is a calf-length skirt with dainty cap sleeves with golden music staffs circling them in a beautiful pattern and repeated in stunning decoration across my soft v-neckline. The pattern reminds me of scalloped lace. The black heels, pearl earrings dangling from my ears, and loose chiffon bun set off my dress perfectly. The final touch Damian adds is a golden music note necklace and black lace gloves. I look ready for a dinner show.

What in all creation does the prince have planned for tonight, a cabaret? I don't have long to wander though as there's a knock on the door before long. When Flur opens the door, she covers her mouth to hide a giggle. Gavril is leaning on the door frame, mocking trying to look cool and calm. He must be nervous for some reason.

"I split the difference at twenty. Was it a safe bet?" he asks Flur. She frowns, not getting the joke. "Sorry, I forgot you weren't in on it. Is she ready?"

Flur nods and steps back to let Gavril in. Gavril steps inside. He's dressed about the same as he was for dinner. Cabaret doesn't seem out of the question by his attire either.

It is nice to see him more relaxed. It's also nice to have a date. I know he goes on far less dates with the numbers down, but a few weeks between is a bit much.

"You look lovely," he says as he looks over my ensemble. There's a look in his eyes I've seen on other men, though Jake rarely looked at me like this. I recognize it from the boys in the theater who had it for many of the girls when we were in better outfits.

I smile and twirl for him to show it off. It wins me a smile that makes my heart flutter. "I need to keep the guards off you," he jokes. "As I've heard, one of them has already claimed a lady." Gavril smiles and winks at Flur who turns pink. How does he know that?

"So that leaves two..." Gavril's voice trails off as his eyes scan the room. He frowns. "Hold on." He notices my missing third maid.

My heart sinks to the floor thinking of her. I say a small prayer in my heart to keep her safe, if she's even still alive. Gavril must not know the rebels took her. I try not to think about it as there's little I can do. The rebels won't talk to me anymore, and my father was tight lipped on the subject.

"I thought each girl had three. She out?" Gavril wonders. He then notices the look on Vivian's and Flur's faces and frowns deeper. "What happened?" His eyes widen in fear and concern with a hint of urgency.

Damian sighs as he steps forward. "She was taken. It happened during the second rebel attack on the castle." He sighs again, this time deeper as he closes his eyes.

"What? I'm sorry. I had no idea." Gavril sighs. He puts his hands in his pockets. "Sadly, it happens a lot. And no news?" I shake my head. "Any family?"

"No, Your Highness. Not really. Just us," Vivian says.

"I'll make sure to check in if we get any reports. They do sometimes show up again," he tries to assure me. "It was... Ro, right?" I nod. Gavril nods at the others too, trying to help. I can see how much his lack of power bothers him in moments like this. If he were allowed in meetings, he might actually be able to tell us something.

"And after that news article, if anyone saw her, they'd likely know she'd need help," Gavril points out. I'd not thought of that. He has a good point. "But I should fix the sour mood I made." He offers me his arm. "Ready?"

I smile and nod, taking his arm. As always, I can't help but admire how strong he feels and wonder why. Gavril doesn't notice, but simply smiles as he guides me down the hall.

He is such a strange man. His strength and temper awe me in good and bad ways. His ability to observe and come up with things others miss, like the news article would help Ro be found, astound me, yet frighten me. And though I know he has quite the temper, he is gentle as he escorts me as always.

I bite my lip before I dare ask. "Gavril?"

"Hmm?" He looks down at me.

"How did you know Flur was engaged to a guard?"

"Oh, I visited him. I like to check on all those who are injured during an attack. Seems the least I can do when they risk their lives to defend us. Don't tell my mother. She'd freak out."

I smile a little and mime zipping my lips. But it warms my heart. Perhaps I should ask Gavril about him. I'd not had the pleasure.

Gavril leads me onto a floor I'd never been on before in the west wing. Gavril opens a door for me, and I step inside and recognize where I am without ever having seen it before. It's a music room. It's only slightly smaller than the one I used back at the theater. There are windows lining the west side to let us look out over the ocean, the rest are shelves or closets for storing music books, sheets, and instruments. The view of the ocean is stunning. Is there a room in the castle that doesn't have a lovely view of the sea?

The walls are seashell white with golden seashells. The grand piano is stunning and shining. There's a cello, a base, an organ in one wall, drums, tubas, even a xylophone, and a stunning golden seashell harp. On one wall hangs guitars, violas, drums, trumpets, tubas, French horns, flutes, bassoon, clarinets, and many other wind and string instruments whose names I can't recall.

It's a magical room. I take a deep breath as I step into it, my eyes taking it all in. It's like stepping back home only better. The instruments here are clean and pristine. Though most likely unused, but still to me, it is as magical as the orchestra pit. It even has the same woody, yet dusty smell.

"Don't get lost," Gavril teases as he closes the door behind him. I notice the door is thick with sealing around the edges, of course, to keep sound in. The familiar ambiance of a well acoustic-ed room falls on my ears.

"Too late." I smile delightedly. Then my face falls a little. "You know I can't play any of these."

"I don't expect you to," chuckles Gavril.

There's a large closet built into the wall by the door that doesn't look like it's for instruments. "Is this where you keep the music books?" I ask.

"No, not in this section. The books are kept on the shelves, so we can see them," Gavril says, joining me by the drawers. "We keep the art up here."

"What?" I look at him as he unlocks one of the drawers with a key in his pocket then pulls it open.

My jaw drops; paintings, hand painted — likely originals — fill the drawers with their own unique dividers protecting them from being scratched or damaged. The smile on my face only gets bigger. Paintings, landscapes most of all, catch my interest.

"See any you like?" Gavril asks, flipping through them.

I see a few I don't like. I'm not a fan of the ones that show too many people. I like sculptures of people far more. I skip over the section with people. Gavril notices and smiles a little. "Aw, not even a few of the Cladio?"

"Not a fan of watching other girls dance," I joke. Cladio is known for his stunning artwork of dancing fairies, almost always unclothed to show off their stunning bodies. "His work is stunning, but I have a soft spot for—" I gasp in excitement. "Are these originals?" I look up at Gavril.

"Some." Gavril nods, helping me pull out a few Rounds paintings. He did the most amazing landscapes of the oceans, ships, beaches, mountains, and Mermaid Lake in Purerah. He'd lived about fifty years before the war broke out, so his artwork showed Purerah at its best.

"Wait, your ancestors were his first patrons," I realize. "Do you have... you must have his theater one hanging somewhere."

"Theater one?" Gavril frowns then his eyes light up. "Ah yes, I know the one you mean, he called it the Chandelier." He pulls open a drawer to the left of the one I was going through, the largest of them all, and pulls it out.

I cover my mouth in excitement. This is my favorite painting. It was done to look like the royal theater, my stage, with the chandelier hanging low and dividing the stage up into sections showing landscape versions of many famous plays: *The Phantom*, *The Witches*, *The Little Mermaid*, *Beauty and the Beast*, *Cinderella*, *The Greatest Showman*, and *The Ice Queen*. It was clearly the original, huge and so detailed. I'd never seen a reprint as large.

Gavril chuckles, watching me with interested eyes. "You like this one?"

"It's... my favorite," I breathe.

"Even with people in it?"

I give him a look. "Yes, it's the characters, and I love how simple their faces are. You can't tell which actor or actress would play them. They are just the character. And the worlds... the beauty of the ice, the shining of the lights on the underground river, the roses... It's just so detailed."

"You really do like this one," he is studying me as I admire every detail.

I notice details I'd never seen before, like the rose actually has exactly twenty one petals, the realistic flutter of the acrobat's skirt, the snowflakes aren't just dots, but shaped flakes all unique. "You sure you don't want to try a few others?"

"Do you have more Rounds?" I ask.

"Lots, like you said, my family bought most of his originals," Gavril says.

We go through a few more, many I know from their reprints. Gavril finds it funny how much I love them, teasing me with other artists and styles, but all I want to see are Rounds. I'd always loved his work.

"Maybe we can have a few put in your room," Gavril says once we've both had enough of the artwork.

"It's too valuable." I flush. "Do you have originals in your room?"

"No, but you're welcome to pick some for your room. Ones that fit, I doubt the big ones have a spot in there," Gavril says.

"Do you have any originals hanging?"

"Maybe in the nursery." Gavril shrugs.

That brings a thought I hadn't had in a while, since the physicals that tested to see if we could even bear the prince an heir. "Have you thought much about that?" I ask. Has he looked to see who would make a good mother for his children?

"Thought of what?"

"Children?"

"I avoid it. The rest of it is terrifying enough," Gavril says quickly.

"Really?"

"Well yeah. I can't pick my own wife. Thinking I can't pick the mother of my children makes it all ten times worse," he explains.

"Sorry." I wish I hadn't asked.

"It's okay. You're not the first to ask," he says.

"Oh." I feel like that knocked me down a peg. The right choice would have thought about children already.

Gavril changes the topic by going over to the music books. I follow. "Top ten songs," Gavril challenges me as we walk.

"For performing or listening?" I ask.

"Hmm, alright, one of each," he says.

I take down a collection of Amian Custod's music. I find a few of my favorites from the Amian Custod book, then a few from the Damian Custod section and a few instrumentals from plays I liked.

"Hmm." Gavril looks them over. "Interesting. Alright, pick your favorite to sing: not perform, just to sing for fun."

"Will you pick some too?" I ask.

"I have mine out already." Gavril grins.

I nod and look them over to pick the top five of each when a stunning piano piece from Amian Custod fills the room. I look over to see Gavril at the piano, playing as if he did it for a living with a soft smile as he watches his fingers dancing over the keys. He hardly looks at the sheet music. He taught himself well. Amian Custod was not known for writing easy pieces.

I pause to watch him for a bit, but Gavril catches me. He keeps playing without missing a beat. "Go on, pick."

I jump a bit. "You are really good. You're telling me off and not messing up." I have to say it.

Gavril shrugs, still playing. "Well, going to make me wait all night?"

"If it means I get to keep hearing that," I retort.

He laughs. "The song is over halfway done already."

"Alright, alright." I go back to finding my favorites to sing.

Gavril plays two more of the pieces I gave him.

"Did you just use your elbow?" I ask as he finishes. The room seems oddly quiet without his playing.

"Yup, it's written in the music." He points at the sheet music that he'd still mostly ignored.

I take a look and see he's right. "Wow. Damian was a weirdo."

"Don't let your attendant hear that." Gavril is still flipping through my choices.

"Oh ha-ha." I roll my eyes. "Not the same."

"You didn't say which Damian." He then mutters the names of my choices out loud. I frown a bit. He didn't normally talk to himself. "Hmm, I think I know this one." He pulls out one of my choices.

"So, you want to play for me?" I smile.

"Yes." He puts up the sheet music. "Let me do one play through just in case." He goes right into it; I start at how strong he comes in. He may not have much faith in himself, but his confidence is stunning in his playing. He plays it through perfectly then smiles at me. "Ready?"

"You are." I beam at him. He plays it perfectly, and I find him easy to blend with for our first song. He's grinning, clearly having a great time. I catch him adding and embellishing here and there, but it goes with my voice.

Gavril then notices a songbook that was on the piano when we came in. He grins and offers it to me. "What about one of these?"

I frown. I shake my head. "I'm not a fan of that show."

"More classical?" he asks.

"Yes, do you even know what role I'm famous for?" I ask.

Gavril frowns, thinking. "I forgot."

I sigh. "Phantom, Gavril. How much more classical can it get?"

"Oh, that... wow," he smiles. "How about one from your last show?" He finds the book for The Hunchback and smiles. "Tambourine?"

I flush. "I'd rather not."

"Come on, you did it every night for a week," he taunts.

"I really rather not."

"Alright, alright, and I heard this one." Gavril keeps going.

He goes to close the book when I notice something on one of the later duets in the play. I take the book before he puts it away. Are these notes? Yes, marked in the proper pencil are notes about how to play the song, handwritten like a performer would do. I flip the pages. There are the normal marks a pianist makes, fingering, reminders to speed up or slow down, but there are others too, ones I know well.

"Gavril," I say slowly, looking up at him, "were you learning this song?"

"What?" He frowns. "I told you I play piano, right?"

"Yes, but—"

"How about this one?" He shows me one from *The Miserables*. Normally, I don't mind, but he'd picked one from a scene I didn't think was very appropriate.

"No," I state blankly and look back at the Hunchback book. "These are breath marks, Gavril. I make them all the time. You don't use those when playing the piano."

"It's not a breath mark," Gavril says. "It's a rest."

"No, it's not. You've got them in all the right places and a rest is written into the music. These are notes for you. You were learning this one," I insist, a bit excited. "You sing."

"No, not really," says Gavril, rubbing the back of his neck. "I will sing along sometimes, but I don't really sing."

"You do too." You didn't make breath notes to just mess about.

"I do not, give me that." He tries to take the book from me.

I hold it out of reach. "They're breath marks, Prince Gavril. I'd know them anywhere. You sing."

"No, I don't. Give me that back." He reaches for it, but I pull it out of reach. "Kascia."

"That's 'lady' to you," I tease as he tries again and misses. I step around the piano, so it's between us. Gavril gives me a look. I giggle. "Say it."

Gavril sighs. "I let you not say 'prince'."

"But you never have called me 'lady'," I tease.

"Not true," Gavril says. "But fine. Giveth me the papers, my lady."

I pretend to offer it without getting closer. Gavril reaches across the piano best he can, but I step back. He laughs. "You missed," I taunt.

"Lady Kascia, give me that." He stands up, and I back up more. He laughs at me. "That's not very proper."

"What? You can get it," I assure him. He steps around towards me, and I still keep out of reach. "What's the problem?"

"You are," Gavril laughs and does something rather impressive. I step to go further away. He goes around the other way, using the piano bench to launch over part of the piano and catch me around the waist with both arms. I cry out in surprise, but not in fright. I'm laughing as he keeps a hold on me with one arm and reaches for the papers with the other. I can feel his rough shirt and neck against my shoulder as he reaches.

"You monkey," I accuse.

"That's Prince Monkey to you. Now give it back," he laughs as he finally gets it from me.

"I just want to see it," I defend. "You are learning to sing it."

"I don't sing."

"You do so," I say flatly. "Don't deny it."

"I don't sing for people," Gavril says.

"You that bad?" I pout.

Gavril shrugs. "No idea." He lets go of me, seeming a bit dejected as he steps back over to the piano with the book.

"Gavril, I think it's great. Just show me how you do it. This one was originally written as a duet. We can do it together."

He shakes his head. "I don't need to find out I'm horrible by the wince on the professional's face."

"I won't wince." I roll my eyes.

"You will too," he says.

"You can't be that bad," I state. "Why are you scared? Other girls make fun of you?"

"No, because they don't hear me, just like you won't. Not even my parents have heard me. Just my guards who don't say a thing," Gavril says.

"I'll be honest. If you're bad, I won't make fun of you, and I'll never ask again," I say. "I like this song. I'll do it with you. It will be fun. Come on."

Gavril sighs. I think he wants to say something but thinks better of it. He turns to the bench and picks up the music and sets it out. "I'm still learning it," he defends again.

I pull up a bench, sit on it, put my elbows on my knees, and rest my lace gloved hands pressed together under my chin, looking at him excitedly. Gavril rolls his eyes and turns to the piano. He sighs and takes off his jacket and tosses it over a bench to his right as if it was as natural as kicking off his shoes.

"Oh, don't look at me like that," he defends.

I look up to the ceiling as if it was more interesting. Gavril sighs again. He hesitates more before starting to play. His playing is spot on like it was before. He takes a few deep breaths as if trying to forget I'm there. But then he starts.

I honestly had expected him to be pretty bad with how he argued with me. But that's not what I hear at all. He has a surprisingly solid tenor tone, a unique blend of soft yet harsh, like the phantom or count. It is warm yet has a strong edge.

I blink as I watch him, eyes closed as he starts into the song, which actually starts quietly. Slowly, a smile climbs my cheeks as he goes on, and his singing gets stronger and more confident.

I sit up, still smiling, and I prepare for my part to add. He's almost fully into it as he sings his last line before I join. He jumps a little to actually hear someone with him, but his eyes shine just a little as a slight smile graces his lips as we join together for the next line.

He looks over at me as he sings his line before we join each other in the harmony of the next section.

A power strike of the piano ends the song before he stops, lifting his foot from the pedal, so the music comes to an almost abrupt halt. He takes a deep, nervous breath, shutting his eyes before he looks over at me, waiting for judgment.

I am awestruck. My mouth hangs slightly open. "Gavril," I say, "I honestly thought with your fussing you'd be average at best, but that was... incredible."

"I thought you said you'd be honest."

"No really, I didn't even realize until after you had trouble with breath placement. You did breathe in a few odd places, but it was... you're good. No professional yet, but..."

"Yet?" He raises a brow.

I flush red and look away. Right, I'd only get the chance to help him be a pro if I won. But my blush makes him smile.

"So, it didn't hurt?"

"No, Gavril, honestly, I'm really impressed. I was sure you'd be just okay, but that was really good for no training," I insist. "Want to do another one?"

Gavril blinks. "Are you serious?"

"Yeah, you get so into it I hardly notice your mistakes. It's just for fun anyway, right?"

Gavril glances left and right before muttering, "Right."

"Come on, it's just me and Sage hanging off a wall somewhere," I insist. "Will be more fun than you just playing the piano. Please? I'll even coach you on what to improve on if you want."

"Well..."

"What others do you know?" I pick up the book.

"Most of the ones from that play," he admits.

"You know it?"

"Never seen it, but I read the book and found the music compelling," he replies. The story of the man locked away in a bell tower likely felt familiar to him.

"So, let's do the other duet."

"There are a few," he points out.

"All of them." I beam, handing him back the book.

Gavril smiles at my enthusiasm and starts with the first duet. He thankfully skips the tambourine scene.

I smile as I watch him get into each character. His acting is slightly over the top and could use some coaching, but as it's just for fun, it makes me smile. I join for the female background too to make it more fun. It makes Gavril laugh as we join each other at the end.

"Okay 'Someday' next." Gavril is grinning like a child as he pulls it up.

I laugh and let him start playing, smiling at how excited he got. I rarely see him get this open and excited about something. I love it.

When the song ends, Gavril closes his eyes smiling while still holding the final notes. When he lets them up, he turns to me. "Thank you, Kascia. I don't know if I've ever managed to get the music to be so cathartic before, and that's all I've ever used it for."

"You come up here to sing as a way of venting?" I ask in awe. And they said the perfect man didn't exist.

"Sure. It's why no one else hears me. I had no idea how fun this would be or... healing." He flushes and turns back to the piano, suddenly shy again. "Um... so what do you want to do next?"

"What can you play?" I challenge.

"Um... most things?" He frowns.

I go right for my favorite play and open it to the famous duet. He pales. "Are you nuts? I'm not that good of a singer. That's..."

"Come on; the same guy who sang Hunchback played this role," I encourage.

"No, not that one. How about... this one?" Gavril finds a different one.

"Alright," I agree. I'll get him to do my favorites one day.

It was really fun to just sing for fun with him, playing with trills, holding notes and even messing with lyrics. I'd never done that before. I always had to do it just as it's written. Gavril laughs at me at times, and I laugh at his changes too.

We have a huge mess of papers that are the songs we'd done and moved on from. I am also starting to "own" my space, moving around him as he plays and even committing the sin of sitting on the piano at times if the music seems to fit. I wasn't rehearsing; I was playing. I'd never done that with music before. I did it in dance when I was alone, but never in music like this. I guess it's because I only had back up when I was rehearsing.

We go on for hours, losing all track of time enjoying song after song, ignoring each other's mistakes and goofs, laughing at ourselves a fair few times. But then one song hits a bit too close to home. There's a bit of a pause as the last note from the piano holds onto the last strand of the night.

Written in the stars indeed. It was right, win this or not, Gavril would be part of me forever, and I doubt he'll escape me so easily. Why I wanted to push him away. I am scared of hurting him that way.

I jump as Gavril gasps in horror and jumps to his feet. I follow his eyes and see the clock hanging on the wall. It's almost two in the morning. Heat rises to my cheeks. How did it get so late?

"I should have had you in bed hours ago," he quickly offers me his arm, "your poor maids."

I try to swallow the nervousness that had entered my chest at the last song and let him lead me away. Maybe the song is right. This whole thing would be easier if we hadn't started to like one another. I wish we didn't know the bliss of being just the two of us.

"Please tell me you're not the one with sleep problems," Gavril's stressed voice cuts into my musings.

I flush, not wanting to admit I am. I have to drink a tea to get myself to sleep each night. "I'll be fine."

“Oh vene, I’m so sorry. I just didn’t realize how late it had gotten. I just kept going with song after song.” He smiles a little. “I had a really good time.”

I force a smile back. “Me too. And it’s not all your fault. I missed the time too.”

“Time flies, right?” He smiles.

But my mind has wandered again. “Have you done that with anyone else?” Why am I so jealous? Or perhaps I’m just hoping that there is someone else who can make him feel like that even if I lose.

“No,” Gavril chuckles. “I told you I don’t sing for anyone but myself. Until now.” He gives me a soft smile as we reach my room.

He lets out a deep sigh. “Forgive the hour,” he bends to kiss my hand, “but thank you for your time. I really enjoyed it.”

I return his smile. “I should thank you for yours. You’re far busier.” Gavril huffs. “I’ll see you tomorrow then.” I wish I had something better to say.

I feel Gavril’s hand tense in mine for a moment before he dares something I didn’t think he’d get the nerve to do again. He pulls me close in an embrace. I thought after my snapping at him when we’d kissed he’d be afraid to. He pauses a moment before he kisses my forehead.

I shut my eyes at the gentle touch. Why does this have to be so hard? I just want to reach up and return it. He’s so close. It had been so easy with Jake. My mind starts to replay those nights by the river Jake and I spent cuddled up, lip locked. But then it changes to that day in the conservatory, Gavril kissing me over and over.

Gavril presses his forehead to mine just a moment. I don’t open my eyes, letting us just be, even if all it is a stolen moment in time. I don’t want him to pull back. I don’t want to pull back.

He tenses again before he lets his head fall, so his lips are near my ear. “You passed.” There’s a tease in his voice. He sighs. “Please keep passing.” His voice is so low, I’m not sure I really heard it as he pulls back and kisses my hand again. I can still feel the tension in his grip. “Good night, milady.” He pulls away with surprising speed before turning away back up the hall.

“Gavril.” It pops out before I can stop it, but he either didn’t hear me or has to pretend he doesn’t because he turns the corner and is gone.

Chapter 9

I wake up to the smell of food the next morning. Breakfast had been brought up. My maids report that their orders were to have the food ready for me, so I could sleep in a bit longer before lessons. I can't help but worry whose orders.

When I join the girls just before the start of lessons, I see Bella smirk and turn to Ericka. "Told you." I glance back to see Ericka handing Azalea and Bella something. Ericka looks truly annoyed. I frown. What are they doing?

Bella smiles at the question in my eyes. "When you weren't at breakfast, some of the girls bet you'd been eliminated. So I took that bet."

"Are you feeling alright?" Azalea asks with a soft frown.

"Someone is feeling sore," Forsythia taunts as she settles into her seat.

"Someone is feeling sensitive," Bella retorts.

"What do I have to feel nervous or sensitive about?" Forsythia smiles that snake-like smile. "I didn't lose his attention."

That was low. I look away and pretend they hadn't started arguing.

"Or maybe you did," Bella hints at what might have kept me up.

Forsythia's laughter was anything but polite. The mere idea I'd had such success is apparently laughable to the others. Forsythia wasn't the only one laughing.

I fight not to redden as I pretend I hadn't heard the exchange. "I'm feeling fine; thank you," I address the others. I don't want to admit I was up late with the prince. They already hate me enough. They'd never believe it anyway. Apparently, me having that success is too funny.

I was right to keep my mouth shut. During break, I overhear Marigold gossiping with the others. "I heard they went up to the music room. That's close to the royal floor," she is saying.

"You're all nervous for nothing." Dahlia chuckles at them as she peruses the sports page of the newspaper. "There's no way someone like her got that lucky. He's not going to take that big of a risk on her."

"Like you've gotten any closer," Marigold shoots at her.

Dahlia's knowing smile makes all the girls glare at her in envy. I turn away.

They're wrong, I remind myself. As much as I often hate it, I still appear to be his favorite. Though he could be making such pronouncements to other girls behind closed doors. It's not like he's public with his affections for me. Not on purpose anyway. *They're wrong. They're wrong.*

At dinner, however, I'm given evidence that perhaps Dahlia had managed to get that close too. I keep reminiscing about my last moments of my date with the prince. I think of him leaning over and whispering in my ear "you passed".

Marigold's is missing at the dinner table. Gavril is missing too, and she's not at breakfast the next day, though of course, the prince is. She'd been eliminated. Obviously, the dates are still tests. But why does that surprise me so much? I'm relieved I passed but also a bit disappointed.

I thought he'd wanted to let me into the one world he felt safe in. I guess it was just for the test. Though what they are testing, I have no idea. How did I pass when we were up so late? I guess we don't really have a rule about how late we can stay up. As long as we are in our rooms after dinner or out with a member of the royal family, we are keeping the rules.

Part of me wants to confront Gavril about it, but I'm also afraid of being disappointed. I'm also afraid of what the other girls might do. What if I am not the only one he'd shared that world with? Or was his shyness about singing just a story for the test he'd made up?

I see a few chances to try to talk to him, but as soon as I get the nerve, he turns and asks another girl out or is out the door. I think it's just bad luck, but then I notice he seems distracted even when I just try to make eye contact at meals, talking to his parents or just eating. Maybe it is a test thing again.

By the time another week has passed, Elice has also been eliminated. We're down to fifteen girls.

It's a week until the holiday season starts, and our lessons change gears to prepare us for the upcoming interviews. There'll be two sets: one before the start of the holiday. Then as a treat for the people, the royal family is putting on yet another round of holiday interviews to be broadcast as well as the decorating and lighting of the main Christmas tree out on the grounds. And as an added gift, the royal family will be interviewed as well.

Lady Keva prepares us by going over interview etiquette and discussing the appropriate behavior for the holiday festivities while Lady Hydrengia grills us on our interviewing skills. I wonder who will interview us. I might look forward to it if it meant I got to cross wits with Fabian again.

There are a lot of other royal events for the holiday too. The one I recall the grand duke mentioning is noted as well. Once we get through the holiday interview, we'll prepare for the Court's Christmas Dinner. The name of it makes my stomach clench. I'm not the only one. I see it on several faces in lessons.

"Today, we are working with Lady Hydrengia for some very important work," Lady Keva tells us.

We all snap to attention. "What?" Erick complains. We'd been preparing but not with both teachers at once.

"Why?" Forsythia demands.

"Well, backed by popular demand, the royal family has decided to open up the Enthronement a bit." Lady Keva beams.

"What?" Zelda sounds horrified.

"No, no, not more Chosen," Lady Keva explains. "But to the public. The event was such a success and the following articles such a hit, they want to do more of them. The people really are getting involved and that's always a good thing."

"The fact they feel like they get a hand in picking their next princess will likely calm down many rebels into submission," Lady Hydrengia adds. "So it's a good political move as well."

"So today we're going to work on more interview etiquette and techniques," Lady Keva says. "We thought using the time shared to hit both at the same time could be helpful." She beams.

It might, but it sure made it all no fun. Lady Keva goes over proper sitting positions and even does a pop quiz to see if we can recall their names. I'm surprised to learn, a lady can cross her legs, but only in a certain way.

Then we go over how to properly behave while waiting our turn, gracefully shuffling in and out of the interview seat, and the basics on how to open and close the interview. Though she admits those are mostly for live interviews.

Then Lady Hydrengia does mock interviews with us to help us prepare good answers. She starts out easy but then starts asking us things we didn't know about to see how we reply. Dahlia gets a smack on the hand for making up facts to answer a question she does not know. Ericka is praised for her beautiful deflection tactic. Bella gets points for being funny and clever in her style.

Lady Keva comes over and corrects our posture or how to say something properly. Lady Hydrengia does the same thing by making sure we never put words into anyone else's mouths: most of all the king, queen, or prince. Lady Keva helps us know how to politely make sure the interviewer also keeps to etiquette, and Lady Hydrengia grills us with more puffy questions, trying to trick us into messing up. I think she likes hitting us with her fan.

I do well but am so ready for a break when it comes. My head is buzzing from trying to learn so many new things at once. I am glad for the tea and a moment to just watch the ocean before we start a fresh wave. We do mock interviews all morning. And I thought preparing for the dinner was bad.

My mind is all brain fog as my maids prepare me for lunch then all through lunch until I finish my meal. I feel better once I change and do my exercises and dance routines. The other girls are too worn to want to play any hard games, and Zelda and I are too worn to want to try to cram more information into our heads, so we entertain ourselves watching Cuppy, Ericka's half rat half adorable curly haired pup, being chased by Ericka as he runs to try to steal the food we throw on the floor for him, making sure Ericka does not see what we are up to.

The next few days are just as painful. Lilly and I start doing drawing puzzles on random bits of paper in the lady's room to relax after my workouts or just staring out of the window at the cold ocean waves. It's only after four or five days of this we finally get used to it and our normal activities start after my afternoon drills.

I start reviewing pieces I'd danced in the Nutcracker during my dance time: the reality of being away from home for the holiday sets in. It will be a first for me. Would it even feel like Christmas? Normally, I'd have been assigned my role in the show by now. I wonder what parts my friends got in the lottery this year. Mother would have told me, but she hasn't written me, and I'm too scared to try to write them.

I sadly wonder what she'll do for the holiday. Likely she'll be stuck spending it with Jake and his father as that's the kind of thing Father would suggest. And without me there, Mother won't have much of a leg to stand on.

"What do you normally do?" I ask my maids one night as they get me ready for bed.

"Work," Vivian jokes, making Flur laugh.

"Seriously," I giggle, "what do you do?"

"Well, the royal family normally do their family thing on their own. Then there is a ball for the court in the evening after dinner. I just spend it with my friends. Nothing exciting," Vivian says.

"I normally spend the day with Karrigan." Flur smiles.

"When does that title finally change?" I tease Flur.

"Depends on when he heals." Flur frowns. "He's insisting he has to be back to himself fully. And that's hard to tell when."

"Was it that bad?" I frown.

"Well, he's on his feet again. I think we could do it any day, but he wants to be at his best for me." I don't miss Flur's frown.

"He is being weird about it," Vivian agrees.

"He likely wants to be sure he can protect you with all the recent attacks." I frown.

Flur shrugs. "I'll take him however he is." Vivian and I giggle. "He seemed to think around Celeste Day perhaps."

"Tell him to hurry up. I want to be there," I complain, making us all laugh.

"What about you? What do you do for the holiday?" Flur asks Damian.

"Oh, not much." He shrugs it off.

"No family?" Flur asks sadly.

"I'll spend some of it with my brother; it just depends on where we are. As I've said, we travel a lot," Damian says, still working on a beautiful white and gold piece.

"But the castle does a lot." Flur smiles. "We'll start to decorate on the first. The whole palace comes to life. The royal family loves to join in the decorating. I suspect they'll invite the Chosen girls to join in too. But they wait to do the trees until the official start of the season. That's when they'll do the interviews. I love that every year." She sighs.

"You met Karrigan doing that," Vivian recalls.

Flur nods with a soft smile on her pale face. "Yes, he was on guard and noticed me."

"I can't wait to finally meet him," I fake complain.

"Maybe when he heals, we can have him added to your door guard," Flur jokes.

"I'm serious. I want to meet him," I say.

"Win, then you can," Vivian jokes. Flur gives her a look while I laugh.

The day before our interviews, the dozens of boxes around the castle are finally opened showing more enchanted evergreen than I'd ever seen in my life, and we cover the stage in the stuff for *The Nutcracker* and *A Christmas Carol*.

We're given the day off lessons, so we can help decorate if we want. Princess Rose, Princess Amapola, Ericka, and Florence decide to do other things. But the rest of us join the servants and royal family in the decorations.

I start off by helping my maids decorate my room while singing Christmas carols. Nothing is more fun than our threesome rendition of "Deck the Halls" while skipping and dancing about as we hung up the evergreen with red and golden bows and phoenixes bedecking them.

My maids laugh at me as I twirl my way between them as I help them place the enchanted fairy lights in the evergreens and Christmas ornaments around the room. Perhaps I wouldn't miss Christmas at home too much. This is as fun as a Nutcracker rehearsal, dancing and singing as we decorate.

"Well, I didn't think anyone could have this much fun decorating." I turn to see Gavril leaning on my open doorway, watching us as we dance about. My maids flush, most of all Vivian.

"Then you're doing it wrong." I smile, not willing to let Gavril's spying bother me as I twirl to prove my point.

Gavril takes advantage and takes my hand and leads me into an under arm turn before moving into a neat Viennese waltz step out the door. Flur and Vivian laugh in delight at our playfulness.

"Merry Christmas, Prince Gavril," I say when we are out in the hall. I kiss his cheek, not caring who thinks that inappropriate as I look around at the boxes. I can't wait to do more.

Vivian is smirking in confidence, and Flur is covering her mouth to hide delighted giggles.

Gavril ignores them, not at all displeased at my mood. "Want to help me wrap some of the evergreen around the balustrade of the ballroom?" he asks.

"I thought you'd never ask," I tease as he extends his arm to me.

Vivian beams, and she and Flur try to back out of sight, but Gavril invites them along too. He gives me a smile as if saying I don't have to shoo my friends away just because he's around. I roll my eyes, still smiling.

We go into the ballroom via the upper entrance. The ballroom is easily one of the most beautiful places in the palace, and likely the world, with its ocean themed floor, stunning golden wave pillars, and most of all, the dome in the ceiling that reflects the sun and the starlight at night. And the balcony that leads off from the ballroom has easily the best view of the ocean I have ever seen.

On the ballroom floor, a few servants, Zelda, Princess Laurina, and Bella are helping wrap the pillars in evergreen and hanging phoenixes and cardinals in the branches and scattering even more of the birds across tabletops.

"We'll work on these." Gavril pulls over a box with evergreen wrapped with fairy lights and phoenix ornaments meant to hang off of the sections of the railing. The smell of the evergreen fills my nose, canceling out the smell of dust.

I bend down with Gavril to help him wrap the evergreen around each stand of the balustrade as well as along the top where we will hang the phoenixes. We pass it back and forth between us to make the wrapping process faster, getting into an easy rhythm.

"So, what do you do for Christmas at home?" Gavril asks once we get the flow down.

"Rehearse," I say honestly.

"Seriously?"

"Yes," I laugh at his expression, "we do at least two shows during the season: *Nutcracker* and *A Christmas Carol* at least, if not one or two more all at once. We perform them on different nights, a show in the afternoon and another show in the evening. On Christmas morning, we sleep in as late as we want before we have a breakfast of cinnamon cake and open gifts. We are able to have a late lunch/early dinner then sit around the fire and read the Christmas story around the fire before we go back to sleep. It's mostly a day to recover from the craziness. But it brings more funds than any other time. We can't afford not to use every moment."

"I wish it wasn't so hard on you." Gavril frowns.

"It's not like I have to endure it this year." I smile.

Gavril shrugs. "True, but your mother and father do."

I ignore the twist in my stomach that comes thinking of them, wondering what they are doing.

"She told you what she'll be doing this year?" he asks.

"No." I focus on the evergreen as if it requires deep concentration. I hum one of my favorite Christmas songs.

Gavril smiles a bit at me, taking the hint. We're quiet with just me humming for a while. Gavril's voice joins mine in humming. I gave him a look. I thought he didn't sing for others. He just smiles at me. "Who doesn't sing at Christmas?"

My laugh rings across the ballroom. Gavril beams at his success. I give him a smile.

He looks back at our work as we slowly make our way towards the staircase. "So, what do you like best about Christmas?" he asks.

"I don't know." I sigh, looking around and smiling, letting my good mood from singing with my maids come back. "The music, the feeling in the air, the magic of it, dancing with that magic." I sigh happily and set back to wrapping the evergreen. "Even though it was exhausting by the time we actually got to Christmas, I've always loved the season, really more than the day itself."

Gavril smiles gently. "That's beautiful."

"What about you?"

He shrugs. "I don't care for it much."

"What?" I take back the perfect man comment from our last date. "How can you not like Christmas?" Most of all a spoiled boy like him?

"Maybe it is hard to understand, but for me, it's because I never got to enjoy the real spirit of it," he tries to explain. "Sure, we decorate like this every year, and the tree lighting that kicks off the season for the kingdom, and gifts, and music, and all that is nice enough. But I thought it was about serving those around you, remembering to be thankful for what you have, the great gifts the Phoenix and Creator first gave us and making sure to share that joy with all around you."

"What about family?" I tease jokingly.

"I'm stuck with them year-round. Not like we have to work hard to get us all together for Christmas." Gavril smiles at me as we finish the first long strand and start on the next one. "And not really gotten a chance to share what I have with those who don't," he goes on as we start wrapping the next strand down the staircase banister, "so I suppose I never understood Christmas."

I give him a sad smile. "Well, you clearly want to, and you seem to know it better than anyone."

"Maybe." He runs his hands over one of the golden phoenixes as he thinks about that.

"What would you like to do for Christmas?" I ask him, taking the ornament gently to remind him about what we're supposed to be doing as we talk.

Gavril smiles. "Spend the morning giving out gifts to the children on the streets. Then I'd go to the town square and give appointments to all who are waiting there. Give them somewhere safe and warm to stay for a while at least. Then have a big dance in the village for all to come and share in the good food, more to go around than anyone could stomach, and that would just be part of the Christmas ball that ends the day."

He'd really thought about that one. "That is very detailed. Why don't you ask your parents to do that? Even if you can't do it yourself, you can at least organize it."

"It's... complicated," Gavril says quickly and focuses on our work like I had when I didn't want to talk about it.

I frown. "Do you ever stand up to them?"

"It's complicated," Gavril repeats, glancing around as if making sure he wouldn't get into trouble.

"How complicated? I know parents can be hard, but honestly, if you want it, shouldn't you fight for it?" I ask.

Gavril gives me a sad smile. "One day, I'll be able to explain, but not here." He strokes my cheek.

I push it away. The man I'd fallen for, my apprentice I'd met that night we met, that is who I cared for. This spoiled prince who doesn't understand how much his dream could do to help end the war if he'd just talk his parents into it is not what I want.

Gavril frowns in confusion. "I'm sorry. I didn't mean it like that. I just meant I can't talk to any of you about it. It's not just you. I promise."

"Are you saying there are some things you can't tell me that you can tell the others?" I ask hotly.

"No," he thinks a moment, "nothing comes to mind that I can't tell you, I can tell the others. Really, it's not about you. I promise."

"So who gets to know?" I ask.

Gavril bows his head. "The winner."

I sigh in disgust. I gave up my life for them and their cause. I betrayed my family, father, fiancé, and all my friends. I have no safe home to go back to. I gave them everything, and I only get to know why he is such a wimp standing up to his parents if I win. It is so unjust. Then again, unjust is what this family is good at.

The Burn District, the ruined cities, starving children: that was all their fault, and his idea could make a world of difference, yet he won't stand up for himself. Even if who he really is standing up for is his people.

"Maybe if you were smarter about that, this war wouldn't have happened," I reply as I wrap the evergreen tighter than I need to.

"Kascia, really, it's not like that. I promise. It's about—" Gavril stops abruptly as a servant walks past us.

I pause, wondering if he would have told me if he wasn't worried about being overheard. "It's not like the kingdom will fall if you said something."

"I might." Gavril looks up at me.

I don't like the longing in his eyes, the tenderness. I look away and start hanging up the phoenixes along the evergreen.

I jump as a black something jumps and takes the ornament I just hung up and stalks off with it. My eyes adjust to see it's the black cat, Nippers. His tail flicks back and forth in pride as he walks away with his catch. "Hey!" I call out. "Give that back."

"Odd he goes for the gold ornaments when the cardinals I have here look so much more like real birds," Gavril says, standing up as I did to chase down the cat.

Nippers sits down at the top of the other staircase and puts down the golden phoenix to lick his paw. He spots us coming after it, picks it back up, and darts out of the ballroom.

Gavril and I chase after him. We almost slide on the floor as we spot the cat, again licking his paw, at the end of the hallway. I try to approach more slowly this time, lure him into giving it to us.

But once the cat sees me, his blue eyes light up against his dark fur. He picks up the ornament and runs right at us, making us both back away into opposite walls. He stops at the other end of the hall again, sitting down and watching us. His tail taps against the floor as he stares us down, the toy still in his mouth.

"Here kitty, kitty; good Nippers," Gavril coos, slowly walking over to him.

The cat meows loudly and trots off up the corridor and into the library. That's when the real chase begins. Gavril and I race to try to catch him, but that cat is fast and smart. He jumps up onto a bookshelf just as I think I have him.

I look up and am about to tell him off when Gavril runs right into me, having thought, like me, he had the cat pinned.

The cat meows happily as he lands next to the pile that is Gavril and I. He drops the ornament next to us and trots off as if he were king of the castle.

"Rude cat," Gavril mutters, pushing himself up then offering me a hand. "I hope I didn't hurt you."

"You're heavier than you look, but I'm fine," I assure him, brushing off my skirts.

"Well, after that adventure," Gavril runs his fingers through his hair, "we should head back."

We go back into the ballroom and finish wrapping the evergreen and hanging up the phoenixes. We then put nests with cardinals along the top of the flat rails. There's false snow about the ballroom and tucked into the evergreen, making a stunning display.

The other Chosen girls are laughing as they sing Christmas carols as they decorate. It reminds me of why I'd been so excited in the first place, and Gavril and I join them, though I can't help but notice Gavril remains silent on the singing front.

Chapter 10

Gavril's refusal to explain has put me into a foul mood and reminds me, I still need to learn what is really going on with this war. I have not dropped it, still spending some days, most rest days, studying in the library, but I haven't found much. There is more to it; there has to be. But what is so bad Gavril couldn't tell any of us? There has to be answers in the history somewhere.

It crosses my mind to go over my father's head and ask the Custod Council directly, but I'm afraid of being disinherited. What would happen to me then? I even debate asking Sage, but that idea is far more terrifying. What if he figures me out?

This frustrating search goes on until the day of our interviews. The Chosen are nervous, hardly speaking all that day. We have worked so hard in lessons to be ready, we're all tense. It's so obvious that the king tries to alleviate it by telling terrible Christmas jokes like: "What type of key do you need for a Nativity play? A don-key!" "What do you get when you cross a snowman with a vampire? Frostbite!" "What is the best Christmas present? A broken drum... you just can't beat it!" "What's a child's favorite king at Christmas? A stock-king!", "What do you call cutting down a Christmas tree? Christmas chopping!" "What's the sleepiest thing at a Christmas table? Napkins!" And my personal favorite, "Why did Scrooge keep a pet lamb? Because it would say 'baaaaahh humbug'!"

Dahlia in particular didn't like the jokes but pretended she did. The king knew she found them annoying because when we leave, he leans over and whispers to her, "What is the most competitive season? Win-ter!" Then he runs as if afraid of being hit.

I cover my mouth to stop my laughter as Dahlia takes a deep breath to compose herself. She deserved that. She's so competitive. And tonight would likely show it.

I am taking deep breaths myself to try to keep my composure, nervous about the interview. I hope it's not the same person who tricked me into pulling Gavril into the last interview. The queen would be quite displeased. What if I make a similar mistake?

I try to distract myself with Damian's stunning work. He went for something elegant but also simple. The skirt is the fanciest part, floor length and off-white; it is beautiful for how simple it is and how it gently flutters with my movements. I wear a white long sleeve shirt underneath that's only a bit more muted than the skirt. On top of that is a stunning knit sweater with a very low cowl neck and some lovely gathering at the back that makes a mini train that goes down my back to just below my hips. The sweater is a lovely golden yellow, reminding me of the fall season. The ocean keeps our season pretty temperate, but a lot of our trees still get stunning gold and red leaves.

The shoes delight me. They're heeled winter boots, a light color to match the rest of the outfit. I have not worn boots in what feels like forever. They put pearl earrings into my ears and then do my hair down, long and curling, showing off the gold and red colors hidden in the layers when the light hits it just right. It goes well to make a waterfall-like look down my back with my hair and sweater train. Two little combs decorated with little white and yellow flowers pull my hair back on each side, so it stays out of my face.

My maids declare it "perfect", and Damian chuckles as he stirs a cup of tea then beams at me. "Perfection. How do you like it?"

"I love it," I say. "At least some part of this will be comfortable." I feel much more comfortable than I had in any interview setting I'd had before, at least in outfit.

"Brilliant." He beams again then offers me the cup.

"Oh." I presumed it was Damian's. He is always drinking tea. I take it though, not sure why Damian is offering me tea. It is nice and warm. I let out a small sigh.

"It's chamomile." He smiles and sits next to me, crossing his legs. "For the nerves."

I nod. It is the most common tea we drink here in Purerah because chamomile grows easily here. But it makes sense. I am shaking a little.

"Now, I want you to do something," Damian says, meeting my eye.

I meet his eyes and nod that I'm listening.

"Forget everything your teachers told you," he says with just a hint of a smile.

I frown. "What?" They just spent weeks getting us ready for this.

"Their intentions are good, but I'm afraid they've overprepared you. You were excellent in the last interview. So, don't lose the confidence you had by worrying about remembering to do and say everything you were taught. You have done it with them so many times now, it's as simple as muscle memory. You don't need to remember what they taught you to do well in this event. Remember, this is your stage, so act like you own it." He smiles with a sort of warm tease.

I smile and giggle a little before nodding. He's right. I hadn't struggled in the last event. There's no reason I should now. I have to be honest and recall my place. It cannot be that hard. I do not need to be nervous.

I finish my tea and set it down, deciding to be confident. "I suppose we're as ready as we're going to be."

Damian nods and stands, offering me his arm. "Shall I escort you, my lady?"

I nod and take his arm. "Thank you, Damian." I smile. He smiles back then leads me out of my room and down to the event.

Most of the Chosen are already there. The born princesses wear tiaras, but the majority of the other girls wear jeweled headbands or something similar to imitate the princess look. They wear fine ball gown-like dresses to try to look more like a princess. I seem to be the only one not dressed to attend the finest dance party in all the land. I don't mind though. I am starting to get used to standing out in the crowd of Chosen girls. I get a few glares, Ericka and Dahlia among them.

There is a name attached to each seat. We're not sitting in order? That is different. I find my place, far stage left.

As I sit down, the interviewer walks in. A new kind of tension fills me. It's not the same as the man who did the last interview. It's Fabian.

He's beaming his wide smile and waving at random people, wearing a stunning navy suit. It's almost good enough to be one of Damian's. His toothy grin and shining eyes turn to me and glitter in excitement as he looks over my appearance then looks over the others as well.

"Quite a party, isn't it?" I jump and turn to Prince Gavril as he pulls up an extra seat behind mine, turning it backwards, so he can rest his arms on the back of it. "You're all making such a flutter, I'd think you were all butterflies."

"You're not in the interviews. What do you want?" I demand.

"A good show." Gavril shrugs.

"You're horrible."

"My dad is watching." He nods at the front where the king is chatting and laughing with Hydie, the Head of Staff. "He likes a lady show."

"That's horrible." I frown.

Gavril shrugs. "I know. But he thinks I should enjoy it while I can. I don't get it."

Someone has been locked away from the world too long if he doesn't get it. I know the habit of wanting to watch girls in pretty rows. Boys came by rehearsals to do that all the time, but I am just as guilty. A line of shirtless men doing their parts was a nice show too when I had little else to do.

"But it gets me out of lessons too, so I can't complain." He smiles. "But meanwhile, are you busy tomorrow afternoon?" He grins.

"Are you just making sure to have a date every afternoon?" I ask. "It's not a test, is it?"

Gavril frowns in mock offense. "I can't tell even if it is," he says. It must not be by his tone.

"Not like the last one?" I try to hide my hurt. "What were they testing for, anyway?"

Gavril looks around. I think he's mentally checking that everyone has had that test. "That your choices in entertainment are wholesome. You didn't like the racier paintings, and you didn't take the bait of the more... base songs left out," he says. "Not many fell for them, just two." He looks around again. "I'm just glad Marigold won't be booming at the table anymore," I laugh.

"Alright, places," Hydie calls out.

Gavril makes a face as if he got caught, whips the chair he'd been using around back into its place. "So tomorrow afternoon?" He checks, playing with the loose curls at the back of his neck with one hand.

I sigh and nod. I can't really say no and not worry about my position in the Enthronement. "Yes, I'm free tomorrow afternoon."

"Don't wear yourself out before," Gavril warns with a small smile before getting out of the way of the impressionor.

The rest of the girls hurry into place. Dahlia sits next to me. She looks down her nose at me as if to remind me I'm still lesser than her. I'm not scared of her. All she did was kick, throw, and catch a ball well. I can do far more than that. Most of all, on the throne. I may not be a true princess, but I certainly am a better choice than many of the girls here. Dahlia among them.

Fabian sits in his armchair, crossing his legs, giving notes to the impressionor. Adam is there, getting stills behind the scenes. That's when I realize the prince and king aren't the only ones watching. There is a small audience, mostly palace staff and reporters.

I watch the impressionist do his normal count down, counting from five and signaling the last two only with his fingers before he flips the impressionor on. We're live for all the people in every town hall and public building in Purerah to see.

"Welcome Purerah!" Fabian beams and gets to his feet, walking to the impressionor the way a narrator walks closer to the audience to introduce a play. I'm impressed by Fabian's ability to own the space and act to the impressionor. I hadn't even learned how to do that.

"To the first of many interviews we'll have with our Chosen daughters of Purerah, the lovely contestants of the Enthronement. Since the last time you saw them, the numbers have gone down. We're now at fifteen girls." He pauses to get the excited reaction from the onlookers. "Yes, yes, I know.

Can you believe it? It seems like so long and so few." That wins Fabian a laugh.

"But today, we're not going to dwell on the pain of waiting to meet a winner or dwell on those who have already gone home," Fabian says, walking about a bit, using the interview space perfectly. He should have become an actor. "We're going to get to know those who have reached such lofty stations in Purerah and which lovely ladies will be our next ladies of the court; one of whom will be our next princess. Let's begin."

Fabian gives the impressionor another dazzling smile. "We're starting off with one of our most honored guests. She is the crown princess of the high kingdom of Emilimoh. She's here to prove she is the princess of princesses as the high princess. Ladies and gentlemen, please welcome with a warm round of applause, Princess Rose of Emilimoh!"

The onlookers give the expected clapping as Fabian waves an arm to invite Rose to come up from her seat into the interview chair. She smiles graciously and nods gently to Fabian as she walks up. Fabian gives her a bow from the waist and kisses her hand before escorting her to the seat.

He sits down and settles in comfortably before smiling at Princess Rose. Rose sat like a queen, perfectly upright, perched on her seat as Lady Hydrengia told us to. She looks regal, yet stiff next to Fabian's casual playfulness as he sits back and crosses one leg across the other, leaning towards the princess.

"Princess Rose, it is an honor to be able to interview you," Fabian says to her.

"Pleasure to be here," Princess Rose bows her head to him. I hold in my frown, but I'm a bit worried. Princess Rose looks almost cold sitting so perfectly when compared to Fabian's warm and casual attitude. The fact she doesn't go on doesn't help.

"So tell me, what possessed the high princess to join such a contest?" Fabian asks. "Is the prince just that charming? I mean, you're the high princess. No one questions if you're really a true princess, so why do you feel like you have to be here to prove it?" His question sounds so playful, polite, and interested, but I feel the slap in it. Did she not feel good enough? What was wrong with the high princess of Eilimohl if she felt she had to prove it?

"Well, the prince is quite charming," Princess Rose smiles, brushing off her skirt as if she was carefree. "But it was because the king and queen asked me to. I am still looking for my ruling partner and thought there was no harm in seeing if this is the place to find him."

"So you plan to take him home with you if you win?" Fabian asks playfully.

"That we can work out if it happens." Princess Rose gives Fabian a playful look as if telling him not to be so hasty.

Fabian just laughs. "Suppose best not to get your hopes up." Princess Rose's face doesn't change, but I see the offense in her eyes at the implication that she not only might not win but would be disappointed if she lost the prince.

Fabian finishes her interview as warmly as he started. "Well, Princess, thank you so much for staying with us, and most of all, for your time tonight. I look forward to getting to speak to you more very soon." She bows her head politely back.

Fabian stands up and helps Princess Rose stand as well. "Ladies and gentleman, let's show Princess Rose how much we appreciate her tonight!" He presents her to the small crowd who clap, but it's not very loud, mostly polite.

Princess Rose then returns to her seat, and Fabian introduces the next girl. "Now, we get a real treat. An exotic princess from a world so full of magic, even the pigs fly!" That gets a laugh. "Please give a warm Purerahian welcome to Princess Zelda of Hyvil!" He waves his arms out again to introduce her, and Princess Zelda steps into the interview circle with a huge smile. She takes Fabian's hand and shakes it before giving him a slight curtsy and sitting down as Fabian did.

"Welcome, Princess Zelda, welcome," Fabian says as the crowd dies down. "So, what made you travel a month by boat to visit our humble kingdom? Did the prince's impression just make your heart sing?" Zelda laughs as Fabian narrates by putting his hands over his heart then making them pop out as if showing his heart bursting at the sight of such a man. "Or are we just that charming?" he asks, leaning on the arms of his chair in interest.

"Both!" Zelda cries, handling Fabian like a pro. "I'm a curious girl, and the chance to come and meet your people, your royal family, and learn about the world my people came from, yet we know so little about, was too tempting to resist."

Zelda is doing better than Princess Rose. She sits properly but crosses her legs, so she is leaning closer to Fabian. So though she also has a more lofty look to her in comparison to Fabian's casualness, it is more warm and inviting, like she is willing to sit in the circle even if she does not fit.

"I hear in Hyvil that the crown is passed down the matriarchal line," Fabian says. "Is that true, and if so, why?" he asks, leaning back with a hand on his chin to listen to her answers in interest.

"Yes, it's true." Zelda smiles. "It's because our first queen, Queen Hyvia, was the principal leader when our people came to live in Hyvil, and she protected us from the demon monster that was mistakenly awakened. Her unique magic sealed the monster away, but he can still emerge without warning, and only her direct daughters can hold the power to reseal him. So those women are given the ruling right."

"So it's a self-defense thing," Fabian says, getting a laugh even out of Zelda. "What a wise choice, wise choice indeed, so different. So does the male led ways here seem strange?"

"Not at all, it feels so the same. Your king and queen rule as one, and that's exactly how we try to do it as well, so though the crown is handed from mother to daughter, it doesn't feel any different at all than here. We do try to keep those traditions that the Custods and Potentates have passed down from the Creator from the beginning. Our law still states a queen cannot rule without a king at her side longer than two years for example. We just adapt it to our unique circumstances. It's lovely to see how it is done for people with difference circumstances than ours."

"Well, at least the prince isn't alone in needing a bride before taking the throne. Even in Hyvil." Fabian smiles. "What is your favorite part of the kingdom?"

Zelda has no trouble with Fabian. They have quite a good time before they move on to the next girl. He interviews Princess Amapola next, and she, like Princess Rose, looks a bit too stiff. Her only moment to shine is when her hot Spearimish looks and speech make Fabian flirt a bit.

Fabian is a born actor. He's wasted on writing. He's perfectly timed, has great lines, and does an amazing job helping each girl shine. Even if they are struggling.

Princess Laurina is almost too fun and free with Fabian. If I didn't know any better, I'd have said she was tipsy, and her comment of how she is so close to her dragon sounds almost like a threat.

But then the born princesses are done. Fabian goes down the other girls in the order they are sitting in. He must have picked it. Florence, Isla, Kamala, Lilly, Azalea, Bella, Jonquil, Ericka, Forsythia, Dahlia... me. I'm dead last. That's why I am on the far stage left.

I worry about why I'm last. I listen to each interview, trying to prepare myself for what he might ask me. There is only one question he asks everyone. "If you could change one thing about the kingdom, what would it be?" The other girls avoid it perfectly. Lady Hydrengia must be proud. They all said something like there was so much to be done, they look forward to the chance to help make those changes. I'd look like a copycat if I said that. So, what am I going to say?

The audience is having a great time. I have to keep that energy flowing. I can either be the best in the interviews or the worst depending on how well I keep the energy.

Finally, Dahlia's interview ends with her telling all her fans she misses "seeing them in the stands" before Fabian helps her stand and presents her for her round of applause and finally turns his attention to me.

"And now, our last lady of the evening, easily one of the most stunning," he says as he walks across the interview circle with the impressionor following him. "Her team does such a good job, they got their own spotlight." I hear a whoop from the audience. I fight not to flush.

Fabian laughs. "And they alone have fans! Look at that. That's amazing. I love that. I really do." Fabian starts owning his stage again. "She is rumored to be the only girl witnessed kissing the prince, and I've been waiting for her all night! So, without further ado or gushing from me," he leans towards the impressionor, "I hope." The crowd laughs. "Let us welcome Lady Kascia, or as I know her, the Girl in Green!"

I stand and join Fabian in the circle, smiling and curtsying to him with a playful look that tells him I didn't like how fancy my intro was. He just laughs with me as we both sit down. I cross my legs, sitting like a proper princess, but also leaning towards Fabian.

He does the same beaming at me. "Yes, welcome, welcome Lady Kascia. I honestly have been so excited to finally interview you. I'll confess folks; I was so excited I went out of my way to try to meet her ahead of time." He turns to the audience. "I know, so naughty."

He turns back to me. "My apologies. I'm so bad. Here, smack my hand." He holds it out to me. I laugh and do as he asks. "No, harder; do it again." Fabian gives me a look.

"I don't like punishing people," I reply and lean back comfortably.

"Ooo!" Fabian looks at the audience. "I never thought I'd hear a royal say that. Did you hear that? I heard it." The people laugh. Fabian smiles. "Yes, I can admire that. I can admire that, indeed." He sits back in his seat and turns to me.

"Now, when we met the other day, I asked you about the green dress. Do you remember that?"

"Of course, how could I forget? It confused me," I say pleasantly. "He asked 'why the green dress', and I had no idea what he was talking about." I look at the viewers. "Do you know what he meant by calling me 'the girl in green'?"

The laugh and reply of 'no' makes me smile. I turn back to Fabian. "So how about you explain it to the audience for us? I need this answer too."

"Why of course, of course." Fabian turns to the audience and leans forward, resting his elbow on a knee. "You see, I was up north with the troops, reporting there as I like to do, and was watching the interviews live, like you all did," he says, gesturing animatedly as he told the story, the perfect performer. He is so wasted on reporting. "And I was starting to zone out at all the blue and casual talk when suddenly, this girl in a stunning green dress that stands out from the rest walks on. She's playful, fun, and actually gave my coworker a run for his money. She handled being teased by him and the prince like a pro. I knew I just had to meet this girl, the girl not afraid to play, be real and honest, and willing and happy to stand out. The Girl in Green." He declares it like he's introducing me again, and the crowd claps their agreement.

"Oh, you're too kind." I wave them off. "I'm not that unique."

"Oh, I disagree. I disagree," Fabian says as if disappointed and yet disbelieving. "What do you think folks?" He turns to the viewers, and they give me a huge whoop. I smile and laugh a little at their praise. I have a feeling Vivian is in that crowd getting them excited for me.

"Yes, you're quite the unique star. Even tonight, look at you. You look so comfortable. You make me feel like I should have dressed down. Perhaps a nice formal sweater and button up. You look so comfortable, yet regal. Doesn't she folks?" He turns to the viewers and gets another round of applause.

"Yes, stunning, just stunning. You told me before it's all on your team. You really do trust them, don't you?" He leans towards me again, turning the conversation to be more between us.

"I do." I smile confidently.

"Even though — now I'm no fashion expert, but your look isn't quite the princess look we'd expect from a Chosen daughter of Purerah. You didn't question that for a moment?" Fabian asks.

"No, and there's no reason I need to look like I'm a princess," I say. "I'm not here to pretend I'm already your princess. I'm here to let you get to know who I really am and for me to get to know you all as my people. You're all my equal, not my lessers. Why should I look down on you?"

That gets a real cheer from the audience. I smile and laugh a little, waving at them. This is one world I could fit into. One part of being a princess I am good at: putting on a show. I also hope it is good enough that Lady Keva and Lady Hydrengia will not kill me later. That and the thought of the grand duke's praise makes my stomach squirm. Is this a good skill?

"So, you don't have to work towards being a princess?" Fabian asks. That tone is new. He's challenging me.

I raise a playful eyebrow. "Did Cinderella or Belle?" That wins me a laugh.

Fabian laughs too. "Well played, well played," he agrees, leaning back a little. "And really, who am I to challenge your award-winning team?"

I laugh as the crowd claps. "I wasn't aware of any awards they won."

"Just working for you," Fabian says flirtatiously. I laugh. "That is its own reward. Its own reward, indeed."

"It's my honor," I say, adjusting my seat, so I look even more comfortable. Damian's choice was brilliant. I'm going to knock this interview out of the park.

"Do you find it hard to have to dress up all the time? It's quite different from a dance uniform for rehearsals every day," Fabian asks.

"No, but it's different. Having someone see to your every need is nice, but it also is a bit of work itself. I want to make sure they are able to enjoy their work too and have plenty to do. They serve me, but I also have to make sure to serve them. I'm not any better than they are. We're a part of the same team. I think that's what's lacking in the kingdom these days."

I can hear the panic that Lady Keva, and even more, Lady Hydrengia are having right now. I am daring to step on that button. But Fabian is laying down the challenge. I'm giving it right back. "If we saw each other as on the same team instead of 'us versus them', perhaps we'd get somewhere."

"Do you see a lot of in-fighting then?" Fabian asks.

I shake my head. "Not among the girls." Not all of them anyway. "Just in the world. I grew up on these streets. I know what it's like to deal with the war-torn kingdom we live in. I'm saying that perhaps if we banded together, we'd find a solution rather than just lengthening it out."

Fabian smiles as if he's hit paydirt. "So, is that what you would change about this kingdom?" he asks.

"Yes, I would," I say confidently. "If I learned anything in coming here, it's that our kingdom needs to be united under a good leader. We need someone who is willing to sacrifice for their people, give their life, time, energy, all of it. Is it possible to have anyone better than a man who's literally dedicated his life from birth to ending this suffering? Most of us act like he's just glutting off of the fighting. I'd change the mentality we have against those that strive to serve us with what they do every day."

The crowd applauds my words, but all I can see in my mind's eye is my father's hurt and disappointed expression as he listens to me say that. He'd call that traitor talk. He's not wrong. I just betrayed my Custod family in front of the nation. I hide my rising feelings under years of acting training. Had I just doomed my people to be lulled into false security?

A flash of movement behind the impressionor catches my eye, but the stage lights makes it impossible for me to see. It stopped as soon as it started.

"A bold answer," Fabian says after letting the applause die and leaving a moment of dead air to let what I said sink in. "You really do feel that the answer to ending this war is not some new way of doing things, but trusting the ways it's been done?"

"No, we've endured the way it has been for five hundred years. We need change," I say, relieved at the chance to make sure people didn't just let the bad state grow worse. "But that change doesn't mean we have to disregard the people who have prepared to help us make that change. I've not met anyone who wants the change more badly than I have here."

That brings a silence that could make a pin drop sound ear spitting.

"Wow, I don't know if I've heard anyone talk like that in a long time. Not one who wasn't rallying for a new ruling family," Fabian says. "I think the last time I heard someone talk like that was when I interviewed a rebel leader at the war front."

"Perhaps the reason the king and queen need to find a true princess is they need to find more people who talk like that rather than look the part." I just offended every other girl in this competition, and I know it. It wasn't my intention. What am I doing? They'll make me pay later, and I'll be powerless to stop it.

"Indeed, is that why you think they decided to run the Enthronement?" Fabian asks.

I shrug. "I don't pretend to know what they were thinking, but I wouldn't at all be surprised. They want to heal our people. They just don't know how."

"You seem to be well trained in these kinds of discussions." Fabian smiles at me warmly. "Where did you learn this? Tell us about your family."

I feared that was coming after several of the other girls talked about their families. But I keep it simple, saying my father helps run the theater with my mother.

"So, your parents are excited to see you getting so far in the Enthronement?" Fabian asks.

I try to be as honest as I can. "My mother was very excited when this started; my father too, but I've not heard from them in a while. I'm sure they're busy with the holidays coming up. It's a busy time for all of us, but for theaters, everything starts as soon as harvest ends. It's odd not to be working on the Nutcracker all fall."

"So, your parents are very proud." Fabian smiles that toothy smile again.

"I hope so."

Fabian catches onto my uncertainty. "You say you've not heard from them. Why?"

"I told you. They're busy, I expect."

"You expect?"

"I'm here doing my duty. I can't see them. I don't know why they aren't writing me," I point out. "I know to keep doing my best here and hope I hear soon. Perhaps there is a delay in mail due to so many rebel attacks." I'm losing control of the interview, and I know it. I don't know how to get it back.

Fabian nods slowly. "Do you have siblings?"

"I'm an only child." I shake my head. "But getting to know the girls here has felt like getting some sisters." I smile over at them. I get a few smiles back, only Zelda's seems fully real.

"You all do seem to get along well for girls fighting for the prince's favor," Fabian agrees. "Why do you think you manage it?"

Because we ignore the stupid ones, I think, but I don't say that. "I think we're all good at seeing one another's strengths and being tolerant of our weaknesses."

"Like sisters?" Fabian raises a brow.

I smile. "Like sisters."

"So, you fight sometimes?"

"Like any sisters. Mostly over clothes," I joke. "Damian's pieces are the envy of everyone."

I can feel the heat of Ericka's glare on my neck as if she had heat vision. That gets a laugh from Fabian though. "So. Everyone wants what you have. You do seem to be a favorite. Rumor has it, the prince kisses you in front of the whole group."

That's right. He mentioned that in my introduction. How did he know?

"A lady doesn't kiss and tell." I smile.

"Even if it's in front of a crowd?" Fabian asks.

I smile this time. "I'm an actress. I've kissed a lot of boys in front of even larger groups." That wins me a laugh.

"Does that bother the prince?" Fabian asks.

I'd not thought of that. I hope not. "We've never talked about it," I admit. "But it was before I came here. I'd not blame him either way."

"So do you feel you're well in line to make the top ten, if not win?" Fabian asks. He'd asked some variant of this to all the girls.

"I hope so, and hope is a feeling." I smile.

"Indeed it is." Fabian nods. "We're running out of time. But there was one more thing I wanted to talk about with you before I have to wait until later to speak with you again." Fabian scoots closer to me in his seat. "You were a famous actress before the Enthronement. Even people in other kingdoms knew of you from your famous Phantom performances. But you also are known for many other shows. Which are your favorites?"

"Oh, I love so many," I say animatedly. I like this topic. I rattle off my favorites, joking, "I'm a dull classical girl, I know." Which wins me a laugh.

"It was a disappointment to have missed your last show," Fabian says. "Will we ever get to see you on stage again?"

I shrug. "Only time will tell."

"That it will, perhaps we can get you to give us a little taste. What do you think?" he asks the viewers. They cheer "yes".

"I think we're too short on time tonight, perhaps another time?"

"I'll hold you to that," Fabian says quickly, pointing at me as if he got me. I laugh. "But with that, we'll have to call it a night." Fabian stands up and takes my hands to help me up. He beams at me, and holding each of my hands in his, he kisses them then turns to present me to the audience. "And that, ladies and gentleman, is our final Chosen girl, Lady Kascia, my Lady in Green!"

I give him a look as the crowd cheers for me, and I give them a reverence.

"Oo, I like that," Fabian says to me then back to the impressionor. "So, for now, Purerah, thank you for joining us for a night of fun, games, and politics. Until next time, good night!"

Then he turns to me, but he's clearly in stage mode, so I stay in it too. "Really, I love how you do that; they should have more girls do that. How do you do that? Show me."

I laugh and show him how a reverence is different from a curtsy.

"And out!" the impressionor calls, and Fabian drops the stage presence at once.

"That's all for tonight," Hydie calls. "Back up to your rooms, ladies. Chop, chop."

"Well done," Fabian offers me his hand, and I shake it. "You really were the most solid interview I've had in years. Not since I snuck in to interview the Custod rebellion leader." Oh vene, he better not make that connection, or I was in trouble. I can see the headlines, "Chosen Girl, Daughter of Custod Rebel Leader Peodrick." I just stop myself shuddering as I smile.

I glance over to see how the king and prince reacted, but they're not there anymore. I guess I can wait to ask until tomorrow.

The crew gets to cleaning up as Fabian asks some extra questions of some of the other girls for their features. Not seeing any reason to hang around, I start to leave. But then I notice Fabian spotted Damian and rushes over to him, likely to get some quotes for my feature.

Damian tries to brush him off, saying he's already done an interview. But Fabian persists saying Damian hadn't interviewed with him. Damian arches a brow. "And what could you possibly ask that others haven't asked before?"

"I have a different angle," Fabian says. "Mostly wanting some help with Lady Kascia's feature."

Damian takes in a deep breath, "Very well. If you must."

I'd rather not be in the room for this, so I step out to let Damian and Fabian have their interview.

Chapter 11

They let us have a break from lessons the next morning. I take advantage of it to avoid the other girls. Hopefully, any hurt egos would heal by the next day. I sit on the balcony to enjoy the feel of the cold ocean breeze. There still isn't any snow yet, so it's not too freezing.

Damian joins me on the balcony and smiles. "I see you are enjoying a well earned break."

I smile. "I like my friends, but after a long day, I'm happier with the ocean," I joke.

Damian chuckles. "I completely understand. I just wanted to congratulate you on your interview. You spoke with the heart of a true Custod."

My face falls a little. "Maybe." Though they all had a different plan in mind. "I try to."

"You succeeded." Damian smiles. "Perhaps your teachers may not have approved, but I do. You said words people have been waiting to hear. They need you, even if they didn't realize it until yesterday."

I look down. "I don't know if they need me." I sigh. "I just hope I didn't make a lot of enemies last night. The girls must be furious with me."

"Only fools hate the wise." Damian smiles.

I chuckle too. "Well, I guess that's true. I did not expect that to come out."

"Sometimes, the best things that happen to us in life are completely unexpected," Damian says. "Regardless, I am proud you had the courage to say it."

I smile. "Thanks Damian. I'm just glad it wasn't a test or I'd be in trouble," I joke. I pause a moment. "You escape his questions alright?"

Damian smiles. "I think I managed."

"Good." I smile. Then I pause. "My next date isn't another test, is it?" Damian would know. Technically, he's not allowed to tell me either, but he'd take pity on me after last time.

"You have a date?" Damian seems happily surprised.

I give him a look. "As soon as we say yes, they tell you so you can prep us," I point out.

Damian sighs dramatically. "I suppose that's fair. I thought I could at least pretend I don't know about every special event." He smiles sympathetically.

I chuckle. "You take good enough care of me to know everything," I joke.

"Fair enough." Damian nods. "But no, it isn't a test."

I smile a bit. "Good." I sigh. The last one still stung a little. Damian smiles gently and massages my shoulder comfortingly. "I wish it wasn't so complicated," I say. "And that I wasn't offended when they are a test."

"I understand. But it's only natural to feel a little cheated. Trust me, Gavril wishes they weren't tests either." Damian smiles. "Though as far as I have heard, you're the only one to get any date to last as long as they have, and you're the only one to have heard him sing."

"I'm sure Zelda got him to." If it were a real 'competition', she's the only one who would make me nervous.

"No, she's not as musically inclined," he says. "She doesn't care about it as much."

I chuckle. "I guess that's true. And we were up way too late."

"Sounds like you were having fun." Damian smiles. "And you know what they say about time when you're having fun."

"It flies." I nod my agreement. I just am starting to wonder how much he really likes me when this seems to keep happening.

"And the way he reacted yesterday when you answered that question." Damian grins.

I frown. "What?"

"The one about what you would change," Damian says. "When you answered, the prince stood up and looked like he wanted to go to you. It reminded me of that night in the safe room. Sage had to push him back into his seat."

I flush. I hope not. That night in the safe room almost got me in trouble, again.

Damian smiles. "Yes, it would not have been good had he acted on it, but it shows how much he cares about you. I think he just wishes for more opportunities to freely show his affection."

I sigh. "And who knows if he'll get the chance."

He smiles sympathetically. "Perhaps, someday."

Damian sits with me until they have to get me ready for lunch. Thankfully, all seems normal though many girls are glaring at me. Most of them really, only my friends aren't. Dahlia and Ericka look the most angry, but I didn't miss the dagger-like glares Forsythia is giving me.

I notice Gavril gets up from his meal sooner than normal, assures his mother he is just getting ready for his long afternoon, kisses her on the cheek and slips out the door with Sage like his shadow behind him. What are they up to? I'd not seen Gavril leave to prepare for a date early before. Then I remind myself I don't have to wonder. I'll find out soon enough.

I realize I should make sure not to keep him waiting and finish my meal a bit faster than might be thought of as polite before I go back up to my room to get ready. My curiosity is further piqued when I see what my maids dress me in.

They do my hair in a nice ponytail, tighter than normal, but make sure to give me a swoop fringe in the front, and they make sure my hair curls nicely down the ponytail. I change into gray leggings, a white blouse, and a corset vest that has a bit of a ruffle gathering going down my back but keeps tight in the front. They even make sure the necklace with my mark as a Chosen goes along with the neckline, but the chain is shorter, to keep it out of the way. What in creation are we doing today?

I put on my long boots to finish off the look. I look like a fancier version of what I wore to train with my father.

I try to get answers out of my maids, but they deflect until the prince's knock comes to the door. Flur gets it, and I step into the hallway to join the prince and quickly look him over to try to guess what we're up to.

He's wearing a tight white jacket that buttons up the side before it takes a sharp turn to go to the collar tight to his neck. The jacket looks a bit thick for being inside. Are we going outside for once?

"Perfect and on time." Gavril grins at me. "Ready?"

"I don't know. I am not sure what we're doing," I admit as he offers me his arm.

"Ah, well, you'll see." Gavril grins that smile that relaxes me. His father can do the same trick. It's like coming home.

I accept his arm, and he leads me in a more roundabout way down towards the bottom floor. We head out the same way we did when he took me to see the ship.

We step into the gym, again void of people. I notice the tall windows that show out to the grounds look like they're in need of being washed. The pool area is clean though as well as the large arena for guards to work on their fighting skills. The weight section looks a little dirty from use. It's like only parts of the room are regularly cleaned, like they'd be cut off in their work. The sting of cleaning solution still hangs in the air.

"And make sure the door is locked," Gavril says to the empty room as if picking up a conversation he'd been having this whole time.

Sage materializes from the shadow — not literally I assume, but I swear he can if he wants — and secures the doors behind us.

"Just hope no one gets annoyed we interrupted." Gavril grins.

"What are we doing in the gym?" Gavril is technically not allowed in here. His mother put it off limits, but Gavril had told me how Sage felt differently, so he would bar others from the gym now and then to let the prince use it.

"Well, I can't get away with using the outdoor training grounds. So, here will have to do. Hope you don't mind. Zelda thought it a bit funny to fence indoors. Though they also get snow where she is from. Can you imagine fencing in the snow?" He looks at me. "I'm sure they'd be freezing. But I hope the inside training doesn't throw you off."

"You're challenging us to fence?" I frown a bit. "I thought that was too dangerous."

"I told you I was taught using wooden weapons. What shame a prince would be who couldn't at least hold his own in a tournament." Gavril smiles.

"As if your mother would ever let you be in one," I state.

He shakes his head. "No, no, I don't imagine she would."

"So, you're making your own," I joke, walking onto the open space.

"Or just a unique date." Gavril shrugs. "You held your own against the rebels. I want to see how good you are." There's an excited glint in his eyes, much like the one he'd had when he showed me the royal flag ship.

I'm a born Custod. I likely will beat him without trouble; the poor thing only trained in show fighting. Though he is strong, impressively strong. That could help him in a fight, but I'm also fast and lithe. That will give me a different upper hand, but I shouldn't use it. A Custod against any prince would be rude. I doubt I'd win points with Sage if I beat the prince so handily. I should at least go easy on him.

"Quiet? Are you nervous?" Gavril teases. "Question is: nervous of losing or nervous about having my mother on your head?" I laugh. "Or both. Come on, pick your blade." He indicates an array of blunted blades, but none are made of wood.

Gavril walks into the training arena, up to the space marked for a fencer to stand. He smiles at me to let me know we can start when I'm ready.

Sage leans on the wall nearby. I roll my eyes and smile at him. It's not like I am going to use this to assassinate him. Most of all with him watching. No smart spy would, and I'm smart, but no spy and certainly not an assassin.

I step into my spot and bow as the rules of polite combat dictate. Sage stiffens a little, not like he'll attack, but poised to move quickly if needed. Gavril bows back, giving Sage a look. He really does need to relax.

I try to remind myself to be gentle as my training is most likely better than his. Gavril shows his inexperience by testing my defenses first. I block all three of his attempts without too much trouble, dodging his third with a sidestep. Gavril tilts his head a little, and a look comes into his eyes I don't think I've seen before. It's like they're sharper, like he sees things more quickly, more observant.

To take it easy on him, I go for a few strikes that he blocks, as I knew he would, but he does a better job than I expected. It seems as easy for him as it had for me. He takes me by surprise by dodging one with a turn that is bigger than it needs to be, putting him behind me. I only just avoid him by dropping to the floor and rolling away.

When I get to my feet and turn to Gavril, he's looking me over as if he's noting that move is in my move set. I have to admit, he is better than I expected. He's testing me, learning me and how I fight. It makes me nervous. Though his jabs, swings, and thrusts are strong as if they are attacks, the look in his eyes tells me he's studying. But just because he could study and read me easily didn't mean he's better.

I decide I've played the game long enough, and I can go ahead and end it. I try to repeat his trick back at him, adding a leg spin to knock him off his feet. I expect him to fall for it, assuming I am just copying him.

If this had been a chess match, he would have checkmated me for my check. Gavril mirrors my move, making us turn around one another as if in a dance, which places him behind me and before I can drop or turn to block it, he's got his sword at my neck.

I shut my eyes as my father's voice fills my mind, screaming, rebuking me for being so weak as to lose to the pampered prince. I'd gone easy. *It's fine,* I try to calm myself. That doesn't mean I am a bad fighter or bad Custod. I'd underestimated him. That's all.

I open my eyes to see Sage smirking at me. Anger fills me. I'd prove them both wrong. I am not going to play easy next time.

"And how did you stop them finding the safe room?" Gavril taunts me. "Just flirted them away?" I glare at him. I am already feeling bad enough. I don't need his teasing. Gavril chuckles, thinking I'm playing. He turns down his blade and backs away to let me go.

"Neat trick thinking I'd not know how to deflect that one," he says as he moves back to the starting position. He's actually good. I guess that's Sage's fault.

I can't believe he read it that easily. I knew he was observant from what he knew about the rebels without ever being in a briefing or meeting with them before, but this impresses me. And the rebels think he'd make a bad king?

"Ready to go on, or you had enough?" Gavril teases.

I smile back and get into position. He gets ready, and I try to get in under his guard before he's fully set. But he doesn't seem surprised at all, blocking and jumping back perfectly to avoid the blows. He really is better than we'd given him credit for.

We pass through a few complicated exchanges, proving Gavril capable, but I'm a Custod. I'm better... I have to be. I dodge an impressive swing and end up with blades pressed together with his face inches from mine.

"Maybe you're not so easy after all," he teases, sneaking a kiss on my cheek before pulling back.

I only just recall myself to reality in time to block his next blow. My swift return to reality is faster than he expected, allowing me to use the classic Custod sequence: stepping on his foot, striking up at his face with my elbow and twisting around, my blade at his neck. He dodges my elbow strike to his face, but he can't dodge it and block the sword.

"Yeah, you got that one. I should have taken the face shot," Gavril concedes without argument. But the way he says it... I frown. *Did he let me take that win on purpose?* Had he just given me the win like I'd given him the last one?

This doesn't make sense. Custods are blessed with increased combat skill. Shouldn't I be able to beat him even without his concession? Or is he being nice? Am I reading too deeply into it? Had my traitorous talk last night or rejecting my father entry at the Harvest caused me to be disinherited? I fight the feeling of my heart stopping, not wanting the prince to notice.

"You are very good," Gavril compliments. "It's been an exciting fight. Best two out of three?" I accept, wanting to be sure of myself.

But he beats me again with his careful observation. And when I do win, I worry he's being nice and letting me.

Now I'm starting to really panic. Have I lost my right, my family in what I'd done? Does that mean I am wrong and my father is right? *No.* I have to prove it. I have to be more, be better. I must prove my father wrong. But after an hour or so, Gavril starts losing heart. He's not as into the sport as he had been. That's when I decide, I have to win this next round. I have to prove it to myself and to my father that I am not wrong. I can't be... can I?

But instead, Gavril beats me so handily he's got me flat on the floor on my stomach, blade to my neck once more.

Rather than being disappointed, I'm terrified. Is my poor performance proof I've been disowned? I shut my eyes, fighting hot tears that try to escape through my tightly closed lids. Does this prove I am wrong? What do I do if I am wrong? I've been so scared of it, I've not allowed it to be true, but is that why I can't find the proof we were wrong in the past? Am I wrong? *Please, no.* Have I lost my Custod heritage?

"You know," Gavril sits back, not letting me up. I keep my face turned away to hide the tears, "this is supposed to be fun. I had no idea you were this competitive. I expected it from Dahlia, but not you." He tries to sound playful, but there's a hint of worry in his tone.

I hate it. I hate him for proving me wrong, but maybe he hadn't. I don't know. I'm angry, confused, hurt, and scared. But he's right. I'm not normally competitive or desperate to win. But I shouldn't lose to Gavril. I'm a Custod. Or was... no, I have to win. Prove I'm still better. I can't have been... Could I?

"Are you normally this set on winning?" Gavril asks, still not letting me up.

"No," I say, trying to keep my voice even.

"So then why are you so tense?"

"Will you let me up?"

"In a moment," Gavril replies. "Is it just that bad to lose to a boy or this boy in particular?"

Neither, and both. "It's not like that," I say. I have to prove it to myself. I'm not lost. My family hasn't been forced to renounce me. Oh no. Was that why Mother hadn't written? I had been disinherited, so she's not allowed to speak to me? *It can't be; please it can't be.*

Anger fills me. *No.* I am not going to have them take more from me. I still have it. I am protecting my people more than my father. They couldn't take my authority. I can still fight well. I can win without him going easy.

"So, if you fenced Sage, you'd not care so much?" Gavril smiles.

"He's a Custod. I'd not stand a chance."

Gavril frowns. "Hmm, so even though you've won about half of them, you're still tense to win each one because..."

"How do you read people so well?"

"Stop doing that thing where you change the topic," Gavril says. "Why so tense?" He does a massaging motion into my shoulder.

"Let me up."

"Why so tense?"

"Please stop," I beg.

Gavril freezes as if recalling something horrible. He immediately gets off of me and offers to help me up. I don't meet his eyes, hoping he won't realize I've teared up.

"Kascia, I'm sorry. I didn't mean to make you feel like that. I promised you I wouldn't. I hold to it," Gavril says, trying to meet my eyes.

Oh, that's what he recalled. During the chastity date, I feared he'd ask me to go further than I was ready to go. I'd begged him to stop the same way I had just now.

I can't help but look at him at that realization. His eyes are filled with worry and confusion. "Why would you... Kascia!" He almost yells my name. "What's wrong?" He sees signs of tears in my eyes. "I'm sorry. I... this was a terrible idea, wasn't it? I'm so sorry. What's wrong?"

"Nothing," I try to brush it off, embarrassed and angry. I can't tell him why. And there is no one I can tell. It only makes me feel angrier and alone. I've given up my family, and they reject me. And now... there is no support for me if I lose. The Custods have rejected me, my family. I am wrong. I am wrong about Gavril, the royal family, all of it. Father is right... but that can't be true. It-it just can't be.

"Please don't lie to me. Did I hurt you? I'm sorry. I guess I don't know my own strength. I didn't mean to."

"I'm fine." I push him off angrily.

Gavril pauses, frowning in confusion. He glances at Sage. I look at Sage to glare at him but then pause. He's watching me in equal confusion, almost concerned too.

I groan. "It's nothing. I got competitive; that's all."

"Is it?"

"Yes."

"Kascia, you may not want to tell me, and I respect your right to do so, but please don't lie. I'm not stupid," Gavril says.

"Just better than me," I say, folding my arms.

Gavril frowns. "Oh," he looks down, "so it is me."

I hear the hurt in his voice. "No... yes, I mean... no, it's not just you. It's... anyone." It's that I am not a Custod anymore. I am no match for Sage. I am wrong.

"Really?" Gavril challenges, getting annoyed now. "It's not losing to the pampered prince?"

I want to snap back "no" without hesitation. It's that he's a prince with no training, and I am a highly trained Custod. Was. I fight not to break into sobs right there. I should win without a thought. I tried and still lost.

"That's what I thought. You can at least be honest with me even if you won't tell me. I'm not a child. I can take it." Gavril sounds angry now.

I sigh frustratedly, fighting hot tears. "It's not you; it's anyone. I'm better than this. I'm supposed to be."

"At least better than the weak prince."

"Well... I didn't realize how good you are, alright?" I defend. "I am better than this." Or should be. I fight more tears. *Please, I can't be wrong.*

"Why..." Gavril stops, huffing through his nose, shutting his eyes and pinching the bridge of his nose. "Never mind, I get it. I just didn't expect... not from you."

My heart crumbles. I really don't mean it like that. How do I explain without telling him the dreaded truth? "It's not you!" I snap at him, shutting my eyes as the tears welled up.

"Kascia, what is it?" To my shock, Sage has stepped up to me.

I look up at him in confusion. His green eyes are filled with concern as he looks me over. Does he know? Does he feel something? This Custod feels the former Custod in me?

I glare at him in hatred. He judged me. He wanted me gone, called me a danger, and now, when I'm not like him anymore, he's kind to me?

I shove him away, surprising him and Gavril. "I don't need your pity." I shoot at Sage. He didn't have the right to pity me for being cut off.

"Kascia, wait. Really, it's alright," Gavril tries to come closer to me.

I don't want his pity either, and I move to shove him away too, but Gavril grabs my wrists as quickly as a cobra strike.

I freeze at his speed and grip, eyes locked on his hands clasped around my wrists. That reaction was instinct, defensive. I'd scared him.

I look up at Gavril and see the panic and fear in his eyes before he pulls away from me. "I-I'm sorry," he says. "I didn't mean to grab you like that."

Sage is frowning at Gavril too. That was the reaction of someone who'd been assaulted before. Someone who'd been hurt by someone doing that and instinctively stopped them. But when...

"Gavril?" Sage frowns deeper as he studies him.

"I'm fine. I shouldn't have been so harsh. We all know I have a temper," Gavril explains, but it feels like an excuse. Something else made him react like that. Maybe he's not as sheltered as I thought.

I'd triggered something.

"Gavril, what..." I start to ask, but Gavril tenses; his temper actually coming out.

"I'm fine," he snaps. "It's nothing."

It's not. "I thought you asked me not to lie," I say softly.

Gavril tenses again and turns away. I can tell he wants to hit something. What have I mistakenly awoken in him? Can I even defend myself from his temper if I won? Without being a Custod, can I even help? He looks so angry, yet scared; I want to help him. But I'd be powerless.

But should he be helped? If I am cut off by the Creator for what I'd done, does that mean Gavril really isn't the one who should rule? I can hardly breathe at the idea. I don't want Jake or those stupid Potentates or me on the throne without him. I can't be wrong. I can't. I fight to control my panicked breathing.

I hug myself, wishing I hadn't pushed them away. "I'm sorry. I didn't mean to freak out either," I say. "I just... I should be better than this." My eyes meet the floor.

"Everyone is supposed to be better than me," Gavril says bitterly. "I'm sorry I tried. I just thought..."

"It's not you," I insist more gently this time. "I... m-my father trained me in the elite ways. I thought I was really good. You showed me I'm not as good as I thought I was, that's all." It is not just humbling; it is humiliating to realize I'd been disowned. "He'd be so disappointed in me." He was disappointed in me and sad for me.

"I can't blame him. It's not your fault." Gavril sounds dejected and sad, using his anger as a cloak to hide under, but I hear the real pain.

"Gavril, honestly, I didn't—" I begin.

Gavril puts his hand up to stop me. "Please, I don't want or need to hear the cover. It's alright. I shouldn't have... I know you have rebel friends, and... how you thought of me before. I should have known."

Tears fill my eyes afresh. "Gavril, no, really I..." How do I explain without Sage pinning me and taking me out, perhaps for good? I glance at him and quickly look away.

"I don't need or want to hear it." Gavril takes advantage of my uncertain pause. "It's fine. I really don't want to talk about it. I just thought you had... Never mind. It's fine. I don't blame you."

"Please, Gavril, let me explain." But how can I? I cannot tell the whole truth.

"It's fine. I will feel better just ignoring it."

I bow my head. I don't want him to. Anger, pain, and hatred well in me. I'm angry that I can't tell the truth, angry I hurt Gavril so badly. I hurt to know I pained him so and cannot fix it. And I hate my father for putting me into this situation where I lost my family, and now, I may just lose the man who was my only hope of getting out of this happy and alive.

"Can I do nothing to prove it's not you?" I ask timidly.

"But it is me."

"It's not." I try to meet his eyes, but he can't. He can't take seeing I still think of him as the useless, spoiled prince I thought he was when I came here. But I don't.

My lip trembles. "Does what I said last night mean nothing?"

Gavril tenses in anger. "Only you can answer that," he almost spits at me.

That is a dart to my heart. He isn't sure he can trust me now? "I meant it," I squeak out.

"For the show, or because you believe it?" Gavril asks bitterly.

"With how it's ruined my life, I'd never do it just for a show," I swallow the sobs that fight to escape my throat. "More than you can know."

That makes both Gavril and Sage stop, looking at me in concern.

"Like what?" Sage demands.

Like I sold my soul for something that's wrong! I glare at him.

"Can't you just go away?" I demand. I don't need his condescending sympathy when he thinks I'm still out to kill Gavril.

"What are you talking about, Kascia?" Sage asks me again.

"Like you care," I shoot at him. "Fine, don't believe me. No one does anyway." I turn away.

"Kascia, wait."

I shove Sage away as he tries to stop me and turn to leave as quickly as I can. But he grabs me like Gavril had before, then lets go just as quickly, and I manage to escape out the door.

He follows and grabs me by the shoulders, turning me to face him. I glare at him and slap him before I can really register his face. I try to get away once more, only to have him grab me again.

"Kascia stop," Sage says, sounding worried.

"Don't pretend you care now," I snap at him.

"I wasn't the one who grabbed you!" he snaps.

I freeze. Did I just slap Gavril? I'm so getting kicked out if I did.

"What's going on, Kascia?" Sage demands.

"Did I just..." Fresh tears fill my eyes. "I'm going home anyway." I push Sage off. "So why do you care?"

"Kascia, you're not being dismissed. I..."

But I ignore him and march off. He stops trying to chase me.

I retreat to the conservatory, thinking they wouldn't think to look there. They'd check my room and the Ladies' Chamber but not here. I just sit on the bench by the waterfall where Gavril and I shared our first kiss and sob.

I lost my family. And I just lost any means of escaping them. I'm as damned as I can be. How long before they dismissed me? Where could I go? I can't go home after being disowned. But I have nowhere else. Most of all if I have been wrong. I can't be, but... what was left? I'd have to find a way to leave the country without any means to do so.

I don't know how long I am sitting there before I hear a gentle voice call my name. "Kascia?" He sounds almost timid.

I start and look up at Damian. I didn't expect him to try to find me. How did he even know? I rub my arms as if to keep warm then try to wipe my eyes on the back of my hand. "Sorry." I must be late for something.

He smiles a little and cautiously sits next to me. "No apology necessary," he assures and puts an arm around my shoulders. "But may I ask what's wrong?"

"I..." I don't know where to even begin. "I don't know where I'll go." I'll be gone by dinner if the queen finds out what I did.

"Were you planning on leaving?" Damian arches a brow and tilts his head at me with a slight frown on his face.

"It's not like I get a choice," I reply, still hugging myself. "After... there's no way they're letting me stay. I didn't mean... And now my family can't even take me back. I-I don't know what to do. I was wrong!" I release the terror.

Damian jerks his head back at my declaration, his brows pinched in confusion with a matching frown. "What do you mean you were wrong? Kascia, what happened? I don't understand what has you so stricken with fear."

My lip shakes, and I look down. "I... I lost it. Damian, they... they cut me off."

"You mean your family? How do you know?"

"I... I couldn't even hold my own in a fight." I look down. I am not enough.

"Really? Sage said you won a few. It sounded like it was at least half. What's bad about that?" He tilts his head.

"I'm... I-I was a Custod." My face falls.

Damian sighs. "Kascia, your father can't disinherit you because you disagreed with him. And losing some of the fights doesn't necessarily mean the Head has either."

"We're Custods. We're supposed to be good at this. I couldn't beat... hardly..." I sigh. "Well, anyone."

"That isn't what Sage told me."

"I'm... w-was a Custod. I should be better than that." I try to stop myself from shaking.

Damian hugs me tighter. "It will be alright, Kascia," he says and takes a slow breath to help relax me. "Just try to calm down. Things always seem worse when you're worked up. Just... take a deep breath."

I nod, still shaking as I accept his hug. "I-I don't know what to do. I-I was wr-wr-wrong." I can't take it in. What is left?

"Kascia, breathe," Damian instructs.

I take a deep breath, calming down a little, but once I try to think or figure out what to do or say, it comes back in, and I have to repeat the process, trying not to feel trapped by the action. I can't think of anything else. I try to just listen to my breathing, but it isn't a calming sound yet.

"Slower. Count to four as you breathe in, and count again as you release," Damian says.

I nod and force myself to do it. It's not easy, but after a few minutes, I get my breath to settle.

"Better." Damian nods. "Now. Why don't you start from the beginning? Gavril took you fencing, did he not?" he says with a kind smile. I nod. "Then what happened?"

"He... I lost. I was impressed and figured I should go easy, but even then... I kept losing." My lip shakes. "I-I couldn't keep up."

"Alright." Damian nods slowly. "So was Sage lying when he said that you won some of the time?"

I try to think. "A few, but honestly, I think he let me."

"That isn't what Sage made it sound like, and he would know. He trained Gavril."

"I'm not so sure." Not with that little smile he gave me.

"So, you think he let you win every time, even when he saw it upset you?" Damian arches a brow. "Coddling you when that is the one thing that he hates most?"

"I don't know." I'm sure he had, but now I don't trust myself to know anything. I am wrong. I feel so lost.

"Very well; we'll get back to that. What happened after you kept losing?" he asks patiently.

"He noticed I was more competitive than normal, and tried to ask what was wrong but when I didn't know how to explain... he got angry." I tense at the memory. "Then Sage had to pretend he cared." He wanted me gone, and we all know it.

Damian gives me a bit of frown as if he disagrees with my last statement but doesn't comment otherwise. "And what did you do when Gavril got angry?"

It's all a blur; I try to recall exactly. "I tried to explain the best I could that it wasn't about him or losing to him. He got annoyed, and he tried to touch me. I didn't want him to, so I tried to push him away, and he... he grabbed me." I swallow. "I knew he had a temper, but I didn't think... it scared me, and I think it scared him too."

Damian nods. "And he tried to follow you when you tried to leave?" he prompts.

I nod. "And he grabbed me, but I thought he was Sage. I pushed him off and when he tried again, I... I hit him." And no matter what else I did, that alone would get me thrown out.

Damian frowns. "So, you hit Gavril and Sage?"

"What?" I frown.

"Well, I saw the red handprint on Sage's face. Believe me, it was hard not to notice. And physically, Gavril seemed fine. So, either Gavril heals fast, and someone else hit Sage. Or... more likely, you hit Sage, not Gavril," Damian reasons.

"But... Sage said Gavril grabbed me." My brows draw together in confusion.

"The first time. Sage said he grabbed you twice after you left the room."

"Oh." Alright, so maybe that wasn't a problem. But I still am soon to be thrown out. "Either way, he'll not want me. No one will. I don't... I-I was wrong." And I don't understand how.

"Wrong about what?" Damian tilts his head as he watches me carefully.

"If I keep losing this badly... h-he cut me off because I was wrong. I should have let them in or not said what I did last night. I broke it somehow." My lip shakes. "I-I was wrong." And that damning thought traps me.

"Kascia, your father cannot disinherit you. The Head Custod is the only person alive who can, and he doesn't simply disinherit people on a whim. These matters are taken with extreme seriousness. You would have received a written notice from him, or he'd have made an appearance to warn you before any action was taken. The only way your Custod right would have been stripped from you without warning is if you had broken your oath in an act of immorality. And even then, there would be a trial to see if you were repentant, and he would offer you the chance to earn it back. I know because I witnessed a Custod get disinherited. But nothing of that has happened for you, unless you have received letters I am not aware of."

"Not yet." But it's not like we have anything to send me a message that fast.

"If you were disinherited at the Harvest, we'd have seen them already," Damian reasons.

"It could have been last night." My stomach twists as I recall the exact moment I knew they were disappointed, but I never thought it would come to this.

Damian gives me a half-annoyed look. "You would not be disinherited for something you said."

"On top of what I've done." I swallow to stop myself from being sick.

Damian rolls his eyes up to the ceiling then stands up and looks at me. "Kascia, stand up."

I do as he asks, not able to look up at him. Without warning, Damian whips his cane out from behind him and swings it at me with the full force of his arm. I jump and duck with a rond de jambe turn while bending, allowing me to get some distance in about a second or less.

I freeze, heart pounding, terrified and unsure why Damian had done that. I fight to calm down and not back away or look for another strike. Or maybe I should. I don't know anymore. I should look up, but I'm scared to. Then again, why did I care if he hit me?

Damian lowers his arm and relaxes, allowing his cane to slide gently until it touches the ground. "There. You passed the test. A disinherited Custod would have been smacked in the face just now, and you evaded me even without truly looking at me."

"What? What does that have to do with it? It's just a dance trick," I say, forcing myself to stand, still shaking.

"Oh, I suppose that is a point." Damian nods to himself. "Which means that if you were actually disinherited, you'd have noticed much sooner." He looks me over again, then carefully bends over and lets his cane rest against the bench, then just as carefully, he moves closer to me and rests his hands on my shoulders. "I'm sorry I scared you," he says with honest compassion in his eyes.

I nod and shove down the emotions. "I-I'm okay." I fight to stop my lip shaking and more tears rising again. He takes me in a moment then hugs me.

I return it, hiding in his support. Honestly, it just startled me, but I'm already so nervous and worked up. I don't understand what happened or what's really wrong with me. "I messed up."

"How so?" Damian asks, his tone is soft and comforting.

"I don't know," I squeak. "I-I'm supposed to be... a-and I'm not."

"You are perfectly fine. You are not disinherited. Please, trust me on this. Dancing and fighting are virtually the same," he explains. "When a Custod is disinherited, they completely lose the ability to fight or coordinate at all because the magic that helps them is gone. You can see it in their countenance because what was light is now empty and dark. Your countenance is not fallen, and your abilities are still swift. My dear girl, you are not wrong. And no man can punish you for being right."

"I-I don't know anymore." I am still uncertain I'd made the right choice. Was this why I cannot find the evidence or support I sought as I studied? Because it is not there?

"Well, I do," he says firmly. "You are as quick now as you were when you fought Princess Zelda. You lost a few times to her, remember?"

"Yes, but she was better trained, and everyone knows they have Custod in them," I remind him.

"And who trained Gavril?" Damian asks. "Custods aren't perfect, Kascia. They can still lose flights. The Merlin lost plenty of fights. Do you think that means he was any less of a Custod?"

"Well, no." But he lost to better fighters than I had.

"Exactly, and no, not all of those fights were with people who knew magic. In fact, the Battle of the Vanishing Mountain got its name from a fight against a man who had no magic at all. The Merlin's opponent was large and imposing, and he and Cedrick were fairly evenly matched until the man threw dirt in his eyes. Blinded and panicked, the Merlin threw a wild blast of magic that not only hit his opponent, but also caused the mountain to collapse. Now most focus on the impressive latter part of that story, but I want to point out that, before that, Cedrick Custod, the most powerful enchanter to ever live, almost lost to dirt."

I'm not sure I would have laughed if it weren't for the way Damian said it. It is a funny thought either way, but his delivery breaks through my fear and stress.

Damian smiles a little to see it then continues. "And I'll remind you that this was to a man we don't know the name of to this day. He was an enemy captain. Who knows what kind of training he had, but it was enough to match Cedrick Custod with a sword, to the point that the only way to gain the upper hand was to throw dirt in his eyes. Now, if this nameless captain can match the most powerful Custod to have ever lived, then why is it so difficult to believe that a Potentate prince who was trained by Custods, one of whom achieved the highest class a Custod can receive, can match you with your blessing?" He tilts his head as he searches my eyes.

My face falls a little. "Didn't really think other Custods had trained him."

"They did. Fencing has been a part of his lessons for years, and it has always been his Custod guard that took that part on, but it wasn't until Sage that he moved from wood to metal," Damian explains.

"But he's not... like us. How did I lose that constantly?" Perhaps if it were only a few times, but... I'm sure he won more than me. And I was trying really hard.

"Well, personally, that says more about him than you. Remember, Sage is not one to approve of a defenseless protectee. That's why he taught Gavril to swim, to fight, and so many other things. He trained Gavril, not only to defend, but kill if necessary because he knows that Gavril's attackers will not hesitate to do so. The prince must be ready. And you have seen how observant Gavril is. He notices the tiniest nuances and quickly determines how to respond. That skill alone makes him a tough opponent, especially in a fight. Even untrained, I'm sure it will help him last a good while in a real battle. And that's all without even mentioning Prince Gavril has his own oath and blessing, which most people forget."

"But it's not in battle." But Damian has a point. Was Gavril right about how I'd seen him? Am I right about anything? Had I thought him not good enough? Was it really him?

"Does it matter? Both real battles and practice or playful fights are geared around the same key factors to guarantee a win. First, skill and training, which I believe you and Gavril are evenly matched. Second, magic, again you are both blessed: you as a Custod, and him as a Potentate. As future king, he is blessed to be a ruler and defender of his people. Not only that, but he has a small Custod gene in which most Potentates today lies dormant, but in training his body, Gavril activated that gene, allowing him to build bulk and develop a keen coordination in his movements. It's part of why he is so good at dancing. And lastly, thoughts and emotions. I wasn't there during the fight, and I can't read your mind, but I'm guessing that you underestimated him and when he won, the embarrassment and thought of being disinherited distracted you more and more from the fight in every round while Gavril kept a cool head.

"Now, I'm not saying this to criticize you, Kascia," Damian says with an even softer tone. "But I want you to see that disinheritance isn't the only reason for losing. In fact, it is the least likely when you consider all the facts. You surely fought well because who you are has not changed. But when your heart isn't in the right place, you may fall. A Custod has more ability because they are fighting for something more than themselves. That ability is a strength that comes from above, from the One who gave it to them in the first place. So where was your heart?"

"At first, I didn't care but then... I-I was scared to be wrong." I swallow and look up at Damian. "What... I don't know what I'll do if..."

"That won't happen," Damian assures me, placing both hands on my shoulders. "I believe in you. And what you have stood for. Gavril is the man this kingdom needs. He just needs to trust himself, and so far, you are the only one to show him he can do this. He needs that support if he is to succeed."

The way Damian says it strikes me. Perhaps it is because it is Damian who I know chooses his words carefully, and he'd said I am needed, or perhaps it is because it isn't from someone who just wants me to win. But this thought hits me differently than it has before.

"Then why do I keep failing?" I ask in hardly above a whisper.

"Because the road is never easy," Damian says simply but sadly. "Roadblocks and pitfalls are going to happen, but it is all part of our journey to our growth. Usually if life seems easy, it's because you're on the wrong road. And just because you fail once, twice, or even a thousand times, it doesn't mean you are a bad person or even a bad Custod. Just because you aren't fighting to help Purerah as your father would have you do, that doesn't mean you are wrong. A Custod is not merely a fighter, Kascia. They are the world's protectors. Yes, that often requires fighting, but you can protect in other ways. Aidan Custod was a horrible fighter, but he helped in other kinds of battlefields. That is what you are doing, isn't it? You are trying to protect the royal family and help your people and that says a lot." Damian smiles. "That doesn't sound like a bad Custod to me."

"Guess not." I manage a smile, backing up a little to rub my arms. My heart sinks a little. "I don't know if I can fix this." He'd been right, even if I didn't realize it. I don't know how I'll get over it, let alone him.

Damian smiles a little. "Well, you surely hit a sore spot with Gavril. I won't deny that, but I doubt it is anything that can't be overcome. Every relationship has their hiccups, but in time, and with patience and work, they often work themselves out."

"Even when he can just pick someone else?" I point out. "Or worse, can't."

"Does he want to?"

"When it might be easier and doesn't matter who he favors, how can I tell anymore?" He'd questioned if I even meant what I said last night. He can't be that sure of me anymore.

"Well, when you phrase it like that it certainly makes it difficult to answer." He smiles sympathetically. "But love is never easy, Kascia. If it was, it wouldn't be worth it. Just give him time, and let him cool his head. If he truly cares about you, he won't let one small thing get in the way. That's what it means to love unconditionally."

I take a deep breath through my nose to stop my lip shaking. "I don't know if I know what that's like." Father's love had been conditional. Jake's too.

Damian's smile glows with a soft warmth as he takes me into his arms again. "Oh, my dear girl." He pauses and lets out a breath, but I can't see his face anymore. "I only hope I can show you."

I manage a weak smile. "Guess I'll find out."

"That you will," he assures me before pulling back. "But with your mindset, it makes me wonder if you're related to my brother somehow," he says with a slight joking tone.

"I'm that much of a goof, uh?" I try to smile but not quite manage it.

Damian chuckles in a way that sounds like two breaths quickly leaving his nose. "In a way. His self-esteem has hit rock bottom many more times than I'd like. I can only hope I can assure you as well as I do him."

"I never thought self-esteem was a problem for me." I force a small chuckle. I really hadn't, not with my confidence on stage. Then again, I also was sure of my family and my husband-to-be.

"Well, let's see if we can get back there." Damian smiles. "But are you alright?" His eyes search my face.

"For now." But I also know this mess isn't over. I'm still not sure he's not about to throw me out. I had really scared him, or worse, disappointed him.

"Can I do anything to make that last?"

"Erase the last few hours," I joke dully.

"Sorry, I'm afraid I have no skill in time travel." Damian sighs with a bit of a playful air. "But I see what Cedrick can do in the memory wipe department."

I chuckle. "I'm sure he has better things to do than worry about a lovers' game." He did work for the king in dealing with the war, after all.

"We'll see." Damian smiles. "Right now, he's helping Gavril."

"What?" Why? What did Cedrick have that no one else did that they called in a high ranking official? What have I done?

Damian grimaces. "As much as I would love to tell you, it's not for me to say. All I can tell you is that when Gavril grabbed you, his mind was not in the moment. Cedrick has had similar experiences, so I asked him to talk to Gavril, so I could be here for you."

I nod, not liking it, but I'd have to accept it. I had no right to demand his secrets when I can't tell him mine. I feel a rush of self-loathing for demanding to know why his family lets this war go on when I can't tell him my biggest secret. "So, what do I do?"

"Do you love him?" Damian asks straightly, looking directly into my eyes.

"I… I think so." I met Damian's eyes as if asking him if it's true.

He gives me a small smile. "Then fight for him. I know there are certain things you can't tell him right now. As there are things you can't yet understand about him. But that doesn't mean that your love isn't worth keeping. Those other things will iron themselves out in time. Until then, remember why you love him and hold to that."

"I can try." I bite my lip. "They're really not about to throw me out?"

His smile grows and becomes warmer. "No, they aren't. Honestly, whether you believe it or not, Sage was actually just concerned about you. He told me to check that you were alright."

I have a hard time believing that, at least that he was worried about me because he cared about me in any way. "Perhaps he did." The motive is the question. He'd never been anything but harsh to me.

Damian smiles with a little chuckle. "Well, he did. But are you ready to go back to your room? Or do you need another moment?"

"We can go back." I had little else to do other than dwell on it and might as well do that in my room than here.

Damian nods then gives me a hug, likely because he feels I need it. I return it, fighting fresh tears. I wish I could just erase the last few hours and pretend they didn't happen.

Chapter 12

I'm dreading dinner like one dreads having a tooth pulled. I let my maids take care of me as always, oblivious to any drama, and for now, I like it. I hardly pay attention to how they dress me. I go down to dinner and try to act like the princess I should be. I take it Gavril has chosen the same course, but I can't bring myself to look.

It's not until we're starting to unwind for the evening that Godwin comes to ask if Gavril can visit me in my room. Even if I wanted to, I couldn't afford to say no, so I agree, and my maids decide to draw up a bath for me to enjoy afterward. If they didn't notice before, they must feel my stress now.

I greet him properly as he comes into the room, Sage with him as always. I give them both the princess smile I mastered from so many years of acting. Gavril manages to return a weak one and bows his head properly to me. I'm a bit hurt, then realize I'd been the one setting that up as I'd waited for him to come in standing up and using my best princess behavior.

"I was wondering if I'd see you tonight," I try to break up the formal structure I'd mistakenly made.

"Me too," Gavril says honestly. "But with how upset you were when you left, I wanted to be sure you're alright."

"I think so." I swallow. Is he about to throw me out?

He forces another smile. "Don't worry. If you don't want to leave, we're not sending you home yet."

Yet. I hate that word.

"I assure you as I have before, you're safe. If you wish to stay, you can stay until you fail or win." He stops at the last word as if unsure of it.

My heart sinks. Does he not want me to win anymore? Have I really made such a mess of things by getting so competitive?

"Gavril, I..."

"Please don't." Gavril holds up a tired hand. I can feel anger and hurt in his voice. "I really don't want to hear the cover up. I respect your right not to tell me."

"I want to." My lip shakes, and I look down, hugging myself again. I glance at Sage, wishing more than anything the little bug was gone. "But I'm ashamed of it."

"Kascia, I may not like it, but you have every right not to tell me." I don't miss the bitterness in Gavril's tone.

"I know, but I want to." I grip myself tighter. "Because like it or not… in an odd way you were right, and I was wrong."

Gavril pauses, looking at me with a slight frown, his brows drawn together.

I take a deep breath. "I didn't think it was you, and it wasn't, but it also was a little bit. It was that you weren't… I'm supposed to be better than this. My father trained me to be one of the best, and I thought I was. I didn't think about how well trained you must be. So yes, I thought you lacked experience, so to lose once or twice was understandable, but not that constantly. Not when I was trying. And yes, I'd have reacted that way to most anyone else too, but… that includes you too. I'm sorry. You hoped better of me."

Gavril stares at me, his mouth slightly open as he tries to take in what I'm saying. At least, I think that's what it is. It's really hard to read his expression.

I wish he'd say something, I feel really stupid standing there like an idiot. I look around at the floor, avoiding his eyes but out of things to say. What does he want? For me to apologize again?

Finally, I can't take his staring anymore and look up at the ceiling. "If you don't have anything else to say, you don't have to stand there."

Gavril shakes himself and clears his throat as if assuring himself he still has his voice. "Sorry, I just… out of all the reactions I didn't expect that one."

"You lose faith in me so quickly?" I ask, heart sinking. I deserve that.

"Do you really think it's that bad?"

"I'm not stupid." I give him a look. I did something to hurt him badly enough he needed unique help, whatever it was. "You believed more of me, and I disappointed you. I'm lucky you aren't kicking me out."

Gavril sighs heavily. "Kascia," he says with a sigh, "unless you want to leave, I don't have the power to send you away."

"Sure," I huff. He has every right to.

A disappointed sigh flutters out of Gavril's mouth as he looks away, shaking his head. "I really didn't expect this conversation to go like this."

"Thought you'd get mad and throw me out?"

"No. Why are you acting like I'm trying to attack you?" Gavril demands, but not with anger, more like irritation.

"Because I know you want to."

"Do I?"

I flinch at the memory of how he grabbed me and hug myself tighter then nod.

Gavril sighs in frustration and messes up his hair. "You were right. Giving in this soon was a mistake."

That hurts more than anything else he could have said, even if he'd just told me to get out. I hadn't known those words would be the worst outcome until it happened. I fight tears. "You wish you hadn't chosen me?"

"No. Yet..." Gavril looks up as he tries to say what he means more carefully. "I wish I could just choose you." He meets my eyes. "Do you understand?"

I nod. I think so. "You wish we didn't have to keep playing the game?"

He nods. "Be easier to fight, wouldn't it?"

I laugh and wipe my eyes from the residual tears. Why does that sound so nice?

"Thank you for being honest with me. Even if that still stings, it's nice you don't pretend it's something else." Gavril gives me a small smile.

"But you're still disappointed?" I frown. I wish I could bring that confidence back to him. It's what Damian said he needed.

Gavril pauses to think about that. "Unique way to say it," he replies after a moment. "I suppose it doesn't soothe the worry I have that perhaps you are too good to be true."

I bite my lips and look down to stop myself saying it. *Maybe I am.* Maybe he just thinks he knows me and created a too-perfect version of me that he loves.

"So that's it? I've lost the trust I gained?" I ask, scared of the answer but needing to know where we stand.

"Not all of it. I trust you, but I admit part of me is reserved."

"Because what if I can't win? What if you're wrong?" Now he plays it smart. Part of me is relieved, the other part full of dread.

"Can I just... not be wrong?" he asks me.

"I... I don't know." I don't know if I can win. "I just wish I hadn't broken that trust." Did I dare ask? "Is it that hopeless?"

"Of course not. I'm sure you can prove me wrong." Gavril smiles weakly, rather forced.

"So, I have to prove it?"

Gavril sighs and drops his gaze as he thinks it over. "I suppose. You did it once. Think you can't again?"

"How?"

"I don't know." Gavril shakes his head in amusement. "I ask myself that every night. Perhaps if you can figure out how you got it in the first place, you can get my foolish heart to shut up."

I look up, not wanting to know I have that much power over him. It is one thing to quiet a fear. It is another to quiet a scared part of his heart. I didn't want the power to break him when I can't even promise him that I'll be able to give him his whole heart at the end of all this.

"Is it really that I saw you as what I'd been told you were?" So, did I just prove I learned better?

Gavril hesitates before he looks back at me. "You want the truth?"

"Yes." My heart lifts.

"I fear I'm falling for the rebel who only ever sees the prince, me, as the man she hated."

I take it back. I don't want him to be honest. I bow my head, hurt, angry with myself, wishing I'd not asked, that I'd not come here, that I'd not gotten so close to him, that I just followed blindly, so I wasn't trapped in this mess.

"Kascia please," Gavril practically begs, "it's not that I don't want to trust you. I do. But you can understand what scares me, right?"

"Yes." He has every right to be unsure now. And I hate myself for letting it be possible.

Gavril watches me, clearly wondering what to say to comfort me, but the truth is I removed his ability to.

After a moment, Gavril takes a breath as if to get up the courage to do something before I hear unexpected music. "Am I making believe I see in you a queen too perfect to be really true?"

My head snaps up, and I look at him, unsure what to say. He just gives me a small smile. The words strike my heart yet also give me hope. "Or are you really as wonderful as you seem?" I reply.

Gavril's smile becomes more real. "There are still fourteen other girls here. Please, prove to be really true."

But I don't know if I can do that. I am a lie. I'm not as perfect as he thinks me to be. He's just finally seeing the truth of what I am now. What if he finds out everything? I felt sure it was safe to tell him, but now?

"Why?"

Gavril tenses. "If you have to ask that," he says stiffly, "then I suppose I have my answer to that question."

I take a sharp breath as Gavril moves to leave. "Gavril, wait. I'm sorry I didn't mean it like that."

He pauses with his hand on my door latch, and he turns to look back at me. "I just..." I bite my lips, "...you don't have to keep doing this."

Gavril smiles with a hint of his father's mischievousness in his eyes. "Oh, Miss Kascia, yes, I do." And with that he leaves, Sage right behind him.

"You know what this means," I hear Sage say as the door closes. I think Gavril swear at him in reply, but the door cuts off the sound before I'm sure.

I endure a restless night, wondering how I can ever prove to him what I had before. How can I win what I hadn't known I'd won until I lost it? How do I prove I don't believe him spoiled or a jerk or a wimp? That thought hadn't crossed my mind. Untrained sure, but never a wimp.

And worse, did I want to? I couldn't even say 'yes, I love him' to Damian. I can't even honestly say to myself that he'd be my choice. I thought the person I would want to spend my life with was someone I'd want to be with no matter their station. Gavril seems appealing when I pretend he's nothing more than the apprentice I thought he was the night we met. But once he's a royal, it gets harder. Is that a sign it isn't to be? Should I fight for it only to break us both if so? And I'd do anything to not hurt him again.

I decide a distraction is what I need. Perhaps a break from these thoughts will help. I join the girls in the ladies' chamber where we play some card games and enjoy the fire with Nippers spooking Cuppy, Ericka's mini terror dog, at random, making him break out into terrified barking as the cat bolts up onto a table, out of the dog's reach.

If cats could laugh, I'm sure Nippers would be laughing maniacally as he lies down, tail wrapping around him and tapping gently as he looks down at the dog tauntingly. At least when he is not taunting the dog, he is sitting with the rest of us, enjoying a lap or some pats. Bella proudly displays his pink "toe beans" to us every chance she gets. I don't think Nippers enjoys that much.

I look over at Cuppy as Ericka strokes him, calming him down from failing to catch Nippers. He is an odd dog. Not what you normally see of a royal dog. He's smaller for one. Most royal dogs are a Custod breed mix, even the smaller ones are part Custod dog. The Custod dogs are bred for security and are majestic dogs. Cuppy on the other hand is a lapdog with curly fur. He'd be adorable if he wasn't so mean.

I wonder how he'd pass as a royal pet. Gavril does not hide, he does not care much for the dog. I don't know how the king or queen feel. But Cuppy is far from the typical princess pet. Princesses often owned cats or the smaller Custod dog breeds, commonly mixed with a corgi or other small dog. But it could be worse. It could be a husky. Custods breed huskies and use them often, but I'd never heard of a royal having one.

In my distraction, I don't notice I am not the only one looking down and gloomy this holiday. Lilly has new shadows under her eyes and is even more quiet and demure than normal. I only notice it because Jonquil complains she's taking too long to take her turn.

When the round ends, Azalea starts reshuffling the playing cards with a bored rhythm that shows we were all a bit tired of these games but have no better idea what to do. Bella lies on her stomach, fiddling with the decorative tassels on the pillow she was leaning on. Jonquil is tapping her fingers on the arm of the sofa.

"You think we'll all be here for Christmas?" Azalea suddenly asks.

"Why wouldn't we be?" Bella frowns.

"It's still a bit away. What if they run another test?" Azalea frets.

"Not before the holiday," I object.

"You'll be fine. It's me who will go home." Lilly frowns.

Azalea frowns. "You don't know that," she comforts her.

"You all would be better at it than me," Lilly says. "You all have better talents than me."

"Doesn't mean we can run a kingdom better than you," I try to comfort her. "A princess is just a queen-in-waiting, right?"

"I suppose." Lilly swallows. "I just can't help but feel this isn't going to work." She glances over at the "elite" girls who are laughing at something as Ericka strokes her demon dog.

I frown at how Lilly watches them. "Lilly, ignore Dahlia and the others." I'm getting sick of how they push everyone around.

"It's not them," Lilly insists.

"What do you mean?" I frown deeper.

She swallows. "I just... don't know if I can handle it, is all."

"Then why compete?" Jonquil asks.

Lilly's lip shakes. I give Jonquil a look who frowns and mouths "sorry" at me. I roll my eyes, but I can't ignore how Lilly's reaction makes ice slip into my stomach.

She sounds like me trying to confess, yet not confess to Damian. She can't be like me, can she? She does look perfect. That would make her a solid plant.

Lilly's answer doesn't calm me at all. "Well, there are pressures too. And I thought it would be fun. But now they expect me to win. And I didn't think about really winning. I just thought the contest itself would be fun. But... I don't want to fight to win. If I win okay, but... but..."

"Okay?" Jonquil frowns. "It's just okay to get to marry the prince?"

"How long have you had a crush on him?" Azalea asks accusingly.

"Like forevers." Jonquil smiles.

"How? No one even knew what he looked like," I point out.

Jonquil shrugs. "I just knew he was dreamy."

We all laugh.

"Why did you sign up, Azalea?" Lilly asks.

"Oh me?" She flushes. "Well... I have spent most of my life struggling to help my mother look after my brothers and sisters. And when mother said I should do it, I realized I could do that for the whole kingdom, you know? And I didn't have many prospects for marriage being so busy supporting my family. So why not try? I still can't believe I'm here," she laughs.

"At least I'm not using him as a rebound." Jonquil grins at me.

I blush.

"You still love him?" Lilly asks me.

Jonquil hits her arm as if to say she can't just ask that.

I bow my head, unable to answer. Truth was, yes, in a way. But even more, I'm angry with Jake. I hate his lies, making me lose my family. I hate him for tricking himself and me and for his inability to realize the truth for himself. When no one speaks, I realize they want an answer.

Panic makes my heart race as I scramble for an answer for them, "I-I don't know. Sometimes, I really hate him, and other times, I wish it could go back to how it was." I hug myself to protect myself and not hurt Lilly.

"Love is hard work too," Azalea says, "because no matter how 'in love' you are, you will drive each other mad sometimes, and you have to go through hard times. It's not easy. It's a fight. So yeah, when you work at it, those moments are real and can be often and maybe all the time, but not without effort."

"So, you have to really want it?" Lilly frowns.

I believe that's true. Do I want it enough to fight for it? How can I decide?

"Yeah, but by the time it becomes work, you want it." Jonquil sighs.

"Like you'd know." Azalea smiles. "You only daydream."

"You know more?" Jonquil challenges.

"I think so. Kascia will back me up," Azalea turns to me.

I flush, but I can back her up; that's true. "It's both," I say, "but sometimes, the hard work comes before love, sometimes after. I guess it's different for everyone." And sometimes, the work is for nothing but covering up the truth.

"With the most real love, it comes first," Jonquil decides.

"Not for sure," Bella defends, finally joining us, "it's case by case."

"But not all couples' love is true," Jonquil argues.

"So, you get to judge all couples from the dawn of time?" Bella challenges.

That gets Jonquil to flush. "Oh... guess you have a point."

Bella starts off on a rant. I then notice Lilly seems to be trying to inch away. Maybe... "If you want," I offer, "we can talk in my room."

Lilly nods vigorously, hugging herself the way I did. I suddenly become aware I'd been doing it too and let go quickly. "Let's do my room," she says.

"Okay."

We get up, and because of the rather heated debate the others are having, we get away without really being noticed. Lilly is quiet almost the whole way. I want to ask, but I don't think she's ready to talk yet. I just hope she's not in the same kind of trouble I am. I can see her being manipulated more easily than even I had been.

We walk into her room, that's as neat as ever, almost strictly so. It's like a hotel room, perfectly clean and neat. But the element of feeling lived in is missing. Her maids curtsy to us as we come in and leave immediately, taking their work with them.

Lilly looks out of the glass doors without really seeing them. Her view doesn't have quite as much ocean as mine. I can see it, but not quite as much, and even my view of the sea is not the best. This view is more of the open rolling fields and gardens of the palace where food is grown. I can see the stables too.

I look back at Lilly. Movement draws my eyes down to her fingers working hard at her cuff, risking fraying it. I try to think of how to ask, but with her so nervous, I'm not sure I'm ready to just jump right into it, so I try to go about it more gently.

"Your view is lovely. Different though. I wonder what the princess's suite will be like. Think it's more ocean or this view? I suppose it would be on the royal floor. Then again, maybe she doesn't have her own suite. Do you think she and the prince would share a room?"

"I don't know. A room to yourself might be nice though," Lilly says, her eyes getting more lost in the view as she doesn't face me.

I frown just a little. "You'd not want to share a room with him? Or just with anyone?"

Lilly swallows and fiddles with her sleeve even harder. I expect her to pop a hole into it any moment. I'm spared trying to find what to say when Lilly finally speaks, still not facing me, "Sadly, I think it's him." She sighs. "I-I don't know if I want this."

"You could tell him. I doubt he'd make you stay if you didn't want to," I say. I don't know what feels worse, losing the girl I feel closest to or that part of me wouldn't mind one more girl down to help me figure out what's going on in this insane game.

Then I get the answer I feared. Her eyes fill with tears, and she looks down. "I can't. I can't go home like that. I won't make it."

Worry creases between my eyes, and I scoot closer to her. "You don't have to tell them you asked to come home." But when more tears flow instead, I put an arm around her. Is it as bad as me? "Why not? What's wrong? We're alone in here. No one can hear us. You can tell me anything. I won't tell a soul, I promise."

"It's my parents." Lilly swallows her tears. "They'd be ashamed of me. I'd bring shame to my whole family to get this far and then give up."

"Well, just admit you don't care much, or even try to fail a test. They are kind of easy to mess up if you try," I comfort her.

"No, it'd be shameful to lose." Lilly shakes her head.

My brows draw together. "So, you're saying the only way not to bring shame is to win?"

Lilly nods. Her fingers fiddle more intently at her sleeve. I'm surprised her sleeve hasn't worn between her fingers yet. Her thumb and index nails are broken and uneven, likely from picking at her sleeve or perhaps when she fiddled with other things in her nervousness. Perhaps, she even bites at them when no one is looking. I have never seen her do it, and I doubt anyone else has. She is such a perfect little lady. I can see why she is so high on the king and queen's list. She is above me. She just looks like the perfect princess. Her story would be a fairytale if she won.

"Your family are farmers, right?" I double check I recall correctly.

She nods. "Yes, we run a rice farm. I help work it, looking after the ducks, helping with the harvest, things like that. It's not easy with times as they are. We are lucky and get orders from the palace and even finer restaurants in the north. So, we're better off than many, but it's still a lot of work. My father was never content with our station and always seeks to elevate us."

"In what way?" I ask, hoping I can get evidence she's like me, so I can tell her it's okay to open up.

"Nothing illegal," Lilly says quickly. "At least I don't think so. He's plotted to have me marry up since I was really little. He makes 'friends' with all kinds of people. People he thinks will get power like city leaders, even rebels I think. I never get to meet them. But if they win, he wants to be in their good graces, you know?"

I know the type. We sometimes get money from those kinds of people, people who won't rebel outright but want power once it happens. Those men likely pay all three groups, but I avoid the kind.

I'm relieved she's not like me, but worried about what other problems she might be dealing with. "I understand the kind, but I don't understand why your parents would be ashamed if you failed. Would getting into the top ten help?" Then I'll do all I can to make sure she gets there. I never understood why, perhaps my Custod instincts, but I feel drawn to her, to look after her, protect her. It gives me a place among the girls I lack otherwise.

"Well, if you know the kind, you can imagine how fast he signed me up for this. I don't even know what he put on my application. I don't know how I got this far," Lilly bites her delicate little lip. "And it was fun at first, and even being in the Enthronement has to elevate our family somehow, but the more I write home and the more I get to know the prince, the more I realize I either have to win this... or feel my father's anger. There is no safe way out of this." She stifles a sob.

"Oh Lilly." My heart breaks as I know that pain all too much.

Lilly hides her face in my shoulder. I stroke her hair a little and let her cry while restraining the pain in my heart I hadn't fully faced. One I knew I'd never fully face, because even if I did, the pain would still be there. There is no fixing this. I just let her cry and comfort her for a long time.

"I know how that feels," I finally speak once I feel it's time. "My father talked me into this too. I didn't want to do this. It felt like betraying all I had and losing the life I'd originally thought I'd have and learned to want. But in the end, it was the only way to escape feeling like I disappointed him and really everyone else I knew." I hug her a bit tighter. "I know how it feels."

"So, what do you do?" She pulls back, looking up at me with tear filled eyes. "If you don't want to be here, why are you so good at it?"

"Uh?" I frown.

"The prince avoids talking to us outside dates, most of all at meals. Then after he spent all day with you, he teased all of us just to get your attention. You pass every test. His guard watches you like a hawk. It's like he's testing you harder than us. Which must mean you're the prince's favorite for him to be so careful with you. You impressed the king and prince at the talent show better than anyone. You seem to just thrive here, but you don't want it any more than I do."

Me thriving here? She has no idea. I don't want to focus on my problems though. "You don't want it?" I ask gently.

Lilly looks down. "I don't know. No. Not really. I mean he's really nice, but... but I don't want to be queen. Not here or maybe anywhere." She finally makes a full hole in her sleeve. She starts playing with the other one. "I just... it's not like the fairytales. Being a princess, or even a contestant, it isn't just about tea parties and looking pretty, is it?" She looks up at me.

I shake my head, still too stunned to speak.

"Right. And I just... I don't think I can do that. And it's not fair to him to make him do it alone. He needs a queen like that. And it's not me. And I don't know if I really love him. I mean... I didn't think about all of that.

He's nice, I suppose, but... trying more makes me nervous. I just... I'm not ready. I thought the game would be fun, you know? Date a prince. Sounds amazing, but this is so much bigger than that. And I didn't realize how much."

She bites her lip. "I just don't feel that way about him, and I'm not going to be able to be what they need. I thought they just hoped I'd get far enough. Sure, I daydreamed I'd win, but this isn't what I expected."

She really is too young for this, maybe not in body but in mind. She's realizing the realities of life all at once, here, alone, with no family and just new friends: girls she is competing against. She's overwhelmed and scared. I don't know how to assure her. Not when I feel the same.

"And there are other girls better at those bigger things than me. And they like it. At least, I hope. Because it's not me. But I can't go home. What do I do?"

I sigh heavily. I hardly know what I should do. "I don't know. Is there really no way your father won't be upset? What if you make it to the top tier?"

Lilly shakes her head. "He's made it clear it's all or nothing to him."

"How do you know?"

"I mentioned it would be odd having a holiday at the palace. And said I missed them and couldn't wait to be with them for it again next year at home. Father was not happy. He lost it. It wasn't 'while I can'; it was 'win this or shame us all'." Lilly sniffs and bites her lip again. "And honestly, I never thought I'd win this thing. I didn't think my parents thought so either. Now... Now, I don't know what to do. I just... I can't do this." She sniffles again.

I give her another hug, but I don't have an answer for her. I'm just as lost as she is. Maybe it's heartless, but... "Have you tried to like him?"

She relaxes and pulls out a handkerchief from the sleeve she made a hole in. "I'm far more scared of the throne than anything. This kingdom needs a real queen. My father wants to climb because he was a starving boy once. He doesn't want to deal with that again. And a queen is supposed to help fix it. And I'm scared to even hold the prince's hand, let alone... anything else. Maybe in other kingdoms I could skate by, but... n-not here." She looks up at me, saying, "Do you think that's why they did this? They know he needs good help so needs a real princess?"

I shake my head. "I don't know." I often wondered why they set this up when I learned they weren't as horrible as I thought, but I know I will never get a solid answer. "Is it horrible I just assumed it was because they were stuck up and wanted only the best for their boy?"

That makes Lilly laugh. "I guess a lot of people think that. With how they take money and all." She sighs. "But that can't be it, can it?"

I shake my head. "Maybe it is. Or maybe they thought it good for security." But even now I know that can't be true.

"I don't know either." Lilly frowns. "But even if I can pass all their tests, I can't do it. And I don't want to. I'm too shy for confrontation and wars and... and all that."

"But a queen doesn't have to do that," I point out. "She often helps with more domestic things. You could help set up orphanages."

"I'd be too scared of the children," Lilly says.

I laugh. I can't help it. She seems like a child herself. The idea that she's scared of children seems quite funny. It's like a rabbit being scared of other rabbits.

"I know, I know. But... I'm not used to kids," she says, hugging her knees to her chest. "I didn't even play with other kids growing up. I just worked and talked to the farm hands who played with me. They were nice, mostly older boys."

I grin. "So, is there someone at home you miss?" I ask. Might explain her struggles.

Lilly laughs. "I don't know. I never thought it was an option," she admits.

"I guess that's easy to do." If her father is so calculating, she just didn't think about it. She didn't get to choose anyway. It's why the prince avoids getting close to us. And in a way, it's the reason I fought to be so close to Jake.

"Yeah, guess so." Lilly sighs sadly. "I just feel sick about everything. I can't help thinking about it. What do I do?"

I ask myself that over and over, and I have no answers. I shrug. "Well, maybe let fate decide," I suggest. "You just do your best, and if you fail... well, what can your father do?"

She bows her head. "For all I know, he'd kick me out. I only know how to work the farm. I'd be helpless."

"But even getting this far makes you a lady," I point out. "If you're in the last ten you are promised a noble rank, the kind that comes with land and jobs." Maybe a good answer to get her out of it. "So, if you can last that long, your father may not be happy, but you'll have more station than him." I laugh. "Maybe if you ask nicely, you can be lady over his lands." She laughs too. "I'll make sure you get out of this safe. I know I can't change your father's mind, but we'll find a way," I promise her.

"How?"

I shrug. "I don't know, but we'll find something." At least if she can get into the top ten.

Lilly nods, not noticing my fears. "I guess now it's Christmas, we'll get a bit of a break either way, so I don't need to worry about it right now. I just wish I knew when and what was next."

"I know. I hate waiting," I admit.

"I just wish I could go home to my old life." Lilly sighs, bowing her head.

I take a shaking breath and hug her again, resting my head on hers. "Sometimes, me too."

There's a timid knock at the door. "Miss," one of Lilly's maids says nervously, "it's about time to prepare for dinner."

"Oh yes." Lilly sighs.

"I can stay until I have to get ready," I offer, feeling she doesn't want me to leave yet. Lilly smiles her thanks.

Chapter 13

I wait for Lilly to get ready, so I can walk with her before going to my own room to prepare for dinner. A few others are already in the hall on their way to dinner: Amapola, Laurina, Dahlia, Isla, Florence, and Kamala.

We hear a sound from the hallway ahead. "I can't believe you've never done that before. Was I really your..." Forsythia's voice fades shyly.

"In a way." My heart stops. Is that Gavril? It has to be. There aren't many males allowed up here who would talk to any of us like that. But his voice sounds unsure, as if debating if his own statement is true. His first what?

"Thank you," his voice goes on. "I needed that more than you could ever know."

"So... it's not crossing a line?"

Forsythia, arm in arm with Gavril, walks into view to her bedroom door at the end of the hall. Neither has seen the group of other Chosen in the hall.

"No," Gavril replies.

Without warning, Forsythia takes Gavril's face and kisses him. He's as stunned as we are as he stumbles back into the wall beside her door, but he doesn't fight it. His fingers get tangled in her long straight locks as he kisses her back. He's relaxed, taking it like a cat enjoying a really good chin scratch. His fingers play with her hair as if wanting nothing more than to feel more of her.

My stomach tightens in a sick knot. That had been me. I'd gotten that first. Now I'm stuck watching how much he's lost faith in me. He's enjoying a kiss with someone else, perhaps more than with me. He looks more relaxed and content than he'd ever felt with me.

His free hand runs down her shoulder, across the arch of her back, then up to her opposite shoulder to hold her more securely. His fingers keep playing with her hair as if searching for something, not getting enough but wanting more of her.

That does it. I have to look away to stop myself vomiting. I'm not the only one who freezes at the sight. I think every girl in that hall is bolted in place.

It finally ends, and Gavril pulls back. "I'll see you at dinner," he says.

"Of course," she kisses the tip of his nose. "Until then, my prince." Forsythia slips into her room, and Gavril turns away, not seeing any of us, and disappears down the hall to the stairs.

The rest of us are frozen stiff in shock.

"She did that so we'd see it." Amapola sounds haughty and angry.

Dahlia is seething. "She wants us to just give up, does she?" She sounds far from backing out.

"Little brat," Laurina huffs.

Isla and Florence look at one another in shock, worry in their eyes.

Kamala huffs, "Little slut making a show of it." But she sounds envious she hadn't thought of a trick like that.

Lilly looks at me, but I can't meet her gaze. I can't turn my head to look at her or take in much around me. My eyes are locked onto the spot on the floor where Gavril had stood as if the marble there were a ghost.

He wants me most? That I will win? What lies. I shut my eyes as hot tears fill them. Lilly opens her mouth as if to ask, but I turn away, fists clenched, eyes tight shut. I take off up the hall, the opposite way to use the back way to my room.

Anger and hurt flood me. I feel like a fool for even trying. I'd broken any chance I had, and Forsythia made sure I knew that I'd been replaced already. She isn't complicated or hard. On the contrary, she is so easy she could just grab him with an audience, and he didn't even see us.

I don't care anymore. I don't care about winning. I don't care about wanting him. I just want to get as far away from him and the hurt he left me in.

I race up the halls with the effect of a gust of wind, breezing past as quick as a breath. If anyone sees me, they only get a brief glimpse before I am already gone. It's like I'm running through a storm made of my own hot tears and the stiff breeze my haste makes.

I reach my room, tear the door open and shut it without looking at anyone or anything, my eyes tight shut again. Why did I waste all this stress and fear on him? I give him one moment of nervousness, and he moves on in a heartbeat. And I didn't even mean it. He said he'd give me a chance.

Instead, he's left me alone, in tears, feeling stupid for believing him when he said he still wanted me and was giving me a chance. Why am I wasting all this effort? Why can't I just forget all we'd had under my desperate spy disguise when he will not even hold out for me?

But even if he wants to, he can't. I know he has to get close to the other girls. So why does it hurt so much? This is why I told him not to focus on me, so he'd not feel hurt when we were taken from him. I didn't remember there is another reason: to protect me. He does not care about that though.

And I am done hurting over a man who is not even mine. No one is mine. I know he cannot be. And unless I can play the disguise well enough, he won't ever be. No matter who he wants to pick.

"My lady?" Flur asks uneasily.

I recall the reason we'd all witnessed the scene and open my eyes. I have to put on a face to get through dinner at least. Will the other girls who saw the display catch on to me being missing? Would he? Would he care? Anger floods me, making my face hot. I doubt it.

"Are you alright?" Flur asks gently.

I take a deep breath. What do I say? Do I prove myself right and not go to dinner and see what he does but risk the other girls using it against me? Or do I put a face at dinner to get no answers? What signal will it send him if I do not go? He will not know why I am ill or upset, so will he check on me? I doubt it, but part of me wants the proof, so I can be mad at him and justify it. But how would the others react to my absence?

Behind me, I hear the door open and close softly, followed by gentle footsteps approaching me. Pause hangs for a moment before I hear Damian's careful, worried tone speak to me. "Kascia, I saw what happened. Are you alright?"

"I-I..." I do not know how to reply. My maids glance at one another, clearly wondering the same thing. "I don't know." I have to be honest, at least.

Damian steps around, so I can see his face. He looks so sorry for me. He lets out a sigh through his nose and pulls me into a hug.

I accept it but don't know what to say or do. I have gotten myself into this. Do I really have a right to be so upset? Yet I still am angry, hurt. He lied to me. I was easily replaced.

"You can let it out, Kascia. This is a safe space," Damian reminds me.

"I don't have time." Unless I try to pretend I am too ill to go to dinner. The other girls will know why. Forsythia will be delighted.

"I'm not sure we have time for anything else. I don't expect you to go down there and ignore your feelings. If you're late, I can apologize for you. If... you want to go, that is." He pulls back to look at me.

"I... I don't know." Part of me wants to have a reason to be angry with him, to prove to myself he doesn't care. If I do not go, he'd not worry or check on me. It gives me a justified reason to be upset. But then I'd have to deal with Forsythia's gloating.

"About what?"

"If I want to go. I should." I know that much.

"That may be. But if you want a grip on things, you have to handle them first. We do have a few minutes. He won't even be down there yet," Damian points out. "Please. I know there's bound to be a thousand thoughts going through your mind. Talk to me."

"You saw it. What more is there to say?"

"Only you can answer that," Damian says sadly. "But I won't force you to tell me if you don't want to." He brushes my hair gently and smiles for me. "You know I never will."

I shrug. "What more is there to say? You saw it."

"But that doesn't tell me what you feel about it," he points out.

"Hurt, angry." I shut my eyes.

Damian sighs and closes his eyes, pauses briefly, and nods. "I understand." He opens his eyes and forces a smile as he pulls back. "Let's prepare you for dinner."

I take a deep breath and nod. My maids set to work. They don't make me talk but work quietly and efficiently. They just touch up my make-up quickly and help me change into a dinner dress: long, flowing, v-cut skirt, tapering into a silver belt that matches the silver streaks across the dress, contrasting the midnight blue fabric.

They are quiet, letting me stand there listless. If I decide to play ill, I am sure my maids would buy it. I am not so sure Damian will.

The second I'm ready, my maids excuse themselves for their own dinner.

Once the door closes, Damian stands from his workbench and looks at me. "Are you ready, or do you need another minute?"

"I..." I take a deep breath. "I don't know. I just... don't want to think about it, but I can't help it."

"Perhaps if you got it off your chest, it would help," he prompts, but his expression reassures me if I don't take the offer, he will let it drop.

"I'm hurt and angry, but that's not really fair. He said he'd give me a chance, but... he wants me to prove it, and... how do I..." I hate to use the word 'compete'. "How do I make that work?" He enjoyed that kiss as much, if not more, than he'd enjoyed our kiss. How do I keep up with that? And he chose her!?

Damian sighs as his eyes dance off to the distance corner. "I wish I had an answer for you. But sadly, I don't. Not a clear one anyway. This situation is certainly unique." Then he huffs a small smile to himself. "If things were a little different, and you my daughter, I would skin the boy alive with my pinking shears for hurting you this way. And it would be done before the dining table was set."

I shudder at the idea though part of me is satisfied at least I'm somewhat justified in my anger. But then my heart sinks. "He didn't... mean for that to happen, did he?" That would certainly make Damian angry.

"From what I can tell, no. He did not," Damian says. "I was at the other end of the hall, so I saw the first part of it. They were walking to her room in silence when Forsythia suddenly started laughing. And frankly, while Gavril is smart, he is still just a man. And honestly, we can be pretty stupid about things, especially when it comes to women. There is much about your sex we simply don't understand, even when we try. And the look of a woman at just the right moment can be intoxicating. And Forsythia has learned how to use that. Admittedly, she is a fairly decent actress too when around Gavril. She's figured out what he likes about you and gives it to him with no strings attached. In another life, she'd have made an excellent harlot."

I sigh frustratedly. "So that's it? I slip for one moment, and that's it?" I fight to keep my face straight as the anger and hurt pulses in my chest, making me want to scream.

Damian comes forward and places his hands on my arms. "Not if you don't want it to be. Don't give up on him. I understand it is hard seeing him with another, especially one you dislike so much. And I don't expect you to get over it tonight or quickly, as that hurt often runs deep, but don't abandon him forever. From what I hear, he isn't too sure of his feelings for Forsythia; that's why he calls her 'fox.' And remember, she kissed him first. And that means something. Or at least it should to you. He doesn't give it to her. She takes it with the illusion of giving him control of the situation. But I fear her goals. And I fear for him if you let him go and she should succeed because no bride should enter into a relationship with her husband without compromise and commitment, and Forsythia wants neither."

"Does it matter when I kindle his anger and he goes to her to soothe it?" I ask. "One moment he's telling me he wants me to be true but then goes with someone else." But is it fair of me to feel that way when that is the game? He has to. Yet I hate him for it anyway.

"Does he though?" Damian asks. "Did he really go to her to soothe his pain, or does it just seem that way? He was out with Bella last night."

At least that isn't as bad as Forsythia. At least Bella would be a decent choice. "I know. He has to." I only feel worse for being so petty. I can't help it. I even reminded him he has to play the game.

Damian puts his knuckle under my chin and lifts it until my eyes meet his compassionate ones. "It's okay to be hurt. I'd be shocked and a little sad if you weren't. I am sorry you had to see that, and to be perfectly honest, I'm a bit annoyed at Gavril as well. He is a smart man, and he knows what she does to him. He avoids Ericka like the plague, but with Forsythia, he doesn't because he enjoys the hormonal high she gives him, and that is dangerous territory. He also put up a wall between the two of you and told you to prove you are true because he can't understand how what happened in the gym isn't about him or how you think or feel about him. At least, not in the personal sense. But he took it personally, when honestly, the mistake you made is not uncommon.

"He is so... afraid to have confidence in his own choices that he wavers at the first sign of doubt, and that hurt goes much deeper than the skin. Now he expects you to give that back to him, when honestly..." His brow furrows hard. "I don't know if that is right. In this competition, you are right that he is required to date around and can't necessarily forget that. But in doing so, he neglects you, and personally, it's no wonder you still have doubts about him. You've likely spent the least amount of time with him of any of the girls still here. He asks you to prove your feelings, but isn't he required to do the same?" He closes his eyes and shakes his head. "I'm sorry, but that feels wrong to me.

"So, you have every right to feel hurt, Kascia. And you don't have to pretend that you are not. If you don't wish to go down to dinner, I will make sure that the king and the queen know you are feeling ill. If you wish it, I will protect you from him. I'll even go as far as to deny him entry should he choose to come see you tonight and you do not wish to see him. Whatever you wish of me, I will do. No man gets to play with your heart like that, not while I'm around."

"Not like it would matter." I bow my head. "Even if I don't go, he won't come."

"Then... I'll stay here to cheer you up." Damian gives me a small smile.

I sigh. "The other girls will know why."

He frowns. "The others who saw?"

I nod. "A lot of other girls still stay on that floor. They were on their way to dinner like us. So, it wasn't just me. Half the girls know, and soon the rest will know."

He nods, taking that in for a moment. "Which is more important to you?"

"I don't know. I have to live with whatever they do." Mostly, I want to stop hurting, to feel safe. I never thought I'd miss him, but that's what I feel.

"You have to live with it either way. So which effect do you want more, or I suppose, less of: Gavril's? Or the girls?" Damian asks. "It's your choice. I won't force you either way."

"I suppose he won't even notice." I don't want to put on a happy face, even less do I want to have to admit what I'd seen him doing. I'm sure he didn't mean for us to know.

"You can't know that for certain. He has before," Damian says.

"What do you think I should do?" I ask, unsure.

"Personally, I want to stick it to him and tell you to stay. But you are right about the other girls talking." He sighs sadly. "And a true princess carries the weight of her people but never shows it. Rightly, you should go, even if I don't want you to." He manages a weak smile.

"I just want the satisfaction of proving I was right. Then I feel right being mad at him even if..." If I still care about him.

"I know." He smiles understandingly at me. "Perhaps you can try another night. Then they can't say you really weren't ill."

I'm not sure that would bring the satisfaction. But I nod. "If I want to stay, I suppose I have little choice." Had my pride doomed me to the gloom I'd brought here?

"You always have a choice. Sometimes, it's not a great one, though," he sympathizes. "Come on. I can escort you if you wish."

I take a deep breath and nod. Damian smiles a little with a gentle nod back and offers me his arm. I take a deep breath and take it. "I..." Will it ever get better? Or will this wild ride keep dealing me blows I don't know if I'll survive? I stiffen my resolve. "I'm ready."

Damian nods confidently. "Yes, you are." He smiles then leads me from the room.

I try to take deep breaths like I'd done in the theater when I got nervous, not because I am nervous per se, but because it gets me in the mindset to put on the proper show. I will be putting on yet another show, one of dozens that aren't the kind I'd been in love with.

Damian takes me down to the dining hall, and unlike before, he takes me right to my seat and pulls out my chair for me. I nod my thanks and sit down, putting on the show of being just another background character to the scene. It also lets me read the room.

The girls who see my entrance are giving each other sideways looks and many of them shoot dark glares at Forsythia who eats with just a hint of pride in her posture, bringing her spoon to her mouth perfectly. The others feel the tension but look confused, glancing at each other to see who else is confused. I decide to join the latter group and gave a small shrug when Zelda meets my eyes.

When the bustle dies down, I dare glance to my right at the royal table. Gavril isn't looking at any of us. In fact, he seems to be trying hard to distract himself in conversation with his parents who seem unwilling to talk about whatever he is asking about.

Damian gives Gavril a sad yet angry look, which I doubt he notices, before sitting at the servants' table. I doubt Sage misses it though. I try to spot him, but his expression is hard to read as he stands, back leaning to the wall with one foot resting on it, arms folded as he watches. I often wonder when the man eats.

"Is something wrong?" Azalea asks next to me.

I shrug, not wanting to spread the gossip further. She frowns and looks at Ericka. I think it's the fact Ericka is also confused that makes Azalea unsure. Wouldn't the queen of gossip know? I'm surprised Forsythia, who sits on Ericka's other side, doesn't elaborate. Isla is sitting as far from Forsythia as she can, but closer to Kamala than I'd be comfortable with, while Florence uses the fact she's on the end with no other girls to give herself space away from it all.

There must be something else going on as the royal family seem blind to the odd energy around the table. They are preoccupied. I think that's what Gavril is interested in, not knowing he'd made quite a show for the Chosen girls. He doesn't look at any of us, so at least I can say it's not personal. Even if it feels personal.

I am more than happy to finish faster than my etiquette teacher would likely approve. But she's not here to judge, and I vanish as just another background character. Gavril is distracted just fine without our help.

I am in such a hurry to escape I miss Gavril spotting me go and a slight frown creasing his face.

My maids aren't even back when I get to my room, but I don't mind. I could use the space not worrying about them. I hate being a burden on them.

Damian comes in a little while later and works on cleaning up his work-space which he normally does while my maids prepare me for bed. I'm not sure I want to be ready for bed yet, but I need something to do, so I try cleaning up my desk, but I use it so rarely now no one writes to me, I have to resort to sorting my vanity, avoiding my reflection.

That's when there's a knock at the door. Damian looks over at it then meets my eye. "Would you like me to see who it is?"

"Yes please." I can't imagine who'd bother to visit at this hour.

Damian nods to me then goes to the door and opens it a crack. His head lifts as if he knows or was expecting whoever it is before he slips into the hall and closes the door behind him.

I frown, unsure what that means. The guards or staff sometimes want to talk to Damian about security. Had something happened? Or perhaps something was planned they had to discuss with him. I wait, pointlessly organizing everything.

A few minutes later, Damian returns and closes the door behind him. When he sees me looking, he gives me a small smile. "Well... he noticed."

"What?" I frown.

"Gavril is outside. He saw you leave dinner early, and he's concerned," Damian says with serenity.

I just stare at him for a moment, unsure I can believe it. "What?" It feels more polite than accusing him of joking.

Damian seems to understand, so he explains calmly, "He was worried that you were ill or upset, so I told him. He wants to speak to you, but given the situation, I only felt it right to ask you first. What would you have me do? Do you want to see him, or should I send him away?"

Dread fills my stomach. "You told him what?"

He sighs. "I told him what you saw in the hallway."

I want to ask why, but I also don't want to sound stupid. I bite my lip. Did he really have to do that? Then again, what else could he say? "What did he say?"

"He didn't say anything. To be fair, I don't think he could. He was... quiet for some time and seemed to still be processing the horror of the situation when I asked if he would like to see you," Damian replies. "He jumped at the chance, and I told him I would ask."

I swallow. Jumped at the chance? Why would he be that eager? I did not want to have to deal with that awkward moment when it's not like either of us can deny it's practically required. "Did you really have to tell him?" I stall for time.

"Would you rather have done it?" Damian lifts his head with the question. "Or could you have done it?"

"He didn't have to know," I point out.

"Yes, he does," Damian says with more firmness in his voice. "And that goes beyond your relationship with him. Need I remind you that this is not a game, and Forsythia is dangerous. If by some horrible chance, she wins this, he will need to be prepared for what he is up against, or he and this kingdom won't stand a chance. That harpy will use her powers of seductive persuasion to manipulate him and the court. It's clearly already working on him, and if he remains unaware, he will be outmatched while she buries his talents to feed her own ends. And frankly, that thought scares me. So, my apologies if I failed as your attendant in this regard, but if he is to succeed, he needs to be aware of people like her. He doesn't need people who will hide the truth to spare his feelings. He needs those who will help him see what he is blind to, like you once did."

I bow my head as I accept that blow. He's right. I was a help, and now I'm just more trouble. I don't know what to say, so I nod, still hugging myself.

Damian lets out a sigh of sad frustration. "Kascia, I'm not trying to criticize you. I simply want you to understand."

"I know." He is right. But that does not make me feel any better. "I do. I just..." I am not who I want to be, or even I used to be, after the mess I made. I don't know how to react. I just want to go back before that stupid night.

"I understand." He gives me a little smile. "I think we all wish we could undo our mistakes at least at one time or another, but that is how we grow."

But what am I growing into? I am not even what I thought I was when I threw it all away. I nod again. "I suppose there's little else to do." What will sending him away do other than delay the inevitable when I cannot say no?

"So, you will see him?" Damian checks.

I nod. "Putting it off won't make anyone feel better, will it?" Not when he knows.

"It's doubtful."

"So, we'll get it over with," I say, pronouncing my decision.

Damian nods and goes to the door, opens it, then stands aside, gesturing to Gavril to come in.

There's a brief pause, likely as Gavril nods thanks to Damian before he steps into the room. He looks at me, and I can't pull my gaze away, but I don't know what to say or do. Formality feels stupid at this point.

The door closes behind him, and I notice Damian has not come back in. My eyes dart to every shadow to try to spot Sage. They have not actually left us alone, have they?

Gavril frowns and follows my eyes, trying to figure it out. It takes him a moment before his eyes brighten in understanding. He looks back at me. I don't like how I feel studied and step back, curling into myself.

Gavril pauses, his eyes filling with compassion, and retreats. He'd moved to go to me but stopped when I stepped away. I hadn't even realized until he pulled back. But still neither of us speak, just looking across at one another.

Why did Damian have to tell him? This is so painfully awkward, and I am not sure how to digest it. Damian was also right about him being speechless. I don't know what to say, and clearly, neither does he.

It's painful just standing there with nothing to say, knowing he's scared of coming closer. I fear what he's thinking, feeling. He's not looking right at me, but down slightly, at my feet. Is this it? Has he realized how dumb it was to invest in me? And now, he has to let me down gently?

"I'm not sure I've ever regretted the past more than I have in the last few weeks," Gavril chuckles after a while. He stands upright and puts his hands into his pockets. I have never seen him do that. I didn't even quite process that his slacks have pockets. "Never thought I'd have to debate which moment of my past I'd want to erase more."

"The night in the garden or on the bridge?" I ask.

I jump as Gavril tenses the way he does when he's about to lose his temper. "Assume the worst, don't you?" I don't know if his tone is more angry or cold. "Neither," he almost spits.

I bite my lip, thinking keeping quiet is safer. It will stop me making a mess of things; that is sure.

"Do you really think so little of... all of it?"

"All of what?" I ask, trying to keep my tone steady.

Gavril doesn't answer right away but is careful with his answers. "What's happened between us. Do you think that our history means nothing?"

"It's not like I don't know that's also happening with other girls," I say quietly. I open my mouth to go on, but Gavril cuts me off.

"If you say 'it should', curse it woman, I will lose it."

I shut up immediately. I don't think he'd ever tossed an insult at me before.

Gavril sighs in frustration and rubs his face with one hand. "Sorry, I just... Please, stop saying that."

But it should. He has to be with them. He has every right and even a duty to have that kind of moment with all of us. He has to keep us all in our bubbles to do as asked. He never wanted us to see into each other's bubble. I wonder who else thinks they are in a special place with him. Forsythia does. I never would have thought her special to him. Does Dahlia think herself important to him too? Kamala, Amapola, Jonquil?

Gavril sighs and rubs his face again. He looks exhausted, his expression drooping, and I'm annoyed with myself for causing it. It isn't his fault, even if deep down I want to slap him. Has he had moments like I witnessed just now with Princess Rose to appease his mother? Is no one special?

"Kascia, please, say something," Gavril begs.

"Like what?"

"Something to prove you didn't lose that beautiful voice." Gavril manages a weak smile.

"Nope, I'm fine." I adjust my grip on my arms before I look down again.

"Where did the fire go?"

"What?" I frown and look to the hearth in the room.

"Not that." Gavril rolls his eyes. "The one you used to demand how I could work for the royal family, or even when you got annoyed with me. You just retreat now. Please, just talk to me."

"I didn't realize you liked talk." I regret it the moment I say it. That was meant as a slap, and I know it, but I regret it. I tense, expecting him to do the same and snap at me.

He doesn't. "I guess I deserve that," he admits with a slightly sick tone to his voice. He takes a deep breath. "My offer still stands."

"What offer?"

"Our first 'official' meeting." Gavril smiles a little. "I told you feel free to yell at me because I knew you'd be furious once you knew the truth of who I was."

That feels like another lifetime, another world. It was so long ago. It feels silly now, almost immature, like we were just foolish children playing a game. It's a lot bigger now.

"You don't deserve to be yelled at," I say quietly.

"Don't I?"

"You have to," I remind him coldly.

"Is that what you want?"

"No." I wish I didn't say it.

"You can't pretend you aren't upset about it."

"I didn't want to see it, but I know it has to be that way." I try to shield myself.

"Does it?"

I glare at him. "We both know it does."

"So, she gets a kiss and gets to make you feel that way, and you don't?"

"You already did that," I remind him of the safe room.

"And you wish I hadn't."

"Yes."

Gavril shuts his eyes and drops his head back as if trying to stop himself saying something. We'd been on a roll; now he wants to be quiet?

"What did you come here for?" I ask, just wanting it over with.

"I came because you looked upset. You don't run off like that unless something is wrong," he says. "And I debated leaving you alone for fear I'm just using it as an excuse to see you because that's all I've wanted to do."

"But you didn't."

"You keep throwing why at me. You have any idea how annoying that is? Every second I spend with you, I get told by five different people I shouldn't be there when that's where I want to be?"

"Is it wrong?"

"Yes!"

I look up at him with a frustrated glare. "You know it's not."

"So, *they* all get a turn, but you don't?" Gavril demands. "Why?"

"I-I do, but..."

"But?" he prods me on.

"But it's different."

"How?"

"No one doubts you'll give me attention." *Or cares if you don't.*

Gavril looks away from me, shaking his head, jaw tense. "And people think I get what I want." His demeanor doesn't change as he looks over at me again. "So that means you don't get a turn?"

"I had my public moment, thank you," I reply as coolly as I can.

"But we're not in public."

"So?"

Gavril looks away again, running his fingers through his hair then puts his hand to his mouth, fanning out his fingers before holding his mouth; his eyes far away as he tries to process something. "If only you knew how hard this is." He sighs and drops his hand. "Kascia, I'm sorry. I never wanted you or anyone to see that. I never wanted to hurt you with it. I know you are always telling me to give the other girls a chance, but that doesn't mean I want you to have to endure that scene."

"It would have happened sooner or later." I hug myself again.

"Kascia, please. I am trying. What more do you want from me when you ask me to do this? I'm sorry I wavered and let this happen."

"Let it?" I snap. "You have to, Gavril. It's the Enthronement. It's not some dating game or a choice you get to make. You remind me too."

"It's so I don't do something we'll regret."

"Like what?"

The snap of Gavril's moment frightens me, but it only makes the adrenaline all the warmer when he's suddenly pulling me in and kissing me harder than I'd been kissed in a long time. His fingers knock the pins in my hair loose, but he doesn't care. In fact, I think he likes it as he pulls more pins loose.

The electricity that generates between us goes from weak static to dangerously crackling electricity as I return his pressure just as vehemently. I regain my senses, gripping his shoulder tightly in one hand, my other balling his shirt into a tense knot.

I don't know how long we stay locked like this, each kiss sparkling lightning between us. I'm so excited and angry, my grip might be painful. Gavril's taken any styling out of my hair by now, and I might have a bruise on my back with how he's gripping me.

Finally, he pulls back, not quite pushing me away, but he does have to force himself back. "Like that," he says angrily.

It takes a moment for me to recall what in creation he is talking about. I flush and run my fingers through my hair to try to get it to look at least slightly decent.

"I'm sorry that's all I really wanted. I'm sorry this stupid game makes me unable to do this properly. I'm sorry I waver, and because of it I'm stuck playing this stupid game. I'm sorry I'm a prince instead of someone more accessible for you. I hate this likely more than you do. I'm sorry I'm not just another poor cobbler or something that makes this easier. I'm sorry that my choices hurt you. I'm sorry I just want to feel something in this cursed contest. I'm so tired of wanting and being denied. I'm sorry, alright?"

"So that's what you want? All you really want?"

Gavril rubs his eyes with both hands with a frustrated huff. "No. Not even close." His shoulders drop. "I told you it would be something we'd regret."

"Then why did you do it?" Though I can't really say I regret it.

"Because it's all I've really wanted. I told you a long time ago where I stood on this. I know you keep doubting it and thinking it has changed, perhaps thinking it should, but it hasn't. I wish for a moment you could understand what it's like to be in my shoes. You try and miss the mark so often. You're not alone. All of you Chosen do it. But if..." he lets out a heavy sigh.

"My apologies. I merely came to make sure you're alright. I'm sorry you or anyone had to see that. Rest assured, I'll do my best to ensure it won't happen again." He clenches his jaw a moment before he goes on. "Know that it doesn't change how I feel about you in the slightest. I doubt that is believable to you, but it's still true. I'll try to behave more properly and prayerfully to stop doing such severe damage to the one person that... well, my sincerest apologies."

He takes my hand and kisses it. The normal tension I feel before he lets go is harsher than it has been before, yet also briefer. "Good night, my lady."

He pulls back to go. I don't want him to go, but how do I justify it? I don't know what to say, and there's nothing I can do. "Gavril," I call before I can stop myself.

He pauses as he has a million times and turns to me. I look at him and struggle with my own longing. I want to just let it out. I want to fight like I had with Jake, be angry, be hurt, cry, and let him apologize and hold me. But he's not mine. I know that. He cannot be.

Our eyes meet, and the longing stretches between us like a tense cord ready to snap and yank us together at a moment's notice. Gavril shuts his eyes, taking a deep breath and forces himself to turn away.

I shut my eyes and bite my lips to fight the different tears that rise up this time. Longing. I want him to come back. I want to feel the wall drop and be able to be the person I missed. I want to beat against the wall, beg it to open and let us in, but it's not to be. Not in this game. Not with fourteen other girls all wanting the same thing.

This room is far too big. There's no small corner to curl up in and hide. I wish I'd done a better job preparing for bed, so I don't have to figure out how to hide my desire to run and hide from my staff.

The door opens, and I wonder if it's just Damian or if it's my maids come back from dinner. I don't have to wonder long as Damian approaches me. He considers me with sad eyes then takes me into his arms and holds me tight.

It opens the floodgates, and I'm able to break down and cry. Damian provides a safe small corner to hide in. I curl into him and just sob out how much I want him. I have to stand there, longing for him, knowing every little treasure I receive, someone else will get too. I have given up everything for the Enthronement. And yet, what I wanted is denied me, and I am losing my ability to help him or be useful in the ways I thought I was. I don't know what to do when the only thing I want, I can't have.

Chapter 14

Forsythia's smugness only gets worse. She walks around the ladies' chamber like she's already queen. The word has gotten around what happened by the time we're at our first break between lessons. Even Lady Keva is proud of her progress, looking more regal, telling her to "own that inner queen". It just makes me want to vomit.

Lady Keva comments to me I'm more round shouldered than normal and suggests some stretches I can do which makes Forsythia even more proud of herself.

"Are you okay?" Lilly dares ask me quietly as we sit apart from the others, sipping tea.

"I'm fine," I reply. Not much else I can say.

"The others just look annoyed or angry, some even jealous. You..." she pauses. "Are you sure you're alright?"

"I'm fine." I have decided to be, so I'm going to be. I'm not going to imagine him doing that with Ericka or Dahlia or Zelda.

"How do you just—"

"I have to." I straighten my shoulders.

"You should win." Lilly frowns.

"Maybe." I let my eyes drop. If I had that assurance, maybe I wouldn't ache so.

After I finish up my practice, I head back to my room, hoping to find some sort of assurance there, only to run into the grand duke. "Oh, forgive me, my lady." He smiles and bows to me, looking over my dance attire.

I clear my throat uncomfortably and fold my arms, holding my dance bag under the fold to ensure it didn't slip off my shoulder. I should have put it across my body. "Your Grace," I greet him, "forgive my intrusion."

"Not at all. I'm always happy to run into our future princess." He smiles warmly. I flush more and try not to meet his eyes to try to escape faster. When he doesn't speak again, I step to the side to go around him. "Assuming that happy event happens," he says just as I step past him.

I freeze. What did that mean? I can't help but stop and turn to look at him. It was like he was muttering to himself, so I wasn't sure he'd even notice my hesitation.

His dark eyes are right on me, turned to face me still. "Pardon my worries. You know I have made it clear who I would choose if it were me. But it seems that may be a slipping chance."

"Perhaps." I turn to go again, but the grand duke steps around.

"Perhaps?" His brows are drawn in worry. "Do you really have no idea of your position? It's all over the palace."

It is? I turn my gaze away from him, not wanting to hear it. But he's going to say it anyway.

"I felt sure our position in this was at least in good standing, but from what I hear from the rumors that is little more than a pipe dream." His tone is concerned yet trying to be gentle. "Or is everyone talking about what happened behind your back?"

When I still don't move or reply, the grand duke goes on. "Rumor has it, you fled from the scene like a fox from a hen house when the dog barks. And that was just the event you witnessed."

My skin goes cold. Who else was Gavril sharing those moments with? How badly had I broken his trust that he's gone back on his word?

"You know I think you a perfect choice, but you have to face your faults and recognize if you want to win you will have to combat them." The grand duke walks around me to try to meet my eyes. I let him but only for a brief moment before I look away. "For example, a princess need not hang her head."

I pull my head up but still don't meet the grand duke's gaze. "Remind him why you're an excellent choice. Help him forget you come with no political advantages, no skills or training above what the other girls are receiving; you come with no monetary value or much that the kingdom needs in the short term. But you are a beautiful woman that will be exactly the lovely image he needs to distract the people to allow him rule."

He's right. I knew that even when I was set to be Jake's queen. I'm not good at ruling. I was simply a woman who could marry their man to unite the rebellions. I didn't expect to help fix anything. Jake would do it all. I was too stupid to even see what a bad idea that was. I don't have the foresight or ability to help Gavril rule anymore than Jake. Perhaps having him move on is better.

"And you have all the skills to do that. Need I remind you how you are dressed." The grand duke smiles at me, but I can't see it. I'm too stunned in my hurt to really focus on anything. "I've always thought you the most beautiful of the bunch. And by the heavens, the most talented. You could put a spell on anyone without magic with that voice. And you can put on a show. That interview should have told everyone you're the best choice. You can charm anyone and everyone. You can calm the people into submission with that skill. Many may think your prima actress background a hinderance, but it's just what we need to stop the fighting. Who'd want to rebel against that beautiful face and voice. Angel of music, indeed."

I shudder at the proud smile he gives me. "Don't let his wandering attention get you down. You must not know much of the ways of young men, but they are easily distracted. The right move or rush of hormones can steal their hearts for good if you don't have a stronger grip on them. That is another element I would recommend. You don't have to stomp on the other girls to tighten your grip on him. You were in the lead. When you are, take advantage of him to make him forget the others."

Then the grand duke laughs. "Forgive me. I'm acting like there is something to worry about. I forget who I'm talking to. You're too perfect to lose. I just know the right princess when I see it and was overanxious to ensure that happens. You're too much of an enchantress to lose. I don't know how someone hadn't already snatched you up before the Enthronement."

The grand duke rubs my arm comfortingly. "I'm sure you'll re-enchant him without much trouble at all. I shouldn't have panicked so. But if you're nervous or in need of help, recall my offer still stands. Anything for my future princess." He takes my hand and kisses it before I can decide if I should pull away or not.

Then he's gone, leaving me standing there feeling sick to the stomach. I'd hide in the practice room if I hadn't just left it. And there's no way I can return to my room and not have my maids ask, let alone Damian. I can feel all the color has drained from my face. I can't act or hide this. There's no way.

My mind still feels numb with the ache of what he'd said, making it hard to think any of it through. I feel like I'd been yanked into the waves when he'd tried to help me onto the raft. I can't even cry. It's a kind of numb pain that tingles across my skin.

A safe place pops to mind, and before I can fully process the thought, my feet turn and go right there: the bridge. I'm in the conservatory and almost throwing myself onto the bench by the bridge so quickly my conscious mind is still processing it.

I had tried to convince myself I was a good choice. I wasn't the best choice perhaps, but I'm far worse than I thought. The grand duke is right. He meant it to be comforting, but he is right. I am not a powerful ruler, gentle peacemaker, or clever courtier. I couldn't negotiate the girls into being kinder to me, Gavril into trusting me (at least when I was trying), not even my father into trusting me. What good could I do to end the war?

Nothing that ended better for my people. What if all I did was make them love the royal family, so they stopped trying to get a better life from them? Sure, the rebels driving people from their homes would stop, and I want that, but then they'd be content in their crushing poverty that would, in time, ruin our kingdom in generations to come. With how bad it is now, likely in my children's time, if not my grandchildren's.

What if I am still as toxic to the kingdom as I was when I wanted to let my father assassinate the royal family? I'd even worried about that in my interview. Is this why the Custods want the royal family gone though they seem innocent? Because it is the only way to shake the people out of revolting safely? Is it a stand off? As long as they rebelled, the royals kept the tax high. Once the fighting stopped, would they let up? Like a parent not lifting the punishment until the child stops the bad behavior. Then maybe I would be helpful. But that is a huge risk if that theory is wrong.

I have no advantage. I am just not as bad as other choices. But would that really solve anything? Not unless the worse choices were gone too. What am I thinking? I'd lost Gavril's affections. I am useless to the crown. I am useless to the prince. I am useless to my people. And even if I have not been disowned yet, it could be only a matter of time.

But I had made a choice. I learned about what the rebellions would do if they were in power. I had taken in all the variables and made a choice. Nothing I stressed about now is going to change that. It is not safe for me to go home, and I have nowhere else to go. For the moment, I'd have to just keep playing the game.

I still have my studies in the library. Perhaps if I find those answers, I'll know what to do. I still have not figured out the prophecy. So far, only my father seemed to know about it. Zelda knew nothing, and she'd been looking too. I'd heard nothing from the court. Though I'm sure it's too dangerous to openly ask.

I'm powerless to stop this course I have started. I jumped into the current, and I will just have to ride it where it takes me. If I'm not the right one, then I'd get weeded out... right? What if I didn't? What would I do then? What would I do if I was?

There had been some comfort in the idea that at least I am a good choice. That if Gavril loves me and wants me that will be more than enough. I don't have to be the best if I am a good choice and the one he wants. But what if I'm too dangerous to wield power?

But I want to be a good choice. I want to be the best choice. I want Gavril to like me as much as I like him, if not more. I want to win fair. I want to have this not just to protect myself from home, and if I'm honest, it's the only happy path forward I can see. Home would be damnation. And that is the choice. It's either the man I'd chosen to trust above my entire past or to be swallowed by my past.

All I can do is try not to be the girl the grand duke said I am. I have to overcome those flaws. Question is, is it possible?

Chapter 15

I use the conservatory to ignore the girls the next day, and I make plans to do the same the following day, but the girls have other ideas. Once I'm dressed and clean after my workout, there's a knock at the door.

Flur answers it only to be shoved aside by Bella who walks into the room and hooks arms with me before I can even take a breath to ask what she's doing. "Come on, we're going to have a good time," she says and starts pulling me, literally, by the arm, not letting me unhook my arm from hers. My maids don't back me up, but not for lack of desire. They look more shocked than I am as I'm marched from the room.

A table laden with frosting, sprinkles, cookies, and other goodies fills the center of the Ladies' Chamber. All the girls but Amapola are there. I can guess where she is. I'm jarred from wondering how close he's getting to her as Azalea races up to Bella and me and drags us to two empty cookie decorating stations. She declares we all need a holiday break.

Of course, she set this up. She is the "mom" of the group. She must have thought we were too stiff and decided to do something about it. I wish she hadn't made me join in though. Not only am I not in the mood, but I never liked this kind of thing. I'm terrible at crafty-things and never had time between performances.

Bella drags me over to the table and has me sit down. She sits on my left and Azalea on my right. Some girls are laughing and having a good time. Kamala and Florence are laughing over the funny shaped cookie they found. Zelda is showing Rose and Laurina what a traditional Hyvian star looks like, and they all look like they're having a great time. Dahlia is smiling as she does up one cookie to look like the two balls used in sparkle ball while Ericka and Forsythia decorate two horse shaped cookies very differently and are giggling at how different they are. Ericka's looks like a white unicorn and Forsythia's is made to look like her jumping horse. Lilly and Isla get extremely artistic in trying to make a phoenix look as accurate as possible with lots of gold sparkles and orange brush strokes.

Azalea tries to help me learn how to do it, offering a Nutcracker shaped cookie, but when that seems too complicated, she offers one shaped like pointe shoes. "That should be more familiar." She smiles. I return it weakly. "Love it!" Azalea declares and takes the nutcracker for herself.

Bella chuckles with a small shake of her head and gives me a look, clearly agreeing that Azalea is not only clueless but a little over enthusiastic. I manage to smile a bit more.

Bella picks a cookie at random and starts to decorate hers. She makes a lovely star. Mine looks like a toddler got too excited to use the pink and white frosting. The "elite" are going to laugh themselves silly at my attempt.

"Oh, I like what you did with the sprinkles," Azalea praises, "very realistic and creative. I'd not have thought of that." She's patronizing me to make me feel better. I'm ready to throw in the towel.

"You can help the bow by outlining it in white like the sprinkles," Bella suggests, showing me how.

"I'm never going to be good at this," I state.

"Why not? This looks fine. You just need to practice. Not done this since you were little?" Azalea asks cheerfully.

"I've never done it."

"What!?" I swear every head at the table turns to me.

"Never?" Ericka sounds horrified, but for me, not judging me for once. That makes the pink flush to my cheeks die down a little.

"What did you do for the holidays?" Florence asks.

I point at the cookie I made. "That," I say. "Two shows a day from the start of December until the end of the day of Christmas Eve."

"You didn't even have Christmas Eve?" Lilly sounds horrified.

"Never?" Ericka gasps.

I shake my head. "It was Christmas Carol that night. It's our best show that evening. We start earlier than on other nights, but that still meant home for my family at nine or ten at night if we were lucky. Our cast got home sooner, but we had to clean up and shut down the theater. It was our tradition."

"Then what would you do for Christmas day?" Isla asks.

"Sleep," I laugh. "As late as we could, then we'd do gifts, a simple lunch and relax before we'd make dinner. Then we'd have a Christmas cake and eggnog before going to sleep and getting ready to prepare the show for the next year."

"You worked?" Dahlia sounds devastated. I'd never seen her look so sorry or compassionate for anyone.

I frown and nod. "A lot of people do."

"No, they don't. Stores close by five," Ericka says, "no matter how much you wish they didn't. Everything, even guards stop punishments by five that day."

"Performers work often," Isla defends me.
"Did you?" Lilly asks as if in horror.
Isla smiles sheepishly. "Well, no, but I know it's common."
"If we don't, a lot of people will miss out on their tradition. It's normal for me, so I don't mind. I love doing the shows." I shrug.
"That is one way to think of it," Bella agrees. "You're helping other families have their special moment."
"And I loved it." I smile sadly. I will never get to do it again. Last year was my last, and I didn't get to savor it.
"Well, you can learn new traditions," Azalea tries to put a positive spin on it. "I'll help you learn some other ways to make the cookies."
That's not my favorite idea, but I'll go along with it. "Still sucks to work," Ericka mutters.
"And let's help you learn why," Azalea agrees and picks out a few more cookies to help me "learn". I go along with it, and all the girls get into teaching me their favorite tricks as if it makes up for me working every Christmas of my life.
It is sweet, but I do not really feel much like being schooled all afternoon on something I am just okay with. I do not dislike making the cookies per se, but I wouldn't have said I enjoyed the task, even as I was starting to get it.
Zelda keeps us entertained by telling us about Christmases in Hyvil. "My siblings and I once tried to stay up all night to see what the Merlin's phoenixes brought." She smiles reminiscently.
"I can't believe how many people still think it's really the 'Merlin's phoenixes' when we all know it's just made up," Jonquil huffs.
I notice Nippers was going to try to sit with her but changes his mind and jumps on my lap with a purr. I smile and stroke him before going back to my terrible decorating. It does make me feel a bit better to have the cat choose me.
"Points," Lilly whispers. I laugh.
"Oh, they're real. Some of my best gifts have come from him," Zelda says a bit stubbornly. "And though he doesn't exactly grant wishes, he sure tries."
"Well, not even phoenixes can top my gift for the prince," Dahlia gloats.
"What are you getting him?" Lilly asks nervously.
"I'm not giving it away, so you can try to trump me," Dahlia sniffs with a playful smile, going back to her cookie.
Azalea rolls her eyes. "Well, I don't know if it's a great idea, but he seemed to really enjoy some of the piano pieces we found in the music room. I was thinking a collection of some more advanced pieces."

"Oh, well let's make sure they don't cross. I got him a collection of Hyvian pieces he won't know," Zelda says. "And I ordered that months ago, so I was there first." The girls giggle at their mock fight.

"Maybe some of us should pull together and see about fixing up some of the other pianos around here," Bella says. "I don't know why they let them get out of tune. Someone fixed the one in here." Nippers purrs very loudly, making us giggle. "But a lot of the other ones around here are out of tune."

"They're out of tune because he doesn't use them," Dahlia drones. "So, it would be pretty pointless."

"After that test, I guess we all were thinking music. He does like the piano." Lilly frowns.

Maybe Dahlia has a point. Maybe by proving how well I really know him by getting him the perfect gift, I could restore his faith in how I really see him. What better way could I find easily?

But what gift would prove that? Their ideas about music is a good point, but that doesn't feel quite close enough to his heart. Perhaps if I focus on vocal, but the others would ask about that. That would end up being more uncomfortable than assuring. I don't want to reveal anything he wants kept private.

Then maybe he should kiss in private, I think but shove the thought aside.

The girls keep debating while I get lost in thought. They have one thing right; the girl with the best gift would prove she knows him the best. It isn't just freedom he wants. What does the prince want?

He needs someone he can trust no matter what. Someone happy to be in his cage with him. Someone who won't leave and will be with him no matter what. Someone perfectly loyal, but it isn't like I could give him that gift. Though I know it's what he wants most in the world, how did you give that? You can't just give someone a loyal friend when I can't magically win the game.

Or can I? Gavril has always wanted a pet. Could I get away with it? If so, what kind of pet? The answer comes easily. A "guard" pet would do well. That would get past his parents and give him the friend he needed. Sadly, I can't offer him sweet little Nippers, but getting him a guard dog might do the trick. Is that even doable? I'd have to ask the king what he thinks. He is the one who'd give the all-clear, right?

If I could pull it off, it would be the perfect solution. Gavril had joked many times about wanting a pet. He even said it would be a dog. I think back to my second date with him. It seems so long ago. We'd had tea in the library one rest day afternoon. It had been my idea to get a chance to talk more privately with him. I can almost hear him laugh the way he did then when he told me, "If I got what I wanted, we'd be keeping a dog off the food right now."

I smile and scratch Nippers behind the ears, feeling confident in my choice. I'd find a way. That's what he wants, needs; someone he could talk to about his problems who does not push agendas but listens. Pets do that, or so people who have pets tell me. I've not had the privilege.

"Bella," Azalea laughs, "you're hogging all the bells!"

"What? I love them," she defends, holding up her latest one. She has a nice pile of them on her drying rack.

"Why?" Lilly laughs.

"It reminds me of my favorite Christmas show." Bella smiles and starts to talk-sing it to herself. I know the one. It's not very popular, but it has some lovely duets Alsmeria and I got to do a few times.

I join her as the second sister in the song, smiling a little at something more familiar to me. Bella stops dead and looks at me in delight. I even made a funny voice for the little brother. "You know it? It's so rare!"

"Of course, I do." I smile. "Actress."

Bella beams in delight and sings the next bit, pretending to ring the bell like the song says, making me laugh and jokingly do the same. I laugh harder as Bella gets up to act it out. Nippers jumps off my lap as she takes my hand to pull me up to do it with her.

She knows it as well as I do, as if she'd performed it too, and it's a thrill to perform it with her, even if to her it is just playing. I couldn't recall having this much fun with friends in a long time as Bella sings and twirls in little Christmas dances with me. When we have to stop to get ready for dinner, Bella hugs me while no one else is looking.

"Thanks, I used to feel silly always doing these playful things by myself. Used to wish I had a sister to do them with, but my sisters just made fun of me," she says.

"I'm a singer and dancer by trade; I'd never make fun of anyone for enjoying it," I assure her. "I'd love to do it again," I admit.

"Anytime," Bella giggles.

"And thanks for trying with Azalea," I say.

"She means well, but yes, she can get a little over excited," Bella says. "It's okay not to be good at everything. And to have never done it before. I think your tradition is sweet, most of all how you think of it." She's holding my hands like I had when I played sisters with someone. It's nice. It's not quite like with Lilly where my bond to her is more protective. I feel like I am suddenly equal, friends, like Alsmeria and I used to be. Perhaps if I gave it time, I could feel that way with more of these girls. Maybe then I'd not be so jealous.

When I get to my room to get ready for dinner, there's a loud tapping at my window that makes me jump. I look over and see a familiar bird.

"Marlon!" I cry in shock and rush to the balcony door to open it.

The falcon-hawk flies into the room and lands on my shoulder, nuzzling me like he did when he brought messages from Jake's father to mine, cawing softly.

"You miss me that much?" I tease, looking to see if I could find a treat. I normally kept a small container of grasshoppers for the falcon at home, but I doubt a Chosen lady's room would have that lying about. "Or did you miss your treats? Sorry, I don't have anything here for you."

Marlon squawks at me then adjusts as if to show me something. It's hard to see with him so close, so I lure him onto my desk. That's when I spot it. There's a card tied to his leg. He looks up at me like I'm dumb for not seeing it sooner.

I untie the note. "For me?" I check with the falcon.

He gives me another "are you dumb?" look. I laugh and stroke his feathers. "You're a good bird." I spot a dish of nuts nearby. "There you go, Marlon. It's not your normal bugs, but I believe you like this too."

The falcon is delighted and pecks them all up in a few moments.

He gives me a chirp of thanks before I open the balcony door again for him. He flies up to my shoulder, nuzzles my head a little, then flies off.

"I've never seen that before," Vivian says in awe.

"I don't know why he'd come to me," I admit, opening the message.

A small smile crosses my lips as a simple Christmas card pops from the wrapping. It's a stunning piece with a ballerina twirling on the front. I open it and a few impressions slide loose. One is the traditional cast impression of the Nutcracker and Christmas Carol with their playbills. The inside of the card is blank.

But with impressions like that, I know only two people it could be, one of my parents. Father wouldn't send me impressions of the cast though. Only my mother would think of that. So though perhaps Father wouldn't let her write, she found another way to reach out to me.

How long had it taken her to get Marlon to warm up to her? I swallow happy tears and hug them to my chest a moment, letting the happy moment wash over me. So Mother, at least, wasn't so upset with me. Perhaps I am not completely alone in this nightmare. I think of Lilly laughing and Bella's giggles as we danced. Perhaps this holiday didn't have to be so dark.

As my maids prepare me for dinner, I float my Christmas gift idea past Damian. I am nervous too, but he's happily humming or singing various Christmas carols to himself. "Damian, what do you think of getting Gavril a guard dog for Christmas?" I ask tentatively.

Damian pauses, tilting his head before smiling a little. I'm nervous of his rebuttal, so I go on. "I'm not even sure it's possible, but I was thinking… maybe… if it showed him how well I know him and what he'd really want, maybe… it might just prove my feelings. And what would be better for him than a pet?"

"Indeed. It is someone he can vent to, and animals are brilliant listeners," Damian agrees. He thinks for a moment then smiles, knitting his fingers together with one elbow braced on the back of his chair and the other resting on the table. "Oh, it is surely possible. I think I even know a place nearby selling puppies. And as for guard training, Cedrick has trained a few in his time. I doubt he'd mind helping."

"Really?" Could it be that easy?

"Sure." Damian smiles. "Of course, you'll have to clear it with his parents first," he reminds me. I smile and assure him I will.

After dinner that very night, I catch the king in the hall. "I… I had an idea," I say, "for a gift for Prince Gavril, but… well, I feel I'd need your permission and that of the queen."

"Oh?" The king grins like the necessity of permission makes the gift amazing already.

"I was thinking with all the security that perhaps it would be good if he had a companion, just a different one. I was thinking of getting him a guard dog. Damian's brother Cedrick said he'd happily train a puppy for it if we got one. But… Well, that's a big deal, so I wanted to make sure I wouldn't cause trouble."

The king smiles and coughs into his handkerchief, making my heart skip every time he does that. "I think that would be a lovely idea. Just make sure it's all seen to upfront and the servants, I'm sure, can handle the rest."

"The queen won't mind?" I check.

"She was just talking about that very idea." The king smiles.

I sigh. "Alright, thank you. You don't need to worry about a thing."

He smiles again. "Oh, I'm sure I won't. It is you who is asking."

I turn pink, flattered but not sure what he means. "Thank you."

The king doesn't miss my uncertainty. "Lady Kascia, you have kept my secret even when there have been plenty of reasons not to. I'm sure your former friends were trying to get it from you. You've done nothing but protected us even though that has put you into a worrisome situation. I trust you. If you are arranging for the guard dog, I'm sure it will be brilliant."

After all my uncertainties, I'm touched by his assurance of his trust. "At least someone does."

"My wife does too; she just panics easily. She is a unique product of years of this war and Potentate culture. She questions out of fear, little else. Deep down, she trusts you too."

"If you say so, Your Majesty." I smile tentatively.

"You'll see in time, my dear." The king smiles once more. "But with all that said, I trust you to make the arrangements and pick the right pet. I look forward to the result."

As if the pressure to do this right wasn't already high. I was hoping to use this to prove to Gavril I believe in him and trust him. And now the king is expecting me to make a perfect choice too. The pressure leading up to the holiday is growing in intensity.

I spend the next day after lessons preparing gift ideas for the holiday for the other girls, telling my guard to turn any girl away who tries to bother me.

As I make plans and list out what we can make and calculating the budget to make the necessary purchases, I'm still not sure what kind of dog we should get. So, I ask Damian for his advice. "I know he'd not like one of those fancy Potentate dogs, and I know he doesn't like Cuppy. And a Custod dog might be too fancy for him too. Are there any other dogs that make good guard dogs?"

Damian smiles softly as he lowers his work. It looks like he is doing some gold embroidery on a beautiful green fabric, but he secures the needle then leans back to think. "Well, though Custod dogs are bred specifically for protection, I personally prefer huskies myself."

"Why?" I ask curiously. They were bred by Custods, but they weren't seen as a polished palace pet.

"They have the best personalities." Damian grins.

I laugh. "Oh really?"

"Oh yes. Any husky will love Sage." He smiles.

"Love Sage?" With that tone, that had to mean it would love to tease him. I'm sure that would just make this gift an extra bonus to the prince. A little hope lights my chest. That would prove to Gavril I didn't think him stuck up, right? But what if the king didn't approve?

Then again, huskies are the second most common dog for a Custod to own. It's said the Head Custod breeds them. Gavril would like a husky. I nod. "Husky it is. So where do we get a husky puppy?"

"I may know just the place." Damian smiles. He then helps me find a few options in a directory and sets up a day for us to go see a litter to pick one for the prince as well as do the rest of the holiday shopping. I'm amazed he got permission for me to leave, but with him and a few others as guards, the royal guard gives their approval.

Chapter 16

I fiddle with my pen, waiting for lessons the following morning to start when the door opens. Damian strides into the room as confident as ever and presents a box to Lady Keva with a bow of his head. I frown. What is Damian doing? Perhaps he made something for lessons?

I'm not the only one wondering. Ericka in particular is whispering about it with the others. Bella on the other hand is intent on trying to see what's in the box. If Damian made it, I suppose she wants to see it.

"Your fans, my lady," Damian says respectively without lifting his head as he meets Lady Keva's eyes.

"Oh, thank you." Lady Keva looks quite delighted. She doesn't seem to know who Damian is as she simply nods at him in thanks.

Damian straightens up, perfect in his form as always, and nods to her. "You are most certainly welcome."

Lady Keva watches him and smiles slightly in approval. Damian gives her a pleasant smile and turns to leave. Halfway out of the room, I notice him grimace, but he quickly takes in a breath, smiling slightly and takes up a place at the back of the room, folding his hands behind him.

I turn to watch, confused at what he's doing. Some of the other girls do too. The snarky little smile on Forsythia's face makes me want to wipe it off. Damian doesn't seem to notice her almost hungry look as she turns to the front, and Lady Keva calls us together.

"Today we're going to work on the art of the fan. We'll mostly be on our feet," Lady Keva calls to us. "Come up and take a fan."

"And she's got a special one," Ericka complains. I look up, trying not to react. Just because Damian brought them, doesn't mean he made them or made one just for me.

Once we all have our fans, Lady Keva shows us how to snap them open with one hand and then has us stand and master fluttering them. The biggest frustration for her is the girls who struggle with posture and forget all their new learned posture etiquette.

"The fan doesn't change anything," Lady Keva insists. "You can make it as natural as any other movement." She looks around as she tries to think of some kind of inspiration. “It’s not about being in the posture for the moment, but about making it natural.” She looks at me.

I know what that looks means. She wants to ask me to show them how it’s done. I press down the panic in my chest. I can’t hide that I saw her looking, so I try to hide how badly I do not want her to use me. I’m done being glared at and picked on for being brilliant at everything. Other than keeping the prince’s attention anyway.

Lady Keva sighs then notices Damian standing at the back. She smiles at him. “Even a member of staff can do it better.” She waves Damian to come forward. I turn away, turning red. Maybe I should have let her pick on me.

Damian takes a deep breath and strides forward to the front of the class. Lady Keva sighs in satisfaction. “See how natural that is?” She flashes a small smile at me. That’s normally what she says about my posture. “Even waiting at the back or just walking forward, he keeps the position as natural as anything.” She smiles wider. “I doubt he’d drop it for anything.”

“I was bred not to,” Damian answers humbly.

“Quite modest. I’m sure you still had to learn.” Lady Keva smiles. “And the posture for such a gentleman is no different than a lady,” she speaks to us. “Keep your shoulders back as you work with the fan. Let’s try this again.”

She nods a thanks to Damian the way she does to tell me I can stop demonstrating.

Damian nods politely and steps to the side. I frown and want to ask him why he’s letting himself be used as a guinea pig,, but instead, Ericka goes over and actually starts asking him for tips on handling her fan when I know full well she already knows. Is she flirting?

Damian puts on a gentleman’s smile and takes the fan from her gently then proceeds to actually show her how it's done. I’m keeping calm just fine until I see how Forsythia is giving Ericka a jealous look too. I want to snap at her, but what’s the point? I can’t seem to win any points with these girls anyway.

That’s when Lady Keva really loses it. She comes over to Damian in interest and begins asking him how he knows how to handle a fan. Most likely because most men don’t have a clue.

Damian smiles with a slight chuckle. “Well, the language of the fan breaks down if the gentleman does not understand it. So yes, I am well versed. After that, logic tells me how I would do myself.”

“If I didn’t know better, I’d say you’ve had to teach it before.” Lady Keva smiles. “They should have you teaching.”

Is Lady Keva flirting now? I look up at the ceiling trying not to lose it. I have no idea what Damian is doing, but I’m a mix of mortified and amused, leaning more on amused once Lady Keva started hinting at flirting.

Damian tilts his head slightly to the side in a half shrug with a small smile on his lips. "I have taught a dancer or two how to wield a fan for a piece of choreography, but in that respect, your skills surely outweigh my own, Lady Keva." He bows his head respectfully.

"You keep their attention better than I do." Lady Keva's tone is teasing as she looks at Ericka. She is known to zone out because she "already knows it all" as she'd insist in apology for why she got distracted. "It seems there's little you couldn't assist me with. You have that mix of confidence, yet humility these ladies would kill for." Ericka scowls behind Lady Keva's back.

Damian's smile grows, but he keeps it polite. "I'll concede to that. I took it upon myself to learn the etiquette of all classes, should I ever need them. As for the former part, all I can say is, it is the curse of my sex."

"I hope not if they want to come out the winner." Lady Keva gives the group a look of amused warning. Then sighs. "Oh for Merlin's sake, ladies, ladies, please focus. Here, as we have a subject, why don't you try using the language?"

I cover my face with my fan as a mix of emotions want to spew out my mouth, sick at the idea of having to flirt with Damian in front of the others and the desire to laugh at how much he's going to hate this while Forsythia and Ericka don't look upset at the suggestion at all. I bite my lips to stop myself laughing.

"Sounds like a brilliant idea." Damian smiles politely, but I know him well enough to see it does not reach his eyes. He believes that idea is anything but "brilliant".

"Come ladies," Lady Keva calls us into a line to practice. "I'll give you instruction on what message to send, and he'll confirm if he got it or not," she says to us. "One at time." The line of girls is rather random. And I'm wondering if I can just be completely ignored for this. It's like flirting with my father. It feels wrong.

I forget about that and have to hide another fit of the giggles to see Ericka is clearly already sending signals. If one girl was going to get thrown out for looking at other men about the palace, it was Ericka. First Cedrick, now Damian, and who knew what other poor attractive guard or courtier. Lady Keva ignores it or doesn't notice, making it all the funnier.

Damian owns the front of the room like it was his stage. He stands upright, but even with his perfect posture, he seems so relaxed. The line of giggling girls doesn't intimidate him in the slightest as he awaits Lady Keva's cue to allow the first girl to begin.

A few are more like me and find it silly, the born princesses in particular. Rose, Amapola, and Jonquil seem to find it beneath them to play this silly game. But they are good sports about it as they try to use the language Lady

Keva prompts. Even if Rose looks bitter about how stupid it is, making it all the more fun for the rest of us. Bella and I keep exchanging looks and trying not to laugh.

The best had to be Princess Laurina deciding if it was stupid, she'd been stupid about it and was far too over the top for her instruction to try to get Damian's attention for a private talk.

"Really ladies," Lady Keva can't help but chuckle slightly as several girls can't contain their laughter. "He's really being very patient. Could you please?" She's trying so hard not to laugh. *Poor Damian.*

But he doesn't react to us laughing. I think I see him fighting a smile, but if he is, I can't quite spot it. As each girl approaches for their turn, it's like he's entering a scene of a play, just looking off into the distance as if watching dancers at a ball. Then a girl tries to get his attention with their fan. If it works, he then approaches the girl and addresses them according to the message they sent him. Though there are one or two that apparently sent the wrong message which makes Damian blush.

There is plenty of giggling when that happens. The only thing that could have made it worse was Bella wanting to add points to the Nippers board when Nippers suddenly flops out of nowhere as if he'd fallen over laughing at Damian trying to understand some of the girl's horrible attempts to flirt with the fan. Lilly quickly moves him to hide the moment.

Damian breaks character for a moment to scowl at the cat then thanks Lilly for her time and gently gives her a few tips before he turns as Forsythia approaches him. He smiles, hiding the disgust in his eyes. Lady Keva may approve of how well she sent the clear "I'm interested" signal, but it makes me sick and want to hit her at the same time. Nippers sneezes in Lilly's arms surprisingly loudly for a cat.

But Damian keeps in character as he bows politely to Forsythia to thank her for her time with the same soft smile he has given everyone.

Kamala is next, but she's having trouble getting her fan open. I think she got it stuck when she was fiddling with it awaiting her turn. Lady Keva goes over to help as Forsythia passes Damian to wait with the others. I am drawn to look over, and I'm not sure why until I see her little smile. She thanks Damian then kisses his cheek. Damian's eyes widen, and his face blanches then looks at her with a mixed expression. She meets his eye then moves on, giving me a clear smug sideways glance with that stupid smile on her face.

Heat rises to my face, and I don't know if I want to cry or kick her or both. I understand clearly what she wants to say. She could take any one of them from me if she really wanted to. And I can't deny that. She'd taken Gavril from me; that seemed almost certain. And I'm powerless to defend myself. I miss being able to defend myself.

A squeal breaks through my rush of emotions, and I look over to see Forsythia and others flinching away from Nippers who'd somehow gotten away from Lilly and literally had a huge slimy hairball, or maybe it's just vomit, all over Forsythia's shoe.

I blink in shock. Bella, on the other hand, has no problem laughing as she joins Lilly in removing the ill cat and helping clean up the mess. Kamala is laughing even more rudely. Even Damian is hiding a smile now. Lady Keva reminds Kamala about being a proper lady and calls for a servant to help clean it up.

It gets worse as Nippers refuses to be picked up and runs up Forsythia's skirt and over her shoulder, ripping parts of her dress and likely scratching her shoulder with his long claws.

Damian smiles a grimace. "Seems like he wants attention. And of course, cats are said to be vain, so he just had to find the finest lady to share his gift with," he says good humoredly. Forsythia gives him a look as a maid starts to help get her shoe and stocking cleaned up.

Once we've calmed down from that, we get back into formation. Bella has the hardest time being serious. If I didn't know any better, I'd have thought Damian was her brother with how she giggled and teased. I suppose she has the same pale skin and straight black hair. Lady Keva has her try three times because she is giggling too hard to take it seriously.

Damian is extremely patient with her. It reminds me how he interacts with Cedrick sometimes, except he wears a gentle smile the entire time. It gets Bella through it with a passing grade at least. The reward she likes best though is she was able to pick up Nippers and enjoy his pink toe beans. Lady Keva can't help but smile in amusement at Bella's energy today. Maybe Bella found some coffee this morning.

Damian chuckles in amusement then smiles at me before getting into character again. A few more girls go before I have my turn. The one I get is the sign of apology. At least that is not too uncomfortable as I stand in a normal position like I would at a party before opening my fan up across my face and slowly spreading it out towards my left eye.

Damian catches it almost immediately, and his eyes become warm and his lips turn in a soft smile. He approaches me and bows low. It is lower than any of the other girls got, except the princesses, but it's inches from it. He then straightens up with the smile still on his face. "Apology accepted, my lady."

I smile back, but a slight flush creeps up my cheeks as a few girls didn't miss Damian's action either. I think I hear someone mutter "duh". That makes sense. He is my attendant, after all. He'd show the most respect for me. But some smaller-minded people like Ericka and Kamala are still offended. Nippers must be happy though. As I go wait with the others, he purrs and rubs against my legs. Lilly rushes to add my new points to the board. Bella giggles that she wasn't faster.

The lesson finally wraps up, and the others go to break. I walk over to Damian, though I have to wait for Lady Keva to finish showering him with compliments and hinting that she'd hire him to help more. It is rather funny how she almost fawns over him.

"You should teach the prince." She smiles as she puts the last fan back in the box and offers it to Damian to put back wherever he got it.

Damian laughs. "No, madam. I thank you for the compliment, but I'll leave that in your capable hands. I doubt I'll hold his attention as well," he teases.

"Oh, you highly overestimate his attention span," she teases back. "But thank you again."

"You are most welcome." Damian bows his head to her.

She finally leaves, and I walk over. "Did you have to make the fans?" I ask as a joking way to ask why he'd come into lessons today. He never had before.

He chuckles. "No, I didn't make them. I only acquired them from the servant who was sent to fetch them."

"So why were you the one to bring them and end up roped into teaching?"

He lets out a sigh with a half frown. "I lost a bet."

"A bet?" I frown.

Nippers meows and joins us, rubbing against Damian's boots. Damian rolls his eyes before looking back at me.

"Cedrick figured I couldn't help but make a dress that makes you stand out from the others, so he issued me a challenge." He sighs and rolls his eyes to the ceiling. "If I won, he couldn't poke fun at me for liking tea or call it 'leaf juice' for at least a month. But if I lost, I'd have to 'make a show in the ladies' chamber' during your etiquette lesson. The conditions were it had to be the dress for your last interview, and it couldn't draw a significant amount of attention from Fabian. I couldn't resist the challenge and the prospect was promising, so I accepted. But," he gestures to the room with a half-smile, "we can see how well that went."

I giggle. "Yes, he made quite a deal out of the dress." I look around. "I suppose that makes sense."

"Yes, well. I think I knew I had already lost when the idea for the dress hit me." Damian chuckles. "But..." He shrugs. "Cedrick was right. I couldn't help myself."

I smile. "Not sure we'd have it any other way."

Damian smiles. "I suppose not. Now if you excuse me, I'm going to wash my face with bleach."

I laugh as he leaves. I shouldn't have been surprised, but it still was comforting to hear.

I endure the second half of lessons with a lot of whispers and glares, but I'm starting to get used to it, so I focus on Bella's smiles and taking notes. It could have been far worse. At least when I get frustrated, I could always threaten to have Nippers vomit on Forsythia again. I wonder how many points that is worth on the Nippers' board.

Chapter 17

The day comes for my Christmas shopping, and I'm giddy with excitement. I have never had a real shopping day. Mother and I had gone out to get supplies for the theater and tried to make a fun day of it, but it's not the same. This isn't work, and our budget isn't stressfully tight.

First, we'll shop for the gift ideas on my list, but with such a large budget, I have fun looking at other ideas in the shops Damian chooses. I had commissioned Damian to make several things for me, but others I pick up as he collects the needed materials.

We start by picking up or looking for gift ideas for the other Chosen. It's nice to shop without being afraid of the small budget. I keep looking at prices, but Damian assures me not to worry. It also is a bit of a refresher to handle money. I'd gotten so bad at giving my gems away to those in need, my father had to use credit for me when I did shopping.

We finish in time for our appointment with the breeder. The breeder's ranch is near the Burned District, allowing the dogs plenty of space in their own open paddocks: some holding puppies, others holding older dogs all with varying colors and patterns but each and every one of them a husky.

I smile at the nearest paddock that houses a litter of puppies. Several of these puppies are trying to pull some junk that sat just outside their area into their pen to play with. The mother dog watches with a bored expression. The puppies are adorable, making "talking" sounds to one another and to anyone nearby. I laugh as a few spot us and bark their greetings.

The barking tells the breeder we have arrived, and he comes out to greet us and leads us into the pen I'd been admiring. There are seven puppies in all: three are a mesh of black and gray, one is black with a white belly, and three are a stunning brown/red color. All of them spot us at once and rush over to the fence to say hello, only moving away from the gate when bribed by the breeder.

They're all so cute. I frown. "How will I know which one?"

"You have to spend a little time with them." Damian smiles.

"But even when I do, how do I know?" I ask.

"You'll know," he chuckles.

There's a chair in the paddock, so I take a seat to observe the puppies and try to figure out which one to pick for the prince, feeling at a loss. The moment I sit, all seven of them rush up to me, but it doesn't take long for most of them to be distracted by each other, or in the case of the black one, Damian.

The black one is determined to get Damian's attention. He sits near Damian and keeps barking or making little puppy noises at him.

I'm distracted from the funny scene by one of the red ones still trying to get into my lap. Unlike the others, she is not distracted. She's too small to jump into my lap, but she's sure trying. I notice her bright blue eyes as she looks at my lap with determination. She's mostly a red and white fluff ball with her ears not quite sticking up all the way yet.

A surprisingly loud yip draws my eyes back to the black one. Damian smiles at me and seems set on 'ignoring' the black one. I chuckle as the black one keeps trying. I wonder if his stubbornness would make him a good fit. I'm really not sure what I'm looking for.

I jump as the red one finally gets onto my lap. I look down at her. She pants in happiness and plops herself down, lying across my lap as if it were the floor. She's a bit tired from her struggle to reach this spot. I chuckle and stroke her soft fur. They all look nice and clean.

The black one barks at Damian, still determined to get his attention. He makes a lot of "talking" sounds at him to which Damian finally turns and looks at him. "Did you want something?"

The dog makes a perfect "hello" sound and sits down, licking his lips before running off to play with his litter mates. I laugh. Damian does too. He laughs harder than I've ever seen him laugh before. I laugh at how hard he's laughing as I stoke the puppy on my lap.

The red puppy had watched this interaction too. She wiggles her backside before she clumsily jumps off my lap, trots up to Damian, sits down, and tries to imitate her brother.

She has to try a few times, but when she thinks she's got it her tail goes mad, looking up at Damian expectantly, likely hoping to get the same laugh her brother got.

Damian chuckles as he tries to calm down then smiles at her. "Why, hello."

She pants happily and tries to say "hello" again. She walks around Damian then comes back to me and sits down at my feet, her tail wagging so hard her bottom moves under her while she sits.

I chuckle and clap my hands to welcome her back up. She has to try a few times before she gets back on my lap. She sniffs up at my ear, climbing up to nuzzle against my shoulder. I smile, liking the feeling, though her quick little breaths make her fur tickle against my skin.

"Get down," I tell her gently. She is trying to steal the spotlight.

She doesn't want to at first. I have to help guide her down before standing up. I walk around to get a better view, but this little one follows me, tail up and eager. She even tries to get my attention by talking like the others did. I giggle. She does not want me to pay attention to her litter mates.

"No, let them have a turn," I tell her, patting her back and trying to get her to stay. I tease her a bit by rolling her over and holding her down to see if she'll fight me to get back up, but she settles down after only a few moments, panting excitedly as she waits to be let up.

Hmm, that would make a good palace dog, right? I stroke her from head to tail to see if she finds any of that annoying. She doesn't mind. She comes up closer to me, moving her paws up onto my knee, so she can lick my nose.

I giggle. "You really want us to pick you." She pants happily, ears up.

"But how can we know we want you when I don't look around?" I ask. The puppy sneezes. I shrug and stand up to try to interact with the other puppies.

They all do much the same as the red one when I try to get their attention. A brown eyed red one doesn't like it when I hold him down, and the black one keeps getting distracted by the other dogs or Damian.

But no matter what I do, the first red one follows me around, sitting and trying to impress me with her talking. I can't help but want to pick her, but I'm not shopping for myself. So, should I pick one that's set on getting my attention?

"You won't go home with me. You'll stay with Gavril," I tell her as I stroke her and watch as one of the gray ones loses interest and walks away.

The puppy tries to copy the sounds I made and flops down on the ground, trying to look cute. I shake my head. "So, are you going to be okay with that?" She just looks at me with her blue eyes that sparkle in the afternoon sun. I chuckle. "You are a handful." I rub her head.

Damian smiles. "Something of note. The others that lost interest will only do the same if not worse with Gavril. While she is begging for your attention now, it may be because you're the one here. So, wanting your attention may not be an issue in the long run."

"But she's not giving you much attention," I point out.

"True. So... perhaps she knows she is supposed to go with you. Cedrick says sometimes dogs just... know," he says with a shrug.

"So does she know me or where we're going?" I joke. I look down at her. "But you do seem to fit what a palace dog will need," I tell her. Her tail goes so mad she has to stand up, so she doesn't knock herself over. I smile and rub her head.

I then test what she does when I try to leave. She follows me as happily as ever until I put my hand on the gate. She stops, her tail slowing sadly. She doesn't look away when the black one comes over to her to try to play, watching me as if worried I'll leave without picking her.

"Alright then." I turn around, and she loses her doggie mind. Her whole body wiggles with her tail as she pants with delight, at least I presume it's delight. Her tongue hangs out in the cold; I can see her breath in the air. "I think you're the one we'll claim." I stroke her again. She makes talking sounds and licks my face. I giggle.

Damian smiles then stands and brushes himself off. "I'll go make arrangements with the owner then."

To mark she's been claimed, they put a little bow on her collar with my name on it. While Damian is working out the details, I play tug-of-war with the puppy until she gets sleepy and falls asleep curled up to my leg. Her littermates are sleepy too. I'm glad she fell asleep. I won't have to see her disappointed confusion when I leave without her.

I sigh as I get into the carriage. It was done. Soon I'd have it running around my room until Christmas day when we'd exchange gifts.

"Ready to get her gear?" Damian smiles. I smile back and nod.

We go to a pet shop and pick out everything our little red puppy will need. I pick out toys, a bed, plenty of food and water bowls, and other fun things on the list while Damian takes the duller tasks upon himself. I also pick up treats for Marlon if he comes back. Hopefully, this time I can get him to take a message back.

"Well, if you'd don't mind, there is one more stop I'd like to make," Damian says as he closes the carriage door.

"Alright." I smile. Damian always has good adventures in mind.

After a short ride, he opens the door then steps out and offers me his hand. I take it and step out. I recognize where we are. I never thought a carriage would fit here, but it does no trouble. "What are we doing here?" I ask.

"Thought we'd pick up new shoes while we were out." Damian smiles wide.

"You make the shoes," I tease.

"Not those shoes." He smiles.

I smile too. "Who said I needed a fresh pair?" I joke as Damian walks me to the door.

"It's always good to have a spare."

"It is," I agree.

We step inside. Wow, the old smell is like stepping back in time. The rush smell of glue, wood, leather is so inviting. The world was so different then. The shop has a few visitors already who pass us on the way out.

Jashon, the cobbler, looks up as we come in. A huge smile splits his face. "Damian, and Miss, sorry, Lady Kascia. What a surprise." He finishes making his note and comes over to us, shaking Damian's hand and pausing before he does the same to me. He smiles and bows instead.

"You'll be princess in no time," Jashon corrects. "Get used to it." I flush. Not if I can't fix the huge mistake I'd made.

"Regardless, there's no need for formalities among friends." Damian smiles.

"Maybe." Jashon shrugs. "But I do have your order ready. Hold on." He turns to get it.

"Thank you, Jashon." Damian bows to him then smiles at me.

"It is so odd to be here again," I say, taking in the unchanged sights and smell of leather, glue, and a sharp smell I never know the name of.

Damian smiles gently. "I understand. Like a different lifetime."

I nod. "But it's kind of nice to see it hasn't changed."

I jump at a click I have come to know well, an impressionor. I look over and laugh. "Are you causing trouble?" I ask as Jashon returns with a box and Adam, holding his impressionor, behind him. A few of my fellow actors come out too, Max for one, clapping as if I'd just finished a show. I flush. I likely look nicer than they'd ever seen me.

Damian smiles as he places his hand on my back. "I think they're here for you."

I laugh a little and am able to step forward to greet them. Anna, one of the dancers I worked with, gushes over how pretty I look. "Your jacket compliments you perfectly. How could anyone doubt you're a true princess in that look?" she says.

"What happens if more than one girl proves to be true princesses?" Max wonders. I roll my eyes. The king and queen won't let that happen.

"Max," Alica, another girl from my troop, tells him off.

"What? Do they have like a cat fight or something?" Max asks.

"I doubt the king and queen would let that happen," I say.

"What? The prince doesn't just pick the prettiest?" Alica smiles.

"Oh, in that you'd win," Anna cues. I laugh. It's nice to recall back at home, even if my family isn't, my old friends are pulling for me. They want me because I'm me. Not because I fulfill some agenda.

"I concur." Damian grins.

"Of course you do. You made it," I point out.

"I didn't make that." Damian smiles as he points to my face.

I smile back and push his hand away. "You made the look," I say. "You designed the hair and make up and all that."

"I only showcase what is already there. I never add to it. There isn't a need," Damian says.

"Don't be silly. You're perfect for it," Anna hushes me. "You fill in the clothes perfectly. That's what makes a queenly look."

"And she always had the heart for it." Jashon smiles at me. "Always so dedicated. I remember the debates I'd hear while people waited in line." I had been in a few debates but mostly with Jake or friends of mine. I don't think those prove me any more of a princess.

"And she played them perfectly. It's why she got those roles." Max smiles at me. He normally was my leading man. "You don't think the prince will get mad when he knows I've kissed you more, will he?" Alica elbows him.

"Uh." As he's kissed the other girls plenty, I doubt it.

"Or has he kissed you more?" Max grins. I turn red as they all laugh.

"He must be really good at it." Alica fawns over the idea.

I don't have a clue how to answer. I'd not even admitted if he'd kissed me at all.

"She just won't tell the papers that." Jashon smiles a little, leaning on the wall, hanging back a bit as he often does. He's with us, but not a part of our group. I realize that's a lot like what Sage does.

"Well, would you want it publicized?" Damian arches a brow.

"Of course not. But I'm not in a contest watched by the whole country," Anna says. "Guess it's part of the deal."

"One you signed up for," I remind her.

"And didn't make the cut." She sighs sadly, overdramatic to be silly. "Why you've got to win for us."

"We'll run the theater for you," Max jokes.

"How is that going?" I frown.

"Weird being one of our biggest dancers short, but don't think we miss your groaning over being Belle again," Max laughs. I laugh too. I did hate that I got that role almost five years in a row.

"Belle is an excellent role." Damian frowns then sighs. "But I suppose five years of it would get dull."

"That's the problem," I agree. "That over and over gets old."

"But a fresh new one every year for Nutcracker. You did great at your first run of Sugar Plum Fairy last year," Max says.

"Alsmeria got it this year," Anna says.

"You got coffee again?" I ask.

"Tea." Anna shakes her head.

"I got coffee." Alica smiles.

"That raffle can be funny." I smile. I'd done both before.

"Makes me miss snowflakes and flowers," Anna sighs.

But by now it must be getting late. I have to be back in time for dinner or the queen may lose her head in worry.

Damian seems to realize the same. "My lady, we should be getting back," he tells me.

I nod. "Alright. I'll... see you when I see you." I smile weakly at them all.

But Anna and Alica lost track of the conversation, looking dreamily at Damian. I think they liked him calling me "my lady". I roll my eyes. They won't miss me long. They might miss him though.

"See you when you're princess. I expect an invite," Max says.

"Just don't stage anything to get me back," I reply.

"The hunchback knows to let Esmeralda go to her knight," Max says playfully. "Or in this case, prince." I want to hit his arm, but that's not very lady-like.

"Then maybe," I agree.

"I'll see you then." Jashon smiles. "And keep you well supplied." I roll my eyes. "No princess or queen dances demi-pointe." I laugh.

"Until next time, Jashon." Damian bows to him with his hands clasped behind him.

"Until then Sir Damian," Jashon replies and goes back to his work.

It was a short exchange, but it helped me feel better, stronger. More empowered. I could do this. My people want me because I'm me. Sure they're my friends, but that's not the only reason. It helps lift some of the doubts and fears I'd been struggling with, making them easier to handle or ignore.

But now we have to go if I'm to be back for dinner on time. The girls sigh and agree they should get back to the theater before my mother realizes they slipped out when their scene wasn't up. I'm guessing that's why Alsmeria isn't here.

Damian opens the door for me. I hear the girls sigh again. I roll my eyes. He's cute, but not exactly anything to drool over.

He seems to ignore them as he waits for me to leave then moves around me and gets the carriage door as well. I smile my thanks and go inside. Once we're both in, I beam at him. "Thank you for that, Damian."

He smiles and nods to me. "You're quite welcome, my lady. I thought you could use a bit of home."

I smile a little. "Thank you. Best I can get." I hold in the sigh.

Damian smiles softly. After a moment, he brightens a little. "I bought paper. So when we get back, you can wrap your gifts if you like."

I smile. "That sounds fun," I agree. "Just no puppy wrapping," I joke.

He chuckles. "No, indeed. Not yet anyway. I'll have to find a box you can use once it gets closer."

"If she'll stay in it." I smile. She is so anxious to be near us. Guess we'll have to have Cedrick work on it.

"We'll work out something," Damian promises with a smile.

I chuckle as we head back. We're almost there when I realize I'd not heard the normal sounds that horrified me before. I wonder if that's the carriage or if they'd slowed. I dare pull a curtain back slightly only to jump and sit back. Nope, the carriage just muffles it. I would presume on purpose. I can't blame them for not wanting to hear it. I avoid the city for that exact reason.

"Are you alright?" Damian asks.

I nod. "Was just curious how it seemed so quiet." I smile weakly. "Guess I was hoping it might have ebbed a little."

Damian gives me a sympathetic smile. "I understand. Though sadly not."

I shake my head. "Not yet." But we'll make it stop. I just don't know how, but I will.

Chapter 18

In our lessons, we're given the itinerary for Christmas week. We'll have the week free of lessons. The first day, we'll have the tree topping ceremony followed by a special holiday interview with the Chosen and royal family. The next day the Court Christmas Dinner in the evening, but the following two nights have surprise events before Christmas day itself where we'll have the traditional devotional in the morning, the gift exchange, then the ball late into the night.

We spend the next day decorating the Ladies' Chamber while an old music recorder plays Christmas music we sing along to; Bella and I most of all, even dancing around each other and laughing.

And all the while, more Chosen features are being released one at a time in each morning's paper. I always look to get my copy as soon as possible and check my desk every time I walk into my room. One evening, when I come back from dinner, I notice a note on my desk. I frown and pick it up.

You're doing great. Keep it up. I'm still rooting for you.

I frown and look over at my maids. "Who left this?" I ask.

"Left what?" Vivian asks, looking up from putting the makeup wipes away.

"This note." I show it to her.

"Oh, I don't know, my lady." Vivian frowns apologetically. "I didn't see anyone drop it off." She looks at Flur.

Flur shakes her head. "Sorry my lady, I haven't seen anyone."

Damian simply shrugs in uncertainty. I bite my lips and look at it. I don't know the handwriting. Who in the palace would leave me a note like this? Or worse, who outside could get in? I'm almost sure it's not Dad's.

I'm distracted from the note the next morning by the next feature. So far, nothing of note or new has been shown in any features. Kamala's had called her a powerful negotiator who wouldn't take any funny business but also pointed out that her loud voice wasn't very princess-y.

Isla's review was good too. In fact, it made a very good point I'd missed. It said she is a quiet woman of faith which is completely true. Those traits would make her a good queen and perhaps that peaceful grace would be what we'd need to end this war. I'd never thought of Isla as one to fear when it came to competition, but the paper was right. She is one to worry about.

Jonquil's was impressive, and that was a surprise to most everyone. Jonquil did not stand out in her interview, but from how the article was written, you'd have thought she did. It called her graceful, poised, with a good head for justice. I have no idea how she'd gotten all those compliments, most of all, when I'm honestly not sure they fit her. I don't want to speak badly of her, but I'd have not called her graceful; poised maybe, but not graceful, and this justice bit came out of nowhere.

I try not to think about it as I spend time in the library trying to find answers once again. It's cold in the library and though the staff lit a fire for me, it's still surprisingly chilling. If we got any rain, it would turn to snow. We often get a few snowstorms at the end of December into early January that left snow that stuck around until mid February most of the time. You'd think the palace would do a better job of keeping itself warm with all the money it takes in. Perhaps I need to bother the resident enchanter about checking that the heating works.

That makes me pause. I'd not met the resident enchanter yet. It's common for the palace to have one and often their household duties are combined with advising the king. How odd I hadn't met him yet. Then again, the only member of court I had met was the grand duke. I saw him still around, but he avoids speaking to me for the most part, apart from polite nods. I work hard to look busy every time to ensure it stays that way. Maybe it isn't that odd. I'd meet the enchanter at the dinner.

I'd ask Zelda if she'd met him, but she joins me less and less in my research. Most of the time, it is because she is out with Gavril. I try not to be envious, but she is getting a lot of them. But she is not alone. I know Lilly, Isla, Bella, Forsythia, and Azalea are getting more dates too. I try not to notice. After all, Gavril has to try to get to know all of us, but I start to fear I'd scared him off asking me out.

It only makes me feel worse when I see Zelda heading back from one of her dates in the fencing gear she wore when we sparred. So he found her easier to fence with. Was that really the problem? He just wanted to have fun training, and I sucked the fun out of it?

Other girls are claiming to have gotten more intimate time with Gavril. which makes Dahlia complain they need to find a way to make the board again and just ignore the Nippers' board.

"The features do a good enough job," Jonquil huffs.

"You say that because yours was glowing," Dahlia snarls, but Forsythia ignores it.

"It's not like it matters. None of it does in the end," Jonquil says. "Let's recall he doesn't pick."

"But he can eliminate whoever he wants for any reason," Dahlia points out. "He can use that to slowly eliminate who he doesn't want until his favorite stands."

"That's what you'd do." Zelda frowns. "Gavril would not be that disloyal and 'cheat' his way through. Not when so much work was put into this."

"He should. Get a backbone." Forsythia shakes her head, muttering to herself. I immediately feel angry. If she wants to be the one he chooses as an easy support, maybe she should support him no matter who she's with.

"A backbone sometimes is knowing when to bend," Zelda retorts. "Backbones don't just hold you upright; they also twist and bend, so you can move. If it didn't, you'd die pretty quick. Perhaps he has the better backbone."

"It's a delicate balance," Princess Amapola says. "You must be as firm as an oak but as flexible as a willow branch. It's not an easy idea."

"Just like any good act," Isla agrees. "Or real balance. You need a balance of all things to get a true center. You don't turn by being flexible alone. You push against the floor to rise up. Opposites make the effect. I have to hold my core firm but also bend each part of me right. It's not being one or the other; it's a balance of all."

Even Isla has a better way of saying it than me. Maybe the paper was right. She is the one we all really should be worried about beating us. She's got everything going for her. She's what my father wanted me to be. Under the radar, so no one thought much of her, but with the power and pull to win.

The thought makes my stomach drop. She's not the spy letting the rebels into the palace, is she? She'd be very good at hiding it if she was. She was in the safe room in the first attack with the rest of us. Or was she? I'd have to check the list I made. It feels like a lifetime ago. But perhaps she just was what my father wanted me to be and has no ill intent. I hope so.

"Guess you'll have to figure it out and make a journal," Azalea says to Dahila. "Then we don't have to keep hearing it." I laugh and so do several others. I think a lot of us are nervous about that aspect of it. We have to spend every day with each other, but we also are competitors.

"It might help to think of it differently," I offer. "We keep calling it a competition or saying we're competing, but are we really competing against each other or the tests? It's more like we're classmates all trying to pass the same test to get into a nice school or something. You know?"

"But isn't it still competing if there is only one open spot?" Dahlia mocks.

"Maybe. But is fighting the other people in the class going to help you get that spot?" I ask.

"No," Bella laughs.

"Um, yeah," Dahlia says. "If they all drop out."

"We can't drop out. We are in a contract to do this now," Azalea reminds us.

"Harsh school," Lilly says, making us all laugh.

"I meant maybe it would be less hard and stressful if we thought of it that way instead of thinking it's all about winning Prince Gavril's favor," I say. "He is painfully aware he doesn't pick the winner, after all."

"Is he though?" Forsythia asks.

"He sure doesn't act like it," Kamala agrees. "It's like the rest of the girls not on the date are just your mutual friends or something. He talks so freely about you all to me anyway."

"Maybe it's unfair, but yeah, we do that too," Florence agrees.

"Not much else to talk about around here," Ericka complains.

"That's true," Florence agrees.

"I hope he's not trying to spread rumors," Dahlia complains.

"The prince wouldn't do that," Lilly glares at her. I'd never seen her glare like that. "It's more facts about each other. Like how we say we've seen so-and-so at their job, like telling him I watched Kascia practice the other day. It's not like we're comparing notes."

"That might be a good way to get to know the real girls better," Ericka muses as he strokes her rat of a dog. "Wonder if he's thought of it."

He doesn't talk about the others like that to me. He mentioned his date with Zelda fencing wasn't as disastrous as mine, but he didn't really talk a lot about the other girls. Just tidbits about what his life is like. At least to me. Perhaps he is more of a gossip with others. Do I know him as well as I think I do, if at all? I need to learn not to join in these group huddles.

"He won't need to if he's reading these," Jonquil says.

"You say that because yours was great." Florence glares at her. "Some of us don't have friends in high places."

"Who said I did?" Jonquil retorts.

"Your glowing review when you didn't do better than the rest of us," Kamala says.

Jonquil shrugs. "So what? They liked me. I can't help that."

"And you're from around here. That helps," Princess Rose says. "That certainly did not do the princesses any favors."

"With that logic, then Kascia will get a glowing one as well, and we all know that's not likely," Ericka laughs.

I glare at her. Just because I had substance to my interview does not mean I am going to get a bad review. I might, but it isn't for sure.

"Do you think how the people react to us will affect our chances?" Lilly asks a bit nervously.

"Only if we get something so bad not even the royals can spin it. If it's not a test, it's a free pass," Azalea says. "The paper is trying to be fair."

"You also got a glowing one," Lark accuses.

It is true. Azalea's was captioned "The Mother Queen" and praised her big sister/mother-like qualities as making her a great fit for a kingdom who needs Mommy to stop the kids bickering. It was a nice piece praising her. I wonder if that's why Gavril has started to go out with her more.

"A wishy-washy review doesn't mean anything. As long as your feature didn't cause a riot, you're fine," Bella assures. She was getting more dates, and her review wasn't exactly glowing, but it wasn't bad.

"At least you all have yours," Forsythia complains. She is right. Forsythia, Dahlia, and I are the only ones not to have our features out yet. I think they saved the two celebrities for last as they will make a splash with their fans.

"Trust me, being last is a good sign," Florence sighs. "Being first means dull. They are saving the real punches for the end."

"Mine was later and wasn't great," Bella tries to cheer her up.

"And they didn't save the best for last." Ericka purses her lips. Hers had come out that day. It was... mixed. They treated her more like a celebrity and got several locals from the area to comment on her. People who had worked for her or knew her from their work with her father, the mayor of the capital. They were either glowing or said she was not fun to work for. I could see that. She was demanding and already thought herself a princess. I wouldn't want to be her maid.

"Depends on who you ask," Florence complains.

"Just recall the people aren't picking the winner. The tests are," says Princess Rose.

"You mean the king and queen are," Ericka says. "Let's not forget that. There's a reason no one numbered under thirty in the line up is still here."

"Um." Florence raises her hand. "I'm still here."

"You are not under thirty," Ericka says.

"I'm thirty-seven," she retorts.

"But most are numbered over twenty, right?" Dahlia asks, now seeming curious. Florence nods, and it's true. I suppose that just means the king and queen actually did a good job in their original interviews to know who is most likely to pass.

"Well, we seem on a break until the holiday anyway," Azalea states. "So how about we all just enjoy a Christmas in a palace instead of bickering over positions we can't change anyway?"

"You mean a normal Christmas," Princess Amapola jokes, making us all laugh.

The end of December marks the six month mark, and no one had been eliminated in a while, and it looks like they will not until after the holiday. Azalea is right, we could try not to worry about it at least until then.

I make sure to have my maids get me a paper the next morning, but to my surprise, I'm not the one being featured. It's Forsythia's feature. I was so sure I'd be next, I check the whole paper and even the date four times before I accept that this is correct.

Her feature talks a lot about her ability to be strong, to make choices, and to execute them perfectly as shown through her career as a horse jumper. It has a lot of quotes from her fans about why they'd like to see her become queen. A few joke they'd rather her not, so she'd keep riding, but couldn't deny she'd be "an asset to the country". It was longer than the others and talked about how she started young and quickly became one of the top jumpers because of her dedication, drive, trust in her horse, and her ability to make deals to get the best mounts.

The article ended with a joke I'm sure Gavril will just about throw up to read. "We'll see if she can negotiate her way into one of the finest mounts yet." The queen will have a few words for the paper over that one for sure.

I'm not the only one surprised in lessons that morning. "I can't believe Kasica's wasn't today," Forsythia was saying. "Why is it me?"

"It's in interview order," Princess Rose says soothingly as she puts her papers in order on her study desk.

Oh no, that's right. I'd not noticed.

"Not perfect order. Mine was out of order," Isla says.

"We got mixed up," Lilly agrees.

"So? One mess up does not break the pattern," Princess Amapola says, tossing her straight black hair over her shoulder as she sits at her desk. "Kascia isn't next; she's last."

Dahlia glares at me. I'm taking the spot she was sure she'd get. End with a bang, and she was hoping to be that bang.

"Maybe it was another mix up, and I'll be tomorrow," I point out.

They all look at me like I'm crazy. They're right. My interview was more dramatic than the others. They are saving the grand finale for me. I am terrified. I thought I'd done really well in my interview, but with how the girls talk, I'm starting to worry it will be a slaughter bad enough to get me eliminated.

I hardly pay attention to the lessons. I hadn't thought the features mattered, but if the interviews do, the features must too, right? I'm starting to fear it might be the feather that brings down the bird. What if it is so bad they send me home?

Chapter 19

"Don't change just yet," Zelda's voice catches me as I head back to my room after my practice time in the studio. "I've not had a good fencing round in ages. Would you mind?"

"No." It pops out before I can think about it. But to tell the truth, after what happened with Gavril, I'm terrified.

"Thanks. I'll meet you in there?"

"Sure." I swallow as Zelda leaves. At least she didn't notice.

I ask my maids to help me get into the fencing gear. Flur smiles, happy I'm doing it again. Vivian looks a little more worried but politely doesn't bother me about it. I am so grateful for her tact. She's quite good at bugging me when she should and leaving me alone when she should.

Zelda smiles at me when I arrive. I force a smile. She offers me the same blade as before. It feels as good as ever in my grip, but I'm terrified of showing how bad I am at this. I know what Damian said. And I hold to it, but part of me still is afraid of being wrong. I don't want the reminder.

"Looks like you could use the pick me up." Zelda gives me a compassionate smile.

I force one back. "It's been rough," I confess.

"It has been rather wild," Zelda agrees with a slight frown. "I know they all told me to leave it alone as they'd checked on you, but I definitely noticed after the Forsythia incident that you were shaken."

It was so close to my botched date; I can see how everyone assumes that's where it started. I'm fine keeping it that way. I shrug. I struggle to come up with an excuse. It would help if that was the real reason I'd been shaken. It wasn't the only reason, and it wasn't even the first. Just the one the whole palace knows about.

"It's hard to have to watch it," Zelda agrees. "The more you like him the harder it is. How did you ever do it when you dated a fellow actor?"

"I've never dated a fellow actor." The reply falls off my lips without much thought. Just the truth rolling out.

"Oh, that makes sense. How did your boyfriends do it?"

My first instinct was to ask how she knew I'd dated before, but not only had I confessed a bit about having an ex at home I was avoiding, in the "I am" game we'd been forced to play on the first day, I'd had to get up when I said I'd kissed a boy.

"They didn't like to come to my shows because of it." Though there was only one.

"So you can understand it's hard on both ends. I can't imagine what I would do." Zelda shakes her head.

"You should be there next time," I say dully.

Zelda laughs. "I don't know if Forsythia needs a next time. Her small hints like taking his arm, kissing his cheek, and that stupid thing she does when she runs her hand down his arm or chest. Ugh." Zelda shudders for effect.

Oh, I'd noticed. Not only did she do it to Gavril in every public setting she could without the queen catching her, but she'd also tried it on Damian. Worst part is, I'm sure she's right. She's so beautiful, tricky, and seductive she could take anyone from me. As Damian said, she'd make an excellent harlot.

"So, it's alright to be shaken. Could you imagine if Gavril saw you all watching?" Zelda shudders again. "I'm at least glad he didn't have to confront us about it."

Oh, if only she knew. *See Damian? She gets it.*

"Kascia, you've hardly said a word. Are you alright?" Zelda frowns.

"Sorry," I say quickly. "I just don't have much to add to any of that. You're right on all of it."

"Well, at least you can let out the frustrations." Zelda gets into position.

"I don't know. It hasn't helped me much in the past," I confess as I slowly walk into position too.

"What do you mean?" Zelda pauses with a frown.

"I've just had a few times where letting it out in fighting has gotten me into trouble," I give a half truth.

Zelda shakes her head. "Don't worry. I don't mind if you're rough or beat me every time. Just no serious injury, alright?" Her joking tone is meant to cheer me up, but honestly, I'm not feeling much cheered.

"I don't know if I'm good enough to hurt you."

"You've fought me before, and you won a fair share of your fights," Zelda reminds me. "We had a good time last time, even if it felt like a lifetime ago. I'm sorry. I should have asked more. I'll confess, I've gotten Gavril on the field. He was so nervous at first, but I think he's grown to like it."

So, it's Zelda's fault he thought fencing would be fun. She dragged him into it. Then once he enjoyed it, he wanted to share it with me. Why does that feel wonderful and awful all at once? He wanted to share something special with me. And I'd gone and made such a mess of it, I'm not sure we'll ever recover.

The image of the little red puppy, so excited to be picked, comes to mind. A little bit of hope at the upcoming holiday. If I had chosen right... though I wouldn't change my choice now, I'm still not fully confident in it. We might recover... just maybe.

"Kascia, are you sure you're alright?" Zelda frowns. "You're zoning out again."

"Sorry." I take a deep breath, shaking myself and getting my mind ready for the fight like I did before fencing training with my father.

It's okay to lose here. It's just training. She's teaching you, that's all. "It's been a while for me too."

"Longer than me I take it." Zelda resumes position. "It's alright. It's supposed to be fun, remember?"

"I'm not used to fencing being fun," I confess.

"You said your father taught you?"

I nod.

"He expected you to need it. I can help you learn to make it fun. You enjoyed it last time," she points out.

I had. But that was before I made a royal mess of it. And before I feared my rights being stripped from me. Zelda is not a Custod though. But she's well trained from a young age I presume, so I shouldn't be so ashamed of losing to her.

I nod that I'm ready and get into position again. Zelda does the same. I'm too nervous to make the first move, but Zelda doesn't make me wait long before she makes her first attempt which I block almost too quickly, too nervous.

Zelda takes advantage with several blows over and over which I block just as quickly as she sends them.

"Very good. You're fast." She smiles. I force one in return.

We run through this style of exchange several times. After five to ten minutes of this, Zelda frowns. "Kascia, are you afraid to go on offense? You've not once made a strike at me unless it was in defense."

"Good offense is a good defense," I quote.

Zelda giggles. "Alright. Fine. I just recall you being more balanced before."

Perhaps I should take the risk. I'm terrified I'll get too competitive and break my friendship with Zelda like I had broken my friendship with Gavril. I have to take the risk though, or I might as well have said no. I wonder if maybe I should have been brave enough to say no.

So far, neither of us has scored a point or taken a win. This will be a long drawn out match instead of my small ones that normally make up an entertaining round of fencing. I know that. I had been told that before, but I am just so nervous. I must get over it.

When we resume, I have to do a few more defensive rounds before I get up the nerve to go into offense. It surprises Zelda more than I thought it would, and I almost score a win, but I'm so surprised by her slip up, I don't take advantage of it.

"Afraid to beat royalty?" Zelda teases warmly. "It's alright to win, you know. Did the queen have another heart attack?"

I laugh at the idea. "No."

"Then what happened?"

"It feels like a lifetime since I've done this. I feel so out of practice."

"Want to do training drills for a while? Will that help and make it more fun?"

"Actually, that would really help." I smile a thanks.

Zelda's kind of drills are different than the kinds my father did, but they are much more fun. We're laughing and enjoying practicing footwork and exchanges. It helps me get over my nervousness about being on the offense.

"That better?" Zelda asks, panting after about an hour or so.

"Much." I smile. "That was a good idea; thank you."

"Well, thank you; we could all use drills," Zelda insists. "Want to try a few matches?"

"If you do." I nod.

We get into position and start to fence. The round is much more fun. I'm back into my normal flow and not afraid of making a detrimental mistake. But even with that, I lose. But of course I do. I'm still nervous even if it's much smaller. The fighting is more instinct again, which makes it fun. One loss is nothing.

Even the second loss is nothing. And the next, and the next... and the next. After the sixth, I admit I'm getting a bit crestfallen. I'm not fighting desperate. I'd beaten her before, but that was before my mistake. Could you be half disinherited?

After another loss, Zelda can't help but notice my disappointment. "I'm sure it's just because you're nervous."

I appreciate she chose to address it rather than ignoring it. "I think so too." It's all in my head. "Hard to win when you're set in your head that something is wrong or you're afraid of being too aggressive."

"You're more reserved. But that's okay. We'll keep going until you're comfortable again or we want to clean up for dinner. Whichever is first," Zelda assures me. "No shame in a losing streak as long as you're learning. No matter how long that streak is."

"You're right." I am encouraged by that. I'm just learning not to be afraid of fencing a friend again. That's all. It was just taking a while to relearn.

The truth is, I was holding up decently well until the loss. It's not like she's beating me within seconds every time. The matches are longer than that.

After two more losses, I'm really getting discouraged. But I appreciate Zelda is still trying, and her words about just learning to not be afraid of it return to me each time and make it easier. I want to learn to fence properly again. And I'm getting there, I'm sure of it.

Zelda recommends a break after a while and so we just sit, drinking water and chatting for a while. "Was your father a strict teacher?" she asks me.

"Oh yes, but he tried to make it fun too." I nod then smile. "He even gave me a unique collapsible blade to carry into town in case I needed it. It was a reward for doing so well."

"That's amazing. I wish I could have seen it. I'm sure they didn't let you bring it." Zelda smiles.

"No weapons." I sigh in mock disappointment. "It had a cap on it to make it look like an umbrella."

"Genius!" Zelda laughs. "I want one."

"I'll have to get it at some point, so you can study how it's made. I have no idea how they did it. I'd never dared study it closely enough. I was worried I'd break it."

"Did you normally fight with that one?"

"Yes, most of the time after I got it. Why?"

"Perhaps part of the struggle is the weight. A blade that can collapse may not be as heavy. Perhaps as you work at it and get stronger that will help." she suggests.

"It wasn't a problem last time we fenced. We were pretty even then," I remind her. I had forgotten who had more wins or losses then. It didn't seem important. It was only important when I was fighting the man my father thought I should beat in five seconds and kill in a heartbeat. I struggle to keep my heart from sinking at the thought.

"Well, you weren't as nervous. I shouldn't have waited so long. The prince hasn't asked you? Not once?" Zelda asks, then shakes herself. "What am I thinking? I had to drag him into it. He'd not suggest it. You should ask him. I doubt he'd say no. Most of all to you." She nudges me playfully. "Then you won't get out of practice if I forget to ask. Or you can ask me, of course. But I would think he'd like another person to fence with."

Her happy tone makes me too ashamed to admit he had asked me, and I'd blown it. So I just force a smile. "Not sure I'd dare ask a prince trained by a Custod."

"He is really good," Zelda admits. "I struggled to beat him for sure. And I think he wins more than loses, but I don't keep track."

So why did I have to keep track?

"Anyway." Zelda pulls me from my thoughts. "Ready to start again?"

I nod, feeling encouraged by the break. Maybe with the mental break and time to get back into it, I'd get into the flow and my normal skill would return. With how many matches we'd had, I should have won at least one by now if I was as good as I had been last time we fought. Even with the gaps in between. I had gaps training with Father when a show was too intense. I'd get a win this time.

I don't expect it to be the first match up though. She'd rested too, and a part of me is still nervous. And I'm right. I don't win that one.

But after about five minutes into our second match, to my surprise, Zelda's sword zips out of her hand as I try a classic little spin style trick. It is a basic one I am so sure she'll just block, the fact it wins me her weapon stuns me. I only just catch her blade to declare the win, almost tripping over myself to get it.

"You did it!" Zelda cries in surprise too. "How did I not see that coming?" She looks at her hand.

I frown. "I didn't get you by mistake, did I? I thought the blades were blunted."

"Oh, of course they are," Zelda chuckles as she finishes checking. "I guess I am now the one losing to mind tricks. I forgot they'd be blunted, I suppose."

Forgot? Something about that doesn't sit right. "You fight blunted all the time, right?"

"Depends on the kind of training at home."

"But most of the time?"

"With my siblings, for sure. It's only with my trainer I'd use ready-for-battle weapons," Zelda assures me. "Princesses in Hyvil may be expected to be able to fight, but they still make sure to protect their precious girls."

We both laugh, but an uneasy, rather sick feeling is bubbling in my stomach. That doesn't make sense. She'd not made a slip up about a blunted blade yet today. In fact, she'd used their being blunt as a tool a few times, just like I did. And fencing with me is much more like a sibling than a trainer.

When the realization hits me, it takes all my self-control not to burst into tears. She'd let me win. I'd been doing so badly, and she felt so bad for me, she let me win. Just like Gavril did. It was after that I got desperate and ruined it.

You won't do that now, I try to tell myself, but the rush of pained emotions is too hard to beat. It takes all my willpower not to cry.

I might have been okay if Zelda hadn't noticed. She frowns at the change in my expression. "Kascia, are you alright? I didn't hurt you, did I?"

For a moment, I hear Gavril asking if I'm alright instead of Zelda. I blink as I recall who I'm really with. The reminder is too much, and the tears rise to my eyes.

"Oh Kascia, I'm sorry. What's wrong?" Zelda steps closer, so much like Gavril did.

I shake my head. "N-nothing." But my shaking voice betrays me.

Zelda gives me a compassionate smile. "Of course, it's something. You won. What's wrong with that?"

"I didn't win," I snap harder than I mean to.

Zelda's face falls. "Of course you did."

I give Zelda a look. "You expect me to buy you forgot?"

"It happens."

Sure it does. Then I get determined to win properly and go too hard, keep losing and then make you question if I'm a rebel or not. My lip shakes.

"Kascia, I'm sorry. I thought it might help snap you out of the rut, is all. I'm sure you can. You have before. It just seemed nothing was getting your head out of it. I only meant to help. I'm sorry."

It's all too much like last time, and the water works are rising faster, and a few fall down my face.

That is too much for Zelda, and the guilt is splashed across her face. I don't want her to feel bad. It's not her fault. It's mine. It's Gavril's. I don't want her comfort. I want to hide and be left alone. I don't want her to help, but not because I don't trust her. I just want to be left alone to deal with this. Most of all, because I don't want her to feel bad for asking, or to know why I really am having a mental block or how jealous I am that Gavril will still fence with her.

"Kascia, please say something. I'm sorry. Really. If I knew it would hurt, I'd never have done it." Zelda puts a hand on my arm.

I jerk away. I really don't want to be touched. I don't want anyone's help. I want to deal with it on my own, so I can control it. When she tries again, I pull back and step back a few steps completely instinctively.

But the hurt that crosses Zelda's face is too much. "I-it's not you," I insist, my voice thick and shaking in tears. "J-just leave me alone, please." But when Zelda comes closer, my fight or flight kicks in, and it wants to flee.

I'm half way up the hallway towards my room before I can take in my location. "What did you do?" I hear Bella's indignant voice demand, but not of me.

My desire to be alone instinctively knows not to go to my room. My maids and Damian will check on me. And I clearly can't control my impulse to get away from anyone, so I go to the conservatory. At home, I'd run to the beach. It's so large I'd hear anyone coming and be able to hide somewhere private. It worked great. But there's no outside I can reach without guards stopping me. So the conservatory in the farthest corner I can find is where my flight or fight response takes me to curl up and sob.

I just need to get control of the emotions. Then I'll be fine. I could face them, but this panicked mode takes over. I need to get control of myself before letting anyone touch me so I'll be able to accept comfort. I can't even justify or control or explain why I reacted this way.

I hadn't done this in a long time. As a child, I did it a lot. I wouldn't let Mom or Dad touch me or try to help me when I got like this. I'd lock my door, hide under the bed, or once I knew it worked, hide at the beach. But once I got a grip on myself, I'd let them come in and get me. I was always glad they would come in to get me. I always feared my desire to get control first made them think I didn't trust or want them.

I'm sure that's what I'd just done to Zelda. I'd broken it yet again, only a different friend this time. I get control, only cry harder as the pain of realizing I'd done exactly what I'd been avoiding washes over me. I should have said no, even if I changed my mind. I could have said I was too tired after dance practice. She'd have been alright with that.

I cry for a long time, getting more control and feeling calmer, but there's no reason not to let myself cry and get the pain out, so I do. It's not like anyone can find or hear me in here. I don't think I used a path. I likely have to apologize for trampling some plants or ruining a beautiful display.

I can't control anything anymore: myself, my fate, my emotions. I'm so caught up in this game. I lost all the power when I made my choice not to let my father kill them. And I'm still unsure that was the right choice. Everything is unsure and not what I'd hoped or wanted. The life I'd dreamed of is gone, and the one I hope to build is starting to flicker away like a candle in a rainstorm.

I wish I had control or hope in anything, but I just can't trust any of the little hopes. And if I had them, I'm afraid like the rest of my life thus far, it will not turn out to meet my hopes at all. I'm trapped doing something I do not want to do to at least survive, get by, and even in trying that I keep making it worse.

"There you are." The voice makes me jump and curl away, not trying to wipe the tears that are running down my face, but not choosing to face the voice either. A small part of me vainly hopes it would be Gavril, but it is a female voice either way. Besides, as comforting as he is, he's still the most uncertain hope in my life.

Bella walks over and sits beside me. "Are you okay? Or better, are you going to be okay?"

"I don't know," I confess, finally trying to wipe my eyes on my sleeve.

"What happened? Zelda is so confused. We don't understand what happened. You can talk to us, you know. We're not trying to hurt you."

"It's not her fault." I try vainly to wipe all the tears away, but more just replace them.

"Then what exactly happened?" Bella asks gently.

How could I ever explain? I look away, watching a bit of the stream go by. A fish swims up the current only to be pushed downstream when it pauses for a moment. I understand the feeling all too well. "I'm not even sure," I admit.

"She didn't hurt you or say something?" Bella checks.

"No."

"Kascia, I'm here to help. Really, what's going on?"

"I messed up. I keep messing it up."

"Messed up what? Zelda is fine. You didn't fail a test. You're still here," she teases lightly, nudging me playfully with her shoulder. It does win a small smile as I keep trying to wipe the tears away. "You beat us all at every interview. I mean it's only two, but it's still strange it happened twice." I laugh at that. "The press eats you up, and we all know your top of Gavril's list."

"I'm not." It pops out of me before I can decide if I want to confess that or not. Bella pauses, watching me gently, waiting for me to go on which lures me into doing it before I can stop myself. "I ruined it with my own uncertainty that I can win. If I even should. I didn't come here planning to win, and now it's the only choice, but is that really what I should do? I was so unsure and desperate to prove I'm what I thought I was, I made him question everything he believed about me."

"What are you talking about? If this is about his moment with Forsythia, we all know she staged it. Who knows how serious they really are," Bella assures me.

"She was only able to because he was questioning everything because of me," I admit, hugging my knees. "He took me fencing on our last date. I got competitive because my father always trained me to be the best, and I stupidly thought I was, so when I kept losing, I felt stupid and was determined to stop losing. I tried to explain that's all it was to him, but he thinks it's because I thought he was the wimpy baby prince his parents, the court, and rebels think he is. And it made him question all he thought he knew about me. And the next thing he does is go out with Forsythia of all people! It couldn't at least have been Zelda, or you, or Azalea, or anyone who'd at least make a good princess? Instead, he goes to her? And I have to watch. It's all my fault."

The tears blind me, and I hug my knees tighter and rest my head on them, letting my tears wet my knees. "All because I was too prideful to just accept I wasn't winning every fight like I expected to."

"What does that have to do with Zelda? I understand how that must really sting, but Zelda didn't do anything to make that worse," Bella sympathizes but tries to understand.

"I told you she didn't. Because I was so nervous about fighting at all after what happened with the prince, I couldn't even win one match against her, even when she tried so hard to help. I thought I was just about over it only to realize she let me win. Just like the prince did to help me feel better. And I just..."

I swallow hard. "I don't want to break anyone, or anything, or mess anything up anymore. And I did. I should have just said no. I don't know how to stop the fighting or defend myself from any of this anymore. It's gotten so bad my friends can hurt m-me without meaning to. It's not her fault, but she'll think it is, and I messed up another good thing I had going."

"Oh Kascia," Bella puts an arm around me to hug me from the side, "Zelda is not going to just drop you because she accidently hurt your feelings. She's much bigger than that, and so is the prince."

"Then why is he running off to Forsythia of all people?" I glare at Bella, though it's not her I'm angry with.

Bella clears her throat. "I don't know if this helps, but Forsythia is being overly confident. It's not just her he's going to."

I blink rapidly, trying to digest what that likely meant. He did go to Bella too. How far did they go? I don't want to know. "At least he's not that stupid."

"This game is pretty mean, isn't it?" Bella gives me a sad smile.

I nod. "More than they ever meant, I imagine."

"I wish I had more to say to help you feel better." Bella frowns, hugging me a bit tighter. "I really do, but honestly, all I can say is I know how it hurts. I thought he was finally getting serious with a few of us only to realize he's likely this way with everyone. So it's not personal."

"If I ever was the favorite, I lost that so badly, I don't know why he hasn't just eliminated me." I wipe my tears and this time they aren't replaced.

"That's not true. One, he hasn't eliminated you," Bella says with a hint of a tease. "You're still here. And you have plenty to offer him and the kingdom. You're clever, pretty, talented, and you care about his feelings and the people more than most of the girls who joined this game. You're willing to act to defend and not just talk about it. You're the only one who's proven what you'll do to help. You killed that rebel and disobeyed orders to help defend the palace. That's more than all of us other girls put together."

"I'm so pretty, I'll lull the people into letting the tax crush them into nothing," I say dully.

"Not you," Bella laughs. "You see how the press eats you up. They engage with you, Kascia. Your charms don't lull them into doing nothing. It makes them more active."

"How?"

"More people are watching each time."

"How does that have anything to do with me?"

"They don't tune in to watch Rose sit there like a stiff overlord." Bella gives me a look, making me laugh. "They want to see how the 'Girl in Green' gets the best of the reporter this time. You wowed them at the Presenting Ceremony, and heaven knows how you wowed them the other day. You'll do just as well at Christmas. You're good with people. You have no trouble with that."

"Yes, I do. I can hardly stand up to the others," I point out. "Let alone the prince."

"If you stand up to him, you're better than the rest of us. We're scared he'll kick us out." Bella laughs. "And yes, you do. You were nice to Ericka the first day. You defend Lilly from the others beautifully. Your problem is, after the Harvest, you feel like everyone else is better than you. Even you said Forsythia is a worse choice. You just lost your confidence. How Lady Keva hasn't picked on it yet, I don't know. She's always picking at mine." She smiles, hoping for a laugh, but doesn't get one.

"She's too busy using me as the example." I think of the girls glaring at me in envy.

"Exactly. You're great at all of that too." Bella smiles. "Honestly, it's a crime if you don't at least make it into the top five."

"Not that anyone would vote me there," I huff.

"The people might," Bella laughs. "And if it came down to it, I think a lot of the girls already gone would. The ones still in the running want to win, so they wouldn't dare vote at all. They don't want to vote themselves out, but it would look un-princess-like to vote for themselves. That could be its own test."

She pauses when my face still is down. "Kascia, I honestly can't understand how you feel so unsure. To everyone but you, you're a great choice. The other girls who pick on you know that, so they want you gone because it makes it easier for them to climb up. I can't pretend I don't want to win, but not enough to try to get you thrown out." Bella hugs me tighter. "I'd pick you if I had to pick someone else."

"You'd pick Azalea." The two are like sisters.

"Are you crazy? I love her to death, but she's a bit ditsy."

We both laugh.

"Zelda would be better," I mutter. "He can fence her without fear."

"She'd be good too, but honestly, as the person who'd be under that ruler, I'd rather a girl who knows what life is like here. You lived on the streets like us. You know what it's like. And I find that comforting far more than a powerful foreign princess," Bella says. "And if you want to go down the list: Isla is too shy; Lilly...Oh, that girl should be given a pass. Jonquil is too forceful if you ask me. And..." Bella looks around. "Promise not to tell?" I nod. "I hate bugs." Bella frowns.

"What?" But she looks at Jonquil's art all the time.

"I'm terrified of them. Long story, but it's so hard for me to look at those pictures. It might be silly, but the fact she loves bugs so much and the prince calls her 'bug' makes me a bit queasy."

That really makes me laugh. Bella smiles at her success. "And we all know most of the others are jokes. Rose is too stiff. The people would hate her. Amapola is just a pretty face. Let's not get started on Ericka and Dahlia." Bella smiles again. "So I suppose we picked our top picks: you, Zelda, Isla, and me. Imagine if we were the top five! Oh! That would make sense but be so horrible."

I chuckle. "It will be someone."

"It will be someone," Bella sighs. "And as we need a top five, we can throw Jonquil in as my reason for not liking her is a bit silly. I mean I like her fine. But as a ruler... It just makes me uneasy to think about."

"I'm not the judge, so I try not to think about it," I confess.

"I do. Maybe it shows that I'm more secure in my place if I lose." Bella pauses. "Isn't it a scary thought to lose?"

"More than you know." I hug my knees.

"Why?" Bella frowns. "Your ex ready to try to kidnap you?"

I chuckle. "No, it's... my father isn't too happy with me. He wanted me to do this, but I think when I got serious, he realized I might actually become one of the royals he despises."

"What? Really?" Bella looks horrified. "Did you know he might react like that?"

"I wasn't worried about it. I never thought I'd get this far or even want to. I didn't want to come, remember? He talked me into it." I swallow.

Bella scowls. "That bites. Why did he want you to do it if he didn't think you'd win?"

"Good court position, I suppose." I shrug.

"That makes sense. There's rumor girls who get into the top five will be in line for other royal marriages. I wonder if maybe he wanted that." Bella tilts her head.

"I'd not thought of it."

"Oh, I have. Amapola has impressions of her brothers and other royals from the east coast kingdoms. You want to window shop?"

I laugh so hard at the term "window shop", I hug my middle.

Bella laughs too. "What? You've not done it?"

"No." I'm still laughing.

"Zelda hasn't either. We'll get her, and I'll explain it all to her. Once she knows, she won't be upset; promise." Bella pulls her arm from around me and takes my arm. "It will be fun,"

I sigh and allow her to pull me up. She lets me get cleaned up in the washroom as she explains to Zelda.

Zelda is quite understanding and hugs me, apologizing for letting me win again, assuring me as she had before that she hoped it would just snap me out of my mental rut.

We all sit in Bella's room, looking at the impressions of other princes for a while, laughing and joking about which we like. Zelda makes sure to add her brothers to the mix. I fake it, but sadly, the only ones who catch even half my eye all remind me of Gavril. I'm in so much trouble.

Chapter 20

Honesty, I can hardly believe things are normal the next day. The only difference is Bella is not as glued to Azalea. She seems to want to make sure I know I'm not in trouble with her or anyone else, which certainly is helpful, but not needed. I try to assure her of that, but she insists it's just for fun.

It helps the staff are trying to help us enjoy the holiday with little activity options in the Ladies' Chamber. I'm sure it's to help us relax before the insanity of the holiday week coming up.

It will kick off with the public tree decorating (as in we'll be doing it for the press to report to the public on) then the Christmas interviews, the Court Dinner, then the holiday itself. I keep running it over in my head. Our teachers are working hard to help us prepare for the dinner. Thankfully, all we have to do is be introduced to the full court and eat properly.

Lady Hydrengia, however, is acting like it's a do-or-die event when it comes to making our impression on the court. It's the only formal event where we'll get to meet them. Those that choose to can come to the Christmas ball, but that's not anywhere near the same. We'll have formal introductions to them all at the dinner. I'm nervous, but if they are even at least a little less intense than the grand duke, I think I'll survive.

There is increased tension in the lessons which often bleeds over into the Ladies' Chamber even after I've done my exercises. Forsythia is still boasting about being the new favorite, and even after what Bella said, I'm still unsure that she's not his new favorite. It's not like the prince has spoken to me since the incident in the hallway.

Bella stands up for me when they turn on me which they like to do, accusing me of having the teachers wrapped around my finger and saying it's not fair I get a leg up because of it.

"The teachers aren't judges," Bella reminds Dahlia. "So it doesn't give anyone a leg up either way. You'd not pick on her if you weren't terrified she'd beat you."

"You're the one who's scared," Dahlia accuses.

"Not of you," Bella laughs derisively.

"No need to argue over me," I mutter, getting up. I would rather sit lonely in my room than endure this.

"It's not just you. She's picking on everyone." Bella looks at me then back at Dahlia.

I don't want to hear it. I close the book I can't focus on and turn to go to my room. I notice Nippers watching me from where he's sitting on Lilly's lap, but Bella is too busy defending me to notice I'd left, even after her comment.

I'm partway to my room when someone almost walks right into me. He jumps and drops the papers he was holding. He swears under his breath and looks up at me. "Sorry. Oh, my lady."

I blink in surprise. "Oh... Mr. Fabian." I realize I don't know if he has a title or not. If he's Godwin's cousin, he should have some kind of title, but I have no idea what it would be.

"Just Fabian is fine." Fabian waves me off, bending over and collecting his papers. "I was just about to clip them. Forgive me, my lady. I should look where I'm going." He smiles as he stands up with his papers. He clips them together. "Can I help you?"

"No. I was just on my way to—" A gong fills the air, followed by another and another each second. I recognize the alarm. Another rebel attack. Though it has been a long time since we'd had one.

Fabian looks around in worry. We're on the second floor still. If the alarm only just went off, I doubt we have much to worry about.

Without warning, Fabian grabs me and pushes me to the wall. I'm so shocked I can't reply. There's a clunking sound, but before I can see what it is, Fabian is yanking me away.

"Hey." What is he doing?

"There's one... there." Fabian spots a guard. His eyes widen, and I follow them to see what he spotted. The guard just narrowly avoids getting his head smashed in by a club held by a sadly young-looking rebel. He looks hardly fourteen years old.

"I have one of the ladies!" Fabian calls.

I gape at him. Fabian isn't... I yank my arm free.

Fabian frowns and looks at me as the guard and rebel looks down at us. "Use the court meeting room," the guard replies before he uses the blunt end of his weapon to strike the boy in the stomach, making him double over and allowing the guard to shove him to the ground and begin tying his hands.

"Come on." Fabian takes my wrist again.

"What?" Was the guard in on it? I'm so confused.

"The safe room. He told me which one is open. It's a code. By Phoenix, do they tell you nothing?" Fabian hasn't stopped leading me as he complains.

We turn a corner only to run smack into two rebels. I tense up for a fight. Fabian quickly pulls me around and shields me by putting himself between me and the rebels, his back to them for a shield, narrowly missing the wild swing from one of them.

Fabian looks a bit panicked and surprised. He is spared trying to figure out how to defend me further when a spear from another guard strikes one rebel, and his falling body knocks over his companion.

"Go!" Fabian pulls back and pushes me forward. I stand there, not sure where I'm supposed to go. He yanks me down the hall until we reach the one where I'd run into him and the grand duke only a few weeks ago. He kicks a panel on the wall, slaps another, then rotates a bust which opens a safe room door.

He looks around before pushing me in and following me. He shuts it behind us. "Now we hope that guard tells the others where to find us." He smiles at me.

"You... how did you know to ask?" I frown.

"I'm technically a courtier. I don't hold a seat, but it still gives me access. My brother holds the seat. I could have had it, but I didn't want to run for it." Fabian shrugs. "Guess getting home on time isn't happening. Just hope the missus doesn't get too upset."

I smile slightly as Fabian sighs and takes a seat. "And I'll have to file this the day after tomorrow. I was hoping it would go in for tomorrow, but it will be too late to get it all together, proofed and printed." He sighs as he puts down the paperwork he'd been holding. "Guess time to relax for a bit then." He stretches.

"You act like it's a treat," I say, starting to pace. I am shocked the rebels were already on the second floor by the time the alarm was sounded. I'm also surprised by Fabian's actions. For a moment, I thought he was a rebel telling them he had me. Next, he's shielding me with his own body.

"It can be if you look at it that way," he replies, flipping through the paperwork. "One, two, three, four, five, six," he mutters under his breath and smiles. "Wow, I've missed a lot since coming down here."

"A lot of what?" I ask distractedly, still pacing.

"Battles. Though not as much as I expected." Fabian glances over the paperwork then looks up at me. He frowns. "You can sit. I don't bite. And it's only on the record if I ask for a quote. I'll try not to use anything you say against you while we're here. I'm sure I'm the last person you want to be trapped with."

I can't admit to him I'm shaken by their speed.

"I thought these happen often." Fabian frowns.

"They do. It's just..."

"You're normally already in a safe room?"

"Not that. It's just they were so fast," I confess.

Fabian blinks. "True. I haven't been here for an attack that actually got inside. Is it normally like that?"

"I've not really seen rebels when they get in other than the Harvest. I'm normally in the Ladies' Chamber or other room with a safe room to quicky sneak into."

"Hm. I may have to see if my guard contacts can shed some light on it. I suspect someone is letting them in if they're that fast, but why report on a rumor? I can't prove it, and that doesn't get people talking."

"Is that all you care about? Getting people talking?"

"Only if it's going to make a difference or cause some fun trouble." Fabian smiles. "If it doesn't entertain with a splash, then it better make history. It's why I'm here."

"'The Girl in Green' made you take the Enthronement seriously?"

Fabian smiles gently. "Yes, in fact, you did. What I took for just another powder puff show turns out to have some real contenders."

"So you went from reporting war to reporting a beauty pageant?"

"That's what I would have said. Truth is, I went from one war to another." Fabian smiles. "My lady, you really should relax. Here, you sit. I'll stand."

"No, there's—"

"You are a lady and perhaps my future princess and queen. I'm happy to let you sit." Fabian smiles, stands up and presents the bench to me like he's inviting me to sit on a stage.

I manage a smile and accept the seat, rubbing my arms.

"I hope I didn't offend you by shoving you to the wall. I only meant to protect you," Fabian says.

"Not offended. Shaken a bit," I admit.

"Oh." His eyes light up, and he laughs. "Sorry, I forget not knowing the code means you were missing many things. You feared I was going to hand you to the rebels when I said I had you?"

"Sorry."

"No, no, it makes sense. If you call out to a guard, they'll tell you the nearest safe room, at least that they know of. Lucky for us, I know this one well as it's the one I normally end up in since it's close to the offices of the court. I will often use my brother's office as he hardly uses it. The truth is most of the court does not use them. They use their home offices. It used to be seen as rude in the olden days, so these ones were made, but there are a lot of security problems with that. And for the court, it's nice not having to pass royal level security to meet with their constituents."

"So no one minds?" I ask, heart settling.

"No one has uttered a word other than Godwin who finds me a liability for his job."

"Are you?"

"I hope so." He smiles a very puckish smile at me that makes me laugh. I am slowly calming down. I wonder if I can dare ask him about the battles he'd seen. "But that's mostly just to tease him."

"Is that how you find your fun? Teasing?"

"Only some people. I am much more interested in recording history. To have your words ever etched in the mind of the people on how you reported what happened that changed the world. I like reactions. And getting reactions is quite appealing."

"So you left a war for this game?" I joke. "I'm sure war is much more history making and interesting."

"Is it?" Fabian gives me a dull look then pulls up one of the papers. "Forty-two casualties, no base found, fifteen rebels captured." Fabian swaps out for another paper. "Five casualties, no base found, no rebels captured." He reads all six papers with the same dull stats. "That sound more fun to you?"

"I'm sure your version of the report would be more interesting." I smile.

"Not when nothing happens. I stayed there through battle after battle, well, more like raid after raid, only to report how many fled and are overcrowding the camps. It's getting quite old. The most interesting story was the mass fleeing a few months ago."

"I heard." I frown. "Which rebellion caused it?"

"Mostly Loyalists, but Potentate sometimes will jump in on the havoc if they can. Of course, it's not organized, so it's hard to accuse them. Though the near assassination of the mayor was certainly Custod work. He's lucky to be alive."

"What?" I gasp. I had heard nothing of this.

"Not long before the Enthronement began, the mayor of Nerine was almost assassinated by a group clearly associated with the Custod rebellion. They put up the phoenix mark and all but didn't realize they got the wrong man. I'm sure that had something to do with those not involved in any rebellion deciding it was better to flee the city than let their lives be next. When the Loyalists took the northeast side, that was enough for them."

"I can't imagine the rebels being that much trouble," I admit.

"After what you see, can't you?" Fabian looks at me. "Look, I'm a reporter, and I try not to take sides, but I've seen more damage come from them than any guard force. The fear is spread by not knowing when your neighbor might cause a riot that causes your home to burn down. You can't trust anyone, not the government, not your friends, often not even your family."

"Why is it so bad up there and not here?" I ask, daring to sit next to Fabian, longing to understand. If the royals weren't the problem, what was?

"Distraction," Fabian says simply.

I pale. "You mean the Enthronement?"

"No. I mean here at the capitol, there's a clear target on who to lash out to, so they're prepared." Fabian waves his hand, indicating the room. "When they get fed up with high taxes, poverty, violence, whatever it might be, they get drunk and attack the palace. Out there, there's not so clear of a target. There, being a Royalist is a real thing."

"I don't understand."

"I mean when you see rebels causing more trouble by attacking guards, Royalists don't just watch. They fight back. They are fed up with it all too, but they don't blame the royals; they blame the rebellions. There's a reason this is called a civil war. It's brother against brother, literally at times. Mothers, daughters, fathers, sons, brothers, sisters, they all form their own thoughts and feelings on who is at fault, and they will lash out at whoever they choose to blame. That's why there are so many rebellions. Potentates, who just want the easy way to get rid of their view of the problem. Loyalists, who see themselves as true patriots. Then Custods... a unique lot. They carry the skill, but their conviction lies in being the only ones who understand and know the truth."

Fabian looks at me. "Custod rebels aren't just dangerous because they are well trained and have actual plans. They are dangerous because nothing can convince them the Creator is not on their side. They're God's warriors, and nothing you say or show them will change their minds."

I quickly pull away, standing up and walking away a few paces, not facing Fabian. "Then why interview their leader?"

"It's news. And that's how I found out why they're so deadly," Fabian replies darkly.

"And what do you think?" I turn to face him.

Fabian laughs. "Does it matter what a reporter thinks?"

"Of course, it does. What everyone thinks matters in a system for the people," I state.

"Few believe that to be true anymore, my lady." Fabian shakes his head. "In a kingdom like this, it's just everyone out for themselves, in and out of the government."

"For others, maybe. But that's how it's supposed to be." I look down, still shaking a little. He didn't know, did he? "So the people who fled Nerine weren't just running in fear of ruined homes."

"No. They fled in fear of when their neighbor decided they were a Loyalist and started attacking them for being Royalist as an excuse to take their property."

"Does that really happen?" I turn to Fabian again in horror.

"Rare, but yes." Fabian nods. "When no one trusts those who have authority, many will try to rise up and take authority themselves. That's what you see around you today. The capitol is unique in that the palace being right there distracts most from turning on each other. When no one agrees on a core truth, it's easy to use any excuse to turn on one another and take advantage if you are stronger. No one calls the guards; they take justice in their own hands. You think theft here is bad, wait until you visit places like Shasta and Astilbe. Wait until you see a merchant ship get blown out of the water for trying to ram into the port that they felt short-changed them as the government won't give them compensation for their illegal practices.

"And they're not fully wrong. The crime and lack of government resources to handle it is out of control. You see the lines to visit the mayor here. Wait until you see those lines. Those who have waited years to have their property returned after their bully friends up the street took it from them."

"Where are the Custods?"

"There is only so much even a family as large as the Custods can do when they handle the whole world. Don't get me wrong; they do their best, but they can't do it all. Most of all, when it's truly the Potentates' job, isn't it?"

"Yes," I mutter, stunned.

"Truth is, they focus on the outlying villages, the places so small they hardly show up on the map because at least in the cities the government can catch up eventually, but out there, it's worse. Though the growing refugee camp is certainly making that more interesting."

"The one full to capacity," I murmur.

"Yes, you do keep up." Fabian smiles. "It's gotten so large; I would go ahead and put it on the map if it were me. Most of Nerine fled there, now many in Shasta, Wellasyth, and Astilbe. And not just their cities, but their provinces too." He shakes his head. "A war gotten far out of hand."

And all just for a little extra funds in the royal's pockets five hundred years ago. I can hardly digest such a thing.

"Though admittedly a lot of the fighting has died down. It seems to go down each time news about the Enthronement comes out."

"Because we distract them," I say hopelessly.

Fabian laughs heartily. I stare at him in shock. How could he laugh like that in a moment like this? "Distraction? No. Power, my lady."

"Power?" I frown.

"They feel they have a say in their government, a voice," Fabian replies. "They cast their vote for favorite, debate over their drinks and smokes in bars and pubs across the nation about which girl they'd want to rule and why. It is a safe opinion to share and argue about without fearing being beat up. A Loyalist and a Custod rebel can sit at peace, not caring which side the other is on as one argues that Lady Kascia is the perfect choice while the other sings the praises of Lady Jonquil's ability to command. It makes them feel heard, a part of the events happening in their own lives and kingdom.

"Government isn't some abstract thing they can't control that is causing them to be poor. It's a powerful force they can use to help rule. Same thing happens every four years when members of court are reelected. But that is so regular and so many people set in their ways, it hasn't had as big of an impact on the people's view as it does now.

"In fact, my sources up north tell me it's become far more common for someone to declare their political affiliation not by titles like Loyalist, Potentate, or Royalist, but as a supporter of Lady Dahlia or Princess Rose. It has made a larger impact than I think even the royal family thought it would. And it started with that first interview. It started when the people got to peek into the inner workings of the contest. Perhaps it was sooner when ladies across the kingdom put in their names in the hopes of breaking free of the poverty cycle.

"It's not distraction that is causing a slow in the violence. It's the feeling of power that doesn't require them to be violent. They have a voice, a say. Those weekly polls for who should win the Enthronement have excited the people. This Christmas has more hope and joy in the air in Purerah than I've seen since I was a boy."

I gape at him. The grand duke was wrong? I wasn't lulling the people into doing nothing? I was empowering them? "I was told it was because they were happy to fall into line for the pretty ones."

Fabian laughs mockingly. "No disrespect to whoever said that, but they're stupid."

I'm not at all offended by that remark. "I don't want the people to just cave in to how it has always been."

"That's not at all what's happening. The people are feeling heard. And they finally have hope their voices are heard and will make a difference. That their casting a vote in the polls may sway the king and queen to choosing a ruler who will change what is happening. They're also finally getting to know the royals locked away for safety. I think girls are more smitten with the prince more than ever now they've seen and heard him. If they wanted to quiet the people with a pretty face, they should have just made Prince Gavril a heartthrob once he turned sixteen."

I laugh at that. Fabian smiles.

"And it's not just the girls still in the running that make a difference. Voices of girls who failed are powerful forces right now. Rachel, who was failed just after the people of Nerine fled, returned to her family there and is an avid advocate for supporting the royal family's attempts to make the camps successful and relocating the lost. She's likely to get voted in as their next representative.

"Though Hanna may give her a run for her money. If either of them runs, the current seat is a lost cause. I don't know if they only qualify for a city seat or higher, though. That could influence their positions. There were two others from Nerine who failed too. I don't think they have a girl left in the running, but Rachel and Hanna are making an impact for sure."

"Who are the others?" I ask curiously.

"Roshan who failed very early on. And Latana."

Who could forget Latana? The sweetheart toymaker with big brown eyes and long black hair that was so sure she was too sexy for the prince to resist. She'd failed the chastity test for dressing too scantily if I recall correctly.

"Roshan tried to get attention, but she lost so early, her fame faded once Latana failed. Latana hasn't advocated much, but that's wise as she has a lot of young courtiers trying to get court positions who are eyeing her. The other two failed at the same time I think, after the people fled the city," Fabian goes on. "And their coming back to the camps and rallying the people to action certainly made a difference. I don't know if they are trying to set themselves up for an office run in a year, but they certainly haven't failed to try to make a difference to their fled-city neighbors."

"What are the other girls doing?" I ask curiously.

"Oh, I don't keep tabs on all of them. Just those of note I've heard of." Fabian leans back, looking up at the ceiling as he thinks.

"Marigold is more recent, but she's making an impact in Formeot. Though what difference that will make remains to be seen. They deal with a lot there with pressure from Japcharia and of course being one of the largest fishing towns in the nation. The largest not in the islands, for sure. They deal with much of the civil aspect of the civil war, mostly dealing with docks being raided or ruined. That's where the angry merchant tried to ram his boat into the docks.

"Jaine went back to Anthurium and is very outspoken against all rebellions. She might end up leader of some Royalist branch up there at this rate, though I'd prefer her get some kind of court seat. She seems to blame rebels for her getting kicked out from what my sources who interviewed her tell me. It's hard when they aren't permitted to say much about the Enthronement until it's over. But she's another one I see making a difference."

Fabian pauses a moment to think. Then his eyes light up. "Though I hear a Lady Violet from Gaillardia is stirring some rebel trouble. She is quite angry with the royal family. Though that area has had rebel trouble on and off for years, so it's hard to tell if she's making that worse or not, but it was quite the story to cover when she came home furious at the royal family and calling them all sorts of names. Most didn't take her seriously, but I can see her choosing whatever rebellion would help her get back at them most."

"She wouldn't," I gasp in shock and horror.

"Oh, a woman scorned is a dangerous thing." Fabian shakes his head. "Thankfully, she's not much of a threat other than getting people riled up. She was a stable hand by trade, and though pretty, too outspoken against the royals for any noble to really give her a serious consideration for marriage."

He sighs. "And the only other girl of note I can think of is Elice, who failed more recently. That girl could command her own army," he chuckles. "She's out there rallying people all over. She was a wanderer swordswoman, you see. She'd do shows and challenge people for money across Purerah. And she's doing it again, but this time on a campaign to stop the wars. The skills she learned in diplomacy and ladyship are serving her well. I hope they give her a good position. I'd never pick her for princess or queen, but she's fabulous! I told my editor to put someone on her, and he did. If you win, remember to have her work for you."

I laugh at that. "But thankfully most girls are choosing to keep under the radar as far as I know. Of course, that's to protect themselves from being denied good positions or drawing attention of rebels. Elice foiled an assignation attempt by some rebels. I'm sure Loyalists or Custods, but I can't say which as I was not there."

My father may have tried to have Elice killed? I shudder at the thought.

"She actually killed the would-be-assassins herself. She is frightful with a blade," Fabian chuckles. "Maybe she can run your security." I give Fabian a look. He laughs again, loving my reaction. "But after that, I think Chosen who leave will keep their heads down. I don't know what kind of transition aid the royal family provides, but hopefully it's that advice."

I sit down, eyes lost in through, rubbing my arms in the cold as I sit down. "It's all so much more complicated than I thought."

"Most people only see their side of it. That's normal." He smiles at me.

I return the smile. "So, if you see more than your part, why are you only a reporter when you could have a court position?"

"I told you, I want to make a mark on history, not by being mentioned in it, but writing it. Like I said, people only see their part. As a courtier, I'd be in that bubble. But as a reporter, my bubble is to see every side, not judge or put my twist on them if I can — easier said than done — and try to understand them all. And so making my bubble inside everyone else's bubbles lets me see more than I would on my own. Besides," he looks around conspiratorially, "you have any idea how fun it is to stir up a scandal."

I laugh. "No. And I don't plan to."

"Aww, my lady, you are missing out," Fabian laughs. "There's something fun about knowing you caused a stir, seeing people react to your work, good or bad. There's just something enjoyable about seeing reactions."

"You should have been an actor. Your job is to get reactions," I point out.

"But they're expecting it, and it doesn't last. It's just the magic that lasts in the realm of the theater. These reactions will cross history far into the future as generations look back and learn about the nutty five-hundred-year civil war of Purerah." Fabian is clearly trying to charm me into it, but honestly, it just sounds like pride.

"A show can leave a lasting impression on a person, good or bad. And I don't have to force them to feel anything," I say with a hint of smugness. "I don't need the world. My audience is enough for me."

"Perhaps I am a little greedy," Fabian chuckles. "But I put those skills to great use in a live interview."

"You're wasted on reporting."

"Ah!" His gasp of offense would make Ericka jealous. "How dare you?" Fabian mockingly clutches at his heart. We both laugh.

"I imagine it's more stable for your family?" I guess.

"For my wife and I, not really. She doesn't come with me when I go up north. She stays here at home." Fabian shrugs. "I think she hopes it will lure me out of it one of these days."

"Well, she married you."

"She used to come with me. I think she found it dull as she didn't have to report. Besides that, it likely made her feel pointless and why put her in danger? She does a wonderful job giving me a home to come back to."

"What does she do while you're gone?"

"Teach, I think. Teachers are rare around here, so I think she pitches in. When I'm home, she just handles the house."

"Does she look like me? Is that why I'm your favorite?" I tease.

He laughs. "You'll have to wonder."

"I hear your cousin works here?"

"He started to work for the prince while I was up north, and no one in my family told me." Fabian uses the tone of mock offense again. "So when I'm in town I'll bug him for quotes or information. Though now I'm covering the Enthronement, it's even more fun."

"I'm sure." I roll my eyes.

"Well, we grew up together. I'm a bit older than they are, but we had quite the adventures. And their father had the seat before my brother did, and though he's retired, he has quite the tirade about the state of things. He'll go on and on. I imagine that's part of how a lot of us in that second generation went into positions that revolve around that. His son is the prince's valet. I'm the lead reporter. His nephew took his position. His niece is a lawyer specializing in tax law. We are quite the civic bunch."

"Isn't that normal for a noble family?"

"It can be. Or not. There are only so many actual court positions to go around. Plus, you have to be elected every so often. And though tradition is that the seat goes to a noble family that held it, it's not required. Back when there were less Custods and less separation between Custod and Potentiate governments, a Custod actually won mayorship of the high city of Emilimoh. He kept the office for two or three terms, I believe. I've not looked in a while. That was back in the Merlin's time."

"Could a Custod run now?"

"I don't think there is an official rule, but it's supposed to be someone with a noble rank, but Custods are considered honorary nobility in every nation. Since the beginning they've been sirs and dames, so technically they could. I think the Head Custod might object. Custods are supposed to not be bound to any one nation or people. Being on one of the courts might mess with that."

I chuckle. "That it would." One of my biggest flaws as a Custod. I am painfully aware of this. "Do you know many Custods?"

"Not on a personal level, no. I've interviewed a few and some who would call themselves Custods. I mentioned the Custod rebellion leader, but I've interviewed many captured Custod rebels as well as those not in custody. They can spout the rules to you as if they are Custods. It's actually rather sickening."

I feel sick at the thought too. Did Father lead those poor men to feel like they were Custods? There are only two ways to be one: marriage or birth. I can see convincing people that they are Custods would make it easier to get rebels on your side. A fresh wave of anger washes over my heart with a mix of sadness for them. The Head Custod really couldn't be allowing that, could he? Did he know?

"Have you ever tried to interview the Head Custod about the Custod rebels?"

"Oh no. I'd love to, but I don't know if he's ever been to Purerah in my time." Fabian shakes his head.

"And you've never left?"

"Well... the army of huskies around him makes that hard."

I laugh.

"The Head Custod is quite busy. His family runs the Armuary theater; they breed the most pure-bred huskies, and of course he's the Head Custod. Admittedly, I'm pretty sure his children do most of the breeding. Though I hear he is particular about being the sole owner of the school and theater."

A big grin slips onto Fabian's face. "I bet you knew that."

"I did." I sigh. I had always dreamed of going to that school as a girl but knew it would never happen. To perform at the world's first full scale professional theater. The idea of being a soloist, let alone the prima actress for that theatre, is the daydream of every little ballerina/actress in the world. And being a Custod made me feel even more connected to it all.

"I bet you they'd jump at the chance to have you now." Fabian is still grinning.

"I doubt it. They have better than me.'" I shrug. "Why would they want a girl from the ghetto of Purerah?"

"Don't sell yourself short. I haven't heard you, but you handle a live interview as well as any actress that silly theater has."

I laugh again. "Still."

"Well, if you don't win, shoot them a letter. I'm sure they'd love to take you," Fabian says. "Unless you'd rather Purerah's stage."

"They'd never take me. Maybe if they did. I don't know if I could ever go home. Things would be too different." Father would never forgive me. I wish that escape was possible. Though I'd rather be here with my people and Gavril, the idea of dancing on that stage, singing under that magical chandelier... is a dream come true.

There's a knock at the door, and it slides open. I get up quickly, ready for a fight, but it's just a guard. "Coast is clear," she says to us. "You better return to your rooms."

I am anxious to make sure my maids are safe. If they got to the second floor, they could have gotten further.

Fabian follows me out and gets my attention before I vanish. "I won't use that to affect your feature," he promises me. "But it was nice to speak with you, my lady." He bows low to me.

I'm so anxious about my maids, I don't realize until I'm in my room waiting for them to check on me that he bowed lower than was needed. That was the bow meant for royalty. And Fabian, as a man from a noble family, knew it.

Chapter 21

There is an odd tension the next morning at the breakfast table. I look at the royal table to see if I can figure out what is wrong, but the tension does not seem to be coming from them. They are acting normal. It must be something from the other girls, but I cannot figure out what. Had something happened in the safe room in the Ladies' Chamber?

That tension carries over into our lessons. Lady Keva does her best to ignore it. We're still getting ready for the court dinner, learning the common etiquette and traditions about how to handle the court. She and Lady Hydrengia often have to tag team lessons when it comes to events like this as they are also helping us learn all the different levels of court. The one that is hardest to keep straight is which committee each member of court is on, but Lady Keva keeps whispering we don't really need to know right now, and to try not to stress.

Perhaps that is the tension in the room. But I cannot help but think that couldn't be it. Something must have happened during the attack I didn't see because I wasn't in the safe room with them. Many girls are giving each other dark looks, more than normal.

I get my normal share, but there's a new air of mistrust between the girls that I'm not sure I'd ever seen before. Forsythia is oddly quiet. Since she'd proclaimed herself the new favorite, she was quite happy to take the spotlight, but not today. She's getting dark looks, and she's giving them too.

No matter how carefully I try to keep track of the exchanges of looks, I cannot even hazard a guess at what is going on. There's no connection that I can see. Zelda and Bella don't seem to be glaring at anyone. Azalea might be or perhaps the expression is more like that of fear or worry. Lilly, as normal, isn't looking at anyone if she can help it.

At break, I try to fish for answers. "Not sure what you're talking about." Bella sips at her tea. "Did something happen to you? We were all fine."

"I was fine. It's just that everyone seems tense," I try to lure her into explaining.

"No. Maybe everyone is just extra envious today," Azalea offers.

She looks at Lilly who quickly pipes in too. "All was fine."

"Are you sure?" I frown deeper. It's like they are trying to hide something from me. "Did someone say something? Like what happened with that one girl, the one who was sent home, after the first attack?"

"Oh no. Nothing like that." Bella laughs it off, but it seems too forced to me. Something had happened.

Zelda is sitting with the other born princesses as the princesses demand. But she and the princesses are talking per normal. Nothing seems wrong. If something had happened that my friends think they should protect me from, at least Zelda would be honest with me about it. She doesn't even notice me looking though.

Lady Hydrengia addresses the tension in her lesson, but she assumes its nerves about the upcoming event and assures us that though it is of "the utmost importance to make a good impression", we need not be so stressed over it that we're as tense as piano wires. But it doesn't seem to help.

The tension at lunch is, if anything, worse. I notice quite a few girls are glaring at Isla, which I find odd. Isla is a sweet, shy thing who'd never hurt anyone. What had she done to get girls glaring at her?

Gavril has noticed the tension too and is looking around at us with his brow slightly furrowed. I notice him glancing at Sage as if asking him if he knows what is going on, but Sage just shakes his head, studying us with that surly look he gets.

I go about my normal afternoon, hoping to catch Zelda to see if she'll tell me what's going on. Had Forsythia made another scene with the prince? No, that does not make sense. She is glaring at others too. She was as smug and cool as a mint when she made the last show. And the way the glares are not just for one girl has to mean it wasn't someone else getting a public display of affection.

Sadly though, when I go into the Ladies' Chamber, Zelda isn't there. I wonder if she's on a date. I sigh and decide to try to get into the book I'd been trying to read with hope that she'd return.

I'm sitting reading for about ten minutes when a huff breaks through my reading. "Look at her just sitting there like nothing is wrong," Ericka sneers at me.

"E-excuse me?" I frown in confusion.

"Everything is normal," Bella shoots back.

"Oh, it's so not." Ericka shakes her head. Cuppy snarls on her lap. "We all know one of us is letting those cursed rebels in, and we're all ignoring the obvious choice."

I pale. "I did not let them in." Why did they think I had? But if they start going to the royal family insisting it was me, what if they find out about my father?

"Oh please, you were the only one missing who could have done it," Ericka jibes.

"She is not," Bella defends. "Dahlia, Florence, and Isla were missing."

"And you think sweet Isla did it?" Ericka retorts.

"I didn't say she did. Just that we don't know. You shouldn't throw around accusations." Bella holds her head high.

"How do we know it wasn't Dahlia?" Kamala demands.

"Excuse me? Keep that big mouth shut," Dahlia snarls at her.

"Well, it could have been. Would explain how nothing more than a ball player got so far," Kamala laughs.

"You're one to talk, grocer," Dahlia mocks back.

"At least it provides skills a princess can use. You being a rebel makes perfect sense. Why everyone just seems to love you and you get so far when you're nothing more than an athletic celebrity," Kamala sniffs. "And we all know you'd do anything to knock out the competition."

"Oh hush. You just want to get on Dahlia's nerves," Ericka chides Kamala. "We all know it's her." She points at me. "She just has the prince so wrapped around her finger they can't bring themselves to throw her out. That's really why she was in the throne room at the Harvest, and why she has gotten so far, and why the press eats her up. I'm sure they're full of rebels too."

"You only say that because your feature wasn't glowing," Azalea accuses.

"Come off it. We all know it's Kascia." Forsythia glares at me. "She's always the one pointing out the people have a point in their complaints and making the perfect face to the press to protect herself. Her family isn't happy she's here? Because they aren't rebels like her."

That one cuts me to the core. It's the other way around. "You think I want him dead?" I shoot back, but my voice shakes.

"See? Even the perfect actress slips when slapped with the truth," Dahlia laughs at me.

I fight not to let my lip shake. They're wrong. I'm not... not anymore. I am trying to protect them.

"You'd not mind doing the deed yourself. Weird kinks and all." Forsythia's tone makes my face flush with anger, and honestly, hatred. How dare she accuse me of such a thing!

"You're the seductress who'd love to murder him like some sick praying mantis!" I scream at her.

The whole room goes quiet, staring at me in shock. "Touched a nerve," Forsythia smirks. "Too close to the truth."

I fight the tears as I try not to release my anger. I'm so tired of being unsure. Having her accuse me of being what I once was and am trying not to be shakes me more than I thought it would. The snake who is trying to win by hypnotizing the prince with her charms accusing me of trying to black widow my way to the throne for the rebels is too low of a blow.

I wish I had a reply. All the ones I can think of would either make it look worse or confess something far too personal. I flounder for what to say or do as I fight not to scream or cry. How dare they? I'm not a rebel. Not anymore.

"You're lucky Sir Sage can't prove anything, or he'd have you out on a gallows before dinner," Forsythia mocks.

"You arrange that attack, so he'd kiss you?" Ericka joins in the mockery.

"You can't prove anything," Bella defends. "She wasn't the only one missing yesterday, remember?"

"You really think it was scared little Isla?" Forsythia asks with a mock baby voice. "Or Florence who's too anxious to even show all she knows about law in class? She's a lawyer, for Merlin's sake."

Florence blushes. "I don't want to be a showoff or make it harder to learn."

But that is a point. Hadn't Florence been one of the girls I couldn't find in the Harvest impressions? I could use that to defend myself, but maybe then they'd just say I was trying to throw suspicion off myself because I'm the rebel.

"No way she'd have the nerve to join the Enthronement just to kill the royals. She'd have to have guts," Forsythia points out.

Poor Florence turns pink but doesn't speak either. How do you defend yourself when defending yourself is seen as evidence against you?

"That's not fair," Isla dares speak up. "Just because they were missing doesn't mean they did it. Kascia was with us in the room for the first attack."

"She could have opened the door and they came in later," Forsythia waves off.

"Then so could any of you," Bella shoots back. "How do we know it wasn't you and you're just trying to deflect attention for yourself?"

"Oh my vene, Forsythia. Really?" Ericka looks at her.

"I've been with you all for every single attack," Forsythia laughs.

"And you didn't just 'leave the door open'?" Azalea points out.

"Not saying you did it, but that's about as strong evidence for you as Kascia," Bella agrees.

"As much evidence?" Ericka laughs. "There's so much that it's Kascia. It's why Sir Sage hates her. We all know he does. He just can't prove it, and it drives him nuts. She almost showed her true colors at the Harvest but used her clever acting to make them all think it was to defend him. She's the one with the most skill. She can kill."

"She killed a rebel!" Bella points out. "Are you a complete idiot? If she let them in, why kill her own guy?"

"Best cover ever," Ericka says slowly.

Bella rolls her eyes. "There's as much evidence its your stupid dog."

Ericka gasps as if mortally wounded. "How dare you. Take that back!"

"Well, there is." Bella turns to the rest of the girls. "We can easily make up evidence that it's any one of us, most of all with the idea that you can return to the Ladies' Chamber after letting them in for a cover. And just because she's not in the Ladies' Chamber doesn't mean it's her. That evidence makes it just as likely it was the prince."

"The prince wouldn't let people in to kill him," Ericka laughs at what she sees as Bella's stupidity.

"That's my point. We have just as much hearsay and evidence for him or the king or queen or Sir Sage or anyone else in this palace," Bella insists. "Pointing fingers isn't going to help anyone."

Bella would be a better choice for queen than me. She is handling their accusations better than I could. I'm still trying not to cry at those hurtful accusations and how close to true they are.

"Yeah, but Kascia said she came to avoid an old boyfriend. What cover would be more stupid? Clearly rebel cover up if you ask me," Kamala huffs.

I want to scream how much I hate Jake, but that will also make me look guilty. Because I am. I am a rebel. I was born a Custod, and like Fabian said, there is no way to stop being a Custod rebel. I am still trapped in that group. I am one of them. My father is their leader. I'm still his daughter. Still trapped in their rebel lies.

"You're just scared she'll do better than you in the tests so want her thrown out," Bella accuses Kamala. "There's no point arguing about it when we can prove nothing. It just makes more bad blood when we have enough of that."

"It's a contest, girl. That's how it's going to be," Forsythia chuckles darkly at Bella's naivety. "And one of us is here just to kill the prize we're fighting for. Of course we're out for blood, bad or not."

"Then get evidence and stop throwing accusations. Or are you hoping to scare someone into confessing to cover up it's you? Deflecting to everyone else to show it's not you?" Bella challenges.

"You think I need to deflect? The prince would never buy it was me in a million years." Forsythia tosses her hair over her shoulder. "I could be the rebel and still win. I'm not, but even if I was, it wouldn't matter. I'd have him and the throne. He'd be so wrapped around my finger, I wouldn't have to kill him to get the changes I want."

"How can you be so heartless?" Azalea frowns.

"I said 'if' cupcake." Forsythia gives Azalea a smile. "I don't need to do any of those things. He's my sweet prince, my knight in shining armor. I don't have to lure him into anything. He does the work for me."

"How is that any different than saying he's your puppet?" Florence accuses.

"Now who's throwing around accusations to look innocent?" Forsythia smiles at Florence who narrows her eyes back. "I'm not accusing just anyone. I'm saying it's Kascia. It's why her parents are mad at her. It's why she suddenly lost all her confidence. She's a rebel and now she's stuck because she can't do the job and can't go home without fulfilling her mission."

"Innocent until proven guilty," Florence snaps at Forsythia. "And you keep on like that, she'll have a right to sue you and win."

"She won't. Because I'm not wrong. Am I?" She gives me a sickly sweet smile.

"Are you? Yes, you are a praying mantis," I retort with the only defense I can think of.

Half the girls burst into laughter. Forsythia's face turns red. "Still distracting and deflecting, rebel?"

I wish I had a reply for that, an answer of any kind, but I don't. So I look down. She's right. If she was wrong, it would be easy, but I am a rebel. I'm a plant. I came here to let my father kill the prince. I have nothing but my change of mind as proof. And how would that protect me in the hungry pride of lionesses ready to attack and remove anyone who stood between them and the lion they wanted?

"Forsythia, seriously, that's enough, or I'll help Kascia sue you while the Enthronement is happening, I swear," Florence warns.

"She'll never agree to it because I'm right. Go ahead. That will get us the evidence we need to get her hanged. I wonder if they'll let us watch."

I can't hide the tears anymore. I move to get up, but Bella speaks up. "You're a sick brix, you know that?"

The whole room goes painfully quiet at Bella's harsh language.

"Is that how a princess speaks?" Forsythia shakes her head in mock disappointment.

"It is when it's the truth. You're just trying to stamp out the only girl you see as real competition. If the prince knew what you were doing, he'd throw you out immediately."

"You going to tell him? Go ahead. He'll have to prove I'm wrong first. Then we'll find the truth of the rebel." Forsythia smirks at me again. "And he knows you all are jealous of me. He'll figure out you're just trying to do what you say I'm doing, 'getting the competition thrown out'."

"I hope the rebels get you before I do if I'm made princess because I'll make sure you pay for this," Bella snarls at Forsythia.

"And win or not, I'll make sure to help. You can't just accuse people this intensely. I'll help her charge you with whatever it takes," Florence agrees.

"Please do. If she's right, we'll finally get rid of all three of you," Ericka laughs. Her dog barks as if he's trying to laugh too.

I'm done listening to this. I get up.

"Oh, the rebel's going to run away to her old boyfriend. Going to let him in to get us?" Forsythia mocks.

I can't muster a reply as I leave. "Kascia." Bella follows after me.

"Just leave me alone," I say through my tears. I can't tell her why it hurt so much.

"No one believes a word of that," Bella assures me. "We all know she is just trying to get to you. I'm seriously going to tell the prince what she did. We'll make her pay for it."

"Please don't." Sage will look further into it and find my father, I'm sure.

"Kascia, she can't hurt you. You need to stand up to her."

"I can't." Because she's right.

Bella sighs. "Fine. Then we'll have to do it for you." She turns around.

"Where are you going?"

"I'm going to tell the prince."

"You can't. You'll be eliminated for asking for his time," I remind her. "Please don't get thrown out for me."

"He won't care. It's not like I'm asking for a date. And someone has to. You're not what she said. You did try to defend us. And I'm tired of letting her bully you," Bella says firmly. "I'll go to the cursed king if I have to."

"Bella, please."

But Bella ignores me and marches towards the throne room. I bite my lip and a few tears slip down my face.

"But she's right," I whisper to myself before I burst into tears. I'm no longer a threat to the prince or these girls, and I was not letting them in, but I was a rebel. Those names she called me are true, and no amount of wishing would change that.

No one is using the practice room, so I go in there to hide. I sit in the far corner and sob. I hate what I am. I hate what my father made me into. I hate this stupid game, those stupid girls, this mess that is my life. I want to go home so badly it aches, but that home is not real anymore. It is a lie worse than the one I am trapped in.

No matter how I change, Forsythia is right. I came here to ensure Prince Gavril died to save my own skin. Alright, to save my people; I am not that bad. I should not paint it that bleak. But if I let those girls defend me, they'd only be proven wrong. I am a plant. I'm just not the one letting them in now.

A sharp meow makes me jump. I look down to see Nippers looking at me with his large blue eyes. He meows more gently and puts his paws on my knees, sniffing at my tear covered face as if asking if I'd mind making room for him to cuddle me.

"Why? I'm just a rebel," I sniff and hug myself tighter.

The meow I get in reply is so offended I can't help but look up at him in confusion. He uses that to jump up between my knees and stomach and rubs my tears away by rubbing my face with gentle purrs. I get a distinct feeling of "no, you're not" wash over me.

It helps slow the tears. I give him a weak smile. "I'm trying not to be, but I can't ever admit the truth to anyone here. I'll be hanged. She's right." I feel sick recalling how she gloated about watching.

Nippers meows as if saying he'd not allow it before he keeps purring and rubbing my face to get all the tears off on his soft fur.

I don't know how it comforts me so deeply, but it does. I need to learn how to handle these girls. If I want to be what my people need, I'd have to grow into the princess who can. I cannot let these women belittle me. Even if I win, I'm sure the court will try to belittle me as well as the rebels or anyone else who wants the power I'll have.

As odd as this thought sounds, the cat is right. If I love the prince, if I really want the life I keep saying I want, I'll have to make the choice to get there. I'll have to work at it, get over it, ignore what I am so I can become something more. I may never be able to get rid of my father inside of me, but I can use the Custod in me to be better.

If I truly love the prince, I'll have to be the girl he needs and not just what he wants. I'll need to do more than just outdo the other girls. I'll have to be so good I'm not worried about them. If I was the favorite once, I could do it again. But how?

I recall my plan. It seems so silly now. Giving the prince a pet is not going to magically make me unafraid of the other girls. It is not going to make Gavril forget how Forsythia charms him or whatever it is about Bella that caught his eye.

But it's all I have. And I have to prepare for this holiday the same way I did the last one. The Harvest was a battle I was prepared for, even if it terrified me. Christmas is going to have to be the same. Though it isn't going to be a battle of arms or letting combatants in, it was going to be a battle of character between my fears and my dreams.

Chapter 22

I'm so anxious about my newfound resolve, handing my feature's release and the tree-topping that night that I forget it's also the day the puppy is being delivered, but I'm reminded as I walk into my room to see her sleeping on the dog bed I picked up for her. She'll stay in my room, hidden until Christmas.

She's just waking up, yawning hugely and shaking her head. I smile. She is so cute. She's grown since I saw her, but only a little. Her ears are more perky, and she isn't as fluffy, more streamlined than a puffball.

My maids are about their normal work, and Damian is too, but surprisingly, Damian's brother, Cedrick, is there. He did say he'd help train the dog. He is leaning on the wall next to my balcony door, one foot resting on the wall behind him, arms folded, watching the dog slowly wake up and yawn.

He and Damian look alike and yet are so different. Cedrick is not as thin as Damian, more muscular and more hallowed in the cheeks. He has stunningly electric blue eyes and an annoyingly charming smile. His hair curls in a wild stylized mess contrasting Damian's perfect straight ponytail. Damian has a friendly warmth, but Cedrick has a caring warmth about him that makes girls weak in the knees.

"Good afternoon. I hope you had a good lunch. You might want the energy," Cedrick tells me. "She's just about ready to find out she's back with you. From what Damian told me, she'll be over the moon about that."

I smile a little as I watch the little red husky shake her head and look around. She's so sleepy she doesn't quite take in that she's not where she expected. She shakes her whole body and gets up, licking her lips before she makes a little nervous sound.

She looks up at Cedrick, and Cedrick smiles at her. It's like he spoke to her without words. The puppy pants a little as if trying to be excited as she walks towards the windows. Cedrick nods and takes the dog outside to relieve itself. I don't know how Cedrick cleans it up, but he assures the maids he did when he puts the dog back down in the enclosure.

The puppy sits down sleepily and scratches her ear with a back leg, too sleepy to quite take everything in just yet. When she's done, she shakes herself and makes a little sound and stands up, tail wagging and looking around for a playmate.

At first, when no littermates appear, her tail slows a bit. But then she spots me. Her tail goes mad; she pants in excitement and makes high pitched "talking" sounds and does a spin on the spot of excitement.

I giggle and walk over to reach into the enclosure and let the puppy sniff me before patting her. She pants more happily and sits as if that will give her more attention.

"Training time." Cedrick tosses me a tug toy.

I take it. "Fetch?"

"Oh no, bonding and getting them tired enough for formal training," Cedrick says. "Get in there with her and play some tug-of-war. Dogs are good at that."

I look at Damian. How are these two so different?

Damian smiles at me. "Don't look at me. I'm not playing tug with her."

I shake my head. "You two are so different," I say as I get in and kneel to play tug with the puppy.

"Of course, we are. It's how I keep him sane." Damian nods at his brother.

I laugh at the idea. Cedrick shakes his head. "It's quite literal," he says. "Now if you want her to let go, hold it still so it's dull, then when she lets go, say 'yes' and start playing again."

I give it a few tries. It works quickly, and we get a back-and-forth game of tug going really well. She's quite energetic, jumping over my lap if I pull the toy to my other side. She yips playfully and play-growls quite a bit. I find it quite cute.

Cedrick goes over a few other training techniques and practices which is a lot of fun. When the puppy is getting more tired, Cedrick asks Damian if there's anything else he should cover.

"Well, as she is going to be Gavril's dog, she should know Gavril's face," Damian says as he hands him some impressions.

"Hmm, are you saying we should play the name game?" Cedrick asks him.

Damian nods. "I think that would be best. There are some images of Sage and the king and queen as well."

"Perfect." Cedrick sits down with his legs crossed and clicks his tongue to get the puppy's attention. "Copy me," he tells her. She walks over and sits in front of him as if she perfectly understands. I frown. That is amazing.

"Gavril," he says slowly, showing the dog an impression of him. It's a nice one. I wonder where it came from.

The puppy tilts her head and starts trying to copy Cedrick's words. It takes her a few tries. Cedrick gives her a treat when she gets close. I'd never seen anything like it before. She is making sounds like talking and trying to "say" names.

After she gets comfortable with Gavril, Cedrick shows him Sage. The poor puppy has a very hard time with Sage. I think more syllables are easier. After a few tries, she makes a 'wo-wro' that makes me think she's saying "weird-do". Cedrick loses it laughing, dropping the impressions as he laughs and looks at his brother, sharing the joke.

Damian drops his needle laughing and is holding his head up with his hand.

"What?" I ask, watching them laugh so hard.

The puppy thinks she has succeeded though because Cedrick drops the treat, and she gobbles it up, saying "wo-wro" over and over to get more.

"Did she just say what I thought she did?" Damian smiles.

Cedrick nods. "Not on purpose, but she is now."

"It sounds like 'weirdo,'" I say.

"It does," Damian chuckles then looks at the puppy. "Is that Sage's name now?"

The puppy tilts her head in confusion.

"Let's try this." Cedrick tries having the dog say my name which turns out really cute. She kind of huffs then makes a little squeak for the second syllable. Cedrick treats that, then tries Gavril again and gets the opposite. A huff then a lower little growl. Then he tries Sage. "Wo-wro," she says right away.

Cedrick is on the floor laughing. He must not care for Sage much either.

Damian chuckles. "Oh, he'll love that."

"I don't know if I could get her to change her mind if I tried." Cedrick sighs. "She likes our reactions."

"True." Damian smiles with a nod. "Or is it because you like it too much?" He smiles at his brother.

"I haven't tried yet, but I have a feeling she'll go for it anyway," Cedrick replies. "She likes the laughs."

"Sure." Damian smiles then starts looking for his needle to get back to his work.

Cedrick keeps working on various types of training until he can tell the puppy has had enough. He sits back and lets her explore as much as she can.

The puppy tries to get Damian's attention. He ignores her until she starts singing. "Sounds like you need singing lessons," Damian teases her.

She pants even more and starts a kind of howling singing. I guess it got Damian's attention the first time.

Damian watches her a moment. "You like that?"

She huffs a sound that makes me think of "yeah". Then her tail wags so madly her whole-body wiggles with it.

Damian chuckles then gets up and goes over to her. "Oh, alright." He pets her head.

She pants happily and licks at his hand in thanks but then tries to bite a little. "Ah, ah, ah." Damian pulls back his hand. "No."

The puppy makes a whiny kind of "no" sound back, as if in question.

"No biting," Damian says. "Well, you're supposed to be a guard dog, so I suppose just – no biting friends."

"Oo?" The puppy questions again. It sounds a lot like no.

"Friends. Nice." Damian starts petting her.

She tries to play-bite again.

Damian pulls his hand away and gives her a look. "If you are going to be that way about it, I won't pet you at all."

I frown as I watch. Perhaps a playful husky was a bad idea. How would Gavril react to her being mouthy like that? The anxious knot in my chest tightens. It's too late now, but what if it just makes everything far worse? I think she's perfect and adorable. But would Gavril? I felt sure as I know he's not a stuck-up royal type like his mother, but perhaps a retriever or something a little more dignified instead of going for the most silly and full of personality breeds I know of.

The puppy makes a complaining sound at Damian and walks along the wall of her enclosure again. Her little talking sounds sound like "oh no" to me as she paces.

Damian chuckles and shrugs. "It's your own fault."

The puppy starts her howling again. I look at Cedrick. Shouldn't he be training her out of this? But he seems to want to watch the show.

Damian sits back down in his chair. "Maybe a little later, if you're good, you'll get waffles. If you're good," he tells her, eyeing her.

The puppy tilts her head and copies the word "waffle" best she can.

"Yes, if you're good," Damian says.

She pants happily and then tries to get my maids' attention again. My maids giggle, having a harder time not listening to her whining. Vivian holds up alright, but after about five minutes, Flur caves in.

Once she's done with Flur, the puppy comes back to play with me. I do a bit of wrestling with her. Cedrick jumps when she accidentally bites too hard, and I give a rather loud little cry of surprise. That really hurt.

Damian looks up, wincing in sympathy. "You alright?"

Cedrick nods. "I'm fine. Just spooked me," he says.

"Sorry, her teeth are sharp," I say as I rub her down more gently to see if we can calm her a bit.

"Sorry, should have warned you." Damian smiles a little.

"I mean, I knew that, but I didn't expect that," I admit, rubbing the puppy down so she'd settle. It works. She nuzzles against my leg, huffing happily.

Damian smiles at her. "You going to behave now?"

She huffs happily again, her sweet blue eyes looking up at Damian innocently. She is a cuddle bug when she wants to be.

Damian smiles at her then pulls out his watch and checks the time. "Blast it. I said I was going to do that..." he mutters to himself then puts his watch away and looks at me. "If you'll excuse me, there's something I promised to do."

I assure him it's fine. Damian smiles at me and leaves. I smile a bit and keep stroking the red puppy until she falls asleep. I then go over the routine of looking after her with Cedrick and my maids.

Damian returns a short time later, smiling gently. "My lady, there is someone here who'd like to see you. Shall I show them in?"

"Oh." I get up and try to get the dog hair off as she sleeps. "Um... it's not Prince Gavril, is it?" How do I hide a dog next to my bed?

"No, it isn't," Damian chuckles.

I nod. "Alright. Yes, you may show them in." Damian nods then leaves then re-enters, holding the door for whoever it is.

I try to make sure I'm presentable. What if it's Sage with questions? Then again, he'd sneak in through the balcony door.

Who I see catches me completely off guard. There's only one person in the world who could have surprised me more.

My mother beams at me, her hair pulled back in its normal dirty blonde French braid bun, her outfit the one I knew from childhood: her leggings, wrap cardigan, and choker style everyday necklace, normally some kind of ribbon.

I freeze, my mouth falling open slightly. It couldn't be. I thought... How did she get here? I can't believe she's here. She's really here.

My eyes fill with tears. I bite my lips. I thought I'd not see her again unless I was in serious trouble. "Mom?" It is hard to resist looking like a real idiot in front of my maids and calling her 'Mommy'.

Mom smiles even wider and opens her arms and steps forward, making it just instinct for me to run up and hug her tightly, still trying to control the tears in my eyes. I'm so happy she's here and not mad at me. It's a relief and a worry at once. There's not a hint of anger or judgment in her, and it means the world to me.

Finally, we let go and pull back a bit to look at each other. We're just about the same height. Maybe she's a bit taller or maybe it's my imagination just being so used to her being taller than me. "What are you doing here?" How did she of all people get through?

"Someone was able to wiggle in the best job we have had in ages." Mother smiles at Damian. I frown. What did he do?

Damian chuckles. "I was only the point man. The king and queen are the ones to thank."

"What do you mean?" I ask.

"Well, you'll be hearing this soon from the king himself, but I suppose it wouldn't hurt to share," Damian says. "They decided since it is the holiday season, to give a little gift to all of you ladies. So, they asked if someone would be willing to reach out to the local troupe and see if they were willing to do two performances at the castle, and because I was already familiar with the troupe through you, they asked if I would do it, and I agreed. I'm only glad it wasn't too much on your troupe to move all of your sets," he adds to my mother.

"No, we had plenty of help, thank you." Mother smiles at me. I hope she doesn't mean Father's boys. Mother smiles her assurance, reading my expression correctly. "Don't worry; it wasn't a problem, but enough about that. Look at you." She beams, stepping back to get a better look at me.

I flush a little as I dab my eyes with my fingers. "They really did a good job with those layers, even when it's up. I told you we should have done those long ago," Mother teases, playing with one of the curls left to hang around my face.

I laugh. "We couldn't afford the upkeep."

"Still, they do it nicely." Mother smiles. "You look like you belong here." She sighs, a strange light in her eyes I'd seen before when we'd talk about my coming here. I want to ask but know it's not the time.

"So, you're doing two shows?" I ask.

She nods. "*The Nutcracker Suite* first then we'll do *A Christmas Carol* on Christmas Eve."

"What about the normal shows?" I frown. They could be out money doing this.

"Oh, we put the understudies on it." Mother waves off. "And these shows are easy to run. We have backup sets if things break, so we're set to go. They'll do the shows in the theater, and we're running our special team here." She's beaming in delight. In that case, they are in to make a lot of money.

"I'm not doing Belle, am I?" I ask. She laughs.

"I will," Cedrick jokes from where he'd been sitting as I sat with the dog.

Damian laughs. "Of course."

My mother shakes her head. "I have my cast just fine, thank you."

"You sure?" Cedrick teases.

"You may want to think about it. He's pretty good." Damian smiles and gives Cedrick a playful look.

"I may have some unique talent," Cedrick agrees.

"Maybe," Mother says doubtfully as Cedrick gets up.

"Have fun, and don't let her bite." Cedrick nods at the red puppy, sleeping away.

"They gave you a dog?" Mother frowns.

"No, she's my gift to Prince Gavril," I say.

"Hmm, kind of serious getting a pet together, isn't it?" Mother smiles.

"Mom!" That is not the kind of joke I expected from her. She just smiles. Damian chuckles as he steps back to give us space. "It's just for him. I don't have to be involved. I got permission," I say defensively.

"You need permission to give a grown man a dog?" Mother frowns.

I sigh. "Did you even read my letters?"

"I thought maybe it was hyperbole, at least a little." Mother frowns deeper. "Well, at least it's something fun, I suppose." She watches the puppy sleep. "But I'll be here through the holiday, and they did offer to let me stay to make sure things go smoothly with the sets and everything, so your father won't have a problem," she says it in a way that makes it sound like she means she's worried about losing the set pieces more than what is really going on.

"He isn't mad?" I ask.

"Oh, he doesn't have to know. I left a note," Mother says. That was gutsy. Father was never violent with us, but she'd deal with quite a yelling match when she got home. Sad thing is, I don't think my father will be that annoyed about spending the holiday alone. I feel like he'll spend it with Jake and his father. That is sad to think. How did I never see how obsessed he was with the mission? Well, I suppose as Custods, we have to be.

"And it will be worth it. I was glad to get to watch your last interview. Have you seen a sneak at your feature yet?" Mother asks.

I shake my head. "No, I haven't." I sigh. "Must be saving it for last. My interview had the most 'fireworks'." I rub my arms.

"You spoke your mind and made more sense than most," Mother says. "Nothing to be ashamed of. I'm sure it will be great." Mother turns to my maids, trying to recall their names correctly.

She then starts complimenting their work and asking me how they make some choices, making me smile to watch my two worlds finally meet in a pleasant way.

Damian smiles and steps up to me. "Good surprise?"

I beam and nod. "The best. How did you talk them into this?"

He shrugs. "The castle hasn't had a show in years. I suppose it dawned on them that it was time to change that."

"Right. Because Gavril never seeing a show was enough to 'inspire' them." I smile back. I don't buy it, but he can have his secrets.

"Oh, I don't know. Life without the theatre is a life of sorrow," Damian says. "Maybe they finally saw the truth of that."

"You've been reading my mother's walls again." My mother has posters with quotes like that all over the theatre walls, mostly in the rehearsal spaces.

Damian chuckles. "Well," he says with the tone of changing the topic, "I did have one more surprise for you, but err... she is flirting with a guard." He makes a face.

I laugh. "Why am I not surprised." That sounds like Alsmeria.

"Shall I see if I can entice her away?" Damian smiles.

"If you're not too busy," I joke.

He chuckles. "I'll see what I can manage."

I giggle too and watch as my maids show my mother some of the dresses she's already seen me wear in impressions.

A few moments later, Cedrick returns. I hadn't noticed him leaving. "Look who I found wandering about the guard," he jokes. "I thought I'd drop it off before it causes more trouble."

Alsmeria is beaming at me with excitement. Her smile lights up her almond face, and her bright brown eyes sparkle. She glances at Cedrick as he leaves and comes over to me and takes my hands like old times. "You are in the hot bed, Kascia. Forget the prince; look at that advisor. He's young, has the dreamiest eyes, and what a job." She beams. I roll my eyes. Maybe it was Jake's fault, but I never really had my boy crazy phase. Alsmeria seems to want to make up for it by never leaving hers.

Then she spots Damian. "And this just hangs out in your room all day." She gives me a look.

Damian smiles in question and arches a brow. "It's there supposed to be a pronoun that goes with that?"

"Not when it's a cute puppy!" She's spotted the napping red puppy. "Oh sorry." She covers her mouth, hoping she didn't wake it up. But no, the dog sleeps on with little more than a huff. She goes over to see her. "So cute." She holds in her desire to squeal. Damian shakes his head, amused, and returns to his work and tea. I sigh my apology for my nutty friend before I join her.

Alsmeria is as excitable as ever. "So? I've not seen him yet. How is it? Did I really miss out not getting in? Your mom tells us what you and that other girl write her."

"Other girl?" I frown. "Who?"

"The head maid, Hydie or something." Alsmeria pauses to think. I forgot she promised my mother to keep her updated too. So I guess my missing letters didn't leave her completely in the dark. But apparently, it gave the girls at the theater lots to gossip about, and my bubbly friend wants to know it all.

I try not to be sucked into her insistence for all the dramatic details. She asks if there are other cute boys there, and I admit I hadn't really looked. But the temptation to set her on Sage floats to my mind. It gets worse when she asks if the prince has any cute staff. "Like a guard or something."

"His Custod guard doesn't like me much. So I don't know how easy it would be to make friends with him," I admit. "But I'm pretty sure he's engaged. And honestly, I haven't noticed if he's cute."

"How do you not notice? Most of all with tall, dark and..." she turns to Damian. "Oh my vene, is he sewing?" Her eyes light up. "And supportive over there?"

I laugh. "My attendant. He's in charge of my look and... I guess, strategy for winning."

"So, he taught you how to interview like that?"

It's hard to listen to her questions while I watch Damian try to hide his laughter that Alsmeria is surprised by his sewing. Damian is fighting so hard not to laugh it looks like he's choking. His face is a little red as he holds it in.

"Hello?" Alsmeria's voice snaps me back.

"Sorry." I smile. "And not really. I mean he picks my look and works with my team, but nothing like that. We talk about things like that, but his plan is just to let me be me. Enhance my look, sure, but why pretend when that would mean I have to pretend to my husband my whole life?"

"A husband who is your biggest coworker in running a kingdom that likes to rip itself apart. I think some faking might be helpful. Then you don't get mad at each other," Alsmeria points out.

"Not sure I could live being fake," I say.

"But once you win you're in, so does it matter?" Alsmeria asks.

"Are you a test?" I demand.

She laughs. "Maybe." She grins.

"What happened to being yourself is queen?" I ask.

"I believe it." Alsmeria smiles. "But do you still believe it?"

"Of course." Though it may not be the best road to winning this.

Alsmeria looks at me doubtfully. "But?"

"But what?" I reply.

"But there's more you aren't saying. We can tell when you do that you know." Alsmeria gives me a slight smile.

"They can?" I try not to let my anxiety at the idea show.

"Well, I can. We have known each other longer than anyone." She smiles warmly at me. "So is it true or isn't it?"

"I just don't know if that's going to help me win anything," I confess as little as possible.

"Everyone else seems sure you're doing great. Are they wrong?" she asks.

I really don't want to talk about it. "I was doing well."

"And now?"

"I have no idea."

"Why not? It's about as complicated as any other relationship."

"Any other relationship where your boyfriend is dating fifteen girls at once," I quip back.

Alsmeria frowns. "I guess that does take competition to a new level. More like who can be the best teacher's pet with the prince as the teacher."

I shake my head. "It's the king and queen who decide who passes a test or fails. The prince has little say in it."

"That's worse." Alsmeria gives me that incredulous look that was her signature expression.

"It is worse."

"But you're doing great. Everyone knows it. I'm making so many friends with the people who join us because you are good at this. It's not just because they are your friend," she reminds me.

But she and they don't know my true past. And the other girls are throwing it in my face even if they can't prove it.

"Come on. You really don't think you're good at this? Have you seen your interviews? I suppose you can't." Alsmeria frowns. "But honestly, you get people talking better than anyone ever did. And I doubt the rumors of how much he likes you are just rumors."

"I honestly can't tell anymore, but I have to try." If I want to win, I'm going to have to ignore these fears.

"Well, we're always ready to help." Alsmeria smiles at me. "You know that, right?"

"Hard to help when I'm in here."

"Hey, rebels keep getting in. We can find a way."

That wins a laugh.

"It's been a while since I've seen you this unsure. Remember when you won your first real lead?" Alsmeria asks me.

"I was so excited."

"And the older girls were envious and made you feel you weren't good enough yet?" Almeria reminds me.

I had forgotten. It was more subtle than even the girls here, but the way they snickered at the smallest mistake or how slowly I learned the part.

"You got over it then, why not now?" Alsmeria asks me. "You've got it in you. Why we'll all vote for you when they present you."

"If I get that far."

"When." Alsmeria smiles and nudges me. "And that's why you need to help me find someone to wiggle me back into your court."

I laugh.

Alsmeria uses the change of conversation to ask how far I'd gone with the prince, had he kissed me yet, what kind of dates have I had? It makes me uncomfortable as I hadn't had many, and yet, we already feel more serious than most. Even if I am not his favorite, I know I am at least among them.

I feel a little sick and look down to see the puppy woke up and is slowly getting to herself. I smile. We take her out to relieve herself then we play with her, making the enclosure a little bigger, so all three of us can play with her until it's time to prepare for dinner and the events of the evening.

After some time, Damian approaches us with his hand clasped behind him. "My lady, it's time to get ready for dinner."

The puppy had just settled down to sleep again, so it was perfect. I get up and go over to let my maids get to work. "Oo, that is so dreamy," Alsmeria says. "How do I get them to call me that?"

"Win a spot in the Enthronement," I reply.

"I tried that. What else you got?" Alsmeria smiles.

"Help her win, and she'll give you a title," Mother teases, going over to see how my maids do their work on me.

"I'll go butter up the prince," she jokes and to my horror she actually leaves the room.

"She's not doing what I think she is, is she?" I look at Damian in shock.

"You really think she'll get past Sage?" Damian arches a brow.

"She will annoy her way through," I say firmly.

Mother nods. She had done it to her enough times.

"I don't think that's a worry," Damian says as he picks out jewelry for me.

I sigh. "I hope so."

My maids do their amazing work getting me ready for dinner then surprise my mother by helping her get ready too. They do remind her she doesn't have to, but she's happy to accept the dress and small makeover. My mother looks as much a lady as any of them. I would think she was Lady Keva's new assistant if I didn't know any better.

Damian beams to see us both dressed up. "You two are the prettiest sights I ever did see."

I flush, and Mother smiles. She takes my arm and whispers to me as we move down to dinner, "Maybe the sight will wise up your father." I giggle. He did like Mom in a good costume.

The dining hall is quiet. I think we're all worried about the interview tonight. I know I am. The girls are distracting themselves, talking about the massive influx of boxes coming into the castle. A few notice I come arm-in-arm with a lady they haven't seen before.

Just before my mother goes to sit where the rest of the servants, Alsmeria shows up holding a purring Nippers.

"Isn't he so cute? Is he the queen's?" she asks me. She always loved cats.

"No, he's a stray that wanders the castle," I say.

"No one catches him? I mean look." She strokes him some more.

"Oh, we can't really catch him to keep him or kick him out. Try either, and he vanishes and reappears when he pleases." I swear Nippers laughs. His purr gets a funny pattern like he's laughing. "Nippers," I scold.

"Nippers? He has a name. That's so cute. He needs a collar," she decides. She takes off the purple ribbon she had in her hair and tries to tie it to his neck. His blue eyes look off into the distance as if asking fate why. I think Alsmeria would have gotten negative points on the Nipper's board.

"Well, you can keep him away from the royal family and enjoy your meal," I say.

"Oh." Alsmeria recalls she can see the prince and looks over. "Oh yeah. Yeah." She nods. "There isn't a bad looking guy here, is there?"

"You can marry Nippers," I say. Nippers coughs as if he has a hairball.

"Aw, you okay?" Alsmeria frowns, stroking him. "You poor thing. I'll let you get dinner." She puts him down. He walks over to the servants' area.

"Just behave," I plead with her. "Don't get me kicked out."

"I'm never that bad." Alsmeria smiles. "And I'm flirting, not you," she assures me.

I return it weakly before I go to sit in my place.

"Who is that?" Lilly asks.

"My friend." I say.

"One of those rebels? We'll have an attack a day," Forsythia sneers.

"Why is she here?" Dahlia demands.

I open my mouth to explain when the king draws our attention. He coughs into that cursed handkerchief again. I wish he didn't. It makes me start every time.

"Thank you for your attention," he says warmly. "Though our guests can ignore us," he invites. Alsmeria's laugh is loudest. "As a special surprise for you ladies who are giving up the chance to be at home with your families for the holiday, and to help the local theatre, we commissioned them to come and perform two shows for us while you're here." He smiles. "First, *The Nutcracker Suite* will be performed the day before Christmas Eve, and we'll get to enjoy *The Christmas Carol* on Christmas Eve itself. Some of the performers will be staying in the castle through the holiday to manage the affairs and to minimize people coming in and out of the castle for security as we've had some breaches lately."

"A few?" I hear Kamala mutter.

"'Some' is being polite," Forsythia agrees. I should hit them both. Then I notice Nippers going under the table. I guess he's reading my thoughts because both girls kick at him under the table a moment later.

"We hope that brings some cheer," the king goes on, ignoring the complaints if he heard them at all, "but with that in mind, we would request you limit your time wandering the castle a bit more to keep safe. Stay in the Lady's Chamber or your rooms as much as you can. You are still allowed in the library, but we'd rather you stay safe with the main locations so if anything does happen, we can make sure you and all of our guests can get to safe rooms in time,

"If you have concerns, let your attendants know, and they'll reach out to us," the king finishes. "But, with that said, when you are done, please prepare for the tree lighting and then meet in the entrance hall, so the guards can lead us out together. Again, for safety." He nods at the girls before sitting back down with another cough. Gavril starts talking to him at once.

I flush as I hear Alsmeria telling my mother he'll be a good parent as he respects his parents. I love Alsmeria, but I had no idea she'd be this embarrassing. Nippers hops on my lap as if to cheer me up.

"Points!" Lilly cheers. She sure loves the Nipper's board.

Chapter 23

My mother and Alsmeria stay to mingle with the staff while I go to change into my first dress of the night. It's cold enough for snow, though we haven't gotten any yet. Damian has prepared a dress for that eventuality. Tonight's dress is a cute red and white jacket-style dress that goes past my knees. They put me in some leggings to keep me warm with a shoulder cape on top, trimmed in the same fluffy white as my cuffs and skirt hem. They then put my hair up in a half up-do held up with long hair pins. It looks cute and very festive. They do my make-up again just to touch it up and make the touches to help with the outdoor lighting they'll do to broadcast the event.

I go down to the entrance hall where only a few girls are ready, all the born princesses mostly, looking irritated at the delay. Zelda is talking to Jonquil about how white and pale blue are also thought of as Christmas colors. "They use the royal blue, even." She's saying. "So it's odd there's not more blue."

She spots me and smiles. I go over and fuss with my skirt, hoping my maids used the hair collector well enough to get any puppy marks off me.

"Your mother is having fun," she tells me. "She's very nice. Said she'd get me a pair of old pointe shoes if I wanted to study them." Of course she did. "She's having a great time with Lilly."

I sigh. "Sounds like my mother."

The rest of the girls filter in. Alsmeria comes over and says hi to Lilly and my mother. Lilly is laughing a lot. I don't need to know what Alsmeria is saying. I'm sure Lilly will tell me later.

Bella walks in wearing one of the most stunning dresses of the evening. I think she might rival me. Its stunning red velvet with an A panel down the skirt in stunning gold and white. The same pattern is repeated as a V pattern on her bodice, her three quarter sleeves have a white and gold flowing cuff. Her curls aren't staying in too well, but at least it gives her straight hair some volume.

"Did you make that?" I ask as she joins us.

"I did," she beams, holding out the skirt to show off its beautiful flow. "I think it came out nicely."

"You look amazing," I say. "Are you sure you'll be warm enough for tree trimming?"

"Of course, I have this." She shows me a red jacket with the same white trim my cape does.

"Well, I'll have an easier time moving around," I tease.

"I was thinking of the interview when I made it. I forgot about the tree trimming beforehand," she sighs. "So, I'll just have to cope. I have layers on under to keep me warm and a clip to hold it up above the snow if there was snow." She shows me where she can have someone pull up and clip the skirt, making a kind of faux bustle to raise the length of her skirt.

"Genius," I praise.

"I hope so," she says.

That's when Alsmeria sees me chatting and comes over. "You're the only one who won't have to worry about keeping her skirt dry. You two plan that?" she asks.

Bella looks confused at Alsmeria joining the conversation. I bridge the gap. "Bella, this is Alsmeria. She's the first soloist in the theater, so we did a lot of big roles together."

"Like the one in the Ice Queen?" she asks me.

"Yeah, we just ignore we don't look like sisters," Alsmeria jokes.

"I imagine that's normal," Bella says.

"So, what handsome thing designed your dress?" Alsmeria asks. I know she's planning on flirting already.

"You're looking at her. I designed and sewed it," Bella says.

"Oh, wow, that's awesome. She doesn't get a friend though," Alsmeria pouts.

"My attendant is female," Bella giggles. "Are you set on joining the castle staff by marriage?"

"There are so many hotties, it could happen," Alsmeria says. "Madder things have happened."

"Like what?" Bella asks.

"Like this thing getting so far," Alsmeria teases me.

"That's not mad. That makes perfect sense," Bella disagrees. "She was a frontrunner right away."

My heart sinks, but not anymore. I may feel closer to Bella than ever, but the truth is, we are still competing for the same man.

"Ooo, who is that?" Alsmeria has spotted one of the other Custod guards.

"The Custod who hangs around my door," Bella says smugly. I didn't even know that.

"Can I?"

"Sure, I'll introduce you," Bella teases. Alsmeria is bubbling in pure excitement. Bella laughs, and I let them flirt on their own. It's not long before the two are laughing and trying to get the guard to smile. He seems nervous by Alsmeria's flirting which just makes Bella laugh more.

"No wonder they think you come from rebels. Your friend isn't exactly very princessy," Dahlia says to me, nodding to my friends and mother.

"Just because I have fun friends, and you have fake ones is no reason to call people names," I reply before I can think it through. I'm impressed with myself and a tad proud.

Zelda laughs and smiles sadly at Dahlia as if to say "sorry, it's true".

Dahlia glares at me. "Just wait, she'll get you kicked out. Finally."

I shrug. "We'll see."

Florence then arrives, and Forsythia is right behind her and takes Dahlia's attention, both complaining about the boxes everywhere. I sigh. These girls are spoiled rotten.

Soon, the royal family arrives, and Sage gives us the once over. I look over to see Alsmeria's reaction to him. She is indeed sizing him up. She sees me looking and nods as if saying, "yup, they are all cute". I sigh. Even Sage gets a pass. Bella is covering her mouth to hide how hard she's laughing.

"The grounds are cleared. We're good to go," Sage says to the king and queen.

I feel a tug on my arm and look to see Alsmeria has come over. "I take it back; take the prince if you can get him. He wears that better than any stage prince, I'm telling you."

I sigh. Gavril is looking. I don't know if he can hear us though. Bella's face is almost as red as her dress with laughter.

I'm guessing Gavril doesn't hear as his brows are drawn together in a question before he turns his attention to Sage giving us directions on getting us to the tree lighting safely. I flush as I see Gavril nod at Alsmeria. Sage glances over with that annoyed look he saves for me, but for once, he's not looking at me. He's looking at Alsmeria. She smiles and waves.

The look on Sage's face makes it hard not to laugh as he looks away. "He dealing with a bad break up?" Alsmeria asks.

"I have no idea. I told you I think he's engaged," I tell her what I said before.

"Oh right, that might explain the face." Alsmeria smiles. I roll my eyes.

Finally, they're ready for us to head outside to the main outdoor tree that would symbolically start the main holiday festivities. I am sure once upon a time this event was open to the public, but now we just deal with an army of reporters. There are a lot of lights going off taking impressions of us.

Alsmeria steps away to avoid being confused for a Chosen in any papers. We do not need that drama. I'm glad she's at least sensitive enough to do that. She isn't normally so bad. The glamor of the palace must just be a shock to her, and she's enjoying it.

"You should hire her as a new maid." I jump as Gavril gets up behind me as quiet as a mouse and speaks. He laughs at me. "Sorry, I didn't mean to spook you."

"What do you want?" I ask, trying to get my heart to settle.

"Not making you jump," he assures me. "Just thought I'd give you a heads up, so you can think about it, but after the interview, my parents are insisting we still have to at least decorate one tree." He rolls his eyes. "Like I haven't done that tradition a million times. Anyway, if you want to stay up, come join us."

"Why are you telling just me?"

"I'm warning others." He smiles. "Just have to check on you first."

But I'm not first, not anymore. I haven't been in a while. I'd hardly spoken to him since the disastrous date, and now he is chatting as if nothing had happened. It makes me nervous. It does not help that I'm still bubbling with hurt and envy at the attention the other girls are getting.

Gavril frowns. "Should I stop?" He sounds disappointed. That gives me a little hope.

"I... no." I mean, I am one of the girls he gets to choose from. It's not like I can fairly deny him that. And I knew he had been close to the others. "Just... this is weird, is all."

Gavril swallows and nods. "I get it. I haven't given up though if..." I hear the "if you haven't" in the stillness.

"Me either," I say quietly.

"Then what's wrong?

"Nothing, I just... you do the same thing with all of them." I nod at the other girls as I hug myself as if against the cold. Though Damian did a good job keeping me warm, our every word hung as vapor in the air.

Gavril nods a bit. "Right." We are quiet a moment. "So, you don't want me to try with you?"

"It's not that. I just... it's awkward. Most of all in public," I admit.

He nods again. "Alright, I'll try to process that. But maybe if you're the only one who shows up tonight, we can try to really talk."

"Do you really want that?" I ask.

"Yes, I'm just still figuring it out too," he says. "Honestly, at this point, I'd rather pretend the last couple weeks didn't happen."

"Can you?"

"I'd sure like to," Gavril says. "Wish I could go back and redo it. Start over."

"Me too."

"And unless it ends with us, we may never have to address it. So why not try to at least enjoy it until then?"

I see what he's saying. Why hurt ourselves if I only leave a few weeks later? That actually is a bit comforting. He just wants to enjoy what he has if I do leave. Then if it looks like I'm lasting longer, we can deal with it. I don't know why that's assuring to me, but it is.

"I think that's a good idea," I agree. "Unless I can't keep awake, I'll be there."

"I thought you had sleep problems." He smiles.

"So, I guess that tells you if I'll be there." I smile. It's true. Without my tea, I could be up all night and just drag on the next day. Gavril returns the smile then moves on.

Though that conversation helps, as I watch him go over to Zelda and whisper something in her ear that makes her giggle, my stomach drops. What is this odd rollercoaster? One moment, I feel sure I'm the only one he wants and have to hold out. The next, I see him being sweet with someone else, and they look so happy and like they're already a couple. I watch as Zelda takes his hand and squeezes it as she replies before she lets go. Well, if it's not me, I want it to be Zelda, so that has to be good, right?

Or not. Gavril walks over to Forsythia next and gets her attention by, no joke, tickling her side. She jumps a mile and slaps his hand, telling him off. He laughs as he speaks with her. I can't hear what they're saying, and I decide I don't want to. I look away.

This game is a nightmare. Who thought this would be fun? Why would they do this to their son and us? They never did say why. Was it just that they wanted a true princess for their son? They should have found a kinder way, maybe test one girl at a time and whoever passes gets to be in the pool of people Gavril picks or something. This is torture. I hug myself tighter.

"Should I slap him?" Alsmeria asks me. "He's sure a flirt."

"No, don't slap him," I say. "He's just doing what he has to. He doesn't pick a winner, so he has to try to like all of us for his own sanity."

"Yeah, but what happens when his tickle friend gets kicked out?" Alsmeria asks.

I sigh. "I don't know."

"Maybe I'm glad I didn't get in. This sounds a lot more dramatic than just trying to get the prince to pick you." Alsmeria frowns a little.

"Yeah, a lot more." I nod. "It's more... political than that."

Alsmeria frowns and opens her mouth to ask something but then looks around as if remembering where we are. "We can talk later," she says. "Look pretty." She gives me a happy smile to give me an example to follow. I roll my eyes but smile. She is good at getting a laugh out of me. But not even the laugh can dispel the knot in my stomach.

Damian comes to my side a moment later. "Well, you seem to be a bundle of joy tonight," he says sarcastically.

I manage a small chuckle. "Guess not." I should be, and it will look better for the impressions and help my chances of a good feature in a few days or whenever it is.

"Anything I can do?" Damian asks, arching a brow.

I laugh. "Teach me not to be jealous," I joke.

Damian smiles and laughs. "I don't think that is possible. But I think I can do one better."

"What's that?" I ask.

"Give me a few days, and I think you'll see what I mean." Damian smiles.

I shake my head. "Not like you can have it all over in a day," I point out, noticing Gavril laughing with Jonquil. I wish I could ignore it.

"No, not even I am that good. But I think my plan will be quite sweet, sweeter than just teaching you not to be jealous. The theory of it is to me, anyway." He smiles. "But if you want not to be jealous, you have to do one of two things. Either teach yourself not to love him or teach yourself to be confident in his love for you."

I shake my head. "I haven't had that since before the Harvest." And even then, I wasn't really sure, just surer than I am now. That thought scares me.

Damian puts his hand on my back to bring me back to reality and looks me in the eye. "Hey. It will be alright. Just because you don't have it now doesn't mean you can't get it back."

"Maybe." I sigh. Tonight is not the time for it anyway. I have to look good in their impressions and get through the event. If I really want to win this, I have to prove I can do that, even if I'm upset. It's what a princess does. Sometimes, what we're feeling doesn't matter in that moment. Later, I'll address it, or keep ignoring it. I take a deep breath. "I can do this." It was the one thing, according to my father, I had to learn no matter what.

Nippers meows at me then runs past towards the bottom of the tree we're going to light. That can't be good.

Damian watches him a moment then turns back to me. "Yes, you can. I believe it with every fiber of my being."

I nod. I have to borrow his faith every now and then, and that will at least get me through tonight. I notice the reporters are trying to get impressions of Gavril with the girls. I hope that doesn't mean I have to see them in the paper later. I walk over to join the group that's waiting for it to start.

Gavril is just finishing talking to Zelda again, for who knows what reason, before he comes over to me and whispers in my ear. "They're trying to guess the favorite. Just pretend I'm saying something cute." I actually do laugh at that. The impression flashes go faster. "See if they can guess." He kisses my cheek, and the impressions are so fast I can hardly see before Gavril steps away. I honestly have to blink, so I can see again. I can't even imagine what kind of face I was making. Was he just playing cute with all of us to keep the impressionists happy?

Finally, it seems we gave the reporters plenty to work with, so we can all gather around the tree for the actual lighting. I notice a few of the players from our theater orchestra are playing some Christmas songs as we add some decorations to just the bottom of the tree.

I pick one up, only to have Nippers take it and climb up the tree to put in a bald spot that must be driving the cat crazy. Why does a cat care?

Damian is chuckling as he watches the cat too and shakes his head at it. "Is he really a cat?" I have to ask. I've never seen a cat do that before.

Damian shrugs. "Looks like a cat to me."

I shake my head. "Doesn't act like one."

"True, but I choose not to think about it," Damian says.

I suppose that's all there is to do as we continue to decorate. Most girls seem to be trying to look the part. Dahlia and Forsythia are clearly using their skills in front of an impressionor to try to shine. They are used to impression shoots, I suppose.

Ericka does much the same, but she's much more pose heavy. I want to throw an ornament at her when she suddenly grabs Gavril's arm to get a cute impression of them all "snuggled" for warmth that the press gets very excited to snap.

Gavril plays the role, but once he gets her to let go, I see the annoyed expression on his face. He knows it's part of the game, but I presume he doesn't like being used as a prop. Does that mean he does not care much for Ericka at least?

I notice the crowds are so busy with us, the king and queen are enjoying a quieter time. They are both laughing, and the king is picking up more unique ornaments and whatever he says about them makes them both laugh. I think the queen is almost teary-eyed. I wonder if they're reminiscing about quiet tree lighting moments. I know they normally do the shoot. So, they must have done this a dozen or more times.

The queen keeps looking over at Gavril while the girls try to use him to get more impression time. I think I know that look. I may not have seen it often, but I've seen people try to replicate it. She might just be starting to come to grips with the fact her son isn't a little boy anymore. How can she when Princess Amapola is hanging off him in a slightly alluring way for the impressionor to capture? When he is standing there being swarmed by girls all after his hand? It almost makes me feel guilty to be one of them.

He is her whole world, and before long that world would have to be shared with the world, her worst nightmare.

I am startled back to reality by Alsmeria trying to get an ornament back from Nippers. Nippers doesn't seem to mind being chased. He dodges her with neat skill before dropping the ornament over by the queen before setting off to be chased some more.

The king laughs and picks it up. I think he says, "there it is", and the two of them look at whatever it is for a long moment before an impressionist shoves me closer to the tree to try to get a shot of more of the girls around the tree. It was rather rude. I doubt they'd have done that to any of the royals.

I think about telling him off, when Gavril comes over to me and offers me an ornament to hang up. "Get them off me," he stage whispers, making me laugh.

"Try Lilly. She's safer," I tease. She is least likely to try to use Gavril for attention. She seems scared of attention.

Gavril gives me a look as if asking why he has to hang out at the little kids table, making me laugh again. "I don't think that's safer," he says instead.

"Zelda can't save you?" I ask.

"She's too busy admiring the unique ornament designs and comparing them to gargoyle designs or something." Gavril shakes his head. "I don't think she's hung up one ornament."

I sigh. It sounds like her. "Then maybe you should get her to hang some up," I suggest.

"Everyone else gets more attention. You can have some too." Gavril smiles a bit, trying to keep our conversation from the impressionists.

He has a point. I do seem to have a problem with that, feeling like he's giving me too much attention when he can't exactly get away with giving me none, even if I feel guilty about it. I am envious of the others getting it, and I'd not had it in forever. I shouldn't feel bad.

"I know. It's not an easy balance," I admit.

"You're one of the few who doesn't get actually mad at me for not giving her attention." Gavril smiles. "Makes me feel like you should get more."

Something falls onto my head then drops to the ground. I frown and look down to see Nippers chasing a small branch from the tree. "Don't break the tree." I laugh at Nippers as he runs off.

"It's a huge tree. What can one cat do?" Gavril asks.

"Who knows, and I don't need to know," I state. "Knock it over?"

"Oh, this tree grows here. It's not in a stand. Want to see?" He nods to have me bend with him at the bottom to take a look. I sigh and take his offered hand. A slight warmth fills me at his touch. It's nice to feel it again.

We have to bend doubled over to walk under and see, but the tree is growing from the ground just fine. I suppose you don't need to find and transport a new tree every year.

Gavril leads me back out, and we get a lovely attack of impression flashes. It is odd to do something like this knowing every cute thing you do is going to be recorded. Gavril ignores it without much trouble and nods thanks for humoring him. "This tree is older than my parents. It was planted to decorate year after year. I have no idea which of my ancestors first decorated it."

"Surprised rebels don't go for it," I say.

"Good point. That is a bit odd." Gavril shrugs. "Guess bloodshed is far more interesting than sapsipping." I laugh at his odd choice of words. "But I better keep at the rounds before they declare I've made a choice of winner." He sighs tiredly. I frown. I guess this game isn't much fun for him either.

"Just cuddle Nippers. That's a safe bet." I smile.

"Hmm, where did he go?" Gavril plays along. Alsmeria is after him again. "Never mind, I'd rather not talk to your friend who keeps hitting on Sage." He smiles.

"Sorry, she's a bit starstruck," I admit.

"Just don't let him kill her. He's still getting over what happened. You should see how red he gets when Zelda teases him on dates." Gavril makes sure no reporters are listening when he says that.

"Getting over what?" I ask, only to be interrupted by Dahlia excitedly showing Gavril a sparkleball ornament and asking how long it had been in the royal collection for the tree.

I use the interruption to escape and find a quieter spot, away from the impressionists to clear my head. Who thought decorating a large tree would be such a confusing activity? But I know it's not that. It's... I suppose Gavril acting normal is comforting, yet confusing. And not just that. I know he does these cute things with the others. Am I really special?

It's nice to work on my quiet part of the tree for a while, cooling off from the madness of the rest of the event. I knew I'd have to go back to it, but it is nice to take a breath. I put up a special phoenix ornament, one of the phoenixes protecting the babe in a manger, when a flash startles me, but I don't let it show. I can pretend the impressionist isn't there. When I don't get any more flashes, I presume I'm alone again and sigh, leaving a big trail of vapor in front of my face as I bend over the box again. I think I'll be ready to join the rest in a moment.

I brush off my dress once I empty the box and debate just getting a new box or joining the crowd when Damian walks up to me with a nice cup of cocoa. I smile. It is cold out here. "Thanks." I accept it.

"But of course." He smiles and takes a seat next to me then looks around to the stars. "It is beautiful tonight."

I look up. I hadn't thought about looking to the stars at all. It is a cold night, so it likely is clear. It is. I can see a lot of stars shining in the night. I'd never really thought to look up much anywhere. I smile a little. "It really is."

Damian smiles gently then looks down into the cup in his hands. "Reminds me of cold nights as a boy. My mother would find me in the back garden, staring at the stars and enjoying the quiet air. She had a way of making the world feel warmer, just by entering the room."

I smile a little. "Sounds like a good mom."

Damian smiles at me. "Oh, she was. During the holidays, she truly shined too. She would have sugar plums made for each of the children. And on Christmas morning, we would find them and eat them until we were all sick," he laughs.

I chuckle. It's hard to picture Damian being such a foolish child at first, but it doesn't take long for me to adjust. After all, we were all dumb children once. It was part of learning. "You must miss her."

Damian thinks a moment and nods. "I do. For a long time, it didn't feel like Christmas without her, but I'll see her again."

I smile a bit. "That's beautiful." He has simple, elegant faith.

Damian smiles warmly then looks at my cup. "I hope it is not too hot."

I shake my head a little. "It's perfect." One of the few perfect moments of the night.

Damian smiles. "Good. I'd hate to burn your tongue."

I chuckle. "Then you'd have to treat me for it." I shake my head a bit. "They do task you with me."

It's like he's my new father in this new life now that mine has left me high and dry.

"Indeed." Damian nods with a smile. "And I wouldn't want to be held responsible for hurting you," he teases.

I chuckle. "You'd have to answer to yourself."

"Oh, dear. We wouldn't want that, now would we?" he jokes.

"No, be quite a mess," I agree. I sip some more and notice an impressionist snapping another impression. I sigh. I'll finish this then get back.

Damian smiles and offers to take my empty cup. "Thanks." I let him take it.

"You are most welcome, my lady." Damian smiles and bows then leaves.

I smile and decide to try to get a new box when someone takes my hand. I look up and am surprised to see Gavril looking around. He puts his other hand to his mouth, finger up to tell me to keep quiet. "Let me show you something," he says and pulls me off into the darkness.

"Um." Is this even allowed? I guess Sage is hanging around like he always does. I let Gavril pull me until we're close to a running fountain around some rose bushes. I think it's close to where we first met. Then he covers my eyes with his hands.

I smile, rather liking the attention, but nervous about what he is up to. "Gavril," I snap with a small giggle.

"Hang on, I'm helping your eyes adjust faster," he says.

"To what?"

"The dark," he says simply. "You'll see it better that way."

"See what? Your hand?"

Gavril chuckles. "No, I have my eyes closed too." I hope Sage doesn't.

We stand there in the dark for a moment. With my eyes covered, I'm hyper aware of his warmth against me, his warm breath on my neck and shoulder, the feeling of his breathing so close. I can almost feel his smile. I hope no one is getting an impression of this. They'd run wild with this. Let alone what the other girls would do. This might be worse than what they caught him doing with Forsythia.

"Okay," he says after a moment then guides my head upward before finally letting me see again.

He bends close to my eye level. His cheek is almost touching mine, making me shudder a little, but not in displeasure, more uncertainty. He's so close, like nothing had happened. Gavril tries to point me to see what he's looking at.

"You can't always see it, but I happened to catch sight of it. I told you I know stars, and I'd show you the Christmas star if you were here. If you look there, those three stars come together and look like one. Can you see it? It's not the brightest in the world, but they only look like that this time of year."

I almost forgot about him telling me he'd do that. I wondered at the time how in creation he'd pull it off. We got lucky. I'm surprised he remembered at all. I had forgotten all about the promise, but I suppose it feels like it was from another lifetime. One where I was still the frontrunner.

But then I finally see what he's pointing at. It takes my breath away. Not only are the stars making it look like one star, I swear I can see more smaller specks of lights around it, making almost a misty glitter effect. I'd not seen anything like it before.

I realize there aren't any lights nearby. We're far from the tree, and the castle hardly has any windows with light in them. There are no city lights here to block the view.

"Can you only see this out here?" I ask.

"In this full glory, yes." Gavril nods. "We're far enough from the city that the lights don't cause a problem. The castle lights as few as possible for security, and the lights of the tree are so dim they don't make a difference. You even have to adjust your eyes to the dark before you can see it this well." He smiles at me, hard to see in the dark, but I can see the light in his eyes. "Some years you can't even see it. I didn't last year. But it's one of the most spectacular views you can get. Winter is cold, but it also has the best skies for stargazing."

I'd take his word on that. But from what I see, he is right. I'd never seen anything like it. I look and see the whole night sky looks different, more brilliant than I'd ever noticed. Are there really so many stars? I really should learn to look up more.

Then I realize what Gavril has just done. He saw the star and who did he want to share it with? Not Zelda or Jonquil or Forsythia or even his parents. It was me he snuck off to show it to. Perhaps it is just because he recalled promising me he would, but it gives me hope he is not giving up on me yet. He'd taken a moment aside, risking getting us in trouble if any impressions got out of this, just to show me something he treasured. That has to mean something.

We don't speak for a while, just looking at the Christmas Star. Even though it is silent, it is still lovely, perfect. I take in his arm around me and how close he is. I have not felt so happy in so long.

Gavril's arm starts to slide down as if to wrap around my waist instead of my shoulders, but he stops himself and clears his throat, securing his hold on my shoulders. But that seems to remind him, we're not supposed to be here. He takes his arms from around me and looks back at the group.

"We should head back before they find us."

"Don't want that all over the paper," I agree.

Gavril takes my hand to help me get back in the dark.

When we get back, they are working on the side of the tree I'd been working on alone, and Nippers is keeping them distracted by stealing ornaments. I owe him a good pat because it is keeping all the reporters entertained and away from missing Gavril and me.

Alsmeria manages to pick him up and stroke him as we join them to help. Unfortunately, the other girls start using Gavril as a prop again, so I try to keep out of the way and help with the decorating.

We finally finish with some help from servants and then they bring out the huge ladder to put the star on top. It is a pretty, golden star, but nothing beats the one Gavril found for us.

Watching him put it on the tree is entertaining. The king holds the queen's hand tightly to prevent her freaking out as Gavril makes the long climb up the ladder. She does insist on five different people holding it up. I think five is a bit much. What if all that "holding" actually makes it worse?

I'm sure the temptation to pretend it is wobbly crosses Gavril's mind, but who could have dared do that to his poor mother who looks ready to pass out any second? Nippers sits at her feet and purrs, watching Gavril as if entertained by him. Once the star goes up, Gavril slides back down, making his mother jump.

I smile as he lands just fine. The king makes sure to hold his wife back long enough for impressionists to get a few good impressions of his son's landing before letting her go to hug him tightly. He just smiles and returns it. How does she not notice how grown he really is? He definitely looks like he is taking care of her far more than she is him. Who wouldn't feel safe in that protective hug? At least I'm not so jealous to be envious of that.

Chapter 24

If the others hoped I'd not outshine them tonight, they were wrong. Damian's dress for the interview is unique, reminding me of Japcharian style dresses. It's a straight piece with a button from my side to my high collar. The edges of this button or tie up section are Christmas green while the main dress is red with golden phoenix patterns on the opposite side. There's a golden skirt under it to cover the slit that goes up my thigh in the button up. They keep my hair up in the half updo with long hair pins and add some dangling earrings for the full effect. I look like a Christmas phoenix.

If it were not for the fact the royal family are also doing interviews tonight, the first in quite some time, I'd stand out from the crowd for sure. As it is though, I'm guessing the royal family will take center stage. I just have to do well enough not to be thrown out.

When we arrive in the reception room, Fabian and most of the girls are already there. Fabian is talking to the crew to prep it all. He is the perfect showman. Many girls were working on drying the hems of the skirts.

Lilly loves my dress. "It's like home!" she declares. "I wish I'd thought of that."

"I have one kind of like this at home, but no gold." Bella smiles. "You pull it off nicely. I should have thought of doing two dresses."

"Thanks. I like that it's different. Though I feel underdressed without as many layers," I joke. "After how much we had to wear to keep warm, it's really nice."

"Oh, that is nice. Not like Ericka. You'd think she thought herself queen already," Lilly mutters. Ericka is dressed in a fancy ball gown like dress with lots of gold, mostly gold really, and some hints of Christmas red and green.

"I hope it's easier than last time. I don't want another two days worth of interview lessons." Bella gives me a warning look. I smile innocently. No promises.

They get us into position, and I sit back in my seat. We are arranged by our numbers this time. It's nice to sit by the girls I'm used to. I'm careful to sit properly, most of all my feet, which are more visible than normal. I'm glad Damian is not an anti-corset kind of stylist. It makes it easier to sit up right and let the corset support my back.

"Good evening and Merry Christmas Purerah!" Fabian calls into the impressionor. He's standing and greeting them as well as before, and the small crowd of staff clap as they get to watch. "Welcome to the Royal Family's Christmas Special for the Enthronement. We've gotten to know most of these girls through our last interviews and the features still coming in the papers. Only a few girls to go. See if you can spot who." He winks into the impressionor.

"Tonight ends with a very special treat, interviews with each of the royal family members. It will be the first in a long time, and the first real formal full length interview with the heir to the throne, Prince Gavril." He smiles wider. "But let's begin with our lovely ladies of the Enthronement. Today, we'll show off the king and queen's preferred order of who was chosen to participate in the first place. Let's give a warm Purerahian welcome to Princess Rose of the High Kingdom of Emilimoh!"

The interviews are nice. About the same as before. Rose still looks stiff compared to Fabian, but she has slightly improved. The rest are much the same, answering questions about their Christmas traditions at home, their family, and all answered the question of what they hoped Phoenix brought them for Christmas.

With Bella, Fabian does note she looks amazing, and they talk about her own design process.

But as we go in Enthronement order this time, it isn't long before I'm up and shaking hands with Fabian before sitting down. I use the same positions as before, feeling quite comfortable with Fabian by now. "Ah, our lady in green didn't go for Christmas green this time." He play-pouts as we sit down. I laugh. "Really, I was hoping you would, but this Japcharian style dress of phoenix red and gold is spectacular as always, Lady Kascia. Will you ever not shine? Though Lady Bella gave you a good run today." He winks over at her to which Bella just chuckles.

"I think people would stop noticing our outfits so much if you'd stop bringing it up," I tease Fabian. "I'm sure my attendant would enjoy not getting so much attention. Not that I mind giving my team the credit they deserve." I can't see where they are with the lights, but I smile at where they had watched before. "Even if they would be happy to hide."

"Well said." Fabian nods. "But we'd still notice the unique choices they make. You just can't help but stand out wherever you go."

"Well, it's less about standing out and more about sending a message," I say. "A lady communicates in many ways. I like this choice. I didn't know it, but it's a popular style in the north of the kingdom. It helps me feel like I get to be a part of them a little. Helps me understand them, you know?"

I am on a roll, and I know it. Not only would my teachers approve of this, but I am still making statements.

"You do like talking and knowing the people," Fabian agrees with a smile. "Is that how you spend your holiday?"

"For us, it's a break at last," I laugh. And I tell him what I told my fellow Chosen about how my holidays usually go.

"Ah yes, what roles did you play?" Fabian asks me.

"For Nutcracker, it's a lottery," I say then go on to tell about all the roles I've had: Clara as a girl, coffee, tea, snowflake corps and solo, flower corps, the super plum fairy, marzipan, and maybe more I forgot. "Then, of course, *A Christmas Carol* is my favorite, but I've been Belle so many times it gets old."

That gets me a good laugh. "How is it being away from home? You're so close." Fabian smiles a bit sadly.

"Well, I at least get my mother." I smile as if I can see her off the impressionor, but the lights make it hard. "The king and queen's surprise and all. Her troupe took the offer to perform."

"Ah yes, they mentioned that." Fabian nods. I should have listened to the opening they did more closely. My mind had wandered at that part, I guess. "That must be nice. Family is here. Most of all when they weren't writing."

"Just busy." I smile, not adding my father still was as silent as a tomb.

Fabian nods, and moves into a cue I had noticed meant he's getting ready to wrap up with the same question he asked everyone. "What would you want from the phoenixes?"

"Well, I got it." I smile, referring to my mother being there.

"So, what would you ask now?"

Oh no, I hadn't thought he'd press that. I think a moment. Wishing for the war to end feels like copying Jonquil. But....

I swallow. "Honestly." I know what I'd ask for. I know it's a sad note, but when I cast my mind about for anything I could reasonably ask for, there is one that stands out, second only to solving this mess in my head. "I'd ask for my missing maid back." The whole room goes quiet.

"What do you mean?" Fabian frowns.

I take a deep breath. "Well, when we arrived, we each were assigned three maids. During a rebel attack, my maid, Ro, went missing. We've really missed her. I hope she's alright. If I could have anything, that's what I'd ask."

There's another pause. "I'm sorry to hear that." Fabian picks it up well. Even the pause felt tactful rather than awkward. "We hope and pray she's found to be alright."

He then thanks me for my time, and it's Azalea's turn. The rest of the interviews go smoothly. I am surprised it's over so fast. I thought that would be much harder. I can't help but wonder why as I take my seat, and Azalea gets up. Then at last, we get to Florence who does really well, standing out for the first time in a long time.

I hardly heard the rest of the interviews. I still do not have my feature up. I thought he did that on purpose and so he could get more out of me today, but nothing. I should be relieved, but I'm more confused. Maybe he's just trying to have fun with the holiday.

"Thank you, ladies, for your participation." Fabian smiles widely as he stands to address the impressionor.

"And now we move on to the royal family. We'll start at the top and work our way down, so don't forget to drink that hot chocolate and keep awake because we're saving the best for last."

Anxiety fills my stomach even though I'm not on. Fabian was saving his punches for the royal family, but all of them, or just Gavril?

I glance at Gavril to see how he's feeling. He's still in the same red and gold suit, brushing some dirt off his pant leg as if nothing was wrong at all. Did he already prepare for this? I hope Sage prepared him or at least Lady Keva or Lady Hydrengia could have done some review with him. They were his teachers first, right? If not, Fabian is going to rip him apart unprepared.

The king soon takes up the seat the rest of us ladies had sat in. He is completely relaxed. He leans back, crosses his legs in a way that helps him turn towards Fabian. "It's so nice to be here and feel like I really get to have a more proper audience with you all as a whole." The king smiles before Fabian can even ask a question.

"Even with about half of them wanting you dead and out of office?" Fabian asks. Wow, he went right for it. I guess Gavril won't be taking all the blows.

"Most of all with that. I understand for security we have to keep tight, but sometimes, I worry it's part of why no one can relate to us. And though such events are expensive, recent events certainly taught me that perhaps finding more creative ways to speak with our people is a desperate need, not a want."

"What kind of events?" Fabian asks.

"Well, the Enthronement for one." The king smiles. "I never realized how information starved our people are. Makes me wish we'd been more open with impressions or events like this, but they are quite expensive and hard to put together, so we never thought of it. But we've seen a lot of good come out of them.

"People are excited for news about the event. They are more open with their complaints. I used to be able to see all those wanting an audience of judgment in a day, and still have extra time in the afternoons. Now, the people seem much more willing to come, though there is still a week long vetting period, but my day fills up so that I need to schedule breaks to handle them all. I'm not as young as I used to be." The king fuses with the hair under his crown a bit. "I am pretty sure the gray is really showing. What do you think?"

He gets a laugh from those watching as he has Fabian try to get a look at it. Fabian tries his best. "Hard to see around the crown."

"Oh here." The king takes it off, and the two men make a bit of a scene looking over his hair.

"Alright, I can see some if I look hard," Fabian agrees, and both men lean back in their seats as the king puts his crown back on. "But it's like baby salt and pepper. I see it more on your face." Funny as the king is mostly gray.

"Yeah, I get a nightly stubble. Can the impressionor see it? Should I have shaved first? I didn't think of that. I'm not used to people coming in and judging my looks." The king looks at me. "Next time I borrow your attendant."

I laugh and so do most of those watching. Ericka glares at me. She's so jealous of me having Damian. Dahlia is doing the same. I didn't realize she cared as much. "He needs to make a list of to-dos before next time."

"Well, I guess you have a favorite." Fabian smiles.

"No, just know where to get good look help. I mean, look at her." The king beams at me, and the stupid impressionor turns to focus on me. I flush and wave the way I'm supposed to. "Pretty no matter what we shove her through, these poor girls."

"So what kind of tests are you putting them through?" Fabian asks.

"Well, I can't reveal what's to come, but we have done quite a bit so far." The king turns back to Fabian. He is so at ease in this situation.

He looks so relaxed, like he's just having a good time with friends over drinks. The only thing missing is the drinks. I also noticed something strange. He hadn't paused to cough once. Was he holding it in? Didn't sound like it.

"But we have had a bit too much fun at their expense, I think. Well, I have. My lovely wife is happy to tell me off." The king gives his queen a warm, loving smile. "It started with the prince finally interviewing them himself. We weeded out a lot of girls then. Then we tested their dating skills right off to make sure there wouldn't be any problems moving forward."

"And how did you do that?" Fabian asks.

"Just observed several dates. Prince Gavril took them for a walk for the first date, and we lost a few then for just not princess-like behavior. Then we had them plan a date to see how good they were. But last one we had was seeing if they could behave when tempted." The king smiles mischievously.

"And you're still a virgin, right?" Fabian turns to Gavril who flushes with a guarded smile. The queen turned beat red at the question though the king just laughs.

"Don't worry; those tests were carefully watched," he assures Fabian, "for that exact reason. Don't need the prince breaking his princely oaths or anything."

"So what else did they do?" Fabian asks.

"I really enjoyed the talent show. My wife wasn't a fan, but I love it." The king grins.

"Princesses on parade, I dare say." Fabian smiles.

"And as an old man, I was happy to enjoy it," the king agrees, getting a laugh from Fabian.

"Indeed so, my lord. So now we're down to twenty after those tests?"

"Well, we had a few more. The first public event we did tested their ability to handle princess duties such as handling the press and diplomacy," the king says. "And the 'royal impressions' you've been using in your articles also were a test to see how vain they were: did they complain about the impressions, did they not like themselves in any, were they overly picky: that kind of thing." The king smiles. "Or were they hogging the impressionist's time."

"And now we're to today?" Fabian asks.

The king nods. "And today, we're down to fifteen from fifty. My wife was right. I thought it would take longer to get to this point, but she had her heart set on a winter wedding." He smiles.

"Still think it might happen?" Fabian asks.

"Hm, doubt it." The king shrugs. "It would be almost impossible to narrow them down that fast. We are likely to see a spring wedding though." The king turns to us. "Note that down for wedding plans like you girls do." Many of them giggle. Zelda plays along so much, she writes it down on her tablet.

"So by the spring, perhaps even the new year, we'll have our princess?" Fabian asks.

"No promises, but I'd not be surprised if we have it down by then." The king nods.

"Well, that's all the time I have to grill you, Your Majesty. Thank you for the time and entertainment." Fabian smiles.

"Always a pleasure." The king shakes hands with Fabian before going back to his throne-like seat, and the queen comes forward. She looks much more nervous; well, I can see she is, but she hides it perfectly.

She gives Fabian a perfectly, happy, queenly smile and sits down with perfect elegance, sitting and straightening her skirt with one hand before turning her full attention onto Fabian, resting her hands together on her lap.

"It's so nice to get a chance to speak with you, Your Majesty." Fabian bows his head to her. "I feel like the last time we spoke was talking about your finally having a child. And look how long it's been." He looks over at Gavril, who chuckles and shakes his head in amusement. "He's sprung up like a bean poll," Fabian says.

"He's not that skinny thankfully." The queen smiles, her crown shining in the light.

Fabian chuckles. "That is true enough, Your Majesty. What is it like having the castle full of girls when you were the only lady here for so long?"

"Honestly, I've been so busy I hardly notice," the queen says. "There's much to do to run a kingdom alongside my husband. Mealtimes are much more noisy, and pleasantly so. And it seems conversations with Prince Gavril are mostly about dating and courting these days." She smiles warmly.

"Are you looking forward to finally having a daughter?" Fabian asks.

The queen misses a beat. Her expression stays the same, but I think he asked a question that the queen hadn't thought of before. It was true. In her son marrying, she'd gain a daughter. I don't think that way of thinking about it had occurred to her yet. It was just finding a bride for her son, not a daughter for her.

"Well, of course," the queen says, recovering quickly. What else could she say being caught off guard?

"So then why wait so long?" Now he was getting her with the hard questions. I can see why he targeted her with them instead of the king. It was easier for him to brush off these questions than her. "Most princes, most of all heirs to thrones, are married by now, long before now."

The queen sighs. "It's not easy to choose a ruling companion in any situation. But in this case it's even more imperative for our nation. We're at a dangerous crossroads, and it will come to full when Prince Gavril takes the throne. He'll need a true princess to help him. This war cannot go on much longer without some drastic changes. And we want to give our people the best chance possible of a more peaceful and fruitful change by providing the best queen for them at that difficult point."

They had to have rehearsed that answer. The queen is almost too poised. It makes me certain it's not completely true. Why? What is the real reason then? I, like everyone else, assumed their pride until I met them. But that's not the case, and they are hiding the real reason.

"So the war isn't going well?" Fabian asks.

"Well, tonight is not the time to discuss that. But it is more of a standstill. And when that happens, something has to give," she says. "And we're doing all we can to make sure it's not the safety or wellbeing of our people."

"Is that why you set up the Enthronement, even to your own people though you seek a true princess?" Fabian asks. He is hitting her harder than even the king, but perhaps it was because she didn't punch back.

"I found myself a true king from our own people. Why not a princess?" The queen smiles. That had to be a quote or something from how she said it. Most people wouldn't know as they didn't hear how she normally spoke, but I can hear the quote in her voice. Odd, it sounds like something she'd have thought of. She did marry a noble of her own people, after all.

Fabian smiles. "That you did," he agrees. "Has the prince confided much on his thoughts of his choice?"

"Even if he did, I wouldn't tell you. A mother's confidence is key," she says.

"And I thought I'd get lucky." Fabian clicks his tongue, making a few laugh. "Do you have any advice for the few Chosen left to help them through the rest of the Enthronement?"

"Not that I'd give the impressionist," she teases lightly. "I'd save that for them."

"Can I ask a question that won't get deflected?" Fabian taunts.

The queen smiles. "I suppose we'll find out." I can see the nervousness in her eyes.

Fabian smiles back. "Do you have a favorite?"

The queen laughs. "Perhaps, but much like the prince I have to be careful about that. What if my pick doesn't pass?"

Fabian's eyes light up like he hit gold. Oh no, the queen escaped, but she did it by handing over an uncomfortable talking point for Gavril. She realized it too late though.

"Thank you, Your Majesty. That looks like all the time we have. We still have one more interview to get to." Fabian bows to the queen.

"Thank you." She bows her head back and stands up. The king gives her a smile and takes her hand as she sits down. They have a whispered conversation.

"Now, the moment I think we've all been waiting for," Fabian says as he walks about to keep the impressionor's attention, "You know him as the Enthronement's heartthrob, I give you Prince Gavril!"

Gavril beams as he gets up to join him, waving at the audience before shaking hands with Fabian. He mirrors his father more than his mother as he sits, even if he looks more like her overall. He sits with his legs crossed but leans back more than his father had, but I can't help but notice he brushes off his pant leg the way his mother fussed with her skirt. He seems relaxed. I hope it's his act and not that he's blind to what's about to happen.

"Welcome Prince Gavril." Fabian smiles. "The man of the hour."

"And it seems I will be until all this is over. You have any idea how hard it is to talk to anyone about anything but this show? I ask how the weather is, and they ask if I have a favorite." The crew laughs.

"Really?" Fabian smiles. "Who would do that?"

"Anyone not a part of it. It's maddening." Gavril smiles. "I could ask the doctor for a headache cure, and they ask who I kissed." It wins him another laugh. Interesting. He is making his jabs first instead of blocking Fabian's. He's going to run out the clock.

"Well, if you're looking for a sore throat cure, he might need to know." Fabian smiles, getting a laugh from the crew and Gavril.

"I suppose he would. I guess that's just the hazard of dating in this mad scene. Let me tell you, the poor girls are having to endure me learning how to date at all. I have made some serious blunders."

"Like?"

"Oh well, on one date, I did the most brilliant thing of trying to be cute and prepare the treat and ended up burning it. I had no idea burned popcorn permeates a five-mile radius, did you?" Gavril leans forward as if asking if Fabian thought he should invade Englaria or not.

"I did. Most people who have dealt with popcorn know that." Fabian laughs with the rest of us. "But some girls may find the clumsy cute."

"Not when they smell like popcorn for hours, and their dog starts begging for it." Gavril grins.

"That may make a lady mad at you," Fabian agrees. "Did that bother you? I'd be most embarrassed if that girl was a favorite of mine."

"I don't know. She didn't talk to me for a few days, but I am so busy dating, I sometimes forget who I went out with. I am just glad I haven't gotten their names mixed up. Can you imagine?" Gavril laughs at himself. "It's a good thing they can't kick me out, or I'd have failed round one." That gets a laugh. Gavril is certainly not letting Fabian let off any bullet questions. The closest he got he deflected easily.

"So, you don't think you're a true prince?" Fabian tries again.

"Well, I'm not a true princess. I failed those tests. I've never taken a true prince test. If you know of any, let me know. If it gets me out of this madness." Gavril smiles. "Your paper run anything like that?"

"No, we don't do pieces like that," Fabian chuckles.

"Good, then no one can kick me out for it." Gavril grins. "Pretty safe here."

"Does being that safe bother you?" Fabian asks.

"You mean not getting kicked out? Yeah, that was the point of the whole joke." Gavril is really playing hard to get. "I guess it helps that none of them can dump me. Most people get in trouble for having twenty girlfriends at once. I'm legally required to. Am I lucky or cursed?" Gavril looks at the crew behind the camera for an answer. They just laugh. "See? No one knows." Gavril turns back to Fabian. "Not even my guard knows."

"Your personal Custod guard? There were rumors you have one," Fabian says.

"Since I can remember. They change all the time too. I must be hard to hang out with. I don't know how these amazing girls do it. Princess Rose is so patient with me. She knows all the laws and etiquette and excuses my newbie mistakes like they're nothing." The prince shakes his head. "And let me tell you, Kascia never misses a chance to correct me on how to be a real prince."

Oh no, he's using us as shields now. And why did he have to add me? "But far worse is Lady Kamala. She has no trouble putting a man in his place. Offer her the wrong date or food, and she'll let me know." Gavril chuckles. "Opposite of Lady Lilly who has to be the sweetest breath of fresh air you can find." Oh, I see what he's doing; he's making sure we all get a comment from him, so Fabian can't pick on a favorite. "Her name is also a delight to say. Just try it, Lady Lilly, the alliteration is just stunning."

Fabian plays along and laughs in agreement that her name is fun to say. "So, are they your top picks?" Fabian asks.

The smile Gavril gives makes me laugh. He was hoping for that question. "There's something to love about all of them. Goodness." He looks over at us. "Princess Laurina knows how to be heard and taken seriously. And a dragon friend is a plus." He turns to Fabian to add the comment before turning back to us. "Princess Zelda." He gives her a special smile that makes my heart skip. I'd not seen that smile before. I love how many different smiles Gavril has. I just wish more were for me. "She has a wisdom few could hope to rival ever, not even me or some of the greatest rulers of our time. Hyvil or Purerah will be lucky to have her."

Gavril's "shake" to reality looked too staged to me, but maybe I'm just a harsh judge as my living is the stage. "Bella has the grace of five queens. Dahlia is a never-ending ball of fun. Jonquil has a strong opinion on everything, even which tea is best. Azalea reminds me of my mother and who doesn't want that?" Gavril smiles gently. "Ericka can command an army with ease. Lady Forsythia has a... power about her. Isla... I've never seen a girl with so much faith. Puts me to shame, that's for sure. And Florence... let's just say she has kept in the game this long through pure talent. How do I pick from so many good choices? It's kind of a relief not to."

I feel like he wants to put a strong emphasis on "kind of" but knows better than to give Fabian the opening. Then Gavril smiles his mischievous smile. "So, which is your favorite?"

I cover my mouth to stop the laugh as Fabian clearly did not expect to be asked that. Fabian returns the smile. "I don't get to pick."

"You sure? Once they leave, they're free game," Gavril points out. "So, if you got to pick? Your wife won't mind the game. Unless you're single. Then you should start with chocolate and flowers." The laughter is infectious.

Fabian takes it with good humor though. "I suppose that's true. But I couldn't begin to choose a favorite. My wife isn't included."

"I don't know, you go on about the lady in green."

"Favorite to win though? I couldn't begin to guess," Fabian chuckles.

"I know what you mean." Gavril sighs heavily.

"So, then what do you hope for this Christmas? What do you hope the phoenixes bring you?"

"Honestly?" Gavril sighs. "Call me selfish for not wanting something as great as some of these ladies, but I just want to know who's going to win so I don't have to keep making them all struggle through this. I make light of it to get through it, but it's not fun to have your heart set on someone and not know if you'll be with them. It's playing with all our hearts. I'd like to relieve that for me and them."

I glance at the clock. Gavril had done it. They are out of time. He adds the serious tone Fabian wants without letting him use his feelings as a toy in this game. For his first prepped interview, he sure handled it like he had lots of practice.

"An understandable wish. I'm sure the viewers join me in wishing you all the best of luck and a Happy Christmas." Fabian turns to the impressionor. "And that's all the time we have for tonight. Keep an eye on the paper for more updates and the final features. We'll see you all in our next broadcast update, but in the meantime, myself and all at the palace wish you a merry Christmas." And the light on the impressionor goes off.

"You are a tricky one," Fabian says to the prince as the crew starts to pack up.

"Nothing personal." Gavril shakes his hand as they both stand.

"You owe me a proper interview," Fabian teases.

"Maybe one day." Gavril claps his shoulder.

He turns and comes right to me. "If anyone asks, I don't call any of the other girls 'lady' in private, alright? And sorry for having to use you.

I had to get everyone in." He shrugs. "Pretend to be annoyed, he's still watching."

I hit his arm like I would if I were annoyed. "Not like that." Gavril laughs.

"That's what I'd do if I was mad."

"Well, that's going in the paper," he laughs.

"I followed your order."

Gavril sighs. "You are trouble." He bows to me and makes his rounds with the other girls.

The crew finally leaves, and the king invites whoever doesn't mind staying up to help them finish decorating the main tree. I don't know how I feel when most girls just go up to bed. Most are in nice dresses that take a while to get out of, and it is already quite late, but that also means we'll have a quieter activity.

"And plenty of sugar to keep us up," Gavril teases as the few of us who opted to stay up go into the main sitting room. I imagine this is where we'll do the main gift change on Christmas day.

There is a tray of tea, cocoa, biscuits, tarts, and other treats set up for us. The king and queen start at their more fun festivities quite happily. Gavril gets dragged in a little more forcefully by his mother. Then I think of something. If this was a test, it was not only rude, but would get us way down. It's just me, Zelda, Lilly, Isla, Florence, and Jonquil. But what did wanting to join a more intimate family activity have to do with being a true princess?

"Nice to have a real family event. We've done this after the formal one since before Gavril was born." The queen smiles. "We save this one for last."

"I was just happy to be invited the year before we were engaged, remember?" The king smiles.

"I was annoyed my father noticed," the queen agrees. I wonder what they were like. I knew her mother died of an illness not long after the two were married, but I don't recall what happened to her father.

"How did you meet?" Lilly asks as she helps string some icicle-like ornaments across the tree.

"A rare palace event," the queen says. "More nobles were allowed at palace gatherings back then, before events became targets for attacks. I was actually avoiding strangers as my parents were hinting it was time for me to date, and being so young, I wasn't sure I was ready. But Aster was thinking the same thing, so we ended up hiding and talking in the back. My parents were upset I'd not danced enough at first, but with how it ended, they were alright with it."

I smile a bit. At least it wasn't as insane as whatever story Gavril would one day tell his children around a tree like this. Either met them in a formal interview or... or me in the garden on a forbidden walk. The latter at least sounded more interesting. I flush at the idea of the king and queen finally hearing that story. If I won, I'm sure they would.

"How old were you?" Lilly frowns.

"I was sixteen. We married when I was nineteen though with... well, just how the times were." She must mean what was happening in the war. The king and queen are suddenly quiet on that topic.

Lilly helps change it only a little. "If you all normally marry so young, why wait so long to do the Enthronement?" Gavril was not in his teens anymore; that was for sure, even if he wouldn't admit his age to us.

"Similar reasons. The times made it difficult. And frankly, not many royals want to exactly come here. And it didn't occur to us that a true princess could live as a commoner around here." The queen smiles gently at Lilly.

What circumstances changed though? It was the same then as now.

Thankfully, Lilly distracts the conversation by admiring a manger set that is set on the tables. The king says it's a gargoyle-make, a gift from the local gargoyle clan.

I start a bit as music suddenly starts playing, a lovely violin. I look over and see Damian playing it. What can't he do? I sigh and shake my head. Of course that's what he does. He's dismissed for the night and still he's at the party playing for us. I don't know what to do with him. I know better than to tell him to take the rest though, so keep helping with the tree.

Zelda seems most impressed. "I suppose it is the most appropriate instrument to use," she says. It is considered more devout for such celebrations and even in services. It does add a nice upbeat tune, perhaps to help us all keep awake, as he plays more lively songs.

We aren't at it long before we notice Lilly is all but nodding off, so the guard sees her to bed. We finish with the tree, and the king gets it lit up. It looks nice. The king and queen sit back in one of the sofas to enjoy the view and sip at some hot drinks for a bit. The fire light helps with the effect.

It had taken us so long, most girls seem to have gone off to bed. Isla, Jonquil, and Florence left after the king lit the tree. Princess Zelda stayed a little longer, but with a yawn, she wishes us a good night as well.

I figure I should do the same, but with my sleep problems, I'm not exactly feeling tired. "Going to make us sit in here alone?" Gavril teases me. I realize that makes me the only Chosen left in the room. I flush a little. I doubt the other girls thought of that. "Come on; we can enjoy it a while." He offers me a spot next to him on the opposite sofa from his parents.

Well, I can't exactly turn that down. I sit by him but try to keep the proper distance. Gavril chuckles and still puts an arm across the back of the sofa behind me. This would feel normal if we were a real couple, but we're not. Well, I guess we are, but he also has fourteen other girls.

There. A distraction. "You did really well with that interview. He hardly got a punch in."

"Thanks. I just figured with how he went after my parents, a good defense would be a good offense. Sorry for having to drag you into it. I hope it doesn't change anything about the feature." He frowns a bit.

"Have I ever gone after you for something like that?" I ask.

"No, but that just means it's about time. Everyone else does." Gavril shrugs.

I frown. "You're not just a piece in this mad board game. And whatever he does or does not do is not your fault. You have to survive those interviews and this 'game' too," I point out.

Gavril sighs and lets his head fall back onto the back of the sofa. "At least someone feels that way."

I recall his frustrations. How could I forget seeing that temper flare at random. I'd not seen it that bad in a while, but I am not going to forget how he scared me that day. We all have another life to get back to after this, well except for maybe me, but this game is his whole life. I have to be kind and remember that. It still makes me wonder why the king and queen put the son they clearly adore so much through it all.

We sit and listen to Damian playing for a while, watching the fire. Gavril moves his arm around me. I want to tell him not to, but if I let the other girls have it, why can't I? I need to be better at this.

I take a deep breath and let myself settle closer to him. He's so warm. I close my eyes as his grip on my shoulders gets a bit tighter, more comfortable, and confident. It is as if I was cold until now, but his warmth warms me right up.

But he's not mine. He's not able to just devote himself to me. And it bothers me more than it should. Is it not better to take what I can get? But I fear letting him love me only to have it taken away if I lose. It would be one more wound in whatever happens to me when it ends. I have nothing to go back to. Or do I? Could Mother really just let me back? Father still was silent.

I shut my eyes again to enjoy the music and the prince's warm arm around me. I get lost in the feeling and Damian's music. He's playing "Silent Night", and I start to hum along without really thinking about it. It's just so peaceful and calm here. I've not felt so safe and warm in a long time.

Chapter 25

I wake up the next morning in my own bed. I sigh tiredly and sit up. My sides are a bit sore from sleeping in a corset. My eyes widen. Oh no, how did I get here?

I bolt upright and look around. My maids had tidied up, and I can see breakfast keeping warm in a heating dish with a lid on it. There's a note saying to ring for my maids when I need them. I can see even the puppy had been taken care of and is now also asleep. I look at my wall clock. It's ten in the morning.

I get up and ring to have Flur and Vivian help me get the corset off and a new one adjusted. I dare ask them who brought me up last night. "We were sent off for the night before you came in, miss." Flur smiles a small apology.

"I don't know who it was." Vivian shakes her head.

Oh no. Was it Damian or the prince? Did I know who I wished it was? I can't believe I let that happen. I never fall asleep in places like that. Not since I was young. I had to feel really comfortable for my sleep disorder to relax enough for that. Oh no, oh no. I try to keep in my nervousness. I can't believe I did that. Even if it was so late.

Lessons are off for the week as it's the week of Christmas. I get the paper and read Dahlia's feature, confirming mine is last. Dahlia's feature is a lot like Forsythia's.

Her fans raved about her ability to lead like she did for her team and her grace under pressure. Though the article finishes by questioning if skills on a ballfield are the same a queen would need.

"Did everyone have breakfast in their rooms?" Or did the prince excuse me again?

"Yes miss, everyone was up so late. In fact, they let us know if you'd like, you can eat where you'd like all week as a holiday treat." Vivian smiles.

I get into my dance gear to do my routine, then realize I could join my troupe for morning warm ups tomorrow and make a note to be up in time.

I sneak into the reception room to see rehearsals. It's impressive how well they're getting the sets done. It is a lot of activity with so much to get ready for a show the next day. The players are in full costume. They are doing the snowflake's dance when I slip in.

They do their best to rehearse around the tech crew setting up. It feels odd not to be waiting for my cue to jump in. I watch them finish up the dance sections and move on to *A Christmas Carol*, and that's when Mother catches me and tells me off for being a distraction. "Shouldn't you be on a date?"

"Only when he asks," I smile.

"How about lunch with the royals?" Mother asks. It is just about lunch time. Why are they getting ready to work on the next show already?

"What about your break?" I ask.

"We will eat in the hall after the rest of you are done. There's not enough space for all of us," Mother points out. "You get to see this all the time. Go enjoy the palace."

"Mom, I did nothing but that until the Harvest," I point out. "I'd rather see you all."

"You can watch the show when it's time," Mother insists.

Alsmeria frowns. "She really can't join in?"

"She's not had time to rehearse," Mother says.

I sigh. "Alright, alright, but in exchange, you will have lunch with me tomorrow, right?" I invite. I can have Damian help me set up a one-on-one.

"Of course," Mother agrees. "But maybe you can do tomorrow with Alsmeria then you and I can talk after that." She's putting off talking to me. I know it.

Alsmeria is too excited at the idea for me to say no though, so I agree.

I get into a day dress then go to lunch, glad to see Dahlia isn't there since I arrive late. The prince and his parents are still there. Lilly smiles at me when I come in. "Sorry I missed out on the fun," she says. "I'm just glad it wasn't a test."

"So are most," I reply as I nod my thanks to a servant who gives me a plate of food.

"If it was, we we'll go down in number fast," Lilly agrees. "I'm looking forward to the show. Have you seen how they're working on the great room?"

I shake my head. "I watch the rehearsals though."

"Your mother let you? She's driven out anyone else who's tried," she laughs.

"I know how to get in." I smile. Lilly giggles.

I help Lilly get a sneak peek, but make sure to run before Mother spots us. After that, I go to meet with Cedrick for the puppy's training. I am anxious about the court dinner tonight. We have lessons off, but tonight is going to be a huge hurdle.

We start getting ready a little over an hour beforehand, getting me cleaned up and ready to get dressed up for the court. They do my hair in a nice half up-do with gold ribbon woven into it. The dress is mostly white with a red underskirt. The bodice is beautifully embroidered with a red and gold filigree pattern down to the waist which comes to a V at the middle with gold and red lace wrapped around the edge of the bodice. The collar is actually made of two parts; the top part is sweetheart neckline while the second is an under layer of red satin fabric that creates an almost off-the-shoulder look, capped with short open sleeves which have a secondary undersleeve of white lace. It goes well with my Chosen necklace and the gold holly earrings that gently hang from my ears. At the A-split in the skirt, there's stunning gold embroidery work on either side with beautiful vine and leaf designs like holly or mistletoe. The full skirt hovers above the floor and floats beautifully.

"Perfect princess," Flur tries to cheer me up. My maids have clearly felt my uncertainty lately and are trying to help.

"She looks lovely in gold," Vivian agrees.

"Indeed, she does." Damian smiles warmly. "You look magnificent, dear angel."

I manage a smile. "Thanks Damian."

"Well, if you're ready we should go assist." Vivian curtsies, and Flur follows her example before they leave.

"Tonight is a big deal, isn't it?" I ask, taking a deep, nervous breath. My first chance to prove my new resolve even to myself.

Damian gives that knowing smile of his, but it's different this time, like he's agreeing with me instead of knowing something I don't. "Yes, my dear, it is. Not in the way of the Enthronement, mind you, but tonight is the first time the governors of Purerah will get to see you as a future noble, just like them. Unfortunately, it also means meeting Ericka's family." He gives me a playful look of disgust.

That does make me laugh. "So, I really better not screw this up?"

He chuckles. "Well, if you were my brother, I might start worrying about that. No telling what trouble that man will get himself into." He rolls his eyes with a smile. "But I'm worried about you." He places his hand on my cheek. "You'll do beautifully; I know it. So try to relax and enjoy the party."

"Like I've had any good parties in a while," I roll my eyes. It's all been one drama after another, "or have good history with the court."

"Perhaps not, but you remember what I said when you were nervous about your interview with Fabian?"

"Forget what they taught you?"

He smiles warmly. "This is your stage; own it. You are excellent with the press, and I imagine the court will be no different, but only if you make it that way. If you let them scare you and get in your head, then I imagine this night will be quite frightening for you. But if you see them for what they are, people looking to learn about you and how they can work with you, I think you'll find them much easier to handle than you think." He smiles again with confidence. "Remember, they want to impress you as much as you want to impress them. So shine like the star you are. And if anyone tries to tell you otherwise, you look them in the eye and show them what happens when they try to touch the heart of a supernova."

"What does happen if you try to touch the heart of a supernova?"

"You burn up," he chuckles.

"Oh." I pause. "But I can't burn them up."

"Of course, you can. You just have to believe in what is inside here." Damian taps my chest, right above my heart.

"I have nothing to hold over them," I remind him. "I'm not even proper nobility yet."

"Perhaps not, but that doesn't really matter," he says frankly. "You are a Chosen, a princess-to-be, and that alone earns you a great deal of respect. The royal family cares about you, and a true princess respects herself as well as others. I'm not saying you must threaten or belittle anyone. Heavens, no." He frowns. "But when some disrespect you, you politely remind them not to step outside the bounds of their own circle because like it or not, one of the Chosen will be queen someday, and they don't want to start making enemies now."

I nod. "Right. Just have to remember it could be me." That feels so fake.

Damian places his knuckle under my chin. "Try to be confident, night angel. You have so much inside of you. One day, you will see it." He smiles with his eyes full of hope. "Remember, those who stand with you outweigh those who don't."

"I'll try to remember that," I agree. "So are you my escort?"

"I will escort you down." He smiles. "But once we reach the banquet hall, Godwin will be taking over from there."

"Why?" I ask curiously as we get ready to go.

"I never took the time to know the court. And I felt you should have someone with more experience. Sadly, Cedrick refused, and we wouldn't want jealous onlookers, now would we?" Damian smiles as he opens the door for me.

"I suppose not." And having the prince's man as my guide wouldn't do that? I suppose less than Cedrick, but still. "Just have to learn to cope." I brace myself yet again. I have to keep to my new resolve. I could do this. I have to.

Damian smiles gently and offers his arm. "Shall we?"

I nod. "Ready as I'm going to be." I accept his arm, and he leads me out of the room.

We go down the staircases to the entrance hall where the other chosen are to assemble. We had to be ready early to form the line in which we'd stand as we were each introduced to the court. It is odd to have a line this long of people to present, so it might be a bit clunky, but there isn't really a precedent for this. I let out a heavy sigh and glance at Damian, wondering when he'll vanish.

"In order ladies," Lady Hydie, the chief of staff, calls to us, "let's get this line formed."

They let us into the banquet hall and line us up in order, born princesses first and down the line. Poor Florence at the end looks extra anxious. Each girl has her attendant with her, some reviewing notes. We get into position and just as I'm wondering if Damian is going to get stuck with me, Godwin runs over, sliding a bit to a stop. "Sorry, hard to handle two royals at once," he excuses, his hair a bit of a mess.

"It's quite alright." Damian smiles at him. "They haven't started just yet." He then turns to me, takes my hand, and bows to me. "My lady." He meets my eyes as if asking for permission to leave.

I nod it's alright, the anxiety creeping into my stomach again. He nods back then straightens up and presents me to Godwin. Godwin smiles his thanks and accepts my offered hand. "You'd do a better job," he teases Damian.

Damian shakes his head. "I refuse to work with politicians."

"I have no idea what you mean. You already are," Godwin jokes.

"Not of the court, I'm not," Damian insists. "I'll be by the pillar if you need me."

"Thank you." Knowing he's within sight, let alone earshot, is comforting.

"But of course." Damian smiles and bows to me once more. "My lady," he says, then leaves.

"He's odd." Godwin shakes his head.

"Oh?" I frown.

"We told them a while ago they'd need to be your escorts and help introduce you to the court, and he refused. He said, like he did now, he won't work with politicians and actually made quite a fuss of it. I'm not sure why. I'm sure he could learn them fine. The other attendants did. And it's not like you aren't a budding politician." Godwin winks at me. Something squirms uncomfortable in my stomach. "It was rather funny. He said I could do it, so I'm doing it."

"The prince won't need you?"

"He knows the court," Godwin chuckles. "And he's alright with it. You know how he is."

"Sadly I do." I sigh.

"You look lovely." Godwin smiles at me.

"Thank you." That compliment is starting to feel wrote or like it's for Damian, not me. "So what exactly do I have to do other than behave perfectly?"

"Just be yourself, let them kiss your hand and bow to you, nothing fancy. Just talk like they're real people. That's what they look like after all." Godwin is looking around as if seeing when we'll start.

"Look like?" I frown.

Godwin smiles. "Well, they are politicians. They could be many things hidden under that friendly face." I roll my eyes, not amused, though Godwin is grinning. "Perhaps you can spot the wolves versus sheep in the crowd."

"Sheep follow without question. Are they really the good politicians?" I ask, confused.

Godwin beams. "No, the wolves are good. You ever seen how a wolf pack works together?"

"No."

"Then perhaps you should learn. A wolf pack is uniquely well organized to look after its members and works as a team under the alpha and beta. Sheep do whatever the shepherd tells them, or they follow the one or two who wander. The wolves are the members of the court who you can work with. Like a wolf, they are not easy to work with, but they do their best for the pack. I'm impressed you caught that." Godwin grins at me.

"So... it's a secret backhanded compliment to the sheep to not be a wolf?"

"Exactly. You'll fit right in."

I wish. I take a deep breath and make sure my hair and dress are perfect.

"Relax, you look great. Everyone else might be a little over the top." Godwin looks over at the girls. I suppose some of their dresses are larger. My skirt is long and full, but it's softer in its lines. I presume it's because at a dinner you sit most of the time so the skirt was designed for that. Ericka in particular would have a lot of skirt to sit on. I also can't help but notice most of the girls went for more green than red or gold. Was it because of the 'girl in green' comment? They hope the court will think they were the girl in green?

"They'd fit right in if they went to Allauisa's party," Godwin jokes and looks back at me. "But they'll know who the real girls are."

"They will?"

Godwin laughs. "You have nothing to worry about. You handle the press, right?"

"Sure."

"It's no different. Though you can hit Fabian, I don't recommend hitting our visitors. Oh! Or Reinold. You can hit him."

"Who?"

"Look for the guy who is the more ugly version of me."

Before I can ask more, Lady Hydie rushes across. "They should arrive any moment, ladies. They will arrive on their own time, so we'll likely have just a few arrive and the rest rush in." She looks us over with our escorts.

"Where's your escort?" she asks me with a frown.

"Oh, Sir Godwin is assisting me," I explain.

Lady Hydie opens her mouth, but Godwin cuts her off. "I was asked and am happy to assist her. Her attendant is not available for this juncture." His tone clearly indicated that Lady Hydie was not to argue it.

Lady Hydie purses her lips and looks across all of us again. "Alright. The royal family will arrive last. Please recall not to sit until they invite you when you are brought to your seat. Attendants, recall your jobs?"

They mutter assent, nodding or muttering "yes" and the like. I force myself not to smile. We ladies are expected to behave perfectly, but the attendants are like a group of grumpy teenagers.

"Will you be her escort the whole dinner?" Lady Hydie asks Godwin.

"No. Just for introductions."

Lady Hydie frowns. "You think that fair?"

"Her attendant refuses. Want to take it up with him?"

"I do."

Ericka, Azalea, and I groan at that pronouncement. Lady Hydie starts looking around to see if she can spot Damian.

"Lady Hydie, it really—"

"Sir Damian, a word," Lady Hydie calls to him anyway. I give Damian an apologetic smile. He just gives me an assuring smile as Lady Hydie bustles over to him with poor Godwin following in resignation.

That leaves the girls to mingle. Ericka in her stunning green dress full of skirts turns to me. "Proud of yourself?"

"For?" I raise a brow.

"You really just have to always stand out, don't you?" Ericka snips.

"Part of her rebel disguise." Forsythia smirks, fussing with her own more lithe green skirt. She looks more like a snake to me than ever, even if it was a Christmas snake.

"How does standing out make a better disguise? An assassin or rebel wants to hide. Look at Sir Sage. He's a trained assassin and knows to hide. Why would I want to stand out if I was a rebel?" I retort, feeling a bit empowered. I suppose my resolve did a better job than I realized at getting me ready for this.

"Because that's obvious, so you do your best to not look like a rebel. It's how I took so long to get it," Forsythia retorts.

"So, are you proud of how much you stand out? You look like a red sore," Ericka huffs.

"The only thing sore is you," I reply coolly. It's like the confidence I had when defending Lilly from them was coming back.

"Well, I suppose the dress does suit you," Forsythia admits, walking over to me. "It is highly decorated and yet..." she touches some of the stunning lace on my sleeve, "delicate."

Then without warning, she grabs a fist full of it and yanks so hard, not only does it hurt my shoulder, it rips the lace right off the sleeve. I'm so shocked she'd actually do something like I don't react right away, taking in the reality of what she'd done.

"Look what you did," Ericka complains, grabbing the sleeve as if to help put it back. "You know it's delicate."

I step back to avoid Ericka copying Forsythia, but she tries to hold me still. "I'm trying to help." But instead, she just rips the lace off and starts to pull at my other sleeve, but doesn't do nearly as much damage.

"Yeah, help Forsythia," I shoot back, looking at the sleeve. At least the main sleeve seemed alright when Forsythia yanked at it, but Ericka's had ripped the seam along the main sleeve too.

"I'm sorry. I was just admiring it." Forsythia's expression may have been apologetic and impressive acting, but I know better.

"And if you'd stop squirming, I could fix it," Ericka insists and grabs the other sleeve. I am only just able to knock her arm away before pushing her back, but her nail had managed to make a small tear.

"I can fix it myself." I glare at them. I can't believe they'd be this childish.

"You don't have to do it yourself," Ericka huffs in offense.

I turn away from them, choosing to ignore them and trying to figure out what to do. If it had just been the lace ripped off I could take it off both and be fine, but Ericka had ripped the main sleeves too.

"I'll let them argue." Godwin walks back over to me. "Once they're done, we'll..." his voice trails off as he sees me trying to keep the sleeve together. "What happened?" He frowns.

I look up at him, still fuming and point back at the two, standing side by side and muttering— I'm sure —about how rude I was when they tried to help.

"Seriously?"

"They'll insist they were just admiring the work." I am still glaring.

"Your attendant is going to rip Lady Hydie to shreds." Bella walks over and freezes too. "Oh my vene, what happened?" She notices the nail rip in my sleeve. She gasps. "Who did that?"

"Guess." I glare back at the other two.

"Ericka always did have evil nails." Bella frowns. "If only it was just the lace."

"Here." Godwin reaches into his pocket and pulls out, no joke, a little packet of sewing needles with small wraps of thread. "I think we can fix this a few ways..." He folds the sleeve so some fabric covers up the hole. "This will make them shorter though." He frowns.

"The first courtiers are arriving!" Lady Hydie calls to us, still looking annoyed at whatever argument Damian had used to win. Godwin bites his lip, clearing wondering how to fix it quickly.

"You could also take more from the bottom to make it more of a cap sleeve, and it will look less like a patch," Bella suggests.

"Then we can take the non-torn bits to make it more of a dangle decoration than part of a cuff." Godwin nods. Bella smiles at his quick understanding. "Help me roll it into that position. Then I can use a quick stitch for now. Maybe if we get a moment we can do something more permanent."

Bella nods and steps over to my side. She rolls and then holds the sleeve in the position they agreed on. Damian comes over with a slight smile and his hands behind him. "Well, I'd offer my help, but you seem to be well cared for, and as they say, 'three's a crowd'."

"You see what they did?" Bella asks furiously. "The other sleeve is worse." It's true that one is in worse shape than the one they started on.

"Hmm..." He squats down to examine it. "I see. Godwin, can I borrow a needle?"

Godwin nods and tosses him the little packet he'd had in his pocket. Damian catches it and pulls one out to start at the sleeve Bella had shown him.

"You know what?" He stops and looks at the other two. "I think it might be better to finish what those girls started."

"What?" Godwin frowns.

"Take both sleeves off, using your needle to rip the seam at the shoulder." Damian indicates with his finger.

"Alright, she could go sleeveless," Godwin agrees. "We are staying inside." He starts fishing for the seam ripper in his pocket.

Damian looks me over a moment. "I'll be right back," he says and dashes out of the room.

"Bet he has an idea," Bella assures me.

"He better be able to get it within two minutes." I glance at the doors, knowing that's how long it takes for someone to arrive from the front doors into this room. They said the first member of court just arrived.

"He'll have a shrug or scarf or something," Godwin agrees. "I think that will work too. This sleeve would run the risk of ripping easily."

"Shh." I glare back at the two jerks who are smirking to each other at the small fuss we're making.

"Perhaps the cover up would be better. They can't rip anything else." Bella glares at them though they can't see her.

Damian returns a minute later, barely even winded, with a thick Christmas-y red, infinity scarf in hand. "Here we are. Glad I had this as an early idea." He smiles as he puts the loop over my head and has me lift my arms. Once the scarf is tucked under my arms, he has me lower them and puts the second half of the loop over my head and shoulders then pulls it down so it wraps around my shoulders like a shrug. He then gently pulls my hair loose and makes sure he hasn't messed up any of my maid's work.

"Perfect," Godwin declares.

"And warmer." Bella giggles.

I smile. It does feel better being covered and knowing the girls can't mess with the dress. Try to rip this scarf off, I'd get it back anyway. "Ready for the court?" I look at Damian.

He chuckles. "More than ready," he confirms and offers his hand to help me up.

I smile and accept it. "Almost time," Hydie calls to us.

Bella sighs. "I am so telling on them," she mutters as she goes back to her place by Zelda.

"Like he'll do anything," Godwin mutters, making my heart sink.

Damian smiles slightly. "If only he could." He sighs then looks at me. "Will you be alright?"

"Yeah." I nod. "Not much we can do if not anyway, right?"

"Maybe." He smiles. "Just remember, they attack you because they feel inferior. That is why they are all wearing green, after all."

I nod. "That's what they were picking on."

"Perhaps I am too good at my job then." He smiles. "But I'll still be right over there if you need me." He points to the pillar.

I nod. "I'll let you know." How I'm not sure, but I would.

"Just call, and I'll be there." He bows to me then leaves.

I take a deep breath and look at Godwin. He smiles back. "You'll be just fine."

Then the doors start to open, and he quickly goes with me back into line. The first few courtiers aren't hard to please at all. In fact, Ericka's beaming from ear to ear. There are three people in this group. One of them I know, the mayor of Roselpa. He always brought his grandchildren to our shows, and they loved having me sign their programs, or sometimes, his granddaughter would get a pointe shoe or two. With him is a young man who looks like a handsome, male version of Ericka: blond, taller than her though, with striking blue eyes, not quite as blue as Cedrick's but strong just the same. And lastly, there's a lovely woman with strawberry blonde hair pulled into an elegant knot. Her dress is elegant too, yet simple, perfect for the holiday dinner.

When they reach me, Godwin smiles. "Lady Kascia, may I introduce the Lord Mayor Victor with his son, Lord Andrew, and his wife, Lady Rina. My Lords and Lady, this is—"

"I know who this is," the mayor cuts him off with a huge smile as he takes my hand and kisses it after we exchange bows. "You fit in lovelily here. My grandchildren were sad to see you missing at the last shows, but when I told them where you were, they started following the news about you religiously."

"The honor is mine." I smile graciously. "I miss seeing them and the others."

"I'm sure you do. They love seeing you and showing off their collections." The mayor's huge smile almost splits his face. I wonder how I never noticed Ericka's is so much like it. "It's a delight to see you here."

"Thank you. It's nice to see you this holiday." I give him a dazzling smile.

"And as he said, this is my son and his wife." The mayor is still beaming.

"Nice to finally meet you. As my father-in-law said, our children love you." Lady Rina beams as she shakes my hand.

"We hear all the time." Lord Andrew bows to me again. He glances down the line towards his sister, who is distracted talking to her attendant. "And between you and me, I apologize for her."

I have to cover my mouth to prevent laughter busting out of me like a nasty cough. Lady Rina's face says she feels the same. The mayor isn't listening but talking to Godwin.

"She's not that bad," I manage to say.

"Not yet," Lord Andrew mutters. "Between us again, we're with our children on who the new princess should be."

I turn red as Lord Andrew and Lady Rina move on to Azalea on my left. Godwin looks at me and frowns. "You alright?"

"Fine." I smile. "Just wasn't expecting that."

"They're not as nuts as her, are they?" Godwin nods at Ericka.

"No. As you heard, I know the mayor's grandchildren and the Lord and Lady's children. The mayor would bring them to every opening night he could manage, and if it wasn't opening night, he'd bring them another time."

"Lovely. So they're nicer than she is?" Godwin says, making me giggle.

"The children are very sweet." I nod.

"Good. Then the next mayor won't be a pain." Godwin rolls his eyes, making me smile.

It's a few minutes before the next courier arrives. Duke Duarte and his wife, Duchess Willemina. The duke is the head of the national budget. He's a tired looking man with a rather sad face, but he smiles as he looks over my attire and bows to me. His wife is rather strict looking with a sight purse to her lips. She lets her husband do all the talking, but even then he doesn't say much beyond what a pleasure it is to meet me before moving on. Godwin doesn't seem surprised.

Next is the Duke and Duchess Severni who are over the north district who are warm and chatty, complimenting everything about me before moving on. The Duke and Duchess Ovest who are over the west district, so my regional representatives in court. They too have all the praise in the world for me. They are followed by Earl Trandafir who is the governor of Rosepla, meaning he covered more than just the city, but also the provinces around it in the court, unlike the mayor who does not have a seat in court. His wife, Earlaness Rosetta, doesn't speak much either. I find this is a common trend among the ruling couples. One of them does all the talking, sometimes the husband and sometimes the wife. Rarely are they both highly vocal.

All the mayors and governors go by in a blur. It's hard for me to keep track of them all. Most all of them are highly friendly and complimentary. I'm sure they're being as sweet to everyone.

"I take it you're the lady in green." The governor of Anthurium, Marquis Kitsune, smiles at me. "You are causing quite the stir in our people."

"For good, I hope." I smile pleasantly as he stands from kissing my hand.

"Perhaps. It is an honor to finally meet you. I hope Sir Fabian isn't driving you too crazy." The marquis smiles at me.

I laugh. "He's not a bother," I assure him.

"He's kinder to you." The marquis laughs. "I hope to see you again." He kisses my hand once more before moving on.

Godwin sighs dramatically at the next group. "May I present the Count Hubert. Count Hubert is retired from his seat as a district head in the court. Where is the current Count Herman?"

"I'm sure he'll be along," Count Hubert says, kissing my hand. "Waste of time doing all this, if you ask me. The funds for this—"

"Dad." Godwin cuts him off. I pause and look the count over. He does have similar features to Godwin. "Not here." Godwin shakes his head.

That makes me have a question. "Is Count Herman Sir Fabian's brother?"

"That's right." Count Hubert looks impressed. "Not that he does much better, mind you—"

"Dad," Godwin says again. "Where is Reinold?" His tone makes me think whoever Reinold is, he's supposed to be looking after the count.

"He went to pick up his girlfriend, but I guess there was some trouble with her job." The count shrugs.

Godwin sighs. "And you didn't ask Ms. Melonie to come instead?"

"I don't need to be babysat."

"Who did you plan on being your second?" Godwin interjects.

"I don't need one."

"Dad, each member has one. Even the single members of the court bring staff." Godwin sighs. "I'll ask someone to help."

"If I must," the count says begrudgingly. "Still a waste of—"

"Dad." Godwin cuts him off and nods at me, reminding him where they were.

"It was lovely to meet you," I tell the count so he can move on.

"Nice to meet the lady who talks sense," Count Hubert mutters as a staff member that Godwin nodded over comes to lead the count along.

"Your family is delightful." I smile at Godwin.

"That's just my father. He is a little odd in his old age," Godwin chuckles.

"I like your cousin too."

"You're nuts."

I laugh at Godwin's playful smile.

"But really he should have someone with him. He's prone to mouthing off. Forgive him."

"It's quite alright," I assure Godwin. It's better than my father would have been.

Next, I meet the Marquise of Shasta, Marquise Lynn who is a gentle and kind lady. She is escorted by one of her staff, leading me to think she's a widow as she still wears a wedding ring.

I let out a heavy sigh as Fabian tries to slip past me without introducing his wife. "Hey! Get over here." Godwin is not shy. Fabien's wife has a golden quality about her. I don't know how else to say it. She has warm dark brown hair that is swirled around the back of her head beautifully.

"I know her," Fabian defends.

"I do rather look like your wife," I tease Fabian who laughs.

"We do somewhat resemble one another." Fabian's wife smiles at me.

"Lady Kascia, you know my crazy cousin, Earl Fabian. This is his wife, Earlaness Orla," Goodwin introduces. "And of course Earlaness Orla, Lady Kascia is Fabian's lady in green."

"Pleased to meet you." Earlaness Orla shakes my hand. "You do keep him on his toes and entertained. Gives me a break."

"The pleasure is mine." I smile back.

"I'm glad to join in during your visit." A man who looks like a more elegant version of Fabian joins us with a rather harassed looking woman shaking her head as they approach.

"Ah yes, Lady Kascia, my cousin Count Herman, the current district head and his wife, Countess Darcie," Godwin introduces.

"Pleasure." the countess smiles at me, her dark hair fluttering around her face. "An honor to have so many wonderful women from our district doing so well."

"Tribute to the city for sure," Count Herman agrees. "Can I confess I have a favorite?" He winks at me.

"Yeah, yeah, buzz off." Godwin shakes his head at his cousin. "Don't need to over butter her."

"Like Fabian doesn't do that already." Count Herman smiles at his brother who resolutely ignores him. I take it they do not get along.

"Well, there are still plenty of ladies to meet and time after," Godwin points out to his cousin.

"There are, indeed." Count Herman sighs in disappointment. "Until next time." The count kisses my hand before his wife and he go down the line.

"I think that's the last of them." Godwin looks around the room. He then does a quick count in his head. "That seems right. We've done the main forty-six courtly couples, and the few city reps that are here..." Godwin spots Lady Hydie waving at us. "That's all of them."

Chapter 26

Our whole line starts to move towards our places at the long tables, forming an upside down U with the high table at the top. Godwin waits patiently for Damian to swap out with him and lead me to my place. However, I recall to stay standing until the royal family arrives, announced by the normal crier. They're all dressed in Christmas colors, like most of us, wearing their official crowns. When they reach their places at the head table, the king greets us with a friendly prepared speech that's less than a minute long before inviting us to sit.

Damian pulls out the seat for me and pushes my chair in before taking his seat beside me. That seems to be how everyone does it. Even those without their ruling partner have a member of staff help them and sit beside them. Godwin had mentioned that to his father. I glance over at the royal table where Godwin has his father with him which sounds like a good idea. Gavril at least looks quite amused.

The governor and governess of Magalleia are seated close enough for an easy conversation. Count Barsat, the familiar face from all the imaginal announcements as the head of public relations, and his wife Countess Ame are also at our table. Duke Quincy and his wife Catherine are also seated nearby. I suspect that was planned because the count and duke seem to get along well.

I glance at Damian as I realize we and the governors are the third wheels here. Damian just gives me a comforting smile.

"What a unique table," the duke is saying. "But I'd not mind the excuse to talk with you." He looks at the governor. "I hear you're more anxious for the upcoming meeting than anyone."

"Ah yes, if it distracts the fighting," the governor agrees.

"Presuming, it does," the governess reminds her husband.

"Perhaps you'd like to choose a topic we're all familiar with, Quincy." The duchess smiles as she pats her husband's arm.

The duke chuckles. "Forgive me, I'm quite used to jumping right into work, even over a meal." He smiles at me. "I suppose you do not know what we're talking about."

"Meeting with different foreign parties, I imagine." I think it through. "Dragia or Gutcha most likely as that's what Magalleia is closest too."

"See?" The governor smiles, leaning back in his seat with a knowing smile. "Only the brightest girls are left. That was a good guess."

"Though both borders struggle with such attacks." Duchess Ame frowns. "I get letters from home about it all the time."

"So not all Japcharians are happy about them, I take it," the count questions before putting a fork full of food into his mouth.

"I am getting mixed signals from their ambassador, that much is certain. I can't wait for the new ambassador to Japcharia to be found. The last retired suddenly and actually has been vacationing in Japcharia since. I don't know if they just plan on moving there or what the case is." The duke shakes his head. "Has made planning much harder, I can tell you. Their ambassador is fine, but as I say, sending mixed signals."

"Unlike Dragia, who is making it clear they are annoyed." The governor shakes his head.

I lean closer to Damian. "Is it normal for meals like this to be mostly business?" I ask Damian quietly, so the others don't hear.

He chuckles. "Frequently, yes. Sometimes, it is the only peaceable situation they can meet under."

I nod slightly. "So... what am I supposed to do?" Do I chime in? Just listen?

"Depends. Are you interested in learning?" Damian smiles.

"Of course. What else would I be interested in?" I ask.

He shrugs. "Ericka would be bored."

I chuckle. "So I just sit quietly like a good little girl?"

"Not at all." Damian smiles then to the duke. "Your Grace?"

The duke looks over at Damian with a smile then he pauses. "I don't believe I was introduced to you. Or is my memory that slow?"

Damian chuckles. "No, my lord, your memory is perfectly fine. My name is Damian Lexus. I was absent from the line, but I serve as Lady Kascia's attendant, and my brother works with the royal family as a military advisor."

"Pleasure; forgive my not noticing sooner." The duke bows his head to Damian then introduces his wife and the rest of the table.

Damian greets all politely then turns back to the duke. "When you say you are getting mixed signals from the Japcharians, are you able to discuss the nature of your correspondence with us? As my lady is to serve in the court, be as princess or another calling, I thought it might be helpful to discuss."

"Ah yes, of course, forgive me. I forget how little the ladies know." The duke smiles good-naturedly. "Much of our work has to do with handling what borders on either end."

"And of course handling public reactions and press around them." The count winks at me, making my cheeks flush.

"But of course," Damian smiles. "Which means you are no doubt familiar with Sir Fabian." He nods over to the man, sitting further up the table.

"Indeed, a playful thorn in my side, even if it's more like being repeatedly poked by a toddler," the count laughs quietly.

Damian chuckles. "That is a fair assessment. But I am curious what recent news is from the Japcharian border. Are they trying to push the boundary again?" he asks the duke.

"We have quite an influx of them trying to get more land, yes, and plenty of those trying to flee." The duke shakes his head. "An odd number in fact."

"Never seen so many," the countess agrees.

Damian arches a brow and glances at me then looks back at the duke. "Did you say flee?"

"That's what it looks like." The count shakes his head sadly.

"Whereas Dragia is just trying to cause tension." The duke frowns. "I'm guessing Japcharia is after the northern lands again?"

"That's the assumption. They just say they want to come, but why come to a foreign country in droves if not fleeing? Most of all, when it seems to be such a panic. It's an age-old tactic. Have your people move in and mostly live in one area until it pretty much is part of your nation rather than the one it should be by law," the count says.

"Though that is only hearsay from letters," the countess points out.

"Where do these letters come from?" Damian asks.

"Well, I hear about it mostly from her family." The count nods at his wife. "Unless the press asks me about it, I don't notice much otherwise. I hear much more about the southern border these days."

"A more active one, it sounds like. The people complain more about them than they do of the northern visitors." The governor raises his brow in question.

"Well, they're not the friendliest of visits," the governess says in disdain. "They may not be properly called raids or attacks, but they certainly will stir up trouble, and it's getting on our last nerves which were already running low."

"They'll take any excuse, and their princess took quite the offense at being dismissed." The count shakes his head. "Might have been wiser to at least keep her around a little longer."

"But that's what the talks are for. To assure them." The duke shakes his head. "Quite a bit of organization, I'll tell you."

"Easier when they have someone who is actually in charge of responding." The count smiles in sympathy.

"Yes, I would say that is trickier, but at least the Dragians are easier to organize with. I don't have nearly as many back and forth letters or confusion or demanding space and times and all of that. Whereas I can't get a straight answer out of Japcharia in good time. I'll have all the others in good order first." The duke shakes his head. "The curse of the position over state, is it not?"

"I deal with people and press." The count waves it off as if his problems are easy.

"When the people are in revolt?" The governess raises an amused brow.

"Domestic is often easier than foreign affairs," the count chuckles. "Fabian may be annoying, but much like a toddler, he can also be endearing."

"He isn't as dangerous either," the duke agrees. As they look over at him, Fabian is laughing warmly about something. Godwin doesn't look overly pleased.

As we watch, I notice the king isn't laughing. He looks like he is, but I think he's using it to cover one of his more hacking coughs. My brows draw together as I watch, worried the stress of the event will cause another episode like I'd seen at the first public event. I look around to be sure someone is keeping an eye out for it. Sure enough, Sage and Gavril appear to be watching more carefully than was needed.

"Just keep him out of my work," the duke says to the count, getting most to look away from the high table.

Though they return to their conversation, I'm still looking at the high table. The laughter has died down, and the conversation resumed as normal, but I can't help but notice the king is drinking more water than would normally be needed for a meal, likely to try to prevent a cough.

I try to remind myself that it is not my job to look after that secret right now. I have to look good and listen to learn to handle the court. That is my job tonight, but even as I think it, I can't pull myself back to the table. The king is definitely hiding a cough or something. He keeps clearing his throat or licking his lips or something to try to cover up his nervousness about whatever is going on.

It could just be a small tickle. I remind myself. It didn't have to be huge for it to be a struggle. I'd seen how sometimes laughing too long or hard would make him prone to coughing, and there was no attack before or after. It didn't mean anything.

"Can't keep her eyes off him," the duke's voice cuts into my thoughts.

I'm able to contain my jump as I turn back to the table with a smile. I don't confirm or deny I was looking up at the prince. I half wish that was what I'd been looking at.

"Oh, she's not alone. I think if the Enthronement were declared today we'd get double the applicants," the count chuckles in amusement.

"That is saying something. I saw that heap of boxes full of applications they gathered in my mansion before moving it along." The duke shakes his head. "Absolutely incredible to think there was a young woman attached to each one."

"I'm sure the prince enjoyed knowing how many were interested." The count smiles.

I'm sure he was anything but excited about it all. But I doubt saying so would win me the kind of points I want in this kind of conversation.

The duke, count, and governor all start talking about what gathering all the applications was like for them. Their wives find it quite amusing and are laughing and joking good-naturedly about the whole thing.

"Ever think when you put in your application it would be like this?" the duchess asks me playfully.

"No. Not at all." *You have no idea.*

"I can attest it's made some changes. I deal with matters of state, of course, but the change in attitude and types of attacks is certainly noteworthy." The duke shakes his head in amazement.

"It's kept me quite busy." The count nods.

"To the point, I'm having to lock up some reports, so he'll get sleep at night or eat anything," the countess sighs. "That is a tool you'll need," she says to me in a playfully conspiratorial voice.

"Forget locking them up. Distraction is better." The duchess smiles.

The governess laughs. "It can be hard when you work with them though. I can get just as caught up as he is. I actually rely on my staff to help keep us from forgetting all about looking after ourselves."

"That is something to keep aware of," the duchess says to me. "Learn to read him to see what he needs. Sometimes, it's that work partner; sometimes, it's that distraction, and other times, it's locking his work away." She sounds like she's giving me advice. "The girl who learns that will get a leg up." She winks.

I force an uneasy smile. I wasn't exactly expecting them to suddenly be giving me tips on how to win the prince, and therefore in their minds, the Enthronement. It is a tad awkward. I suppose this is the part of the game where they try to get into my good graces, so if I do win, they have the princess as one of their allies. I imagine most all the girls are getting this kind of treatment or perhaps the intimidation I'd seen from the grand duke.

This talk continues as the small orchestra plays Christmas songs in the background of the chatter of the court. The conversation grows more light as the courses go on. The tempting aroma of the feast fills the air. I glance up at the royal table now and then. The king is definitely fighting at least a lingering cough. I wonder if they have an excuse for him before he gives the toast at the end of dinner. I suspect many courtiers will stick around to socialize a bit longer. That is what our teachers prepared us for. As we start on the second to last course, I feel confident I got through part one. Now I just had to make my way through part two.

At least the food is a good treat. I try to focus on it as the talk gets into territory I'm not as comfortable with. Apparently, politics and the tension of a rough court is easier for me to handle than the slightly tipsy banter between court members joking about what "fun" the Enthronement must be. It's nothing crude or even anything that anyone but perhaps the queen would find out of line, but perhaps because I am stuck in the middle, and it is my heart on the line, I wish I could get them to talk work again.

But I do find a distraction. "I don't know if I've ever had so many courses," I joke.

So far, we'd enjoyed a simple fondue, a wonderful hazelnut soup, a light fish with lovely green seasonings, the main course was a fine turkey (a rare Christmas treat in Purerah) with creamy cheesy potatoes, and a fine green bean salad. Presently, we are enjoying an intricate cheese platter that is honestly one of the best things I'd ever tasted.

"Only one more," the duke chuckles at me. "I suppose that is new for many of the ladies." He looks around the table at the random placement of chosen girls. "Makes it quite a treat to have a royal holiday." He takes a small sip of the wine he'd been enjoying with the cheese. That is what they're all doing. The ladies in particular look a bit tipsy. I'd managed to avoid breaking my Custod oath and drinking any alcohol by using the water glass that sat beside my wine glass. I'd hoped to make Damian mistake my glass for his, but so far he's not even glanced at his, let alone mine.

"This simple old fare to you?" I ask. "I've never had such a fine turkey before." Our family rarely had the extra money or time to prepare a turkey. I'd had it once or twice at holiday parties I'd attended, but it was much less than this and not nearly as delicious. In fact, until now, I didn't know I cared for turkey.

"Oh, it's as fine as it's ever been!" The countess laughs. "Not to put a bad name on the royal family, but I'd never thought the food and variety quite as good as it is this year."

"That is true." The count nods. "They do seem to be making extra effort this year."

"Because more people came for the Enthronement." The duchess giggles behind her hand. The duke laughs more openly.

I force a smile. "Perhaps." That does seem a bit odd. I thought that's what the royals always spent all the tax money on, lavish parties like this. So either they'd gone extra extravagant this year, or my dinner company is more drunk than tipsy. "Either way, it's the finest turkey I've ever had. And those potatoes were a treat I'd never had the like of. And these cheeses are divine."

"Surely from the farms to the north east. Fine dairy farms there." The duke nods slightly bigger than he needs to. "They also have some of the best cheesemakers there. They make so many different kinds. It's family tradition there. Amazing how many impressive artistries we have in Purerah that are fading into obscurity because of this blasted war."

The countess huffs. "And Purysia acts like they are the center of art and culture in the world."

"Allausia certainly tries to keep up with that," the duchess laughs. "Though they are far more good humored."

"Puryisians aren't that stuck up, just certain they are the best at everything." The countess takes a small sip of her drink.

"Unless you want a good sport." The governor laughs loudly, almost making me jump. "Those are fun loving people. Those lads know how to play a good game of sparkleball."

"Reason their team is most often world champions. I would be quite happy to see them lose more often than they do," the count agrees with a slightly rougher edge to his voice.

And the conversation diverges into talk of the sport. I keep my composure, but honestly, I hardly know the rules of sparkleball, let alone have any points or comments on Purerah's national teams strengths and weak points versus other nations.

My mind wanders, wondering if it was expected of royalty to attend such events and trying to picture myself sitting through a match (something I've *never* done or thought I would) when they bring in the smooth chocolate pie that is one of many traditional desserts for the holiday.

"This they never get wrong," the countess declares. "The palace is known for doing pies well."

"Is it?" I'm not sure I've ever had a pie from the kitchens here. The idea they're famous for it is a surprise.

"Oh, it is." The duke gives me a smile. "You'll understand when you taste it."

I take a bite, and my eyes widen. Is that a hint of egg nog? And the crust is so perfect, buttery and just the right amount of flakiness.

The duke laughs at my reaction. "And I don't think anyone else in the world knows how to make this unique combination and make it work. It's perfect." He takes a huge bite of his and washes it down with more wine. I can't imagine how that tasted good, but I don't comment on it.

"It is a delightful treat we only get but once a year," the countess agrees, but she savors each bite more than the duke does who I'm pretty sure is getting close to having too much to drink.

"You know, if this is how these events will go once we finally have a princess to handle the events properly, then we should have thrown this Enthronement ages ago," the duke declares. "Easily the finest banquet we've had in years."

"The queen has her hands full with other things and doesn't get as much time to organize such things," the duchess chides gently. "It's not her fault."

"If the kingdom weren't at war, I'm sure she'd handle fine on her own," the governess agrees.

"True, true," the count agrees with her. "In fact, most of these parties are just templates of the years before. The queen just makes final approvals."

"Not the standard sadly," the governess says as if explaining to me. "But it is also traditional for the crown princess to help with such things."

"Did the candidates help at all?" the countess asks. "Might explain the upswing in quality."

I shake my head. "No, we've been too busy learning the ropes."

"Be a good way to test for that," the countess says as if to herself.

"There's no need for that." The duke wags a finger at her.

"You may need to take a breath." The duchess takes his hand and gently lowers it. "Loose lips, darling."

"I can say as I like." The duke gives his wife a look.

"You should really take it as a compliment that they feel comfortable enough with you to get tipsy," the governess whispers to me. "They aren't always so relaxed."

I force a smile of thanks. It might be a compliment, but I have *no* idea how to handle someone who has had too much. Custods don't drink because of their oath, so the only drunks I ever saw were fake on stage, someone I avoided on the street, or in the audience being shown out by security.

We'd all finished our desert by now, and the staff is slowly taking away plates until every last one is cleared. A gentle ringing makes the players halt the music, and everyone in the room turns to the high table. I do the same, admittedly with some anxiety, as the king gets up to give the final toast. I glance at my glass, wondering what is the best way to look like I drank the wine.

"Thank you for humoring our little tradition yet again," the king smiles around at everyone, holding his glass in one hand. "And I mean enduring this toast before you get to enjoy mingling with those you want to instead of those you were assigned to sit by. I'm sure you're all happy for free food."

That wins a friendly chuckle all around and one rather loud "here, here" from Fabian or Godwin's father, or maybe it was both. I spot Godwin elbowing his father in the ribs either way.

"Another year has passed in our court, and a lot has changed. We've had struggles and changes. The war still rages on, but at least it's not as virulent as it has been."

I frown at his phraseology. That isn't the kind of word I'd normally expect to hear from the king. Either someone else had written the toast or he was quoting something, or perhaps, he really is smarter than he lets on and slipped up.

"But there is certainly hope this Christmas season with how the people are responding to the Enthronement, and of course, the hope of finally having our crown princess in our court." That gets more positive reactions. I can tell the duke isn't the only one a bit tipsy.

As the room cheers at the king's comments, Damian casually leans over to me and gently whispers in my ear. "Your glass is safe. I had it filled with cranberry juice," he says then pulls back.

I start a bit in surprise and look at him, but only sideways to not draw attention, not quite managing to fully restrain my smile. He is quite good at what he does, seeing to things before they even cross my mind. He certainly has kept me competitive in this game.

"And of course, we have the pleasure of our fifteen lovely Chosen ladies here with us, giving up time with their families and friends during this season. So this year's toast, I'd like to add a toast to them for all they have and will do, our princess-to-be, whoever she may be, and a successful season that we will continue to work together as friends in this royal court to end the fighting so that this time next year, we can have a much more peaceful holiday."

The king raises his glass, and we all stand. The part we'd been warned about starts, the long interlude of music. When it ends, we drink. It really isn't that long, but it feels like forever as they play before we take our drinks. I find I rather like cranberry juice. I can't help but smile at how the duke and governor down their drinks quickly.

And with that, the formal sections of the dinner are finished. But that still leaves the tea portion, the final course that is really just a beverage to enjoy as we mingle as we like. It is not even presented at the meal tables. A round table is placed in the center of all the tables with various teas that staff members prepare as requested and serve. There also is coffee and cocoa for guests to enjoy if they prefer. After a meal that large, I'd rather not have anything too heavy, and a light tea is just fine for me.

I notice a few members of the court trying to get their rather drunk spouses to drink something heavier to help with their tipsiness. Some members go up to the royal table to speak with the king and queen, likely thanking them for the evening, and heading straight out. Others mingle. The governor and governess thank me for a lovely time that evening and go right out.

I can't help but frown. They didn't bother with the king or queen at all, as if I was a proper substitute. *That's a good thing. You're competing now,* I remind myself. *Be happy about it. You're winning. It's fine.*

I fuss with my dress as an excuse to get my nerves under control before I brave whatever wave of socialites I'd deal with next.

The duke, duchess, count, and countess have vanished, likely to socialize or speak with someone they needed to for work or would have chosen to speak to if they picked their own seats. I am unsure where I'll end up, but I know this is part two of the insanity so go get my drink and decide to let them chase me as there is no one here I'd like to chase.

The crowd I gather is quite interesting. I'm not too surprised Fabian came over, but he didn't come first. Instead, Godwin's father, Count Hubert, approaches me first. Fabian takes the excuse without question as does his wife, Earlaness Orla. Just before they reach me, Marquis Kitsune also comes over to me. I can't help but fear that, as he came with staff and not a spouse, that he's looking for a Chosen cast off to try to court.

"Lady Kascia, I know you must hear this all the time, but you look perfect." The marqis grins at me.

I nod my thanks. "I do hear that a lot," I confess. "But it's still appreciated."

"Well, I still don't know why she has to be 'the girl in green' when she's the only one not in green."

"No, Princess Zelda didn't bother." Fabian grins.

Count Hubert mutters, but I can't hear what he's saying. I can't decide if he's just drunk, old, or if this is just the way he is. Now I take the time to look at him, he isn't as put together as many of the others on the court. Perhaps this is because he is retired, but his beard and mustache aren't as perfectly trimmed as it bustles about in his grumbling.

"I trust you aren't causing trouble." Godwin appears between his father and Fabian, wearing a clearly fake smile that he keeps on as he mutters to Fabian. "You're keeping an eye on him, right?"

"He doesn't need—" Fabian starts to say, but his wife interrupts.

"I'm keeping an eye on him."

"Thankfully, someone is." Godwin smiles. "Next time, no matter what his girlfriend says, bring his normal caretaker."

Fabian waves Godwin off. "She needed a day off, and you can't blame him for not wanting to have what he could have had rubbed in his face."

"You'd be the only one rubbing." Godwin sighs.

It's not hard to tell they are all family. I can't help but smile.

"If you mean me, I don't need watching after," Count Hubert blusters.

"Of course not," Godwin says, but it's clear he doesn't buy or believe a word of it. "I just wanted to make sure you're alright. I know you are used to Reinold helping you out, if not Melanie."

"I'm just fine," the count insists. "You attend the boy you're supposed to handle."

"Dear Uncle," Fabian says with the utmost graveness, "I'm afraid to tell you, you are no longer a boy."

I wish I could say I didn't laugh, but I do along with everyone else. Even Damian couldn't help but chuckle. The count mutters more nonsense indigently as Godwin sighs and excuses himself to attend the prince.

"You should show more respect." The poor marquis is smiling though trying hard not to.

"How couldn't I? It was right there," Fabian chuckles good-naturedly.

"Your poor uncle," Earlaness Orla sighs tiredly. "And of course he's no longer on the court, so it's harder to take shots at him in the paper."

"I can handle whatever he shoots at me," Count Hurbert insists.

"Of course you do." Fabian pats him on the back rather patronizingly which was clearly intended as it annoys the poor count even more.

"Perhaps you should run again just to show him up," the marquis jokes.

"Not like anyone does much good on the court these days anyway," Count Hurbert complains rather loudly. "When I had a seat at least people were trying. Now a days—"

"We just complain about other people trying." Fabian grins. That makes the marquis laugh. "No offense, uncle. After all, I'm even more guilty than you. I do it publicly and get paid for it." Which wins another round of light laughter.

"It is easy to complain sometimes," The marquis also tries to excuse it.

I have to force myself to verbalize my thought. "I prefer action."

"Indeed, my lady in green." Fabian bows to me dramatically. "Why we love you."

"I haven't seen her do much yet," the count mutters then starts to mumble under his breath again, his mustache twitching and bustling about as he did.

"Speaking of doing," Fabian turns to the marquis, "you're up for re-election this next cycle, aren't you?"

"I am. And some foolish rebel sympathizer is on the other end," the marquis sighs.

"Hmm, not one of these former pretty ladies, is it?" Fabian's tone goes into reporter mode at the drop of a hat. I just sip my tea, raising my brows at the sudden interview taking place.

"No, no, just some foolish boy who thinks his rank, yet being poor would make him better in court than someone with the skills I have. The normal kind that never wins." The marquis shakes his head.

"You do have a very torn area. You run for... just the city position or governor position?"

"I'm working to keep my governor position. District is not quite in my reach, and that's not up for a tad longer." The marquis glances at me. He better not be thinking to improve his rank with me. Apart from marriage, how does one improve their rank?

"Do you plan to try?" Fabian asks.

"Not something I'm thinking about. It's about one election at a time, and of course, the people I've promised to serve until they promote me or throw me out." The marquis smiles the perfect public relations smile.

I sigh, thinking this might get dull for me again quickly, sipping at my tea and wondering when it's safe for the Chosen to slip away. So far, all fifteen of us are still in the mingling area.

"You don't sound at all worried for your seat." Fabian raises his brow in question.

"You should always worry about your seat. It's when you don't, you lose it," Count Hubert says forcefully.

"Too true." Fabian nods. "You never let that happen. He retired. He was not voted out," Fabian informs the marquis and me. He then winks at Damian as if sharing the secret that Damian already knew. I roll my eyes. I highly doubt Damian knew that.

Damian simply smiles, but I think I catch a very slight roll of his eyes. I wonder if anyone else saw it as Damian puts on a more gentlemanly smile and turns to the count. "You must have served the people well to have kept your seat until retirement."

"That's how you stayed in office in those days. Not by war mongering like they do these days," the count complains.

"We do no such thing. It's just gotten much more intense since your time," the marquis explains. "Rebels are not the only problem anymore. The people who want nothing to do with it are just as bad."

"Nothing to do with it?" The challenging tone pops out of me before I can think it through. I don't like what he's implying.

"Yes. Of course, those are the votes that matter because it's the only time those timid people offer a vote. They're too preoccupied in their little lives to bother with actually assisting in solving the problems that are causing havoc in their lives," the marquis says with a tone I don't miss. He's speaking like he's explaining something rather complicated to an inexperienced child. He may be trying to hide that's how he sees me, but I don't miss it one bit.

I'm not the only one. The way Count Hubert starts muttering to himself makes it quite clear he disapproves of his tone as well. Fabian's eyes are alight as if he'd just found gold in his wine glass, and his wife is looking at him sideways with a small smile like she's making sure a child doesn't hurt himself having too much fun.

"So what do you think they should be doing?" I ask.

"Those who do nothing are no better than those fighting against us," the marquis says with the firmness of a teacher dispelling a common myth to his pupils.

"So they should, what? Take up arms and fight off the rebels themselves?" I challenge.

"You misunderstand. I do not mean they need to physically go out and fight them, but standing up and stating their loyalty, if they have any. That would do more than being silent to reach those who are roped into rebellion because they are drawn to anyone with an opinion. They're too busy with the day-to-day to see that is how they'd break free."

"So what do you think they're doing instead?" I ask, trying to hide my indignation.

"Mostly complaining about the problems to their officials instead of doing something about it," the marquis huffs. "I get more demands for help with food or extra security than I do reporting actual crimes or rebels which is how we stop the problem for the need."

"Excuse me?"

The marquis sighs as if tired of trying to explain something simple to a child. "The best way for them to help themselves isn't to keep crying about it. It's to do something. Stand for their loyalties, or for Merlin's sake, get some."

"You mean campaign for you."

My quip makes a sudden quiet come over the group, but I'm too indignant to care.

"What exactly do you think they're trying to do when they come to you for help? They're not saying 'help me because I don't know what to do', it's that they cannot help themselves. They'll be punished if they fight back. You know as well as anyone the only way to really fight back is to be a rebellion member yourself or go to the people you trust to help you. What you really want is them to prove that they want to be loyal to the current ruler: you. Not the royal family but you so the rest of the scared sheep will do the same.

"How can you be so blind to what it's like for them? You're from one of the most rebel stricken cities in the war. What can a man who's hardly making enough to feed himself, let alone his family, do against rebels taking his wares under the name of true patriotism? You're no better than they are, holding what they need over their heads before you'll lift a finger for them, and you call them the child. How can you be so blind to those who need your help?"

"Excuse me? For one with no rank, you've got a big mouth. Getting a bit ahead of yourself, aren't you, Chosen?" He raises a brow at me. He's still looking at me like a child, likely how he looks at his people coming to him for help.

That only makes me angrier. "I'm speaking as someone who's needed the help of her mayor or governor. I'm standing up for the people you should be happy to defend, happy they are coming to you instead of causing more crimes or worse on your streets by trying to take care of it themselves. You speak of loyalties. They have loyalties to their families. I know how dangerous it can be to speak your mind, most of all for the royals. They come to you for help because there's no other choice. They will only be persecuted worse if they speak up for you. And why should they? Your loyalty should be to them, and instead, you blame them for the problems. How many of their problems or requests have you met, marquis?"

"How many have you?" he challenges back. "You know nothing of these matters."

"I know when to stand up for my people when those who should provide justice only offer it at a price. If they want real help, they have to make themselves targets or your campaign scouts. It's people like you that fuel the rebels. It's people like you that have taken all the trust the people had in the royals and their system because you're using it against them."

"How dare you? Where do you get the right—"

"To defend those who are defenseless? By being a decent human being. You're *elected* to a position where that's your job. How can you complain about doing it? How can you run for the office you clearly don't really want? I think the real cry baby here is you."

"My lady, you are out of line."

"Is she though?" Damian arches a brow. "You best be careful, marquis. She is in the running to be your future queen, and you don't keep your seat by burning bridges. And even the runners up will receive court positions. I'd choose my words with great care tonight. High chances are you'll be working with her in court by the end of next year." He smiles that knowing smile of his and looks at me with pride.

I try not to smile as the flush creeps into my cheeks. This kind of outburst is exactly what I'd been afraid of. What if he turned around and called me a rebel? What more could I do? But I couldn't just stand there and listen to him belittle those who came to him to escape that exact treatment from the "holier than thou" rebellions.

"One who still has much to learn." The marquis folds his arms with a huff. "But who offered a good debate and practice for that fool of a rebel sympathizer. You sound just like him."

"Then you better hope your people are too busy crying to listen. Because if they hear a candidate speak like that, that's who they'll go to. They want someone to help protect them. If they hear someone protecting them from you, they'll make you the enemy faster than you can blink. Perhaps I'll see you in a year." My tone clearly indicates I doubt it before I put down my finished tea.

Honestly, I'm afraid I'll lose control of my mouth again and get into more trouble. At least angering a lowly marquis from a city too far to be a problem in day-to-day court wouldn't hurt my chances in the Enthronement, but if higher members heard that, I'd be investigated for sure.

"But perhaps this isn't polite talk for such a party. Forgive me, my lord, I'll let you enjoy the evening." I give him a bob of a curtsy before walking away.

"Comment before I go write that down in my 'never to forget' journal?" I hear Fabian ask the marquis as I go.

"Not heard someone bold like that in decades," Count Hubert mutters but more clearly than I have heard him all night.

Damian joins me with a smile. "I'd say you turned a few heads. I'm proud of you, night angel." He beams with fatherly pride.

"You mean I just burned a bridge?" I smile back though. I honestly can't say I'd go back and undo what I did even if I could.

Damian shrugs. "No one was going to cross it anyway."

"I suppose a simple governor isn't someone a princess would have to deal much with. And it doesn't sound like he'll be in office long anyway." Though do I want a more rebel sympathetic governor to deal with?

"With that attitude, likely not," Damian agrees. "Especially as the royal family will need to place the Chosen girls in court positions. If he is causing the kingdom that much trouble, he could lose his seat before his reelection. I think the courtiers are so focused on the princess-to-be and the 'show' of the Enthronement they forget that, but the royal family has not. They may use the end of the Enthronement to make necessary 'adjustments' to the court," he says as he glances around the room.

I look around too. "Seems wise." I look over at the high table where the royal family are still stuck. I frown at Forsythia standing beside Gavril with a dazzling smile. She's using him as a prop. To Gavril's credit, it's not like he let her take his arm or anything. "How much more do I have to endure?" I ask. I can't tell if any other girls have left, but the crowd is smaller.

"We can return to your room if you like." He smiles understandingly and offers his arm.

"That sounds lovely." I smile and accept it. He nods back and leads me from the room and up to my own. My maids help me get into my night clothes and clean up. They play a Christmas music box as I sip my night tea and relax, surprisingly proud of how I'd done. That was the last feeling I'd expected to have this evening.

After Damian and my maids leave, I sit on my bed, finishing the last bit of the tea, watching the puppy sleep. Perhaps I could still have that fire. I may have rejected my father, but that passion for my people does not have to be rejected too. It could be my motivation when other motivations fail.

I wonder how Gavril would have reacted to my outburst. It wasn't too different than when I'd asked how he could work for the royals. Perhaps there is more hope in standing up than I thought. The marquis didn't call me a rebel. He hinted I'm a sympathizer, but that's a far cry from being an actual rebel. Perhaps Forsythia really is just trying to intimidate me.

I need to stop being intimidated. I have to learn to be the princess before I am. Tomorrow, I'd have to work up the nerve to stand up to my fellow Chosen. It was one thing to speak up to a courtier I'd never met or may never meet again. It would be a whole other game to stand up to the other girls.

Chapter 27

The next morning, I avoid the paper at first and just go to enjoy participating in lessons for dance again with the rest of the ballet. Mother does not mind one bit. It is nice to do a routine where I didn't have to make up myself, getting back into the drill with everyone else. I feel it does me more good than a week of my own lessons. Maybe I could have Mother leave me a book or something with how I should do lessons and drills when she leaves.

But I can't avoid the article forever. I go to have breakfast in my room, so I can avoid the other girls' reactions until after I read it. I step into my room nervously, having my maids help me into a day dress before I dare ask where my copy is. Vivian points at my desk.

I take a deep breath before I pick it up. Unlike the others, my feature is on the front page. That can't be good. I scan it to be sure it's not outing my rebel past, but no rebel-heavy words stand out and the title is just fine.

The Lady in Green

Lady Kascia, the lady in green, is the girl who taught me this game was worth taking seriously. If you missed the interviews, you need to tune in next time to get the full story, but her ability to be fun and talk about real issues struck me as the exact kind of queen we need. Before that point, she was relatively unknown apart from her already devoted fans. Lady Kascia is world renown for her portrayal of Miss Daae in *The Phantom* and other stunning performances of other famous shows.

Lady Kascia is the daughter of Peodrick and Chryasinth Thorapple. Her friends say she was always a dedicated performer and had a knack for playing the roles of princess or fair maiden turned princess. Her first major role was playing Clara in *The Nutcracker Suite* when she was eight years old.

But that's not all that helped shape contestant number twelve in the Enthronement. The local cobbler reported, "As soon as I heard of the Enthronement, I thought of her. I knew she'd be good for the kingdom and the experience would be good for her. I told her the moment I could, she should go for it."

And he isn't alone. The impressionist who took her first impression for the competition reported much the same. He told reporters, "She just struck me as different. She didn't ask for a retake like most girls. She even apologized for the others giving me a hard time and told me she'd hope and pray they were nicer to me. I watched, hoping she'd get higher in the rankings. I haven't met another girl I thought better for the position."

It seems anywhere and everywhere Lady Kascia goes, she inspires confidence. She's grown a following being the only contestant to have a fan club formed supporting her who did not have one when the Enthronement started. The group started with personal friends, but after her interview, it grew to include many more. Her ability to capture attention on and off stage has brought a crowd who before had no interest in the Enthronement.

Sources within the castle even report she takes it on herself to help protect the other girls during rebel attacks. Rumor also has it she was among the initial girls to be kissed by the prince, if not the first, though no such rumor could be confirmed. However, sources can confirm she's inspired quite a bit of jealousy from other girls who feel threatened by her ability to generate support. Such a quality is vital for the future queen of our war-torn nation that few others can bring to the table.

But her most glaring difference is her courage. She was unafraid to talk about real substance in her first public interview on the castle's steps as well as in her latest public interview. And in many conversations outside the public eye, she does the same. Unlike other contestants, Lady Kascia was willing to make comments that could be seen as offensive but had real meaning and intent to unite the kingdom once again under its current Potentate ruler. She brought something to discuss while others played the role of faithful contestants, saying what we wanted to hear. Despite her perhaps controversial statements in the interview, it seems from reports inside and outside the castle that Kascia is one of the very few that has support from all sides.

The only fear from her is the fact she seems too perfect. She is a public favorite, a friend to everyone, a favorite of the prince, perfect all around. She has the conviction, courage, and talent to lead. But perhaps there is more hidden about this Chosen lady than meets the eye. Time only will tell if it's as true as we hope.

This contestant has changed how the public sees what the Chosen queen should be. If the interviews were any indicator of what we're dealing with for the future queen, one thing is for sure. Others may be willing to play the role of princess to win the crown, but this actress is done acting.

I stare at this for a good five minutes after I finish it. Well, apart from being "too perfect" — which is frankly true. I likely have the biggest secret — I got a stunning review.

My biggest fear is the other girls. They are going to eat me alive. Dahlia is going to be furious. Forsythia will be ready to get me from behind at any moment. The other girls are going to say it's just a sign that it is me. I'm the paper's favorite; that's for sure. Would I be the people's favorite?

The puppy makes some happy talking sounds at me to get my attention. I look down to see she's trying to be cute and rolls onto her back to get belly rubs. I giggle and give them to her. "You don't care what any reporters say, do you?" I cue, picking up a toy to toss for the puppy. She races after it happily.

There's a frantic knock on the door. I nod at Flur that she's allowed to get it, but Alsmeria barges into the room in a way that would make my teachers scream in horror.

"Did you read it?" she demands, holding her own copy of the paper. "Kassie! Oh my vene! Can't you believe it? You dominated." She rushes over to me and sits on the vanity bench. "And they mentioned us! Our little fan group. It's amazing. I didn't know they interviewed some of us. And my goodness, they were so nice. Adam gave a great quote too. No wonder you just flew through the preliminaries." She laughs in delight and hugs me. "Oh, and you have questions to answer." She snaps the paper in my face. "Did he kiss you?"

"Mira." I laugh.

"No joke girl, spill it," Alsmeria insists. But I refuse to spread the gossip no matter how Alsmeria begs. "Dog," Alsmeria says to the red puppy, who looks up from chewing the bone I threw for her. "Tell her it's okay to share."

The dog tries to copy her last few words sounding like "to share" in a squeaky huff, but her head tilt makes it clear it is a question. I roll my eyes. This is not going to help.

"Miss Kascia is a lady. She doesn't gossip," Vivian says approvingly as she puts a pair of shoes away in my closet.

Alsmeria keeps trying though until she has to go before Mother finds she's missing.

"Excited, isn't she?" Vivian says.

"Don't they make teas for that?" Flur says, making me laugh.

"Shall we prepare you for lunch?" Vivian asks. I hesitate. Do I want to face them?

"I have an idea." Flur beams and goes into the closest. I am afraid of her idea.

"You should go, miss. Don't let them scare you," Vivian says. "I'll help Flur." She steps away too.

Damian smiles at the maids then turns to me. "I don't blame you."

"What?" I look up at him. That is not what I expected him to say.

"Well, I am pleased you received a glowing review, but I don't blame you," he repeats. "I would be just as nervous in your shoes. No one likes knowing people are waiting for you to make a mistake. And that's what Fabian's done. He couldn't find any dirt, so being the annoying rascal that he is, he decided to point people in a different direction and make them worry about you, and that isn't fun or fair. Especially when he didn't do that to anyone else."

"He had something to pick on for everyone else," I point out.

"Not Jonquil," Damian counters. "Though I did overhear him griping to his cousin about that not actually being the one he wrote."

"Really? I thought he was assigned to do all of them." I frown.

"He is. But it sounds like his editor included more than a few changes on hers," Damian says.

"Oh." I better not spread that around, or the gossip would be a nightmare.

"Still. What he did was extremely rude. He didn't have to do that." Damian rolls his eyes. "And he shouldn't make claims he has no sources for. But I know his kind. He's a troublemaker. As Cedrick's wife used to say, 'he's the spoon'." He can't help but smile at the memory.

I smile a little. "You don't think he had evidence to support what he said? He sure had plenty of quotes."

"True enough. Perhaps not the evidence he wanted though. He did say it was you that made him take the Enthronement seriously." Damian smiles at me.

"That doesn't sound like a good thing," I point out.

"And why not?" He arches a brow.

"You said he's a spoon. And I'm the one who made him leave whatever other shiny toy he had to come here. Sounds like he finds me a trigger or something."

"Maybe, maybe not." Damian shrugs. "From what Godwin told me, Fabian is as mischievous as he is excitable. He loves his art, and most of all, he wants to be the one to record history. He wants to be where the most important thing is happening. For a while, he believed that was the war up north, but after he saw your first interview, he left the battlefront immediately and came here. Something about you made him believe this is where he wants to be."

"Wouldn't the Enthronement just make sense to be the most important place to be for history?" I ask. Fabian sure convinced me that's the case.

"Not when everyone writes it off as a powder puff show about doe-eyed girls falling for the dreamy prince charming. You showed him it was more than that."

You mean he wants to tell the world what I really am, I think, but I keep that inside. "So now he's waiting to break the biggest story since the war began." He just doesn't know the story is I'm a rebel.

"He's waiting to see how this contest will change the course of the war," Damian replies. "How it will change this country, and its people. But you can bet he'll be there with a quill in hand, waiting to guess or predict the smaller turns of events along the way. The paper doesn't choose who the true princess is, nor does he, but that won't stop him from trying."

"So, he'll make the biggest hay he can?" Of course he would. I was just hoping otherwise. Damian had said what Fabian thought almost word for word. And Damian says he doesn't know everything.

"Partly, but there is also something he pointed out you have to remember." Damian meets my eyes.

I look back into his deep green eyes.

"Your friends are loyal to you. Yes, you have your share of mistakes and secrets, but your friends, the people he talked to, would not share those things with him. You have people here and at home who love and support you. And they will do so no matter what anyone else says."

I smile a bit. He's right, even if that too is terrifying. "So how do I not let them down?" I ask.

Damian smiles. "By being the best 'you' you can be."

I nod. I hope that will be enough. "Now I just have to somehow handle the girls," I say.

"By being you," Vivian says as she and Flur come out with their arms full of whatever I'm wearing to lunch.

It's a beautiful dress. Then again, are any of them not stunning? This one is a soft gold with a hint of pink with amazing bead and embroidery work making the look of winter branches across it, shaping the bust and arms and neckline of the dress in a look I'm sure is even more beautiful when it's able to actually outline my shape rather than just being on the hanger. The sleeves and top part of the collar are slightly transparent looking, but as it goes down to my wrists, I imagine it would keep me warm even in the cold castle. The skirt is the kind I'd see a queen wearing but not over the top.

The color contrasts my skin so perfectly, making it look a bit darker than it is by contrast, but the makeup they use gives me an almost golden glow, and the choice to let my hair down is perfect. It curls down my left shoulder and back, making me look soft and gentle yet powerful at the same time. I really do look like a queen, but not a harsh one. A quiet grace, meek, powerful but controlled. But anyone could dress like this and look that way, right?

"You fill it out perfectly." Vivian helps arrange my hair on my shoulder a bit more perfectly.

"And not just anyone can. You are just as much in line as the rest of them. Don't let them make you feel otherwise. Make sure they remember it," Flur says. "No one is going to forget you."

Damian chuckles a little and looks at me. "They are right, you know. You have more power than you realize. I have said it once before and I'll say it again: I never add anything. I only enhance what is already there. Anyone can wear a dress, but only you can take that dress and make it the look of a queen. So, look in the mirror and tell me: what do you see?"

I blink a few times and manage a smile. "I-I see grace, power. I see a gentle and meek lady."

Damian smiles. "I agree. Those qualities come from you, and no one else."

I take a deep breath. I'm not sure that's easy to believe. It's not easy to believe that the woman in the mirror is really me. But it cannot be anyone else. Even I saw the dress lacked something on the hanger. It needed the right person to make it come alive. And I need to stop pretending it is not me. These people have faith in me for a reason. It is time I test their faith and mine. If I am going to deal with the drama of the other girls, I am going to have to own up to myself and them about who I am and be willing to own it instead of hiding and apologizing.

I shut my eyes a moment and nod. "Do you really want me to do this?"

"I do." Damian nods and looks at the other two.

"Win or not, you're my princess," Vivian says. Flur blushes too hard to answer and just nods.

Then maybe it's time I learn to do what I came here to do. Be what my people need. I'd started on that road, but I have to dedicate myself to it. No matter the consequences.

Damian escorts me down to help give me courage. I take a deep breath before stepping through the door.

"This isn't stupid, is it? Is there really a chance I can win this?" I ask.

Damian smiles at me. "Only if you are willing to take this chance. I have every confidence you can win this, but you have to believe it to truly succeed."

I nod again. "Then let's do this." He nods then leads me into the room.

I look around to see who I'm dealing with. It looks like my preparation took a bit longer, or longer than anyone else. I think everyone is here.

Dahlia may have snapped her fork in half, but I try not to pay her or the others any heed. Instead, my eyes go to the head table. The queen is appraising me with a soft smile. The king is smiling, holding back his reaction. He looks away and tries to tease Gavril as a distraction. Gavril's face is frozen as he looks at me. I can't read his expression. His father's nudging shakes him out of it, and he looks away. I smile a bit.

Damian lets go of me. I turn to face him as he bows low to me. I bow my head and give him a small curtsy back before he heads to his table. I walk over to my place. A servant scrambles to pull out my chair for me. I sit down, and he pushes me back in before going back to his place. Another servant places my meal in front of me. I feel surprisingly comfortable eating properly in this getup. It's really becoming second nature.

At first, I think everyone is afraid to speak to me. I don't mind. They can deal with their own problems. I'm going to play this game. I want the throne. I just need to get myself to finally decide I have to let go of my old life and want the man who comes with it. I sigh a little in relief. At least, that should be easier if we can get over our rough patch. If my plan for Christmas works, it will be. I restrain my nervousness.

"Your team is so talented," Lilly finally dares speak to me after the initial staring dies down, and people return to their meal. "You look perfect. That on top of your article, and you're sure to be going to at least the top ten."

"I don't know. Think she's made her poor prince a bit shy," Azalea jokes, looking at Gavril who's grinning to himself and trying not to look at me while his father nudges him teasingly now and then.

"I can deal with that as it comes," I reply.

The girls look at me in surprise. "Wow, what happened to you?" Jonquil asks. "That article go to your head?"

Lilly, Bella, and Azalea glare at her. I smile a bit and shake my head. It's not that big of a deal.

"Just because she decided to fill the part more doesn't mean you have to be jealous," Bella says.

"It's not that. She's talking like she's already won," Jonquil defends.

"I just... decided I actually want to win," I say honestly, taking a bite, so I avoid having to answer right away as they all gape at me.

"And you weren't decided before?" Jonquil demands.

I shrug. "I was just letting it happen, I suppose." I didn't think this would happen, but winning has become as much about the people as for Gavril as well as the reason I let my family bully me into coming. I had to win this for Ro, for my other maids, for those who have hope because of me.

"Dahlia is going to eat you," Azalea says.

"Let her try." I am surprised how easily the attitude comes. I'm not scared of her anymore. I feel confident I can handle her or whatever comes. I'm not alone.

Bella smiles. "This is going to be almost as good as watching them go up against Princess Zelda."

"Hey." Zelda laughs. "Who is going up against me?"

"No one. I'm just expecting a good show when Dahlia loses her cool," Bella says.

"I see." Zelda smiles at us, looking me over again. "You really wear it well." But I see more in her eyes. I didn't expect that. Her green eyes meet mine. She doesn't have to say it. If she doesn't win, she wants it to be me, perhaps even more than I feel that way about her.

I open my mouth to ask, when Lilly runs a hand over the beadwork on my sleeve. "It's so pretty. Who did it? Your maids?"

"I don't know. Either they did it or Damian," I say.

"I wish they'd teach me." She sighs.

"You like needle work," I recall. "Do you like to sew?"

She nods. An idea comes to me, but I don't say anything. When she leaves, I think I may have a way to spare her, but we'll have to see. "You can ask them. I'm sure they'd teach you, whoever it was."

Lilly smiles. "Really?"

"If you really like the needle work, I'm sure my staff would teach you," I assure Lilly ."Unless it's a rest day, they're always working in my room. Feel free to ask. You can ask them anytime."

"So you can be a servant too?" Dahlia finally snaps out of her gaping to sneer at her.

"Leave her alone. Just because she can do something useful doesn't mean you have to get jealous," I say coolly.

Dahlia glares daggers at me. Zelda is grinning as if I presented her favorite flavor of cake. "You should talk. Compensating for his attention slipping away?" Dahlia jeers at me.

"Well, you keep starting fights, you'll get his attention. He wasn't pleased with you last time this happened," I remind her, taking another bite. The same confidence from last night while I defend my people has returned. I hold on with both hands to ensure it doesn't slip away.

"What are you talking about?" Dahlia demands.

"Keep trying to fight, and you'll find out." I look up at the royal table.

Sure enough, just like the last time something like this happened, Gavril noticed the raised tones and is watching with concern. I smile a bit, trying not to smirk. I am not scared of her or any of them anymore. Gavril can see all he wants.

"Fine." Dahlia puts on a fake smile. Her acting could use work. "We'll talk later then."

"Look, I didn't pick the order of the features, " I state. "I'm sorry if you really wanted to be last, but I don't have control over that. Maybe if you write the paper, they'll be more accommodating." Jonquil laughs at that.

Dahlia huffs and rolls her eyes. She starts talking to Princess Amapola and Princess Rose instead. I smile a little. I had no idea I could do that. That wasn't hard at all. I take another bite, a slight smile still on my face. I could do this. They were right. I just had to believe it. I had to hold on to it.

After the meal, a servant hurries to help me out of my seat before the others. I smile and nod my thanks to him before I turn to go. I'm thinking I'll see if I can catch Mother in a free moment. I just hope Alsmeria doesn't catch me first.

I'm almost out the door when I notice Gavril moving quickly as if to catch up to me. I pause to see if he is. To my surprise, his father catches up to him first and puts a hand on his shoulder before saying something to him I can't hear. Gavril immediately looks nervous, but his father passes him and moves towards me. Oh no. I'm not sure I'm ready for whatever this is. I turn and step out, hoping that I was perhaps wrong in my guess.

But then it comes as I leave the room. "Just one moment." The king catches me in the hall after only a few steps.

I take a deep breath and turn to him, curtsying as deeply as I should. The king gives me a small bow back to my surprise. Does he normally do that? I feel like he doesn't. "Thank you for stopping. I'm old. I don't chase girls well anymore," he jokes, making me laugh. "I may not have heard what they were saying, but I did see how you handled them and how you decided to handle their envy over the feature. You did well."

My heart stops, and I hold in tears. He's looking at me with a look I'd only seen on two other people: my mother and Damian. Mother would look at me like that when she was so proud, she couldn't even say it. When she was doing all she could not to just hug me in joy. I'm certain that's exactly what the king is trying to say.

I fight hard to keep in my reaction. I'd lost my birth father, but perhaps if I could do this, I'd gain one better. I smile, tears slipping into my eyes, making them over bright as I curtsy once again. "Thank you, Your Majesty," I manage to say around my throat catching. I hope he can hear or see how much his stepping out to speak to me like this helps me. It gives me hope of a new life, a new family, no matter what else happened.

"Well, I'll see you at dinner then. I have work to do." The king sighs then coughs into his handkerchief as he does before going over to the throne room. I watch him go, almost not wanting to let him leave. I watch until he steps inside. I look down, thinking, perhaps my chances are not as slim as I'd feared. I have the king's favor.

"He didn't give you a hard time, did he?" I jump and turn to Gavril. He smiles sheepishly. "Sorry, I do that a lot, don't I?"

"More than you mean to," I agree. "And no, he didn't give me a hard time."

"Good." Gavril sighs. Then he smiles. "You really do look magnificent."

"I'm learning to own it," I thank him.

That makes Gavril smile a brighter smile. I love all his different smiles. I feel like he has so many you couldn't even count them all or make any kind of guide. I hope to find and count as many as there are. "That's even better," he says gently. "But mostly, I wanted to say thank you for actually putting them in their place. Do I need you to even tell me what they're up to?"

I shake my head. "You can guess pretty well. They just want to scare us."

"And they don't anymore, do they?" Gavril asks.

"A princess has no need to fear a ballplayer," I say.

Gavril gives me the largest smile I've ever seen on any human being. It makes me smile and laugh just a little. "No, no, she doesn't." Gavril's admiring me again, looking me over. "Keep it up," he says it the same way he whispered to me that night, begging me to win. Or perhaps I'd only imagined it. I still wasn't sure.

"You done?" Gavril takes his turn jumping as Sage appears out of nowhere. "We have places to be."

"Right, have to patch up egos." Gavril sighs.

My face falls. That can't be good. The only egos he might need to patch up were all sitting at the two long tables. I try not to get angry about that. He liked me putting them in their place, but then he goes on a date with them to make them feel better.

"Not exactly what I had in mind, or you I believe," Sage sighs.

"I know. I'll go get ready." Gavril brushes Sage off. Then he smiles at me. "I'll see you soon." He takes my hand and kisses it. He does that strange thing where he tenses before letting go. But by now, I'm just used to it. Maybe they're supposed to do that. Maybe they were supposed to give it a squeeze or something, but no one else had at the dinner.

I watch him go with a slight smile. But then it too leaves when I see Sage looking me over. "I'm still watching," he warns me.

"At least I give you something nice to look at," I say calmly. But inside, my heart is pounding as if to get away before Sage reacts. I can't believe I managed to say that out loud. I suppose it's alright to speak up, even through the fear. That is true courage, right?

Sage actually gives me a rarity. He smiles. "That you do." Then he slips off after his protectee, his cloak fluttering behind him. Was that a compliment or a pick up line? I flush deeper.

I try to see if I can catch my mother free as I know they have lunch after we do, but she seems a bit frantic. Their first show is tonight. I can see it's all in hand though. It always was.

"Mama." I giggle as she looks over to make sure all her troupe is eating. "You have it all. Have you eaten yet?"

"Oh, I'm fine. Just need to make sure they're all set, so we can do the last run through with all the set pieces, then we have to do the *Christmas Carol* runthrough," she rattles off.

I laugh again and take her arm. "Mama, it's fine. Come sit with me while you eat." She's so frantic she's not even noticed I'm dressed nicer than normal. She must really want to impress the royal family.

"Alright, alright." She sighs as I drag her over to sit down where the food is laid out for them before I sit across from her.

"Everything is going smoothly. Even I can see that from out here. Oh, thank you." A servant must have seen I wasn't eating, but brought me a cup of tea anyway. "Your warm ups today were great. Was really nice to have a proper lesson again," I try to distract her.

"You know, perhaps I should make little outlines and mail them to you," Mother says. "Keep you working on the right points."

"I'd like that." I smile.

That's when she finally notices how I'm dressed. "You look marvelous," she almost cries. "What are you dressed up for?"

"As funny as this might sound, battle." I smile a bit. "Did you see the feature?"

"Are you kidding? Alsmeria and the others won't stop talking about it. They really are hoping you'll win." Mother smiles softly. "A lot of people are."

"I know." I sigh.

"Do you?" Mother studies my face.

"For them, yes, but..."

"But?"

"Well, with Father and all." I stir my tea absentmindedly. "And... what I am. But I am going to try." I can't back down, but those thoughts will make it all the harder.

"Yes." Mother frowns.

"I know it's what's best, but..." I swallow. "I do fear what they will do." Meaning the Custod Council who ordered my family to overthrow the current royal family. My parents were given that mission before I was born.

"Yes, we do need to talk about that," Mother sighs heavily. "But not today." She shakes herself.

I smile a bit. "You are a bit too stressed for that." I have to agree. "What about after the show? Oh, right, then you have one the next night." I bite my lip. "How about after the last show? Then you can relax. You can even spend the night in my chamber with me. We can get a nice bed in for the night, I'm sure."

"And make Alsmeria jealous?" Mother smiles.

"She's going home to her parents. Who cares?" I smile back.

"Which reminds me, I'm letting the crew rest during the day between shows, so make sure you give her at least a few hours, so she doesn't go crazy," Mother warns me.

I nod. "I'll give her the morning after lessons."

"Alright, we'll run lessons," Mother agrees. I sip my tea as Mother starts to eat at last.

"Mother," I finally say after she's eaten more. "Do... Do you think I should do this?" I look up at her over my tea.

Mother smiles gently and puts her free hand on mine. "Kascia," she says, "I think you should do what you feel is right. I told you before, if you decided to run off with your guard or the kitchen boy after being here, I'd be happy and proud of you. Do what you feel is right."

"But this is more than that," I say. "It's a job as well as a marriage. It's a lot more than that. Do you think I really should do this?"

"You mean do I think you'd make a good princess?" Mother asks.

I swallow. "More like a good queen." That's all a princess was, a queen-in-waiting.

Mother smiles tenderly and strokes my cheek. "Sweetheart, I always knew you could. There's a reason you were good at the roles. And besides that, you have what it takes, and a lot others don't. You know the people on all sides better than perhaps anyone in this palace." She looks around. No one is listening. "From the common boy on the street, to all three rebellions, and now you even know the more elite and royal family as well. Who else would be better, more prepared, and more gifted? I honestly believe you were born here and put into this position for a reason. You were prepared for it long before your father tried to use it for political gain. It's about what you can bring. If you love him and want to marry him and take the throne, then yes. I know you can do it."

"What if I don't love him and still want to help?" I ask.

Mother smiles. "Well, that's up to you. But yes, I think you can do the job. I suppose it's up to you if you want him to rule with you or if you'll follow the path many others have tried and find someone else. That is up to you."

I shake my head. "No, it's not, but I see what you mean." I could take any path I wanted. I could easily get any rebellion on my side now after that feature. I shudder at the idea. Damian was right; I have a lot more power than I thought.

Chapter 28

I'm excited to watch my troupe perform *The Nutcracker Suite* that night. I had felt their pre-show jitters when I joined them for morning lessons, but I'm sure they are ready.

When I get back to my room, I find another note.

Have a merry Christmas. Hope it goes well.

But yet again, no one knows who left it. I frown and use the puppy to keep me happily busy until it's time to get ready for the show. It would be my one break in trying to actually show myself stronger and better than I'd been. I could be more, but it was taking a lot of work. Tonight would be fun, as well as Christmas Eve.

This dress is lovely. It has transparent sleeves like my one for lunch, but this one is a lovely midnight blue with stunning embroidery work like growing flowers on the sleeves, bodice and under skirt. The top skirt has slits on either side to show off the embroidery on the under skirt and is made of a lovely smooth silk, I think. I don't know fabrics well, but it's nice and floaty.

I smile. They really are doing a wonderful job of helping me see myself being able to do this. I just had to get over myself and believe it. I slip on the heeled shoes and am ready to go. Luckily, the little red puppy had fallen asleep again, so I can slip out without trouble.

"Perfect as always," I compliment. "Do I wear the same one twice?" That's not happened yet apart from day dresses.

Damian grins. "You think I would ever allow that?" he jokes.

"Oh, so it is forbidden." I smile back, making Damian laugh, and he claps his hands together. My maid pulls out a smooth, velvet red dress that's almost off the shoulder but not quite. With the right jewelry, that will make a nice statement, and likely long earrings. It must be for tomorrow's show. "Stunning," I declare.

Damian smiles warmly. "I was hoping you'd like it. I thought something more simple would be good for a change."

I smile my agreement. "I'd like that." Yet I'd still be the best dressed in the crowd I felt sure.

At dinner, I have to smile. The other girls are done up fancy again. They look even more fancy than I had at lunch. All but for Lilly and Zelda who wear more simple gowns, a bit like mine, but Lilly's had a lot of gold trim and designs throughout it, making it look more busy. And Zelda's looked like something I'd see her wearing to judge court, with the quarter force symbol on her chest. I like the braids they used to pull her hair back with her simple sparkling tiara.

"I thought Ericka would need two seats." Zelda sighs.

"Can't be too over the top," Dahlia huffs, though I have to note she dressed fancy too.

After dinner, we all make our way to the theater. I hear the orchestra warm up, and I get the oddest feeling. I pause by the door, listening as the others sit. I'm used to this sound. I know it like I know the sound of the ocean out my window or my mother's voice. But it's a different setting. I'm used to being on their side of the stage. I don't know how I feel about being on this side. Left out? Out of body? Excited? It's such a strange feeling.

I stand there for a moment, taking it all in. Then I feel a hand on my shoulder, and I turn. "You alright?" Gavril smiles at me.

I nod. "Yes, sorry. Am I blocking the door?"

"No, but you're so still you could be mistaken for scenery." Gavril smiles gently. I like that smile.

"Sorry, it's just so strange to be on this side of the stage," I try to explain.

"Ah." He smiles. "I guess that would feel funny. Would you rather be up there?"

"Honestly, I have no idea. I've only ever been up there."

"Well." He looks around. "Looks like most spots are taken. You took too long," he teases. "So, guess you'll have to endure sitting by me."

"Oh, that's so sad," I mock back.

"I know. I'm a horrible theater guest." He rolls his eyes. "I don't know what I'm doing."

"I'm sure most people here do and can guide you. Just follow their lead," I say. "I'll try to help, but I don't really know what I'm doing. I will just have to try to be the ideal audience member I always wanted when I performed."

"We'll see how we do." Gavril offers me his arm.

I smile and take it. "The girls will be mad at you."

"How? You're the only one not in a seat," Gavril points out as he helps me settle into the armchair next to his. Did this undo what I said about this being my chance to relax? Gavril and I had hardly spoken since the insanity of the hallway incident. Yet I can't seem to feel I have to put up my guard.

His father sits on Gavril's other side with the queen on the other end. "And being front row will make it easier for you not to mess up the others on how to behave." Gavril smirks at me. I giggle and shake my head. The king smiles over at me but doesn't say anything. The queen is fussing with her dress and hardly notices. I am alright with that.

Gavril takes his seat, crossing his legs casually. "They don't explain anything in ballet, so I have to read this to understand?" He's taunting me, I know he is, as he holds up his program.

"We don't talk, but we explain fine," I counter.

"So how do they tell the story?" Gavril smiles a bit.

I sigh. "Dance. That's why it's called a ballet."

"But then why write the story in here?" He had clearly been hoping to tease me with this.

"Do I have to explain it all to you as they perform?"

"Might be helpful," he teases as the orchestra slowly comes to a stop. A cue they're getting ready to start. Then the lights flicker. Gavril frowns a bit.

"Means they're starting in a minute," I explain.

"Oh, helpful." Gavril nods. I hope I don't spend the whole time laughing at him.

Then the lights dim until only the stage lights are fully on, and my mother steps onto the stage. She does the normal opening the girls and I normally talked over or were too busy getting into position to listen to at the start of the show:

"Your Majesties, ladies and gentleman," my mother begins. "We want to start by thanking you for sharing your home with us to allow us to perform. It is a unique time and setting. It is a true honor to be able to participate in this historic time and performance.

"Thank you all for being a willing audience. Just a reminder that if you need to leave for any reason *during* the performance, please use the exits at the back as we have a lot of moving parts towards the front using the hallways and other rooms behind us. Anyone who isn't in the show going that way might be confusing and possibly dangerous. We don't want anyone falling or hurting themselves as we move actors, sets, and props back and forth. I'll remind you, please unwrap any goodies you might have now, but I doubt that's a worry at the palace." That wins her a warm chuckle of laughter. "Please refrain from speaking, and if you must speak to someone, please whisper as to not disrupt the show for anyone around you or the actors.

"This show was originally performed in the Golden Age not long after the opening of the Armuary Theatre. It was among the first ballets to be performed. It is based upon the ballet created in Damian Custod's homeland. It's based upon the story of *The Nutcracker and the Mouse King* which was later rewritten by another author we love here in the theatre, Alexander Dumas, who wrote the original novel *The Count of Monte Cristo* as well as *The Three Musketeers*.

"Though the ballet was not well received when it was originally performed in his homeland, Tchaikovsky's stunning score was pure Christmas magic and is the main factor that turned this classical ballet into the holiday classic it is today. It is a tradition so beloved, there isn't a theatre in the world that doesn't perform some version if they have the dancers, and even if they don't, they will often adapt it.

"So without any further delay, the Purerah National Theater proudly presents Tchaikovsky's *The Nutcracker Suite* as inspired by the choreography of Layla Reedman, adapted by Chryasinth Thorapple."

Mother bows to us as we applaud. She then slips back behind the curtain as our applause starts to fade. A second letter, that magical score fills the air of a happy, snowy Christmas Eve afternoon.

I settle down as the familiar overture starts. I smile as the curtain rises and shows the dancers. I relax and watch, feeling quite content and almost more enveloped in the world of the story than I did on stage.

Gavril enjoys the show, though the sillier points — like the attacking mice — confuse him. But he settles into his seat comfortably as the show goes on. At the start of the battle with the mice, I feel something glide across my hand, resting on the armchair as I lean on it a little. Gavril laces his fingers through mine. I smile a little. I don't know if he's held my hand before. Not like this. I don't mind, just hoping the others can't see it.

A sudden joy at finding some success through fighting for this assurance again floods me. His displays of affection don't terrify me. I feel confident in allowing them. The smell of the wood, the feel of his firm hand in mine, the magic of the music, make a moment I won't soon forget. Perhaps one magical Christmas memory I can keep no matter what else happens.

He lets go quickly as the lights come on for intermission. I get up to stretch my legs and refresh myself like everyone else. When I get back, Gavril is standing, leaning back against the ledge that marks the end of the audience space, talking with his parents.

"I was worried you'd slip onto the stage," the king teases me. I laugh.

"Nope, she has to explain to me exactly what happens in act two," Gavril jokes. "Far as I can tell, the story is over."

"You'll see," I chuckle.

"Alright. Keep your secrets." Gavril smiles. "Can you really do all those things they were doing? Those turns seem insane. I can't imagine jumping like that."

I flush. "Yes, yes, I can do those things," I say. "Trained my whole life for it."

"Wow." Gavril shakes his head. "Sage can't do that."

"Hey." Sage gives him a look.

"It's okay. He can win in a sword fight," I joke.

The lights flicker to warn us the show is about to resume. Gavril sighs and helps me into my seat before taking his. I hear some girls mutter behind us.

Well, maybe they should wait until the last moment, then they can sit with him. Then I realize that this is odd. The chairs are arranged this way. Every other row has five seats, but the royal row royal has four. Someone chose to have an extra spot.

I'm distracted by the show resuming. Act two is my favorite with all the dances inspired by nations around the world. I know all of them and enjoy seeing their talents shine. We're part way through the tea dance when Gavril leans over to me, using the moment to take my hand as he says in a low voice. "Your secret is it's just the rest of the show is dancing in thanks."

I smile. "Yes." I lean closer to whisper back.

"Isn't that cheating?"

"Depends on your definition. Maybe Damian can explain it to you," I say.

Gavril pouts. "I'd rather you explain it. He's not as fun."

I give Gavril a look. I am not more fun than Damian. Gavril rolls his eyes, smiles, then squeezes my hand before leaning back in his seat again. We enjoy the rest of the ballet like that.

When it's all over, he claps with the others. Though I think Alsmeria appreciates Gavril whistling at her when she bows with Max at the end. I give him a look. I do not need more drool from her, thank you.

The curtain drops, and the lights return to normal. Gavril sighs and stretches tiredly. "Now we need to find a way to shoot right to bed from here."

"Sleep in your seat. We'll be right back here anyway," the king says. The queen sighs and hits his arm like I had Gavril before.

"You'd get a crick in your neck," Gavril says as if explaining why they shouldn't have fish for lunch.

The king sighs. "That's true. I'm too old for that."

"And I doubt it fits a king to sleep in a theater seat," the queen reminds him. I think she spends half her life telling him to behave like a king.

The king nods, stands up and offers his wife his hand to help her from her seat. Gavril smiles at me. "Will you be mad if I don't want to get up to help you up yet?" I laugh so hard, I have to cover my mouth. "Damian will come get you for me anyway," he jokes.

"Will not," I say.

"If I make you wait too long, he will." Gavril grins. "Unless he heard me, I'd bet on it."

I wonder what I could win if I took that bet. Damian might have heard him and then I would win.

"He's not that close. I doubt he's listening," the queen says as she takes her husband's arm.

"You never know," I state. It is Damian. What can't he do?

"What if I need help up?" Gavril mocks, finally getting up with a sleepy sigh.

"You're not that helpless," a new voice joins in. I look over to see Cedrick grinning. I fight to hide laughter as I see that charming grin. He's looking at Gavril. He's daring him. I've not seen Gavril make that expression before. I'd compare the expression to an annoyed cat: eyes half open, glaring with irritation back at Cedrick's big grin.

"But I can see you to your chambers, milady." Cedrick offers me his hand.

"Darn, I should have taken the bet." I sigh and take Cedrick's surprisingly smooth hand. It's not super soft, but I expected it to be rougher, like my father's from using a blade so long.

"I'll be faster next time." Gavril winks.

"Perhaps." Cedrick bows to the prince then the king and queen. "Until tomorrow."

The queen is looking at us as if in shock. The king sighs and whispers something in her ear before wishing his son a good night and leading her away.

"What was that about?" I frown.

"Don't worry. You're not in trouble," Cedrick assures me.

As long as I'm not in trouble. I smile a little.

"Well then, until tomorrow night at least." Gavril smiles and bows to me. I curtsy back. "Good night, Lady Kascia."

"Good night, Your Highness." I bow my head and let Cedrick lead me to my room. I thank him with a small bow before going inside and letting my maids help me change.

They buzz with questions, asking about what it's like to actually perform those things on stage and what I liked best and who my favorite was tonight. I answer all their questions, but their questions wake the puppy, so once I'm dressed for bed, I play with her to get her to settle. I pet her to sleep as I drink my tea and get into bed myself.

Tomorrow is the magical day of anticipation: Christmas Eve. I wonder what magic will actually happen.

Chapter 29

I wake up to Nippers purring at me. I sigh and sit up. I would normally worry the puppy would get upset, but Nippers oddly seems to make everyone, even the dog, like him. The puppy plays with Nippers as I get dressed for the day.

At breakfast, Lilly is beaming which is not what I normally see. "Did you get any mail?" she asks.

"No," I say. "Only people who write me are here."

"True." Lilly smiles as she finishes her last bite of food. "My mother wrote me. It was so nice to hear from her. She said not to worry about losing now. Father will be upset, but she'd be happy to have me home. She has a plan and assured me not to worry."

"That's a relief." I smile. What had her mother said to turn Lilly's confidence around so fast?

Though a part of me is sad too. Will she fail on purpose now? Will she ask Gavril to dismiss her? I'd miss her if she did. It makes me wonder about when any of them leave. Our numbers are so small now, it is only a matter of time. What if Bella, Jonquil, or Azalea go home? I can't imagine life at the palace without them to talk to.

"Yeah, a huge relief. Just what I need to cheer me up this season." Lilly smiles.

I smile back. "I can only imagine." That does make the season brighter, and it brings such a change in Lilly I hardly recognize her. She's much more open. She must have been stressed about this longer than I realized.

I spend most of the day playing with the Nippers and the puppy. My maids have the bulk of the day off at my insistence, and I need a break from the Ladies' Chamber. Besides, I would be social enough tonight. Mother is coming to my room after the show to enjoy a Christmas Eve night together.

My maids come in before dinner to help me change. Tonight's dress looks elegant but comfortable for the long show. The velvet is divine against my skin. They put a nicer chain on my necklace to really get the V shape of the almost-off-the-shoulder dress to pop, and they pull my hair back in a nice half updo. The dangling earrings finish it off perfectly as I expected when they showed me the dress. They also add short white gloves.

At dinner, I find the girls did try to dress down a little, apart from Ericka, Dahlia, Forsythia, Isla, and Kamala. I think they thought the rest of us would dress down, so they'd stand out. They don't really. In fact, even with the step down in fancy apparel, I still look the most appropriate for the evening. They really should have learned large skirts are just a pain when you are sitting for three or more hours.

I hang back again, admiring the sets done completely differently. I can't imagine how busy they were handling this all day. I expect the prince will sit with someone else like a good boy, but as I head to a seat in the second row, he catches my hand. I actually expected it's Cedrick at first.

"Oh." I pause when I see it's Gavril. "Sorry, I thought you were Cedrick."

"I don't blame you. It's why I had to get here first," he jokes.

I laugh. "You're not really playing this game with him, are you?"

"I think it's more him playing with me," Gavril admits.

"Gavril, trust me, unlike the others I'm not drooling over him," I say.

"Or his brother?"

"That's rude." I glare at him, debating if I should yank my hand free.

"Perfect answer," Gavril says. "After all, you talk about him a lot."

"You talk about Sage a lot."

"But he's a guy." Gavril fights a smile.

"So is Damian."

"But you're a girl." Gavril laughs.

I sigh. "I know," I say as if it's a great burden.

Gavril laughs again. "Well, I still have your seat for you."

I look around. "Shouldn't you... give others a turn?"

"I can ask who I want. It's not like everyone is going to get a turn anyway," Gavril says. "And you're the best person to explain the things I don't understand."

I suppose that's an excuse to make the other girls shut up, so I nod. The queen doesn't look overly pleased, but the king whispers something into her ear that makes her laugh, and she whispers back. That's rare. The king smiles and kisses her cheek.

From the music the orchestra is playing, I gather they're doing the musical version. I love this one.

"These are lovely gloves." Gavril admires my white gloves. "They're so soft."

"I assume they're silk. I'm sure you have many clothes like them," I say.

"True," Gavril says quickly. I frown a bit. It was almost too quick. "But they're really soft on you." He runs a hand over the gloves, up my arm a little. I shudder at the touch. Okay, this is not the time for that. I turn to face the stage to get him to stop. I swear he's smiling at me.

There's an odd sound from behind us. I turn to look at the other girls in the second row. I frown. They don't look like anything is happening. Then I turn back to the stage. I must just be hearing things. Or maybe Nippers is running around.

The king and queen settle into their seats. I notice they get comfortable. I hadn't noticed how close they sat before. They are leaning towards each other. As the lights dim, the king uses the excuse to put his arm around his wife's shoulders. I smile a little. If his parents are any indication, Gavril would have no problem being affectionate at least. Unlike Jake who didn't like to sit quietly like that. If he had his arms on me, we were going for more.

I shake the strange thought as my mother comes out, dressed as Mrs. Cratchit. "Welcome once again, ladies and gentlemen and Your Majesties." She bows to the crowd then to the royal family in particular. "It is with the utmost excitement that we join you for a second performance tonight. For a show that is performed during this season, most of all this very night, across the world. This performance is one of the most cherished and beloved of Christmas stories. In fact, many credit its performance for how quickly and universally the world joined in to celebrate Christmas after it was first celebrated by the royal family in the third year of our Phoenix's rise. The Armuary Theater took a bit of time releasing this particular piece as they decided which version they wanted to perform. But the theater was already famous for other musicals such as *The Greatest Showman* and *The Phantom*, so the musical version — which you are about to see — was the first performed. However, the following year, audiences were met with a surprise of a non-musical version that was perhaps a greater success to the surprise of many.

"Following that version, copies of the original book by Charles Dickens sold like wildfire, mirroring what happened when it was originally released in Damian Custod's homeland. The original book was written in just six weeks and sold out in record time. It is still in print and one of the most popular Christmas stories on stage, on page, and in the heart. The original author and Damian Custod both loved Christmas for the special season that it is. They saw it as a time of goodwill and charity, and both strove in their day-to-day lives to help others feel of that magic as well, both at Christmas and year round. As the song says, 'where's there's love, it feels like Christmas.'

"It is a testament to the story and how well it encapsulates the spirit of Christmas that it's remained mostly unchanged as far as we know, from the original performed two-thousand years ago. We hope this performance helps you feel that magical spirit as well of joy, love, hope, goodwill, and most of all charity at this special season. And with that thought in our minds, the Purerah National Theater joyfully presents the musical adaptation of *A Christmas Carol*." Mother bows once more as we applaud and vanishes backstage.

Gavril claps with everyone else but moves right into taking my hand. I smile a little. He relaxes even more as he's sucked into the story of the old miser. It's almost just as fun to watch Gavril react to the play as it is to watch the play itself. He seems confused by Scrooge, unable to understand his obsession with riches.

Then Bob Cratchit comes out of his workstation. I frown. He looks familiar, yet I don't know him. Had he been hired since the Enthronement began? But then why is he familiar?

Cratchit mumbles and mutters as Bob should, being submissive to Scrooge. It's when he claps at Nephew Fred, I realize and gasp. *It's Cedrick!* How did he wiggle his way into the play? Then again, he was a great actor. I couldn't recognize him until he did something more like himself.

I see it even more as he steps out of the office and starts one of the two songs that this role is known for. He's so sweet with little Ted who plays Tiny Tim. I hear several of the girls sigh over Cedrick as he behaves the perfect parent on stage. It does make him more attractive.

Just as I think this, I feel Gavril take my arm. I look over, only to realize he hadn't even realized what he'd done. He is so relaxed with me, he wrapped his arm in mine before taking my hand again. I take a deep breath, losing track of the show for a moment. It is not just that he'd done it. He still has not looked at me, still enjoying the performance. It makes my skin tingle, and I feel pleasantly warm. I bite my lips to repress my smile as I turn back to get caught up in the show again.

His arm wrapped in mine does make it that much funnier when he jumps at the ghost's yelling at Scrooge. *Well done, cast.* He settles down fine though and enjoys the rest of the show.

We finally reach the last song before intermission, the one I always performed. I think Alsmeria does a good job. Scrooge does a great job dismissing the Ghost of Christmas Past with all his pain and anger before the curtain closes for intermission.

"Do you not know this story?" I ask Gavril as the girls start to get up for the break.

"I read it, but seeing it is quite different," he says. "It's so strange to see someone actually be so cruel, you know? Even with that history, how could anyone be so selfish?"

I give him a look then sigh. "I forget how sheltered you are sometimes."

"Makes one of us." Gavril smiles. "Do you really meet people that rude?"

"You will. Just wait." I shake my head. And our people thought him and his parents some of those rude people.

Gavril lets go of my arm to get up and stretch. The king does the same. I go to freshen up, and the queen follows suit. She gives me a smile and actually walks with me. "Your group is very good," she says.

"Thank you. I think they are," I agree.

"Do you miss doing it with them?"

"More yesterday than today. I was sick of playing Belle," I joke.

She smiles. "Well, I'm glad you're both enjoying it." She pauses a moment. "Sir Cedrick seems to like you."

"Oh, he just likes to tease. He's just having a go at poor Gavril," I say.

The queen nods. "I suppose that is true. He is oddly a tease." She pauses as if in thought.

When we return to our seats, the king and Gavril are talking animatedly. The king is laughing as we join them. He takes his wife's hand and kisses her cheek before they sit down.

"We could copy them," Gavril suggests to me.

I glance back at the girls. I don't think that's a good idea. Gavril laughs but helps me sit like a gentleman anyway. He takes his seat, taking my arm right away without a thought, crossing his legs and relaxing as the lights flicker.

"Do you mean to do that?" I ask him.

"Hmm?" He looks at me.

I hold up our wrapped arms a bit. "This."

"Oh." He looks at it. He rubs his thumb along the silk of my glove. "I suppose so."

I smile. It really is subconscious. I guess he'd have done that no matter who sat next to him, but it is nice he did it for me. I just hope it's hidden enough from the other girls.

The lights dim, and the second half of the show begins. Cedrick really shines as Cratchit. And my mother gets something my fellow Chosen would kill for. Cedrick puts down Ted and kisses my mother on the cheek in greeting. Almost the whole theater gasps as if in envy. I stifle a laugh. So does Gavril. We exchange a glance before quickly looking away. I see the queen looking back at the girls disapprovingly. After all, we all are in the running for her son's hand. But we're promised, not blind.

Once we get over our amusement, I look over at Gavril again. His reactions really do remind me, and perhaps really teach me for the first time, the magic theater has on the audience. He reacts just the way we'd hope the audience does. I see him look at Tiny Tim with that sad longing, even knowing that in the end it turns out well. He does seem a bit creeped out by Christmas Future. I always loved the tall, cloaked figure we manage to make every year. I wonder which two poor souls got stuck on the inside this time.

I get a good laugh at the end when Cedrick acts freaked out by the sudden change in Scrooge and how legitimately freaked out he looks. I laugh and clap with everyone else.

When the show ends and everyone bows, I don't think anyone gets louder applause than Cedrick who doesn't look too happy about it. I forget he doesn't like this kind of attention. He's such a goof, you'd think he'd love it. He does his best to give the orchestra their due as well before the curtain closes.

"Of course he's a good singer. He's your attendant's brother," Gavril jokes as he gets up.

I smile. "True. He has to be good at something." I let Gavril help me up.

He smiles wider and opens his mouth to speak, when Dahlia, who'd sat behind us, cuts in. "Thank you for helping get this set up. It was a wonderful show, don't you think?"

Gavril smiles. "I really do. I certainly enjoyed it. I'm glad you did too." He looks at the clock. "But with it being late, I'm sure you'd like to be getting out of that dress and into bed." Getting out of the dress would not be a quick task.

"Of course. Until tomorrow. Merry Christmas, Your Highness." Dahlia curtsies before going.

"Do they not all—" I begin but am cut off by Ericka this time, doing much the same.

Gavril replies with almost the exact same wording too. Oh, I see. He's prepared for the flood of girls trying to get his attention on Christmas Eve night. After all, it's a night of magic, right? Anyone could get lucky.

Once Ericka is gone, he sighs. "Mind waiting for me?" he asks. "If I make the round, it will be faster." I smile and nod.

After what feels like forever, likely about twenty minutes, Gavril comes back with a tired smile. "Call me silly, but I feel after yesterday I should escort you to your room."

"Oh." I can't say no, but what if the puppy is awake and noisy? I'll just try to make it quick. "I suppose that is fair. Can't have you being sore," I joke, accepting his offered arm.

We leave the room before I dare ask. "Why does it bother you? You know, I'm really not one of the girls dewy-eyed over him."

Gavril shrugs. "Call me jealous." I smile a bit. He's not really that jealous. I know what that is like. "And he was challenging me."

"He can be a twit that way. Or so Damian says."

"'Twit' is a good word," Gavril agrees. His grip tightens on my arm. It reminds me of the tension that ran between us in my room after I'd seen him kissing Forsythia.

I don't want to talk about it, but the fact we can both forget it is a bit of a relief, even if I worry it is a secret wall between us. But if it isn't right now, at least I can pretend it won't ever be.

"Damian likes it." I smile.

"You know, there are a lot of girls I have to deal with, and after the ball, I did have to focus on them to keep my mother from freaking out, but... I haven't changed on that point." Gavril has a bit of trouble looking at me. I think he's painfully aware Sage is watching nearby.

I force a smile. "Well, as much as you can help it." I can tell he hasn't given up on me, but I'm not as sure of my place, and I don't think he is either.

Gavril swallows. "That is fair. I've only managed one unassigned date. Just... I hope you know I'm still hoping."

I glance nervously back towards where I imagine Sage is. "Me too." Can this moment be really happening?

Gavril sighs, clearly hoping for more, but I'm just not that comfortable saying more with Sage glaring at my back. Then again, Gavril's isn't either. Sage still is sure I'm dangerous. Even if Gavril trusts me. I almost feel guilty not telling him everything with how he trusts me, even with his lead guard so against me.

What if I could tell him? I feel his gentle pressure on my arm, wanting me to keep close. The assuring pressure makes my heart dance. Could my new found confidence really fix things?

We stop outside my bedroom door. I'm glad I can't hear the puppy inside. Gavril tenses a little. He pauses as Nippers jumps down from some decoration on the wall and trots down the hall, meowing loudly at what I presume is Sage's hiding place.

Gavril chuckles. "That cat likes to point out Sage." He turns to me as Nippers keeps bothering Sage, ignoring the cat like background noise. "But thank you for giving me tonight and last night. I know the girls will likely be on your case once the holiday is over."

"They already would be." I smile. "I'm just learning to deal with it. It's only going to get harder after all, right?"

Gavril smiles. "As you get further, I suppose that's true." I see the hope light his eyes. It's better than any of the Christmas lights.

"But we'll have tomorrow no matter what." Nothing is going to snap that badly at Christmas, right?

"We will," Gavril promises and kisses my hand. But as he goes to straighten up, something falls on our hands. We both frown and look up.

Oh no. Who thought it a good idea to put mistletoe up there? Would I be snapping at Vivian, Flur, or Damian? Perhaps all of the above.

Gavril laughs a little. "Oh boy, someone thought they'd be funny." His tone makes me wonder. He didn't put it there, did he? I noticed it was over the Lady's Chamber door, but I hadn't looked at my bedroom at all. And I am pretty sure it was Dahlia who'd put the mistletoe over the Lady's Chamber door, hoping to win a kiss from the prince. She and Ericka had argued about it.

"No one is around. Who's going to make us?" I smile a bit.

"Oh, but then you run the risk," Gavril says. "Don't you know the story?"

I shake my head.

"Well, it's said if you don't kiss under the mistletoe and take one of the berries, it will poison your love," Gavril explains. "And with how dramatic our lives are, I don't really want to run the risk, do you?"

Not really, but at the same time... Then again, no one was around. But each kiss and action made the hope deeper, and what if it is ripped away if I lose? What then? But what if I didn't get that assurance that I can win this. That reminder of why I wanted this, why I threw my life away. I want it, yet I'm terrified of it.

"I won't make you," Gavril says gently, not looking at me but rubbing my hand again. His tone hurts. He's trying to hide it. I can't blame him. But I fear him choosing me without the ability to choose me. I fear letting him and me down, and...

I inch closer, not able to look at him until I'm almost too close and look up nervously. Is this smart? I bite my lower lip. I thought he may not do this again after all that's happened. Would he really? I want it. Is it so bad to let myself have something I want?

I don't even finish the thought before he gently puts his hand to the back of my neck and kisses me deeply. His lips are so soft, yet firm. He's so warm and soft and gentle. I close my eyes as I return it, my hand pressing into his chest as my other wraps around his shoulder from under his arm. It takes me back to that night before the rebels attacked, the magic of where he could take me. Jake had never done that.

I lose myself in that moment. I'm lost in his scent like fresh rain on the pavement and some rough smell I can't name, the smell of his breath, keeping me warm against the rain he envelopes me in. I slip and allow myself to settle in that soft cloud and forget the risk and the truth that this might all be ripped away. I let my other hand slip under his other arm to wrap around him and pull him closer. A tingle runs up my spine at the pleasure of feeling his firm body against me. He feels so solid against me.

How could it all just vanish? He's right here. I feel certain he wants me as I want him. I don't want this to end.

The oddest part is, I thought he was relaxed with Forsythia, but he's also relaxed with me, in a different way. With Forsythia, it was like a cat enjoying the best pets. But with me, it feels happier, genuine, deeper perhaps? Like he is content and happy here rather than just enjoying the sensation. He doesn't fight to pull something out of me or find something in me. He has what he seeks and drinks it in with joy.

There's a final tension before Gavril pulls back. His eyes are still closed. He rests his forehead to mine, breathing deeply as if trying to absorb and not forget the moment. I feel the same. I resist the urge to kiss him again. It's so tempting. I can still taste him on my lips.

I move just a bit closer. Gavril tenses in anticipation, and that does it. Before I can fight it, I kiss him again. It's not like the gleeful excitement of the first kiss in the conservatory. This is more tender, almost more mature, and real… intimate. Like we're linked, hearts beating steadily together rather in a wild rush: smooth, united.

We both pull back with a deep breath. Gavril smiles a little before he opens his eyes and stands upright. "It's late. I know how you struggle to sleep. I should let you go, so you're not too sleepy to enjoy tomorrow."

I'm alright with that if I can enjoy tonight. I think it so I can stop myself saying it.

Gavril brushes my cheek tenderly. "Thank you, Lady Kascia." He kisses my forehead. I shut my eyes. Oh, that touch… I lose all train of thought for a moment. "Sleep well. I'll see you in the morning." He smiles and huffs a kind of laugh to himself. "And… Merry Christmas, of course."

I laugh a little too. "Merry Christmas, Gavril."

He finally pulls back. His fingers twitch instead of tensing like he normally does before he gives me a proper bow and heads for his own room.

I smile as I watch him go and bite my lips. I didn't know it until I got it, but I think I got the only Christmas gift I needed. A glimmer of hope. Whatever Forsythia got, what I just got was far better and being private, felt far more magical.

Chapter 30

But the fun isn't over. I almost forgot in the excitement that tonight is my night with my mother. My maids get me into my night clothes with my robe on, all excited for me. I wish them a happy Christmas with their friends and family and sit on the mess of cushions we'd laid on the floor to imitate how mother and I spent Christmas at home.

I'm only waiting about ten minutes before she arrives, looking tired but happy. I can tell she's glad to be done.

"All went well, and you're done with the strange stage," I say cheerfully as she comes to sit by me.

"Yes, and hopefully one day we'll do performances for the royal family and not need to adapt," she says, giving me a look as if telling me I better make sure that happens.

"Mama, we have no way to know I'll win or if I can even do that if I do," I laugh.

"I'd not be so sure. He looked pretty cozy with you." Mother smiles. I huff and roll my eyes, making my mother smile. "You never made that face with Jacek."

"There's a lot I didn't have with Jake."

Mother frowns. "Do you miss him?"

I hesitate. "Yes and no," I say carefully. "I don't want to go back, not really, and I won't pretend I'm not angry with him, but... he was mine so long. I miss how simple it was sometimes."

Mother smiles sadly. "Is the palace so bad?" she teases.

"No, not at all... well, sometimes. It's just the fear. What will they do to me? I can't just go home, can I? You'd let me, but Father... I am scared to think on it. And what options do I have? It's not like Father will just let me back with open arms after this. He may not even be allowed. And though everyone says I'm sure to win, I'm not so sure. And it's stupid why I feel that way, honestly, because it's not Gavril's choice anyway." I miss the slight smile that crosses my mother's face. "But I am never sure if he really does like me or if I've made him so offended he'll have me kicked out, because technically, he can, but technically, he can't. And what if Sage finds out why I came? What if anyone finds out? Will they believe I'm not letting them in? Then it comes back to what happens if I lose, and I try not to think 'when' I lose. I just..." I pause to find a word. "Am so unsure. I want to feel secure, and sometimes, I do. But then I question it all again when I see the prince give more attention to other girls, but then I'm stupid and tell him to because what happens to him if he does 'choose me' but I fail or get found out?"

I stop. I hadn't vented like that in a long time. It's amazing what a mother can do. Last time I vented this much, I'm pretty sure I was in tears, having to yank it out myself. Now it's just tumbling off my lips like water. It was nice to just say it without feeling worried about how I said it. I knew I could trust Damian with anything, but I suppose I valued his opinion enough to want to make sure I say it right, so I don't come off as a horrible person. With my mother, I can say anything and not care how she judged.

"Hm, sounds like one huge mess," Mother comments, leaning over to try some of the Christmas chocolates my maids left out, giving me permission to start on them too. "And it sounds like one leads into another. Does he really seem interested in the other girls? Is that why it bothers you?"

"Well, honestly, I'm just stupidly jealous," I admit. "And I hate it, but I can't help it. And until recently, I tried really hard to avoid the drama with the other girls. Because I might be jealous, but it's nothing to some of them. Dahlia can be really competitive, and I just hate the drama."

"You always did avoid it with the other girls in the theater," Mother agrees.

"So when I stood out or did well, all I wanted to do was hide. Because they just want to win too," I say.

"But try to remember that perhaps their reasons aren't as good as yours. After all, did Dahlia join to help her people, giving up the life she loved and led? I doubt that." Mother smiles a bit. "And what happens after winning for them compared to you? You don't have to feel guilty for wanting to win. They certainly aren't going to feel guilty for wanting you to lose."

"I guess that's my problem. I don't want to lose, but I don't want them to lose either." I sigh.

"You never were very competitive. Why it was easy to give you bigger roles once you earned them because you didn't flaunt it like some girls do. But even then, there were times I'd give the big role to someone else, and they would, and I'd wish you were good enough for the part. I suppose I should have better prepared you for that when I told you to do this." Mother gives me a sad smile. "I'm sorry I pushed as much as everyone else, but at least I had different reasons."

A smile lights my mother's face. "But my goodness did you handle them well the other day. I heard about it, rumor mill. I can see how they were envious of that dress. You weren't joking about dressing for a unique type of battle." I laugh. "I'm proud of you. You stood up to them better than you ever did to the other girls at the theater, and you were pretty good at ignoring them or snipping them back. But it's nothing to what I heard or what I've seen the last few days."

I turn pink and look away with a smile. "Thanks Mom."

"But it's still hard?" Mom frowns.

"I just wish... I don't want to go back to what life was like fully, but I didn't want to lose the life I had." I sigh. "And on top of it all, I feel guilty not being able to explain it all, and sometimes when I can't help but compare them, I feel guilty for never giving Jake the chance. I promised him... begged him to save me if this happened." I sigh, angry with myself.

Mother frowns. "Well, I don't know if he'll be even trying that."

"Why not?" Jake would keep his word. That is one of the best things about him. He at least keeps to what he says.

"No one has seen him," Mother says. "I saw him a few times after that night but not in a long time now. You haven't heard from him? You're sure?" Mother checks.

I shake my head. Not a word. Unless... I shake off the thought.

"Your father is quite annoyed with him. Perhaps he just wants to use Jacek as a way to talk you into his will again." Mother sounds a bit bitter.

"I've not heard a word, unless he sent the falcon," I hint.

"No, that was me. I wanted to ask you, but we're never alone," Mother teases.

"I know. That's life in the palace."

"How are you ever going to get some intimate time with him, even married?"

"Mom!"

"What? It's a real question. Even married, you're always watched if there are people in your room," she laughs.

I sigh. "I don't know. I am not thinking that far ahead yet."

"Why not? Makes it easier to endure, right?"

I shake my head. "I don't want to be shattered with disappointment. Less daydreaming to break if I just don't think about it, and the terrors of the now keep me plenty busy."

"What do you mean?"

I give my mother a look. "Did you hear anything I said before? I'm not a true princess. I'm a would-be-assassin with a terrible track record. A failure of a Custod." I fight to keep my emotions in check.

I jump a bit as the puppy walks over with a huge yawn, flopping onto my lap with a content sigh, looking up at me in sympathy. I smile and stroke her soft head.

"You're not a failure of a Custod," Mother says firmly. She sighs and sits back. "I should have told you sooner."

I frown, still petting the puppy. "Tell me what?" Mother looks uncertain and slightly ill. She pops a chocolate into her mouth as if to prepare herself for something. "Mom?"

"Kascia, you are doing this because you want to, right? Not out of duty?" Mother checks, her eyes shining with sincere care and concern yet also worry.

"When I came here, it was duty, but I stay out of choice. If it was just duty, I'd have let them in."

"And if you could go home?" Mother raises her brows slightly.

I think it over. "Just would be a comfort if I lose," I say honestly, looking at the puppy on my lap and mixing my hot chocolate. The truth is, my heart longs to stay. The idea I might lose it all makes my heart ache. I want him, this life, and I want answers.

Mother watches me another moment. "Even if the Custods would do nothing to you?"

"I already told them to get out. I said it to Father's face. Mom, what's going on?" She's acting really odd.

"That's true." Mother sits back with a sigh. "Well, I suppose it will be easiest to start at the beginning."

"Start what at the beginning?"

"I think explaining what happened will make telling you the truth about your duty clear." Mother gives me a sad smile.

I close my mouth to listen, anxious and confused.

"I met your father when he was first assigned here. His chosen profession to support himself was the arts, so he auditioned and got the part."

"Of Rothbart when you were Odette. I know that story, Mama." I sigh. They loved to joke about it.

"Yes, and he was here to help quell the rebellions," Mother says. "He'd been working on it long before I met him. Your father had dealt with this war from the time he passed his Test. The fact it couldn't be so easily solved drove him crazy. Back then, there were only the two main rebellions, though there were others scattered about. He'd argue with his fellow Custods and the royal advisors. He thought their way of handling it wasn't enough, and the other Custods agreed with him, but didn't believe the royals should be overthrown. The prince was an infant, and none of the royal family had left the palace since the queen's pregnancy with him progressed further than the rest." Mother smiles a little. "So I don't know if he ever met them. But seeing so little action from the royal family and finding no end in sight convinced your father, he was right. As he saw it, any of the Custods he dealt with handled the war better than the king ever could. He was certain that they could do a better job. And a Custod has gone from Custod to Potentate in the past. He felt that's what Purerah needed. So, he tried to convince the council of that."

"So that's when they sanctioned the branch-off?" Father must be well respected and powerful to be able to talk the Head Custod into something like that.

Mother sighs. "No. We were married only a few weeks when your father started to form the Custod rebellion. The council was not happy and told him to stop. He didn't. He was sure the royal family had to go and the best way to fix it was not other Potentates with their royal customs fixed, and not a common man with no blessing or skill, but a Custod as the Creator gave exception for. All his discussions fell on deaf ears. The Custods saw no reason to remove the royal family. And as your father would not stop in his attempt to get public support after what must have been longer than I even knew, they told him to stop or be disinherited." Mother's face falls even more, and she shakes her head, a lost kind of sadness in her eyes. "They never did sanction it."

My stomach drops into a sudden emptiness that fills my mind. All I can say is, "What?"

"Your father tried to tell them it was best, but they disagreed. He tried over and over, and they warned him over and over. They even told me what would happen if he didn't, and if I didn't want to be cut off too, I'd have to let them know, so they could help me stay a Custod: make sure I was trained and joined in the classes properly and all of that, but then I'd have to be separated from your father as he tried to come back or... divorced if he didn't. I never went to them, so... whatever your father chose, I went with. It was him I'd made a vow to. I actually was turned off by the Custod part when we were dating. But being a support Custod was alright with me. So I finally decided I loved him enough for it. Then this... well... As you know. He never stopped, so..." Mother's eyes flick up to mine in anxious concern.

I gasp and cover my mouth as a flood of emotions I can't name washes over me. Father didn't stop. That meant... my fear of being disinherited was stupid because I already had been. Father had lied to me. He'd somehow faked the test. He tricked me. Used me. Made me a Custod when I wasn't. *Just like he does to his little soldiers.*

"Oh Kascia, I'm so sorry. I'm not sure you ever were a full Custod. I found out I was pregnant a little over a month after he was disinherited. I thought that might soften your father's opinions on this war, but it didn't.

He's stuck to his plan, sure he was right about how to fix this kingdom. We've had to avoid Custods since. He faked your test, and heaven knows how he did it. But he was always good to me, and I saw no reason to leave as he doted on you, apart from the training, but I knew you'd not believe me if I told you the truth.

"Your father and I fought about it many times. I begged him to stop, but he's convinced he and you are still Custods though he had to retrain himself to fight, and other Custods treat him like a ghost story to get their children to stay in line. He's certain that the Creator knows he's right and supports him into deluding himself into this mess."

'*He had to retrain himself to fight.*' But then... that means, he's not as good as I thought he was. And I'm better than I thought I was. I fought that well with no blessing, but my teacher wasn't as amazing as I believed either. Perhaps Gavril would stand better than a slim chance against him. The concept feels wrong and makes me feel woozy, like the world is out of balance.

"He made me promise to keep my 'opinion' to myself, and I learned to play along. It made life easier than keeping up a fight. I never told you or encouraged you to be what he said you were, but I didn't disagree in front of anyone. I did what little I could to stop his actions or slow him. He knew I did it." So did I. I knew full well Mother was unhappy or at least impatient when we talked of duty or raids or whatever Father planned with me. "We compromised. I got to raise you in the theater lifestyle, and he was able to train you, and it was your choice to do anything he asked you to do for the cause.

"I made sure never to lie to you, but with my promise, I had to hope you'd find the truth yourself, or I'd get a chance to get you away from him, but you were always such a daddy's girl. I couldn't bear to take that from you. That's why he didn't want you to tell the Custods in the castle about your mission. He thinks they're all wrong and would turn you against the 'truth'."

Mother pauses, studying my face.

I'm taking careful breaths as I try to digest it all. *It was all a lie?* I was never... that duty I never wanted was never mine? Father lied to me more than I knew? But he lied to himself just as much, and my poor mother had to stand by and watch, hoping I'd find a way to break free on my own.

"Kascia?" Mother's tone is tender, yet worried.

"I-I... i-i-it's just a lot to take in," I admit.

Mother nods, lips pressed together as if trying not to cry as her eyes sparkle. "And that's why I wanted you to join the Enthronement on your own. It didn't matter to me what choice you made, but this could get you away from your father's web to learn the truth for yourself. And in many ways, you did.

"I'm sorry for all his lies. Please understand why I had to stand by. I still love your father for all his pride and faults. I know it's foolish, but perhaps I hoped with someone there to keep him grounded, he'd come around in the end. As you know, he's been nothing but loving to us in every other way. He's never hurt me or come close to any abuse. I firmly disagree with his rebel actions, but I made a promise to stay with him no matter what for all eternity. I kept my oath and did the best I could. I'm sorry."

I shake my head. "I-it's not your fault. I always knew you didn't like it; I just never understood why."

"It also allowed me to protect you. I was afraid if I openly tried to leave, even taking you with me, that he'd try to get at you anyway. That he'd talk you into it, most of all, when you were young. I almost left with you after he made the arrangement with Jacek's father." Mother scowls. "But when you agreed... I didn't know what to do. That was the deal, but I knew you hated it and that your father was pressuring you into it. I didn't want to do the same and leave you torn. I never thought in time you'd grow to like him. I hoped that might be what shook you, but it didn't. If you were happy, what could I say? When I tired to pressure you as he did, though I tried to be more gentle and kind, it never worked."

I shake my head. I don't know if I could have done any differently in her shoes. How did you argue against that or fight for it? Most of all, with a young, confused child in the middle?

Mother studies me with a worried face. I realize she's waiting on an answer. "It's alright, Mom, really," I assure her. "I don't blame you. I'm just... t-trying to take it all in." I'm in shock, stunned, unable to feel anything apart from that rush of feelings that leaves me too frozen to know what they are or do more than just listen.

I'm hurt. I feel guilty and relieved. I never wanted to be a Custod. Not being one was not a let down. What was disappointing were all the lies. The pressure Father always put on me, the things he'd told me to do were just what he wanted, not duty. My father had tricked and lied to me and himself. Even my being dutiful to my people was a lie.

That thought brings angry tears, and I wipe them away quickly. The man who meant the world to me used me. He had always used me. No wonder Mother never had any other children. It was likely on purpose. She feared giving him a boy. He'd done enough to me, and I'm sure being his precious daughter did make him softer on me. He did let me have my dream job as a performer. I have a nasty feeling he'd not have been so kind to any brother I might have had.

"I'm sorry if you felt pressured into doing the Enthronement because of me, but I knew it was my best hope of helping you break free. I do not agree with why your father or Jacek wanted you to go, but I knew if you went, you'd perhaps see the truth from the gifted Custods around you."

A small, watery smile crosses Mother's face. "Though perhaps in a twisted way, your father was right. You've done better here than most. You would make a wonderful princess. And if the papers are to be trusted," she winks at me, "you might get more friends on your side to help stop the fighting than anyone else. And you do know the rebellions better than any other princess who could sit on the throne. Not that I am saying it must be you, but it gives me hope. And if so, I'll admit that perhaps your father was right. It's not magic or authority that does it. It's just you, being you."

She's right, and that frightens me just as much. All my talents for the royal duties in this game, my ability to fight, my desire to serve my people, it is not some Custod magic working in me, and even less, some Custod oath. I am normal. I am Custod by blood, but not in magic or oath. I may never have it. Yet I am able to keep up with Gavril in a fight as well as I did. I got this far. And it is not because of a Custod blessing.

"Don't be afraid, sweetheart." Mother smiles sympathetically. "There's no reason to fear the other Custods. They don't even know your name. I'm still unsure they know you exist. Your father has kept off their radar for a long time. They are too busy to chase him anyway. Custod rebels have worked behind the curtains enough that they focus on the main wars up north. I even heard a rumor that they think we left Purerah after he was cut off. I think it's true. Everyone in his immediate family went as far away from here as they could to try to forget."

I have other family? Do I have aunts, uncles, cousins? What about my father's parents? Are they gone? Not that they could acknowledge me. I'm cut off, never one of them.

That's when the tears come. The family, the sisterhood, the group I'd used as my purpose and identity was a lie, and it was all because of my father's lies. I try to blink the hot tears away, but they keep coming as the fire rises in me. He lied to me about everything!

I try to wipe away the tears. The puppy whimpers and tries to lick them away. I turn my face and stoke her with one hand, putting down my mug to wipe my eyes with my other hand.

The man who meant everything used me. He had always used me. Had all the love I'd felt just been his way to get me to follow "Daddy" anywhere? I thought even his willingness to let me have the theater was for me, but it was just to keep his compromise with my mother. I feel so used.

Mother gives me a sympathetic smile. "Are you alright?"

"I-I don't know!" Mom jumps at the anger in my watery voice. "He used me. He lied to me. Does he even care?"

"Of course, he does." Mother scoots over and puts an arm around me. "He just... really does believe what he told you about being a Custod, sweetheart. He was formally disowned, but he feels only the Creator can really decide that, and he's certain that's who called him to do this work. He didn't want to push you. He honestly deludes himself into thinking that you would be happiest with Jacek as queen. But he also really wanted the Loyalist numbers under his command. He lied to you the same way he does his 'troops', but he always loved you. He just... believes it his duty to get the rebels all under his control."

"And I almost helped him get it." The idea of giving my father that power makes me shudder. He'd have done it. He'd have killed the whole family, tried to kill Sage likely, then the rest of them would be at his mercy. He wouldn't have cared. That's why he didn't promise. If hurting Lilly or Bella or even Zelda helped his cause, he'd have done it. And I hate him for it. He'd almost made me just like him.

Mother feels my shudder of grief and hugs me tighter. "Oh sweetheart, you didn't know. It wasn't safe for you to know until you were free of him." She strokes my hair. "And you got away. You didn't even need to know the truth to know it was wrong. Even early on, you told him 'no' unless he promised only to hurt those he targeted. When he didn't... Oh Kassie," Mother hugs me tight. "I was so proud when your father told me. He was furious, yes, and a bit dirty mouthed, but even he was impressed you could turn him down like that. I knew you had the power in you. I just feared you'd not trust it."

She sighs and hugs me tighter still, letting me silently cry into her shoulder. "You did the right thing. And now you're free to do as you like. Honestly, your father adores you. Sooner or later, he'll come around to accept you no matter what you choose."

"Even if I win?" I ask through my heavy tears.

"Even then." Mother nods. "Besides, he gets what he wants, right?"

"But I'm not—" I sigh and drop my head on her shoulder again. "I feel so stupid."

"Honey, you had no way to know," Mother says. "Really, how could you?"

"Not just that." All the signs I saw of the truth happened here, and one in particular makes me feel awful. I struggle to explain about the moment that broke Gavril and me in my fear of losing what I was... what I never was.

Mother nods. "I think I understand, at least a bit. Not all of it though."

"Well, I knew Father would be mad. They asked me about my ability to fight," I explain. "But then the prince thought it a good idea to try fencing as a date. And for a boy who only has fought with his guards, he's really good. I was... confused why I had such trouble. I mean, I won some of the time too. But I just was frustrated I wasn't doing better. But then the prince noticed. He was hurt I still thought him little more than a spoiled rat, but it wasn't that, and I couldn't explain the truth, so he'd believe me, and it ruined everything. He isn't even sure he can trust what I say anymore, and it was stupid and for nothing!"

"He took it more personally than it was meant," Mother guesses.

"It wasn't that it was him. It was that a Custod was losing so badly to someone who wasn't," I say. "Now I feel extra stupid." Because for not being a Custod, I held up to him pretty well actually.

"Well, one day you can explain, but if you've moved on, as bad as you feel, I'd advise leaving it that way for now. Once you win, it can be a funny joke between you," Mother says.

"Mom." I sigh. "That's not funny."

"No, but it's a solution. Like it or not, if you win, you will have a lot of explaining to do. And if you don't trust him to be alright with the truth, then I don't think you want to win." Mother gives me a serious look.

She has a point. If I can't tell him without Sage being able to drive me out, what kind of marriage or even ruling relationship would we have?

"I wanted to tell him that night after the date, but... Sage would have had me in a moment." I sigh. "He looked so hurt. He didn't even want to talk about it later when I tried to explain and apologize." I pause. "I never felt that way with Jake. We could scream and let out our feelings, and no one cared."

"Despite popular belief, that may not be a good thing," Mother says. "After all, don't you care about how he felt after being yelled at?"

"Of course not. He'd understand," I say.

"Like when you didn't want to do this and had to tell him you were upset he thought you should?" Mother asks.

"Well, yes and no." I guess I didn't want to just dump it on him. I tried to be tactful.

"And when you're angry, you likely want to yell to hurt them with it. And that's not good. If you are comfortable enough to tell them anything, wonderful, but enough that you can just yell your feelings at them and think you're fine might be a disguise for a good relationship." Mother shrugs. "But perhaps you two did make it work. All couples and all relationships are different and grow and thrive in different ways, but there are key things they all should have. Yes, that trust and openness should be there. But it should also come with concern for the other's wellbeing and often that means their feelings."

I smile a little. "I guess that's true." I swallow. "I just wonder which relationship is better. Sometimes, I feel sure Jake was the best, but then... there never were butterflies or nervousness with him. I knew we belonged no matter what. So why be nervous if he likes me?"

"A blessing and a curse," Mother agrees. "All these situations are different. You'll figure it out. Just don't win because you think you should or you fear what happens if you lose. Make sure you want the throne but even more you want him. Because plenty of kingdoms struggled through a king and a queen who couldn't be more than coworkers. A kingdom can survive but not thrive. They need to work as one and frankly love between them and faithfulness are the only things that make it work. Perhaps that is a part of what this kingdom has lacked."

"Not their current rulers." I force a smile. "The king and queen make me envious sometimes. They're so different, yet so... one." I don't know how else to say it.

"Then let's hope their son learned that from them." Mother smiles and enjoys another chocolate. That action brightens the mood slightly, and I do the same. It somehow tastes better after all our talk.

"So that's why you're so jealous?" Mother asks. "It's because you felt you had purpose and lost it?"

I nod, trying not to have more tears rise to my eyes, but they do anyway. "Doesn't help how he dates fourteen other girls."

"Well, they also didn't give him a lot of experience." Mother smiles. "Does that make it hard? It seems like you two get along. What makes it so easy?"

"Um..." I have to tell her the truth now. I tell her about how we actually met and how it made it easier for us to talk. "And even that first night there was just... something." I recall how I flushed and felt so understood. We both had to escape the castle walls. I felt so understood by that stranger. He made me feel understood and yet unique. It was nice to have someone to relate to and just open up to. "We could talk and understand each other. I was so mad when I learned the truth, and it just never stopped. We like some of the same things. And the way he sees the world." I think of when he showed me the Christmas star formation. "It's so beautiful and different. He notices the small things. He thinks to look up." I laugh. I should be better at that. "I don't know if I have words for it. He just makes me feel... better."

Mother smiles in understanding. "We'll just have to see if you can both keep it."

"And just hope Jake doesn't barge in to save me?" I ask.

"Better hope he doesn't. Your friend Sage will catch him and eat him in seconds," Mother says. "He never was good at being quiet. I swear I could hear him muddying my floors." I laugh. "But as he's not been around who knows. I just hope he's alright."

The puppy whimpers and noses towards my face to lick me and try to help me feel better.

"Do you have to let the prince have her?" Mother jokes, and I can't help but smile.

The puppy likes that and makes a loud squeak of happiness at her success. She zooms off and comes back with one of her favorite toys and throws it, rather violently, onto my lap, looking up at me to see how happy the toy would make me.

I laugh and scratch her ears. "You're a good girl, thank you." I throw the toy to make her happy.

It does help me calm down. "So now you know... you're not going to sneak home with me, are you?" Mother teases to try to help me stay upbeat.

I shake my head. "No. I don't want to go."

"So, do you like him or someone else? Is Cedrick your apprentice?"

"Mom!" I laugh. "Did you not hear what I said or see my note?"

"Note?"

"I wrote on the back of one the impressions saying it was the prince, remember?"

"I never thought to look at the back." Mother flushes.

I laugh, and Mother makes another cup of hot chocolate for me and has me take more treats. "I don't know what's going on with him anymore." I sigh as I accept the fresh cup.

"Well, your attendant was right. Cedrick was worth giving an audition to. He seemed eager and needed very little rehearsal before he had it down pat. I doubt the original did any better. The girls oddly thought him cute in our first scene together." Mother frowns in confusion.

"Mom!" I laugh. "The gasp when Bob Cratchit came in wasn't just because of him. It's that you got a kiss on the cheek from him. You should have seen how the girls behaved when Cedrick came to breakfast once. They were almost drooling. They'd kill to get the kiss on the cheek you got." Mother laughs. "At least I don't have that jealousy problem. They can have him." I sigh and hold my cup of hot chocolate tightly. "Which I guess makes it all worse."

"There's no reason to feel bad that you want to win or are trying," Mother says. "The fact you're not falling for Cedrick's charms is a good thing. Shows you actually do have your heart more in the running than many of the others. Though he does have a unique charm, my goodness."

Mother shakes her head. "I don't know how almost drooling over Cedrick wasn't a test."

I shrug. "No idea. I'd be happy if they all gave up to go after him. Then I don't have to feel odd wanting to win yet not wanting to beat them. I know that doesn't make sense."

Mother gives me a sad smile. "But the other girls fawning over Cedrick like that. They should be eliminated if they don't want the prince as much."

I think about who'd still be in the running. "Do they have to be borderline drooling to fail?" I ask. "Or just interested?"

"I'd have to say drooling to be fair because that man can make any girl have a heart flutter." Mother sighs. "Even if she doesn't want to. He has some unique magic, so to speak." She's right. Even he'd made my heart skip a beat.

"Then I guess we'd only be a bit smaller now." I sigh. "Though not all would be good ones to keep."

"I haven't paid much attention," Mother says. "Far too busy, but perhaps I'll see more tomorrow before I go home. But I'm sure in something like this not all the girls are shiningly perfect."

"No, and of course, they hide it from the judges," I say.

"And while on dates," Mother presumes.

I nod. "I think so, but I can't really bring myself to say more because it feels like being a snitch."

"Even if it spares him?"

I groan. "Mom, don't side with him. He already got on me for that." Our first real disagreement. "My maids dressed me up like a queen once before, and I was so embarrassed. The girls tried to belittle me. Gavril saw something was wrong and asked, but I didn't want them getting worse on me. He lost his temper and snapped at me."

"What?" Mother frowns. "Does that happen often?"

Suddenly, I feel defensive for him. "Not really. Now and then, but who could blame him? He's never had to deal with social situations where he had to control it, and he has a lot of pent up frustrations with not being allowed to help run a country, so he can learn how when it's his turn. And he's in a contest where he's the prize but can't pick the winner. I sometimes forget how sheltered he is."

"Doesn't mean he gets to lose his temper with you." Mother's brow furrows as she sips her hot chocolate.

"He's never done worse than snap at me," I say. I will not mention he hits things. He's never shown a hint of hitting me, but I can see my mother freaking out about that. I stir my chocolate a little.

"Yes, but there are more formal walls up now. What happens when they aren't there?" Mother demands.

I flush a little. "Well, I still know how to knee a guy in a pinch." That makes my mother laugh.

"Still, I wouldn't have stayed with your father if he lashed out at me or you. Just because you like him doesn't mean you should take that abuse."

"So you and Father never fight?"

"Of course, we do. But the way you said it, I'd have thought he was ready to attack you." Mother frowns.

Perhaps she read into that without my needing to say it. "He's never shown a sign of hitting me, even when he loses his temper. It's crossed my mind, but I can defend myself, and honestly, I think he'd be horrified. Not sure he'd forgive himself."

"Well, he better. Just be careful. I won't stand for even a fine prince having a swipe at you."

"I will. I promise." I sigh and put down my empty cup. "If that ever is a worry again. Like he'll ever be comfortable enough to get upset with me again."

"Don't lose heart." Mother smiles sadly at me. "Instead, tell me more about him, so I don't run off only thinking about how he loses his temper."

I laugh and settle into the pillow I'm leaning on. The puppy lies on my lap to be pet, gnawing at one of her toys tiredly.

Mother and I stay up late, talking about all the little things I enjoy: Gavril's smiles, dancing in the ballroom, how passionate he is about doing right by his people, reminding me exactly why I want to stay until we are finally too sleepy to stay up a moment longer.

Chapter 31

I wish I could say my Christmas Eve dreams were as magical as the day suggested they should be, but magical is far from the truth. The dreams I have are mixed and confusing. I wander the darkened hall of the palace, trying to find something, but I'm not even sure what I'm looking for. I open every door I reach only to see empty room after empty room.

Some doors don't open easily. I have to yank and tug, kick and pry at them. I have to dig my fingers into a few doors only to have them rip and tear at my hands painfully, making them shake and bleed. I grit my teeth and yank and pull and kick at the doors, getting splinters into my hands, feet, and in my chest. No matter how hard the door is to open, when I finally do break it open, the room is just as empty as the last.

I move from door to door, wondering several times not only what it is I'm looking for but why am I fighting so hard to get into empty room after empty room. Each room provides just as much success or fulfillment as the last no matter how hard I fought to get into it.

"I know you can do it." Father's voice will say now and then, encouraging me to get into each room. "Only you can do it", "We're counting on you", "We'd not ask you if you couldn't do it".

Pain-filled door after pain-filled door is all I find, and each time the pain only gets worse. "Why can't you find it!?" I snap after what feels like a lifetime.

"I have every faith in you."

"If only I can do it, why can't I find it?" I demand.

"It's there for you; just take it."

"It's not here!" I claw at the most difficult door yet, getting blood across the polished wood.

"You're the true princess. You can see what we miss."

"But I'm not!" At that moment, the door somehow opens. I stumble inside, but this room is just as empty as the others.

"Of course you can see it," Father's voice still assures me, though I can't see him.

"Only those worthy can see it. And you're not." It's Sage's voice this time.

I try to see him, but the only thing I can see is the painful emptiness of the room. It's nothing but black shadows. I can't see through the darkness.

"I may not be a princess, but I'm like you," I insist.

Sage's mocking laugh makes me shudder. "Like me? I'm not a cast off Custod, little actress. I am a true Custod. You're no more than an actress putting on whatever face you're asked to. Look."

I turn around and see a mirror. Why am I in my Christine costume?

"Whatever we ask you to be," Sage's voice carries on. "Naive and deceived little actress."

I jump. In the blink of an eye, I'm a mermaid, fins and all, like the night I dressed as one for the Harvest; only this time, I'm really the sea creature. "You put on whatever mask is set upon you, little mermaid. Strong hero." I blink again, and I'm Cedrick. Not even a character that looks like me.

I gasp in fright and back away from the mirror; Cedrick's wide blue eyes staring back at me in horror... my eyes.

"Innocent maiden."

I'm transformed into Cinderella in her rags. "Stop it!" I cry.

"Cold ruler."

I'm transformed into the ice queen, lost dead eyes and all. I shake my head as tears rise to my eyes. I want it to stop, but I can't stop it.

"Perfect temptress."

"No!" I scream and stumble back into the shadows, but the mirror seems to follow me. I'm Forsythia in the temptation dress made for me. "No, I'm not!"

"Then what are you?"

"I-I..."

"She's my daughter!" Father's voice challenges Sage's.

I'm suddenly myself, dressed as I did when we practiced.

"She's a Custod."

The outfit changes to the perfect Custod armor in stunning gold and red.

"Our best weapon in this war. Our royal assassin."

More tears fill my eyes as I'm changed yet again, this time wearing the traditional black hood with black and silver designs stretching across the long coat that's open at the front and the vambraces with those horrible blades on them, just like the dagger my father sent me to kill Gavril with. I can't recognize myself. I don't want to be this.

"She's not strong enough," Sage scoffs, and without warning, all the strength goes out of me, and I collapse to my hands and knees, gasping in weakness or from the pain in my heart as tears drip from my face to the floor.

"Stop it!"

"She's going to change the tide of this war. She's our perfect weapon."

I gasp as I'm suddenly yanked to my feet, and I'm nothing but the dagger Father gave me.

"She's nothing more than the prince's foolish temptation."

"I'm not." I sob as I'm again painfully changed into the starlight dress that my maids put me in that made the girls envious and started my first fight with Gavril. "I'm not."

"Then what are you?" Sage challenges. "Show us."

"She's our Custod assassin." At my father's command, I'm back in the assassin uniform. I'm so pale and my eyes so dark and cold, I'm not even sure I'm me anymore. My hair is black and fluttering under my hood like a billowing shadow.

I don't want to be this. I shake my head in more tears. "Please stop."

"Then tell us what you are and be it," Sage snaps. "Are you a true princess?" I'm transformed into Zelda.

I sob and shake my head, trying to wipe the tears.

"She's a Custod!" Father argues. Each time he says that I'm changed back into his assassin with the dead eyes.

"She is not! A Custod doesn't go against their oath and refuse to uphold the Creator's ways. She doesn't sneak into a princess contest with nothing but lies. She doesn't betray her orders and impede her army. She's no Custod!" Sage screams back at my father.

"She is."

"Stop it!" Each time, I'm painfully changed back into that assassin, only to have Sage deny it and change me into something different: defeated Cinderella, beat-up street rat, sickly girl, none looking at all like me.

"She's our spy!"

"Please, it hurts! Stop it!" I beg.

"Then decide. What are you!?" Sage demands.

"I don't know."

"Who are you?"

"I don't know!"

"She's mine!"

I tremble in sobs as that horrible assassin reappears in the mirror. I can't stop them pulling me back and forth. I don't know what I am.

"She's a cheating snake," Sage accuses.

I'm painfully twisted into a lithe green snake like the one I always associated with Forsythia.

"She's a Custod following orders."

"She's a liar!"

"She'll be your queen."

I'm transformed into the queen's younger sister looking just like her impressions that inspired my portrait.

"She's your puppet."

I'm now a wooden marionette version of Esmeralda, tambourine and all.

"She's my assassin."

I'm back to that monster.

"She's heartless."

I scream as the pain intensifies as if my heart is literally being ripped out, and I wake with a horrible start.

I sit up and look around as reality slowly filters back in. Why is it that when you're dreaming, even though it should be obvious it's a dream, you never notice until it's over?

Mother is still asleep in her guest bed. The puppy is asleep in her little bed nearby. The moonlight shining weakly through the clouds is the only light in the room.

My heart is still racing, making me feel sick with how sleepy I feel. I get up quietly and carefully, tip-toeing to the washroom to put cold water on my face which feels amazing. It helps clear my head which also brings tears. I take a few tissues from a box on the washroom counter and put them into the pocket of my robe and slip my slippers onto my feet.

I step outside and shiver. It's remarkably cold still, but I need a moment to get my head, and I don't want to wake my mother. I'm fine. I'd dealt with harsh wake-ups like this with and without nightmares with my sleep disorder. I just get over it and get back to bed; that's all.

But how do I just get over the fact that I've been lied to about who I am at my core my whole life? I don't sit on the rail like I normally do. I put my arms on it and lean over it, looking down at the dark grounds and the darkness where the waves crash into the shore below.

I shudder as a cold breeze glides across my skin, and I hold the robe closer, feeling instant relief from the cold. I don't have words for the anguish and confusion in my heart. I wish I did. It doesn't matter if that nightmare did tear my heart out. It's already broken. It's damaged from so many lies and tricks.

No one has been fully honest with me. My mother wasn't allowed for fear of what my father might do. Gavril isn't allowed to either. Perhaps Jake is the only one who didn't lie to me. *Apart from when he said he loved me.*

I furiously wipe tears from my eyes and look up at the sky where there are patches of stars and patches of clouds. It looks like a thick cloud cover is rolling in from the sea. It could be rain or snow. It sure feels like a storm is coming though the weather has little to do with that.

Father lied to me. What am I? I'm still a rebel and a plant, just not a Custod one. Well, a real Custod. I'm one of many young men and women my father diluted into thinking they're Custods. He lied to me as he lies to himself. I'm not a strong fighter. I'm not a defender. I have no duty. I'm a no one. I'm an empty lie. I'm the prop and puppet changing into whatever they wanted.

It's exactly what I did. I was my truest self for my mother, her actress who adored her work, her friends, her team, and yet, I still pretended. I pretended I was perfectly happy with my father's plans. How odd to have faked it when I really wasn't. But I was so proud of my duty and the skill it gave me, I wanted to keep it. I played the perfect daughter, follower, and asset to my father. I wasn't always perfectly compliant, but I made sure to make my point but accepted what he wanted anyway. I'd even done it with the Enthronement in the end.

In the Enthronement, I played the part too. In interviews, I was the perfect candidate for princess and played the role, even if I didn't like or believe a word of it. For Yarrow, I was his perfect mannequin. For my maids, I tried to be exactly the girl they wanted to serve. To Damian, I was the uncertain follower, but he demanded nothing of me. He asked me to be me, and I questioned everything to follow what he gave me best I could.

Who are you!? Sage's demand from my nightmare cuts into my thoughts and makes me shudder once more and hold the robe closer.

Who am I? I don't know. I think over what everyone would say. The other girls would say I'm a talented actress performing her way to the top. I don't belong here. I'm drowning under the pressure. I thought I had to do this, and it was my strength. But it's not true.

But does that matter now? It didn't matter if I wasn't a lady of her people before this game. Before the Enthronement, that horrible feeling of being without duty and without purpose was completely true. But not after I was Chosen Number Twelve. I am a candidate for the throne now. Does it matter I am not a Custod?

I am perhaps even more powerful and noble than a Custod born into the expectation. I'd taken it by choice, even if I didn't know it. And looking back, I'd not change that.

A determination fills me. I may not have done well so far. I struggled as I tried to rely on the Custod authority I didn't have. That's why it failed me. And my father's support had been the tool used to fake that power and support. Once it was gone, I floundered. I was expecting a float to help me swim, but it wasn't there. But I'd started to swim on my own, even though I didn't know it and felt I was drowning.

What exactly a candidate is, I'm not sure. I don't have the balance or talent of a Custod as I was brainwashed to believe. But doesn't that make me more impressive, not less? Without that magic, I'd survived letting them rip me apart and make me what they wanted to get deeper into the game. I had defended the others from the invading rebels without the aid of any Custod magic, made choices that lead me here while relying on my own heart and thoughts and not some inner Custod compass.

I look up over the water. I'm going to learn this. They aren't going to break me, even if I have to keep trying over and over and patching up each crack they made until I am unbreakable. I don't have a Custod duty, but I still love my people. There's no shame in how much I love my people here in Purerah because they are mine. As a chosen candidate, they are my people, and my duty is to them. And I chose that. I know I did because even if I knew then what I know now, I'd sign up. I'd go through the same motions to get here.

They are my people, and I need to be their candidate, their princess. Be their lady in green. Be the hope they are looking for or point them to whoever that will be. *It will be me.* Because I was prepared for this, born for this. Not because I'm a Custod who has to fake it. I choose to be their girl. And I'll be their representative to the royal family. I'll be the royal family's representative to my people. I'm going to help save them, no matter what that takes without the chains of the Custod council, my father, or anyone else.

I look up at the stars and smile. I know who I want to be. I'm not her yet, but I am growing into her right now. I'm going to be his starlight princess. I'll be his night angel.

Chapter 32

When I awake in the morning, my mother is already waking up, and Damian is setting out dresses for us. Dresses? Oh, of course, they had asked Mother and I to do parts as well as a duet together for the service this morning. I thought I'd be more tired but perhaps my newfound resolve is giving me more energy than I normally would have.

Though Mother and I are both sleepy from a late night, we aren't too groggy. It helps that services didn't start too early to allow us some rest from a late night. I get up with a huge yawn, but I feel more awake.

I frown as I slip my slippers on, watching Damian work. "Do you have elsewhere to be?" He has his brother at least, right? Shouldn't he get to spend the holiday with him?

"Not really." Damian smiles. "Afraid Cedrick woke up a bit stomach ill this morning, so I thought it best to let him rest. And after all, while Flur and Vivian are with their families, someone has to be here to help you ladies."

I smile. "We could help ourselves, you know. But is he alright? Should we do something?"

"Don't worry about it," Damian assures us with a warm smile. "Cedrick seems to get sick around this time every year. I'm sure he'll be fine by evening. I just leave him some strong peppermint tea, not telling him it's tea, of course," he grins, "and let him get his rest."

I chuckle. I forgot about his dislike of tea.

Mother frowns. "How does one just get a stomach flu this time of year?"

Damian shrugs. "Too many sweets, not enough fiber? I don't know. I don't exactly have an eagle eye on him and all he does. He just seems susceptible to these sorts of things."

"Is that why he doesn't like tea?" I tease.

"What?" Mother frowns. "He doesn't like tea?"

Damian smiles and shakes his head. "No, he calls it 'leaf juice' because that's all it tastes like. Or so he says."

Mother looks from me to Damian a few times but doesn't say anything. Damian meets her eye but doesn't comment.

"He'll bring Damian tea if he's bored though," I say.

Damian smiles. "That is true. He knows I enjoy it and tends to dramatize how much I do."

Mother just nods and turns her attention to getting ready for the day. It's odd how she's surprised by Cedrick's dislike of tea. I can't quite place what it is that makes it feel so out of place, so decide it's Christmas, I can let it go.

Damian smiles at her then turns to me. "Well, I suppose now is as good a time as any to give you this." He brings a small, wrapped package out from behind his back and offers it to me. "Happy Christmas."

I smile and accept it. "You give me things all day. You didn't have to get me anything."

"That is not the same," he insists. "This is Christmas; it's special."

I smile a little and open the gift. It is a red hardcover bound book with gold spectral writing engraved into the cover. The book doesn't exactly look new. The feel of the cover tells me it has been in print for a while, though it is otherwise well cared for. The gold lettering reads *A Christmas Carol* by Charles Dickens.

I take a sharp breath. This is not an easy book to come by. "Damian..." He really shouldn't have. "Thank you, but... this is..." It is too much on top of everything else he did for me.

"Do you like it?" he asks.

I smile and nod. "I do. It's just... I know how rare this is."

"True. Original copies are hard to find, but I want you to have it. Please, accept it." He looks into my eyes.

I look back into his eyes and smile. "Thank you. It really is too kind." I hug the book to my chest, looking forward to actually getting to read it. We didn't have many books as they are expensive. I'd never gotten to read the original story, just the scripts.

Then I recall. "Hold on, I had to get help with yours." I look around. It takes a moment to recall where we have even hidden it. Finally, I remember the spot and go to my desk to pull out the wrapped, square package before giving it to him.

He smiles down at it then up at me. I'd had my maids and Cedrick help me make a scrapbook with copies of the different impressions of all the different pieces he'd made me. We chose more fun photos, like the one for the harvest ball being mostly us, and even one Cedrick must have taken of Damian and I dancing.

He beams as he flips the pages then looks at me again. "It's wonderful. You did this yourself?"

"Mostly. I had help getting copies of the impressions and some suggestions." I smile.

He returns it with gratitude. "I shall treasure this. Thank you," he says sincerely.

I smile. "I owe you all the thanks, and it just seems to keep coming." I giggle as Mother comes out from behind the changing screen, impressed by how she looked in the dress Damian made.

Damian turns and smiles at her. "Well, if I didn't know any better, I'd say I was in the presence of an angel."

Mother does look lovely in her dress. I trade her, letting her do her hair and makeup while I change then do the same.

We are a stunning match. My dress is a white, floating dress, like an angel, but there is a nice red sweater with a clasp at waist level to secure it over the dress to keep me warm. Mother's is similar, only her dress is red with a white sweater. It makes me think of an angel, snow, and the cozy red of the holiday. It's perfect.

I check in with Damian to be sure I do the hair and make up right. Damian comes over to do my hair for me. I didn't know he knew how to do that.

He pins parts of it back, and at certain places, at the back, so it drapes nicely down and around my shoulders. I smile and nod my thanks and ask him if he wants anything particular with make up as I put on the basic parts.

"It should be light. Like... freshly fallen snow, crystallized and glistening on a crisp winter morning, but warm like the hearth around a Christmas tree," Damian says.

Mother chuckles at Damian's phrasing, but I'm used to it. I know exactly what he means. When I'm done, I check with Damian before putting on the protective powder to keep it on.

Damian has me only wear my Chosen pin for jewelry and then we're ready to go. We still have about half an hour before it starts to make sure we have all ready for our parts in the devotional.

"Are you alright?" Mother asks me quietly.

"Of course." I smile back.

She frowns. "Just... after last night."

"I understand." I smile. "I'm fine, really."

"Good. Hope I didn't ruin the holiday." She smiles back.

I almost smirk as I look over at the puppy. "Don't worry; you didn't." But failing to win my battle today might, but I'm feeling confident. Perhaps it's just giddiness from the holiday and lack of sleep.

Once we're ready, Damian picks up his violin.

"They're making you work again?" I tease.

"Again?" Damian arches a brow.

"After the tree decorating, you were 'working' then too," I remind him.

"True, but no one asked."

"I'm sure they did this time," I say as we head to the door.

"Well, I volunteered. Only seemed fair when their every option for violinists were in every other country." He smiles and opens the door for us.

"Why am I not surprised?" Mother sighs as we walk out the door. I nod a thanks to Damian as always, and we make our way down to the meeting room.

The room looks stunning with garland and red flowers all about and the normal golden phoenix marks about the front area, choir seats, and podium. I smile a little. There is piano music, playing appropriate Christmas songs. I look over to see Gavril playing, in a nice red suit for the occasion.

"See, there's nothing wrong with him," Mother teases me. I nudge her.

Damian chuckles. "I should go set up. Shouldn't take long."

I nod, and we let him prepare. My mother and I find our places. Gavril smiles and nods at us as he keeps playing.

"See? He can even do two things at once," Mother teases.

"Mom." I sigh.

Mother and I sit in the seats for performers. I glance over at Damian who's making sure his violin is ready to go when I notice Zelda and Azaela join us. I smile at them. Soon Damian sits down, and we're ready.

Gavril runs the meeting as he always does each second rest day of the week. The meeting runs less than an hour but does not feel that short, pleasantly so. Azalea performs a lovely flute piece first, then Zelda plays a stunning harp. I perform my solo; Damian performs his; Gavril plays a spectacular piano solo, then we finish with Mother and I singing a duet with Damian on the violin. It sounds lovely.

Mother smiles at the end as Gavril jokes with Damian that he should have let Damian back him up. Damian chuckles. "You did fine, Your Highness. Best I've heard in a while in fact."

"Alright, then I guess I shouldn't have left you to back up the singers alone," the prince jokes.

"Perhaps not." Damian grins. "Your piano pieces surely would have covered up any scratches I made."

"I guess," Gavril chuckles. "Will you be joining us the rest of the day, or better places to go?"

"I'll certainly be joining you. Cedrick may too if he ever decides to get out of bed," Damian says the second part like it's a joke.

"Alright," Gavril chuckles. "See you in about an hour then."

"Until then, Your Highness." Damian bows his head to him.

Mother is still smiling as Gavril leaves. I think she is starting to warm up to Gavril. At least more than she ever had to Jake.

Now the real work begins. We'll meet in the main sitting room, where we'd decorated the tree after the official tree topping, to do the gift exchange. The real work is getting Gavril's gift ready. The puppy has to be quiet until presented which isn't going to be easy to do. Mother and I try to wear her out, so she'll be quiet. Maybe she'll nap until the right moment if we're lucky.

Damian says he will handle bringing her in at the right time. I had my maids put all the other gifts under the sitting room tree two nights ago, so it's Gavril's to manage.

Mother gets up to help Damian as I stroke the puppy to calm her down. She's settling down nicely, looking sleepy. "Are you ready?" I ask her softly, so the others wouldn't hear. "I'm counting on your help to help him feel better." And prove I know him. I swallow. This is going to work, right? What if it doesn't? What will I do if it doesn't?

My heart trembles, ready to crack at even just the thought. It had to work. It just had to. I need this. If I can't do this, I'm nothing. I'm just a Custod wanna-be. A girl with no true identity or path because of the lies of her father. I don't want to be that assassin. I shake at the memory.

The puppy whimpers and licks my hand comfortingly before she finally falls asleep. I smile. Who could think dark thoughts like that with a sweet little ball off floof like her to keep them happy?

I change into the dress Damian prepared. It's red and gold with amazing detailing on the bodice, little shoulder bows, and cap sleeves. Its skirt is pulled up on one side with a bow making the whole dress remind me of a wrapped gift.

We wait until the last moment to put the sleepy puppy into the box. Damian puts a bow on her neck before getting her settled. It wakes her up, but she settles right back to sleep with our gentle strokes and comforting whispers.

"We have everything?" I check, nervous and excited. I fear it not working, but what would happen if it does? I push aside the thought of the Enthronement just ending now. What a Christmas gift to all of us if it could, but it's mere fantasy, I know.

Damian nods as he double checks the sturdiness of the box. Both the box and its lid, which lays on a nearby table, are gift wrapped red and green; a large green bow top of the lid with a tag bearing the prince's name and who the gift is from. Once Damian is satisfied, he nods to himself. "Alright, this will be sturdy enough to hold her, and I wrapped the box and lid individually, so he'll just have to remove the lid and take her out. There'll be a toy in there to keep her quiet until it's time. Though the plan is I'll keep her and the box in the next room and when you give me the signal, I'll bring the gift inside for the prince."

I nod. "Alright. I guess that's all ready then." I smile. I hand Damian the lid to the box.

"Thank you." He smiles, puts on the lid, and picks up the gift, then looks at the door and sighs before turning back to me. "I know I normally get the door, but can you this time?" He smiles, somewhat embarrassed.

I laugh. "Oh, for heaven's sake, it's not that big of a deal that I open a door once." My mother is laughing too as I open it to make room.

"No, but it's my job," Damian says as he leaves through the open door.

I shake my head. "You take this to a unique extreme," I say as Mother and I follow him out the door.

The sitting room is done up beautifully. There are lights in all of the garland along the edges of the room making a nice light effect. The rich smell of the pine tree and glowing fire cracking in the hearth add to the Christmas magic.

A few girls are there already. Ericka sniffs at me, smirking to see my hands empty. I frown, unsure why. But as other girls arrive, it becomes clear. The girls had opted to carry in their gifts for the prince, in an attempt to intimidate the rest of us, I think. But none of them make me worried. I doubt they'd get him anything so fun or perfect.

The king is smiling at me each time a girl tries to show up the others. He knows what I brought. The question is, is he excited to see his son's reaction or the drama that would ensue? How badly could this go for me?

Gavril is among the last to arrive, but that was clearly because he was handling last minute gifts. Poor boy has to have an idea for each girl after all, and the pressure for what it should be had to be intense. I giggle at the idea. Poor thing. He could have skipped mine if it made life easier.

The proceedings aren't extremely formal. They popcorn in taking turns, grabbing a random gift and handing it out to make it harder to keep track of who has how many and who gave what to who. I can tell the royal family had done their exchanges on their own, likely before this even started.

Damian slips in as the proceedings begin. Not long after, I hear a meow, and a sluggish Nippers wanders in as well, tail twitching a bit as he sits at Damian's feet. He is such a weird cat. Damian looks down at him, smiles and strokes him a bit as he watches us pass out gifts. Mother is watching nearby with an entertained smile.

It is fun to see what everyone got one another. A few stand out to me. One is Ericka's really funny choice in giving the prince a plush dog as if that would help him like her dog more. I wonder if the red puppy would like to play with the stuffed toy or not. I have little doubt that Gavril would let her.

Zelda gave amazing gifts to everyone, bits made by her people she'd sent for a month before. Most are amazing bits of jewelry or decorative artwork. I am amazed by the craftsmanship. The most impressive being a diamond-like necklace made of gemstones that glow for Princess Rose, a similar bodice for Bella to build into a dress, and a stunning Hyvian style rapier for me, though I have to let my guard keep it for me until the Enthronement ends.

Bella gives everyone a dress she made for them personally, each one perfectly fitting their personality. She even nailed the Hyvian style. And the dance dress she gives me is perfectly playful and flowing for playing around in the practice room.

The prince did a good job with most girls. He seemed to use their skills and interests as bench posts. A nice pair of new sport gloves for Dahlia. A really sturdy-looking riding jacket for Forsythia. Lilly got some stunning thread and needles with beautiful crystal-like beads. Things they already had, just nicer ones.

But when I open mine, I have to admit they take my breath away. I'd had pointe shoes dyed for an outfit, but I'd never owned a usable pair of decorated pointe shoes like these. They're expensive and really not very useful, but I always loved to look at them and imagine things to go with them.

Gavril had to have custom designed this pair. They're a stunning blue, like the royal color, with embroidery mostly rather than jewels, though some jewels were sewn on. The sewing was not easy to do, but it would last a lot longer that way, done so it looked like my feet were part of an ocean wave.

I blink and stare at them in awe. They're stunning. I can't believe it wasn't something Damian made. I pull one out and admire the needlework and gemwork. And they clearly are designed to be used. They have all the parts and even marks and tips on how to break them in without ruining the artwork. Gavril is smirking to himself at my speechless reaction. I can't imagine how long it took to make these. He had to have thought of this at least a month or more ago.

"Thank you," I finally say. "They're stunning." He knows me well. I don't know if I'd ever mentioned the thing I'd love most are such stunning pointe shoes like these.

"I hope so," Gavril says. "I hope you get to enjoy them for a while."

“Oh, I will.” I’d save them for special events. Gavril smiles with just a hint of that smirk.

Next, the king and queen open their gifts from me, and what I asked Damian to help me make for them are a hit too. The king laughs pretty hard at my gift. It’s a music box with a little ballerina twirling that’s supposed to look like me with a note inside that read “For when you want to watch us”. I’m glad he is not offended by the joke. On the contrary, he happily shares the joke with anyone who would listen — the rest of the day.

The queen’s is a bit quieter, and she has to hide her reaction. It’s a little jewelry box with a quote on the inside of the lid done in Damian’s amazing artwork that reads “Two amazing women can love the same man in completely different ways. One is his wife, the other is his mother, and that never stops.” I figured with it being hard for her to let go of Gavril, perhaps a kind daily reminder that just because he’s to be married doesn’t mean she has to lose him would help.

She’s clearly touched as she struggles to hide her reaction with a quick “thank you”.

Time passes quickly by as more gifts are exchanged and opened, but soon the only thing left is for Gavril to find his puppy. An anxious knot fills my chest. This is it. The moment of truth. I’d been building up to this since that horrible day in the gym. A day I loathe and wish I could take back more than ever after last night. Yet another cursed chain my father had made to hold me that kept me from the one man who might truly love me just for me. I want to bury that horrible moment and all it had done with a burning passion that I’d never felt the like of before. I need this moment to rip apart all the walls that had gone up to do what I need to do.

I steel my nerves and nod at Damian a few minutes before as the last two gifts are being opened. He nods back and quietly slips out of the room. A few minutes later, he returns with my gift in hand, assessing whether he should step forward yet or wait.

I give him a slight nod to tell him to wait, but once it seems we’re all done and everyone is quieting down, I smile. I need to time this perfectly. This is more than just giving a gift. It’s a bit of a performance, looking to get just the right reaction out of the prince.

For a split moment, a rush of emotion comes over me: longing. I suddenly realize how long it felt since we were last together and safe to do so. I suppose it wasn’t that long ago, but it feels like a lifetime. I’m beyond ready to get that back again.

I smile warmly. “Well, I had to ask for this to be last,” I admit, breaking up the bustle that had just started as everyone assumed we were done. “But I didn’t forget,” I tease Gavril a little. He chuckles. “So, here you are.” I nod at Damian. He smiles and steps up humbly to Gavril and offers him the present.

"Thank you." Gavril smiles a little, but he's wary. I suppose it is an oddly large box. And he's not the kind of person who wants a big gift, but then again, he also doesn't want small ones filled with fine jewels and finery of the world. He puts the package on his lap, having to balance it. Oh no, I think the puppy is moving.

Red puppy, please just another moment, I beg.

Gavril does not catch on right away. He holds it still with one hand and lifts off the lid. His jaw drops instantaneously, almost comically, as the puppy pops her head out and starts sniffing excitedly.

The anxiety tenses into a knot worthy of any talented sailor as I watch for Gavril's reaction, biting my lower lip anxiously.

The motion of being put down on Gavril's lap must have woken the puppy. I recognize the signs of her waking up and getting ready to play. She makes her squeaky talking noise that sounds like "hello".

Gavril blinks in shock, staring at the dog as she sniffs around. His expression is blank other than shock. What I'd give to know what he was thinking. Then she looks at him. Her tail goes mad, making the box wiggle. Gavril grabs it to stop it from falling. She makes the sound that sounds like his name.

"What?" Gavril laughs a little, looking at his dog in utter surprise.

She makes the sound again and jumps out of the box which falls off his lap as she kicks it out of the way in the leap at his face. Gavril laughs and tries to push her off.

She makes more sounds and turns to the rest of the room. Her tail is going mad, making her lower body wiggle back and forth. She makes her noises at me as if making sure I know that she found the real Gavril and then turns to him again, licking him more.

"Okay, okay, down," Gavril says. His smile is brilliant. I can't help but smile as the glow of joy fills me as I watch the pure happiness spreading across Gavril's face in easily one of my most favorite smiles I've collected so far.

The queen is giving her husband a look. "She asked me. It's fine. A guard dog," the king defends.

"You're joking." Gavril looks at them; his face falling in hopeful shock again. I think he just realized he's keeping the puppy. The light of it comes into his eyes and grows like a steady fire.

"No. I asked. Cedrick is training her as your guard dog. They've already gotten started," I say. "She's yours for good. No matter what." I fight not to flush at the last bit.

The puppy says Cedrick's name before she realizes the room is full of people. New people. Her tail goes mad again. Gavril grabs her to make sure she doesn't jump around. That smile that I treasure more than anything is back on his face as he restrains her gently. She's so happy and "talking" like crazy with a lot of "hello" sounds.

She sees the king and queen. She has a high-pitched squeak that's for "mom" that Damian and Cedrick taught her and a huff for "dad". She's so excited she can hardly contain it. She looks at Gavril again, licking his nose as if thanking him for all the new and wonderful friends and life before looking at the room again.

"I can't believe you got away with this," Gavril tells me. His eyes meet mine with not just the surprise and impressed energy, but a warm gratitude that makes my heart glow further in joy. I didn't know it was possible to feel that much joy. He's impressed, touched. Perhaps I'd pulled it off. There is clearly hope. This might have gone better than I hoped and be the best Christmas I'd ever had or would ever have.

I beam. "She's all yours. Servants should be putting her pen and bed and all that in your room, and they're used to feeding her. She's trained to use a little potty box that's kept on your balcony that the servants clean up. She's good to go; just keep working on her training."

"Calm down," Gavril laughs happily at the puppy, his eyes crinkling, as he tries to get her to sit, but she's just too happy.

She makes my favorite sound, sounding like "I love you" as she licks Gavril again.

"Oh, and you get to name her," I say. "I just call her puppy or red puppy as she was one of the few red ones in her litter."

"Oh, um..." Gavril pauses to think, his face pulling in simple concentration, another expression I love. He finally lets her down as he thinks, setting her gently on her feet on the floor, so she can let out her curiosity. She doesn't run off though. She sniffs everything, starting with whatever was nearest: the box she'd been in, the sofa, the floor, Gavril's shoes, then she sniffs her way across the floor. She smells me and comes over to lick me in hello before she wanders the room.

She likes Ericka. Well, her smell. She stays around Ericka for a long time. She must smell Cuppy on her. Ericka is so shocked she just stares, stroking the dog a few times, but mostly gaping. The puppy noses around as if trying to find the other dog.

"Maybe something with a Christmas theme," Zelda suggests to Gavril.

Her voice draws the puppy's attention, and she trots over, tail wagging to say hello to Zelda. She makes her "hello" sound and sits to let Zelda pet her a bit before she starts to attack some wrapping paper.

"Like what? Holly?" Gavril frowns.

"Phoenix?" Lilly halfheartedly suggests. Nippers makes a funny sound in the corner. Damian chuckles and strokes him gently. The dog jumps on Lilly's lap, licks her face then jumps off, making Lilly jump and laugh.

"Not that." Gavril watches as the puppy's tail wags madly, his face still scrunched ever so slightly in thought.

She calls "I love you" to the sky and then runs around to try to get all the wrapping paper. We all laugh.

"Look, she's even cleaning," the king says to his wife, who gives him another look.

Then I remember Nippers is in the room and wonder why he's not chasing the paper. I look over to see what he does, but he's just watching the dog as if making sure she behaves. I chuckle. I love that odd cat.

"So happy." I coo and smile at the dog as she wanders back to me, and I give her a good rub down, inspiring her to want to play, and she lets me push her over to wrestle. "I'm glad you're always in a good mood."

"Is she?" Gavril asks.

"Well, most of the time," I admit as I rub her belly which she happily exposes to me.

Gavril has to think. "She does need a good name." He's clearly thinking hard, watching the puppy with those observant eyes.

His voice gets her attention. She sees Gavril, yells his name to the room then rushes over again to try to leap onto his lap. She fails, like she did when I first met her. I laugh.

"Need help?" Gavril asks with an amused chuckle.

She huffs "no" back, making Gavril truly laugh. She tries twice more before reaching his lap.

"That's a good girl." Gavril rubs her down like I did. It makes the puppy so happy, she flops backwards against his stomach. We all get a good laugh out of it.

"You are happy," Gavril says to her. "One happy puppy, one..." His eyes light up. "I got it. One joyful puppy. You're a little Joy, right?" He rubs her belly. She pants and noises in happiness. "Yeah, I think it's Joy. That's who you are," Gavril agrees.

Joy is right. She'd brought a more joyful moment than I'd ever known. I watch Gavril beaming with his dog, filled with how much I care for him. Work or not, I'm glad I thought of this, gave him this. I don't know if I'd seen him happier or at least more excited.

"Hyper might be better," the queen says.

"Nah, she's Joy. She's full of it, and she is a joy," Gavril says. "You'll be a good girl, right?"

Joy huffs "yeah" as she lies down more calmly on Gavril's lap, panting in excitement. It won't take us long to wear her out.

Damian walks over and shows Gavril how to train the puppy to learn her name. "She'll know her name in no time." Gavril smiles.

"Indeed, she will. Happy Christmas, Your Highness." Damian bows to him and steps back.

"Thank you," Gavril chuckles as he rubs Joy. Then he looks at me. "And you. That was pretty gutsy," he admits. The admiration in his eyes makes the glow in my chest brighter.

I smile. "I thought you could use a friend to talk to," I joke. Gavril laughs. Joy tries to lick his face.

"And she is chatty," Gavril agrees.

Joy then recalls there are other people in the room. She jumps down and sniffs around. She finds a unique scent and starts to follow it. I laugh. She's found Sage.

She looks up and sees his face. Her tail wags so madly, it's almost a blur. "We'wo Wo-ro," she cries. I laugh. I forgot she calls him "Weirdo". She pants in delight then does a howl that I think is "I found weirdo".

"What?" Sage looks at her.

Joy pants then says "wo-ro" again. It sounds just like weirdo.

"Are you calling me weird?" Sage demands.

"Is that his name?" Gavril manages to get out, laughing so hard, he's doubled over.

Damian is laughing too. "Sorry, we couldn't get her to call him anything else."

"She picked that name?" Sage almost shrieks.

The laughter in the room is everywhere.

Joy pants then does her talking. I think she says, "I love you, weirdo." But I'm not sure.

Sage glares. "My name is Sage."

"Wo-ro," Joy insists.

"No, Sage," he says.

"Woooooo-wroooo," Joy howls.

Sage sighs. "Dumb dog."

Joy makes her "thank you" sound and trots over to see if she can find more treats and cuddles from other girls. Dahlia doesn't want to pet her, but Azalea does with great enthusiasm.

"Hey, she can play with Cuppy," Lilly says brightly.

"Oh, I suppose that is true." Ericka manages a smile. She's almost green with envy. I guess that's why Dahlia doesn't want to pet her. I won yet another round, and many hate me for it. Well, what else is new? I'll handle that like everything else.

"Yeah, be a good girl," Gavril says. "Joy," he says, trying out her new name.

When Joy turns, he says "yes" and tosses her the treat. She misses and sniffs around for it. Sage sighs tiredly. I think he isn't a fan of my gift either.

I was right about Joy getting tired quickly in all the excitement. She yawns and puts her head on the queen's lap as she lies down. She makes her 'I love you' sound and nuzzles in. She's trying to get the queen to like her. The queen melts and strokes Joy's head.

The servants and some of the girls help clear away the mess and organize gifts into piles to be brought up to the different rooms later. When they're done, Joy jumps down. I worry she'll come to me for nap time, but she goes over to Gavril and lies down at his feet for a nap. A few girls cue at how cute it is.

Gavril smiles and scoops her up. "How about a nap before the ball?" he says to the dog. Joy "speaks" back to Gavril happily.

"Be good," I tell her.

She pants and talks in what I hope is her saying she will be. Gavril smiles at me. "Thank you again. I don't think I'll be forgetting this in a hurry." I laugh. But there's deep intent in his eyes, and I'm excited yet terrified to find out what it means.

Chapter 33

I go to my room to change into a unique dress for the ball. The style of the top reminds me of many a dress I wore as a ballerina. It has the lovely red Y shape I like made out of beads and sequins down the center of the bodice. The white skirt is long and flowing, much like a Juliet tutu, with red V-like petals around the skirt, edged with gold. It twirls nicely with the floating tulle and other more silken fabrics that flow beautifully. It'll make a lovely dancing dress for the Christmas ball. They put my hair into a half bun, leaving some down to flow down my back. They add a beaded tiara that goes on the bun, again reminding me of many I'd worn as a dancer.

"Not quite." Damian smiles and looks to Vivian and Flur who bring over a longer, dark green top piece.

I frown a bit. "What is this?"

"Your dress." He smiles wider and nods to my maids to help me slip it on. They help me slip my arms through each of the arm holes and carefully fit my short flutter-y sleeves over the shoulders and then snap the top piece into place along the gold trim of the Y, hiding the white underneath. The skirt is longer but much of it is made of the same material as the first shorter skirt with the same red V-like petal patterns on it as the first, only it is green instead of white. It overlaps a little to avoid a split down the center of the dress, and Damian makes sure the overlay portion is fastened correctly, so it'll hang right.

"Why the double layers?" I ask. "I mean it's beautiful and will twirl wonderfully in the dances but... seems a bit much."

Damian smiles and hands Flur my shoes, so she can help me with them. They remind me of the glass slippers in the Cinderella plays with a red tint to them. "It's a surprise." He grins.

I give him a look as I put on the shoes. "For who?"

Damian smiles again. "A few people."

"Alright." I smile a little. "I suppose that is alright. I trust you."

"Do you?" Damian's grin hints at a tease.

I chuckle. "Of course, I do. I'd not let you run wild if I didn't, would I? I'd be more demanding."

Damian nods. "I suppose that's fair." He then looks at my maids. "No jewelry this time. Let her shine." He beams at me.

I frown a bit. That is strange. Normally, I'd have something for a ball.

Damian smiles. "Well, I did give you a tiara."

"Still suspicious," I smile back.

Once we're ready, we head down to the ballroom. That anxious bubble returns. If my gift worked and he's going to say anything, it will be at the ball. It runs the rest of the day. The only break will be to pause for the fine dinner, but as we had a Christmas dinner with the court, it's not as formal this time.

The ballroom looks really nice and festive. I'd seen it in normal mode, but for the holiday, it's lit up with garland lights, holiday candles, and plenty of green, gold and red flowers to bring it all together. It reminds me of the ballroom from *Beauty and the Beast* with its golden glow.

My mother pauses to take in the amazing view. This ballroom is world famous for its two unique features. The balcony at the far end that looks out over the best ocean view known to man, and the huge dome skylight above that lets light in but not out. I'd had my moment to stare at the Harvest Ball. I giggle to see my mother staring at it open mouthed. It is some amazing work.

Cedrick is out and about with an impressionor. It looks like most everyone, but the royal family is here.

Damian sighs and gives his brother a look as he lets go of my arm. Cedrick notices us. "Oh, hi. What's surfaced?" he asks Damian.

"You point that thing at me, and I'll tell you what's surfaced," Damian says in wary annoyance.

"Oh okay." Cedrick points the impressionor at him.

"Cedrick Michael...!" Damian swats the thing away.

"What? You said now you'd tell me what surfaced."

"You did. You great twit," Damian replies.

"I knew that. What's with the faces and trouble?" Cedrick says innocently.

"I'm remembering last time."

"Hmm, guess that's true. But you chased me that time."

"I know because I was trying to get you to behave," Damian says dully.

"How is volunteering to take impressions misbehaving?"

Damian pinches the bridge of his nose. "Never mind."

"Hmm, I point it at him and still don't know." Cedrick sighs. He smiles at me. "How are you?"

"Fine. Glad to see you're feeling better after this morning," I say.

"I normally can sleep it off." Cedrick shrugs. He notices my mother looking at him. "What? I was fine for the show. No need," he says. She flushes and looks away. Odd. My mother is not shy.

Damian smiles a little. "Shall we join the others?"

"I don't know. They might be talking bad." I glance over at the group which is Dahlia, Ericka, Florence, and Forsythia. I doubt they are happy with me.

"Then we'll hope Gavril doesn't bring his new puppy, or she may learn some naughty words," Damian jokes.

"Like what? I don't teach naughty words," Cedrick defends himself.

"You're not the only one she learns from," Damian points out.

"What are you teaching that poor puppy?" Cedrick demands playfully. Damian rolls his eyes.

Not long after that, the royal family finally arrives with their normal introduction. My mother is a bit slower than the rest of us to stand and bow or curtsy, but that seems to be the only thing out of place. Gavril's red and green suit looks nice, and they tried hard to get his hair to look neat.

The king smiles, and as the royal family joins us, he calls out for the ball to begin, giving the players permission to start the opening song.

Damian suddenly comes up to me and leans to my ear. "Remember that surprise I mentioned?" I nod. He grins and puts something in my hands. "You'll need these."

I look down to see my red pointe shoes. "What?" I should have asked questions when they put me in tights.

"Well, I figured you didn't have a gift for your mother, and she didn't get to see you dance this year." He smiles.

"What am I doing?" I ask, a bit alarmed.

"One dance from *The Nutcracker Suite*. Unless you absolutely hate the idea." He meets my eye.

"No, I'm just surprised," I say. "So... what am I doing?" He had to have an idea.

"The Pas de deux." He smiles. "Cedrick volunteered to be your partner."

"Oh." This is going to be tricky. He's lucky I'd done it enough that I'm almost certain I have it memorized. *Surprise!* I have to perform it now, but... it is a bit of a challenge. One I want to win, so to speak. "Alright then." I look for a chair to change out my shoes. I am going to prove my skill beyond a doubt. We'd shine with no rehearsal. I try not to chicken out at the thought.

Damian pushes a chair up to me then nods at Flur and Vivian. They look nice in matching red and green dresses, though for each of them, the red and green is swapped. Vivian has red with green highlights, and Flur green with red highlights. They run over and use a pretty shining hairnet to make a nice little hairdo for me in a pinch that will keep my bottom layer of hair up.

Damian smiles and loosen the overlay and the snaps, so the top piece will come off easily. "Cedrick knows to take it off. Meanwhile, I have an announcement to make."

I nod. I hope they're not going to do anything too crazy. I'm just ready to move, so Cedrick can slip it off over my arms.

As the music hums, Damian steps out to the center of the ballroom. "Ladies and gentlemen, if I could have your attention, please!" he calls above the noise and chatter. The noise quiets down as everyone looks. I glance at the musicians. They knew this was coming.

Damian waits until the room is practically silent then smiles. "Thank you. I hope I am not being too forward, and I know this may seem a little irregular. But where I come from, we celebrate this holiday in a variety of ways. Some being to perform musical works like we had this morning. But I am truly grateful to be here, and to our wonderful hosts King Aster and Queen Dalilly." He smiles, gesturing to them. "They have worked dutifully to make every day here pleasurable and run smoothly. So, in a way of showing thanks, my team and I have prepared a special performance for this evening.

"So, with that in mind, I hope you all will relax and enjoy." Damian smiles to the crowd. "Dancing the 'Pas De Deux' from *The Nutcracker* Ballet, Lady Kascia Thorapple with Cedrick as her partner." He bows out and leaves the floor.

I find it a bit odd, Damian didn't use his last name, but it looks like everyone is happy to clear space and let us do the dance. Cedrick comes over to help me take the over dress off. Damian had unsnapped it, so all I have to do is hold my arms back, and in one smooth moment, Cedrick pulls it off, drapes it over his arm, then sets it across a chair.

I get to my spot, hoping Cedrick knows what he's doing. He seems to; he stands across from me as I do my part. I give him a weak smile. I have done this a million times or more but having not even done it once with Cedrick makes me a bit nervous. I lift up on pointe and start the dance.

Cedrick's a steady partner, holding and supporting me perfectly and making it easy for me to hold positions and turn with his support. I just worry about the lifts, though the version I know doesn't have too many. There is the one dip, but I know he can do that.

When we get to the first lift, I'm not too nervous, as in reality, it's more like he's supporting and guiding my jumps. It's the last fish lift I'm worried about.

But I shouldn't have worried. As I do the run up and leap, he catches me easily and twists me into position as if it were as easy as helping me turn. I can't help but beam as he pulls me back up, and we slide back and do the second lift which is easier as it's on his shoulder. Once that is done though, the hardest parts are over.

When we strike the final position, there's a lot of clapping. I think I hear the king whistle. Of course he did. Cedrick smiles and presents me like a proper performer should before I give reverence and then Cedrick does the same. "Thanks for not dropping me," I say so only Cedrick can hear.

"Damian wouldn't let me," Cedrick replies, giving me a last bow of thanks. Mother is beaming. I return it then give her a curtsy too. She chuckles at me.

Damian claps too, beaming at me then nodding thanks to his brother. Cedrick returns it and glances at someone, smirking a bit before blending into the crowd. I sigh as everyone starts to mingle.

"Well done, even without warning," Mother approves, kissing my cheek.

"Well, you made me do it a million times," I remind her.

"True. I liked the change effect. We'll have to use that." She smiles.

"Mom," I giggle.

Damian chuckles then holds my top piece open, so I can slip back into it. "My lady."

"Thank you." I let him slip it on me like a jacket.

"Of course." He smiles as Flur snaps the latchets closed, and Vivian fastens the overlay. Damian checks it then nods. "Like nothing ever happened." He smiles as they take the net out of my hair.

"Um, apart from the red pointes," I point out. Vivian pulls up the chair Cedrick had set the top layer on earlier.

Damian chuckles. "Of course. Flur has them, I believe."

She comes over with my ballroom shoes, smiling a little as she puts them down for me. I start working on my pointe shoes.

"I do believe I've outdone myself this time. Do you have any idea how difficult it was to make that top piece?" Damian says, looking it over. "Had it been off an inch, I would have had to rip it apart and redo the whole thing." He shakes his head. "Never doing that again."

I giggle. "So, we get a good template, but you won't make it."

"Maybe, if you ask really nicely." Damian smiles.

"I don't know if I'll need this again," I say.

"Make a nice wedding dress idea if you want to do a dance there," Mother hints.

"Mama," I sigh. She was never like this before I was chosen.

Damian chuckles. "Well, I'll let you ladies enjoy your evening. I better find that brother of mine before he causes trouble."

"What could he do?" Mother smiles.

"Many things. He gets bored easily," Damian sighs. "Until then, ladies." He bows then leaves.

"So, what do you want to do?" I turn to my mother.

"As horrible as this sounds, your father was so strict on treats, I'm quite ready to try out what's laid out on that table." She smiles.

"They'll bring out a nice dinner later." I smile.

"Then I'll make sure I have space. Go find the prince and get a few dances." Mother nudges me with a smile before going over to the table.

I chuckle. She's wrong though. I don't get to ask him. The rules haven't changed. But that doesn't mean I can't have a good time.

The dancing resumes. Gavril has asked Ericka to dance for some mad reason. I guess he has to court her too. As long as we're in the running, we're part of the dating game.

I walk around to find a different partner when to my surprise, the king taps on my shoulder.

"May I?" he asks pleasantly.

I smile and accept his offer. He's not the most brilliant partner I've ever had, but he's pretty good. "I realized with things being so far, we've not really spoken to most of you," the king says as he gives me a twirl.

"You're busy," I say as I tilt my head with the swing movement before he spins me out again. "No one is surprised or offended."

"One of you will be our new daughter. We should do more," the king argues.

"Well, you know me well after asking me about the last attack."

"Both of them." The king acknowledges the thing we can't say. "But it's still important to take the chance." I turn to a lower cape position. "And call it a stickler move of me, but we did promise if your family wouldn't let you home, you'd have a place here. So, I should learn to like you anyway."

I laugh. "I don't think that's a problem."

"Even if I have a smaller version of you to remind me." The king smiles.

"I'm glad you like your gift." I smile back.

"But with that aside, how are things? I see your mother was happy to come and stay through the holiday." The king glances at her over my shoulder as we get back into a closed position.

"Yes, it's been nice to have her. Thank you for that." I give the king another smile as we travel across the floor.

"Our pleasure as well," the king assures me. "I'm a bit surprised your father didn't come, though."

I swallow hard. "He's... not overly happy with me," I admit.

"Is he the real reason you're unsure you have a place at home?" he asks. I nod. "I understand. Well, if it comes to that, don't leave without speaking to the queen and me first," he says seriously. "We'll try to sort it out."

My heart drops. Could I ever tell them the full truth? Could I now? It wasn't a risk I could take. Without this... I have nothing. If I confess who my father is, most of all a disgraced Custod, I'll be locked up for sure or worse. I doubt the king would want to, but it's the law. He has to. I am able to hide my shudder of fear in another turn. "Are you sure you're alright?" I think the king noticed my shudder anyway.

I force a smile. "I just fear it coming to that." I can't run the risk. If it isn't safe, I could be dead or worse.

"I understand." The king smiles and kisses my cheek as the song ends. He must have picked a short one for his health's sake. "It's going to be alright. No matter where this goes."

I manage a watery smile. It makes me miss the days when I felt I could trust my father. I miss the man I thought I knew. I wish my father really was that man. "Thanks," I manage to squeak out. His care means more than I could ever dare tell him. I blink back tears.

The king smiles and actually gives me a hug. I try not to hold too tight or long, but it feels wonderful to have such a hug, like having my father back. "We're happy to play substitutes," the king reminds me. I laugh a little, taking a breath to make sure they don't turn into tears.

"Even if I don't win, I'd like that," I admit. Gavril or not, I want this man in my life who changed my world view by not being the monster I expected. And I could help more than just entertainment. If I work for them, perhaps I will not be tried for coming here as a spy, and I can tell them what I know. Maybe I can go home and pretend to have changed my mind. I might be a good spy. I have no idea. Though admittedly, having to put on more masks makes me feel sick. I try not to think of my nightmare.

"Good." The king kisses my hand. "But I have to make the rounds with the others."

"And make them all the same promises," I tease.

"Oh heavens, no. There are a few I'm still hoping will lose," the king openly admits. "I'll talk to you later." He leaves as I laugh.

I sigh and go over to the refreshment table and find some Christmas cake with the vanilla cream in the middle I like so much. I'm almost done when Gavril smiles and picks up a chocolate-filled tart with snowflake patterns on it. "Enjoying yourself?"

"Your father keeps me entertained," I reply. My heart pitter-patters in my chest hopefully. Was he about to make or break my hopes? Had I succeeded or would I have to come up with another idea? There is Celeste Day coming up in a few months. Perhaps I could use that.

"Was that hard to take off?" He looks over my dress.

"They took it off. Damian did have to kind of unlock it along the decorations here." I indicate to the Y.

"Hmm. That is weird," Gavril says, admiring the dress. Then he smiles. "But it was nice to see you dance. Only bummer of you not being in the performances with your troupe. I got to see it anyway." He smiles again. "I may not know how to do that stuff, but would you like a dance?"

"I have to finish first." I smile, taking the last bite of my cheat treat. Also stalling in case this is the moment I'll dread most.

Gavril beams. "I recall you said you like those."

"You went for a tart."

"My mood changes more." Gavril shrugs.

I sigh. "You can finish with the other girls if you'd rather." Stall, and perhaps if I'm last like before, I'll get more time.

"I don't want them mad at you if I steal you all night," he teases. "But if I strategically put other girls on the dance floor between our sessions we can still have most of the night."

"You are clearly showing a favorite. First the shows, now this," I point out.

Gavril sighs. "I know. I'm trying not to, but if I'm smart they won't notice."

"Do you even care?" I ask quietly.

Gavril takes a deep breath. "Yes and no," he says and swallows. "I..." He looks around. I realize he really wants to talk. It would be easier on the dance floor. There is hope. My heart beats faster. Do I dare put all my hopes in this? Could I find a back door? What would I do if it failed?

"Do you really want to talk about this?" I ask. I thought he said he wanted to pretend it didn't happen, but that might help me know if what he has to say is good or bad.

"I don't look forward to it, but you deserve it, yes," Gavril says. Great, his answer is as clear as mud.

I fiddle with the chocolate in my hand, thinking. "I don't want to force you." *And if it's bad, I don't want my heart broken today.*

A small smile crosses his face. "I'm not sure if avoiding it will help us. Can't exactly do that married, can we?"

The emotion that floods me makes it hard for me to know how to react, so I pop a chocolate into my mouth to distract myself. The idea he wants to treat us like we'll be real, that he still wants it, that he's thinking that way. My heart glows. Anxiety fills my stomach. My face flushes with heat.

"Would it help if I cover like I did before and take care of everyone else first?" he asks.

I think about it. "Perhaps," I admit. More time and an easy excuse to run to my room if I couldn't hide my heartbreak. I just pray I can hide it from Gavril at least. He'll feel so guilty no matter what if he saw it hurt me.

"Done," he says as if promising to cut off his hand if he fails me. My cheeks turn red. He makes it worse by kissing one of those red cheeks. "I'll see you soon." He squeezes my hand. "Merry Christmas," he says before he goes and does what I ask.

To my heartache, he goes to Forsythia first and bows, asking for a dance. She smirks smugly at the others before accepting.

"Did you just send him away?" Mother suddenly is next to me.

"No," I say. "He just asked me to wait while he handles the others."

"That's good," Mother beams.

"I hope."

"Oh," Mother gives me a look with a half-smile, "don't be that way. Come on, we can enjoy some treats and dances."

So that's what we do. After some treats, we do a few Christmas dances as we had in the rehearsal space when we decorated and closed up on Christmas Eve in the past. We enjoy this until dinner is announced, and we sit to eat.

It's a lovely turkey meal that is full of things I normally don't get to eat on a dancer's diet. I enjoy a bit of everything. The vegetables are perfect, the meat perfectly juicy. The potato mash is top notch. These are foods we rarely eat at any other time, just like the court dinner. But they do have some wonderful dumplings, a seafood mix with water chestnuts I love, and wonderful sauces that cleanse the palate between the courses. It is a nice change after the court dinner. I think we're all a bit overfull when the meal is done.

Though the music keeps playing for us to dance if we like, most of us just sit and talk for a while. My mother, most of all, looks ready for a nap.

She stays long enough to have some of the pies and tarts for dessert, but then she figures Father should at least have her Christmas night.

"I'll send Marlon with a message soon," Mother promises as I walk her to the door. "Even if it makes it take a bit longer. Just give him the letter back as soon as you can, so he'll get it to me. He knows to only give it to me."

"Treats work," I smile, trying not to be sad at the moment of parting. When would I ever see her again? It didn't help that I'm nervous for my talk with the prince.

Mother hugs me tightly. "It's going to be alright, no matter what. I love you so much." She pulls back and puts a hand to my cheek. "No matter what, you'll make a difference for good. I'll make sure you're kept safe. I'll keep trying with your father. He did come home swearing and upset that night, but he also was proud of you. He still loves you; don't forget."

I nod. "I'll try, Mama." I hug her once more. I didn't realize how hard it would be to say good-bye again. I fight the tears. "And if I win... will you come stay?"

Mother sighs. "We'll have to see, but I will certainly visit often," she promises. "Now have a merry rest of your Christmas, and keep writing and sending those impressions. Alright?"

I nod my promise. Mother kisses my cheek and gives me one last hug before she goes to pack up her things and go home. I sigh sadly and watch her go before going back into the ballroom.

Chapter 34

I do my best to dab away the tears without ruining my makeup or revealing I had cried at all. I bite my lip to stop it shaking and take a deep breath to fill the sad hole in my chest. I can distract myself.

I think the king notices I'm down because he asks me for another dance which he just makes as silly and fun as he can. I dance with a few others too. Several courtiers I recognize from the dinner ask for a dance, but none of them say anything truly interesting. Just more kind words and flattery. I take a break to enjoy a drink when the grand duke comes up to me. I notice Godwin's eyes lighting up as he notices, but he does not look pleased about it.

"You were splendid!" the grand duke declares with a large warm smile that, as always, doesn't quite meet his eyes. "You live up to your reputation and far beyond. They understated your skill."

"Thank you, but it wasn't me alone," I point out over my drink.

"Indeed." The grand duke's face darkens a little. "That Sir Cedrick does get into everything."

"Well, he does prove talented, and what would we expect of Damian's brother?" I smile as I take a drink.

The grand duke smiles at me as I do, as if admiring me. "That doesn't quite cover how invasive he can be."

"He got a part in one of the plays and did one dance with me." My smile is quite amused. How is he bothered by Damian's brother getting into the shows?

"Ah," the grand duke nods one slow large nod, "I see. You don't know how dangerous he is?"

"Dangerous?" I chuckle. He's a charming handful, but apart from maybe trying to get us kicked out if he ever actually tried to hit on us, he's not dangerous.

"He has little skill or place in the Covere where he works with the king with no background and surprising sway for a nobleman with no skill or graces of a lord of any sort. Military background no one knows about. Perhaps others know more and trust him, but I wouldn't be sure to fully

trust him, even if I knew his background. There is no experience that should give him the sway he has in the Covere or with the royal family."

"Sway? I think you're confused." I'm still smiling. Cedrick? Dangerous? The only danger I see in him is the kind a toddler poses. Sure, they get into trouble which could ruin parts of your home, but it's not like he's going to start assassinating people. "I know he likely has secrets and a darker side, but it's clear he's done his best to murder it."

"He's a stranger who has the same authority as a courtier who has been here his whole life." The grand duke frowns and raises his brows. "I'd be wary of him. He might come off a charming goof, but that is often an easy disguise for something far worse."

"You need to relax." I shake my head, still smiling over my drink. "You may know more of court life than I, Your Grace, but Cedrick is as dangerous as a kitten to any political aims. He wouldn't have the ability to hide his smile at the mischief he's up to."

"My lady," Godwin finally comes to my rescue, "Pardon the delay. Thank you for waiting." What a smooth lie I accept, putting down my empty glass and accepting Godwin's hand as if I'd been waiting for him to return for a dance the whole time.

"Merry Christmas, Lady Kascia," the grand duke wishes me before Godwin whisks me off.

"I told you to be careful of him," Godwin reminds me as we turn to a closed hold.

"I know, but I can't just shove him off either."

"I'll try to be faster next time."

"Gavril hold you up?"

"No, other matters; he was trying to hurry me up."

I laugh.

As Godwin escorts me back to my place, Gavril comes over to catch me. "Are you alright?" Is his first question. He must have seen the pain in my eyes when mother left.

I nod. "Just... hard to say goodbye again." Most of all when I know it might be forever.

"It's just your father who doesn't like how you're doing?" Gavril checks. I nod. "I see..." His eyes wander into emptiness for a moment. "Well, may I?" He bows, offering me his hand for a dance.

I take a deep breath and nod, taking his hand. This was it, and I'm excited, yet terrified. He smiles gently and guides me onto the dance floor, going into a basic and mostly keeps it simple which isn't normal for us. He loves to dance, and I do too, so he'll use all the unique steps we know. Not today. Just basic turns, twirls, and steps, so it is a second thought as we focus on words.

"I'm sorry it's been so long. It's been... complicated," he says, going a bit pink.

"I'm sure it has." As he's kissing other girls.

"After... what happened, I was unsure you were what I thought and hoped you were. I thought perhaps I'd do as you asked and give the others a real try," he goes on. "And though I really did and do want to give you a chance, I was afraid to."

"Afraid I'd be false?" Did he have to break my heart at Christmas? He's trying to tell me he's still unsure. I try to think of how to hide my severe disappointment.

"No, afraid I'd ruin something," he says. "I knew I was being stupid with how I felt about you, but I was sure I'd prove right. When I lost that surety, I tried to think logically. I hadn't done as you asked and tried around, so I tried to find someone, anyone who could compete with you.

"I always planned to give you the turn I promised, but I wasn't sure how to have a date where I kept my head. I felt getting close would make me lose all sense of intelligence as perhaps I have done in the past. I was fighting to find the best situation to do that in when..." He pauses. "When you all saw that."

I can't meet his eyes. "I understand. It's the game." I'm already desperately trying to think of a plan B.

"I really wish I could take it back. I never wanted you to see that. I didn't want anyone to see, but you most of all. I knew you would be hurt most after all that's happened. I couldn't even take in the truth when I heard. I wish I could make up for it or truly apologize to you. I would do anything to take that moment back."

"You enjoyed it. No harm in that," I say.

Gavril sighs in frustration. "Not that much," he says. I look up at him with a frown. "When I said I wish I could take back the last few weeks, I meant it in so many ways. I wish I could take back that day in the hall. I wish I could take back what I said in your room. I won't blame you if you don't believe me. I struggled to believe you when I wanted to."

"But I can't prove it," I say hopelessly.

He smiles gently and holds me as close as he can dare in the dance and with others watching, but thankfully, our rotation keeps our conversation private, so I doubt a soul can hear us. It leaves us free to talk, but we have to be careful in body language.

"I wish I didn't have to ask you to prove yourself. I wanted to believe; I did, but it was my own desire that made it so hard for me to believe." He smiles and again repeats what he'd said in my room, only softly singing the tune. "Was it safe to believe as I so badly wanted?" He finishes before pausing, coming even closer to me, his cheek almost pressing to my temple before he wisely backs away and pulls me into a twirl to cover up the movement.

Was there hope? I want to close my eyes as I take in the gentle pressure and warmth of him so close, but I can't dare. I just can't lose him now. How could I handle the darkness that would be my life?

"I've wanted to tell you the truth, yet not be foolish. I wasn't sure how. I couldn't talk openly at the shows or take the time last night. I only hoped... you felt the answers," he says.

Wait. He'd been wanting to say this to me for a while?

"Then..." He pauses as if trying to speak around his emotion. "I still can't believe you even thought of it, let alone had the courage to ask my father permission to give me a pet." My heart thunders in hope. "The one girl I know I'll get to keep through the Enthronement no matter what," he jokes, making me laugh. It's what I'd hoped for.

"It's the closest I could give to what you really wanted," I say. "Someone you could be open with and play with without the pressure and stress. Even if I know you want what you told them in the interview, it was the closest I could think of." I meet his eyes. *Did it work? Please, let it work.*

"If you really thought I was the way I feared you did, that gift idea would not occur to you. What prince who wants the finest is happy with such a simple, base animal? Huskies aren't known for their elegance or prestige. You wanted to give me something that would stay with me and care no matter what."

"I hope it works. She was quite attached to me. I pray she is just as close to you." But inside my heart is dancing in more joy than we are in our simple waltz. Perhaps it had worked, at least enough to take down the wall, so we could start building again. I'd done it. Oh please, let it have worked for good.

"And that's just it," Gavril says. "I'd already decided to trust you anyway, and... you proved it. I'm still in shock. I could hardly take it. She made sure I couldn't with her endless energy," he chuckles. "She is a joy."

"That's all I really wanted to give you," I say. I still don't face him out of nervousness. I'd proved it before? How? When? I succeeded but I didn't have to? I'm confused and now less certain.

I feel him tense, and I tense too, worried he's getting angry again. "And not one person really thought of that. Only you knew me well enough and had the courage to do something you knew may not be the best."

"I got permission."

"But you had the courage to ask," he replies. "I had decided to take it on faith you were what I thought. Then... when I was just unsure how to say it, you went and proved it with something so simple."

"Taking care of a puppy is not simple."

"That's not what I meant." Gavril gives me a look. "And you know it. I... Thank you. I still want you. You're still one of the girls I want to win most."

"Just not number one anymore." My heart sinks. I proved it, but I'd still lost his favorite spot. How would I get it back?

"Am I allowed a number one when favoritism makes you nervous?" he asks.

"I wasn't sure it was true. And you were just playing up to the press," I cover as I do an under-arm turn.

"Not when we slipped away," he points out.

I had noted that. It was something that was just us.

"And let's make sure all our interactions are private if you don't mind. I know the only incident we've had was my fault, but if you wouldn't mind not trying to rub it in the other girls' faces, I'd be thankful."

"So, you know Forsythia did it on purpose?"

"I don't know," he says carefully, "but the idea seems likely."

"Can you really not see through her?" I ask, annoyed.

"It's not that simple. And as much as I'd love to discuss those problems with you, with how the girls are acting, you included, I think perhaps it's best we don't discuss such things."

I groan. That just means he does not want to believe it.

"Kascia, please, I really don't want this to be about that." He frowns. "I know you all are competing, and that brings out the worst in some people, and though I don't believe that's a good trait for our future queen, it's not a test, and I can't use that to throw her out."

"You could let me free whenever you wanted," I remind him.

"Yes, but only if you want it. I have limited eliminations, and I want to use them only if I'm sure I have to," he says. "I wish I could explain why, but that's privileged information."

"And I'm not privileged anymore." Did that mean he had to use one soon? If he doesn't want to discuss it, that seems likely. It was more important than ever to stay in his favor.

"No, for that information, you never have been. None of you girls are." He frowns. "I really was trying to make this a good apology and then enjoy the Christmas magic. Am I that bad at it?"

I chuckle. I forgot how inexperienced he is. But he finds ways to remind us in cute ways.

"Just know that is something I've not told anyone: Forsythia, Zelda, Bella, Florence, anyone." Did I just get a glimpse at the other girls he's interested in? Are they ahead of me, equal, or just behind me? I know two of those are girls he likes. Zelda and Bella pretty much said so. "But if you win, I'll explain all of it. I promise," he goes on. "I really do still want you.

I gave you another chance, even if it took a while with how many I have to get through. Can I not have that in return, or do you..."

"Please don't ask if I want to go home," I beg. Did he not see how much I want this now?

"You could just go with your mother, but no, I wasn't. I stopped myself because when you seem to not want me, I want to free you. But I understand it only hurts you."

"Thank you," I say quietly.

"You're welcome," he replies as if I were thanking him for a pair of slippers. "So can I not get one more try?"

"I wasn't the one who put down the ultimatum," I remind him.

He sighs, shutting his eyes for a moment as some tension leaves him. "Then we'll just forget that conversation ever happened?"

"I'll try to." I nod as the dance called for us to move closer together. It was bliss, yet frightening. I want it, but I forgot one thing. What would I do to him if I lose after fighting for him?

"Then I'll do right and prove it to you." He kisses my forehead. I close my eyes in joy at the brief touch.

"Will you at least admit who else you're looking at?" I ask.

"All of them," Gavril says with an apology in his face.

"You know what I mean."

"I can't. Honestly, I'm still not sure," he confesses. "I suppose that stupid board can tell you."

"It's all about Nippers now."

"Maybe we should change it to Joy. Then it will kind of show you how the running is going," he suggests.

"I think Nippers would change it back," I point out. Of course it wasn't actually Nippers. The board is little more than a running gag. I don't even know who's been filling it out.

Gavril nods. "Half and half?"

"With less girls, there is more space," I agree. Maybe I can get my answer in a more roundabout way. "When are we going to see more of that? We've had the holiday off. Does it just start again?"

"Well, as you ask," Gavril says, "the next test is a big one. I am alright to tell you that because they will give you warning. They'll wait until after the rest days, I presume." That's in three days. Three days until I know what's coming.

"Are there girls you hope leave like there are girls you like better?" I ask, staring at a spot on his jacket.

Gavril sighs. "Yes, I have opinions on both ends, but none I can talk to you about."

"Or anyone else?" I wonder.

"Once I thought Sage, but he's increasingly biased these days," Gavril says. "So no, not really."

"Tell Joy. She then can give you girl advice," I tease.

"If I can understand her," Gavril says with a smile. I think he's glad we're moving into more casual conversation. "Sometimes I can understand her perfectly, and other times, it's just puppy noises. I hope she's adjusting alright. She went right to sleep before I got ready and came down here."

"She'll sleep a lot. Puppies are growing. She grew visibly in just the week she was in my room," I say. "And some since I picked her out."

"You made a good choice. Sage will get over being 'weirdo'." Gavril grins. "I love it."

"We tried to get her to say Sage. It did not work." I smile.

"I don't plan on changing it." He smiles at me. "Thank you. You have no idea how much that gift means to me. No matter what they force me to do with you or the others, I'll have something of yours forever. Her happy attitude will always make me think of you." I turn red again for a different reason this time. It worked but not how I intended. Things are getting even more complicated and interesting. I have his trust again, but if I've got a good hold on him remains to be seen. I could get it back without playing by Forsythia's rules?

Gavril has me do another turn to the music when his eyes light up to something over my head. "There it is," he says.

"What?" I turn to see he's looking out the window. I gasp. "Is that snow?"

"Let's see." Gavril takes my hand and goes to the door then pushes it open. I feel the cold breeze and shiver a little. Gavril takes off his jacket for me as he goes out to see. I step out once I put his jacket on and see he's right. It's starting to stick to the railings and the balcony floor.

Without warning, he pulls me further out onto the balcony, making me laugh. The snow is falling so rapidly it's already sticking to my hair and eyelashes. The storm I'd seen hit will full speed.

"What a great way to enjoy the end of the holiday." He pulls me into a closed hold for a waltz step around the balcony, making me laugh as we go.

Soon, we're both covered in the snow, sticking to his jacket, parts of my skirt, his hair and shoulders. He twirls me, and I feel and see snow fly off me. I laugh again. It's magical.

Soon we're pushing through the snow in each of our steps. We're already wet and will get so much wetter.

Once it's too thick, Gavril stops, wrapping his arms around me from behind as we watch the snow fall into the ocean.

I can see Gavril's breath as it floats into the air as he stands behind me. I can even see it go down as he breathes it out before it goes up. I look up at the falling snow, mimicking the stars that are hiding behind the clouds. It is a different kind of pretty. I smile and try to catch a flake on my tongue. If I wasn't sure of the words he'd said, this close moment gave me hope he means it.

"Snow is one of the few things my parents would let me outside to see," Gavril says. "As it only lasts a few weeks. Because of it, as a kid I thought outside was always super cold and wondered why guards wanted to take their jackets off in the summer. Silly, isn't it?"

"Make sense if you don't know," I say.

"Yeah." Gavril sighs. Then he laughs. "I wonder what Joy would make of snow."

"You can show her when she wakes up. You'll have to tell me all about it," I say.

"Or maybe I can show you later." His voice is low, his breath warm on my neck.

I close my eyes and take a breath I perhaps shouldn't have. I feel Gavril pleasantly tense. He lets go only enough to turn me around and meet my eyes.

My breath hitches, and my heart races. We hadn't felt this much electricity between us since he came into my room after he'd kissed Forsythia in front of us all. I don't dare look up at him. I study the detailed yet rough patterns on his waistcoat.

"You're stunning tonight." Gavril's voice is gentle and low. "Far more than even this stunning snowfall. When I think I've seen the extent of how beautiful, you surprise me with more. Just like a star. And you fit so perfectly." He smiles as he looks down at me, his warm arms secure pleasantly around me. "Always have, even when I doubt it."

He pauses and gently puts a knuckle under my chin to guide my eyes to his. "Even when you doubt it," he says quietly.

The tone of his voice and rush of emotion tells me what he's about to do before he does it. I close my eyes and relax to accept his warm, enchanted kiss as it sends warmth through me no snowfall around us or piercing wind could cool. And it only grows warmer as I feel his warm lips and skin on my face, his gentle hand warming my neck as he cradles me close as he holds this magical kiss.

We are locked in this warm cocoon we created together, holding that kiss and the joy and magic of the day in this crystalized moment in time. If I had more moments like this, I know I could survive whatever they threw at us. If only I knew this lasted. In all the insanity, uncertainty, and uncovered lies, I'd almost forgotten how this man and his sweet, gentle passion for me, his people, and the world around him change my mind about the core of my being. I needed this reminder. I needed this small bubble of joy to remind me why. And it is going to be worth it.

The words I don't dare speak almost float to my lips as they part from his, but I can't dare say them. If it got taken away, it would scar us both, but I feel them, and I believe he does too.

He leans in and kisses me again, cradling me, protecting me as I dip back ever so slightly to enjoy his cradling hold. We've had a lot of missteps and falls on this odd road of romance we're on, but at least this Christmas, we are one step closer to making this work. I was going to do all it took to be his starlight princess. And I'd gotten the best gift I could get for Christmas. Hope.

Can Kascia win the Enthronement now she's ready to try?
Find out:
Read book 3

And if you enjoyed the book, help others find the book and join the community:

And if you haven't yet, join our community for exclusive content, updates, and more!

Character Guide

The Chosen Candidates (In Chosen Order)

1. **Princess Rose:** High-Princess heir to the high throne of Emilimoh.

2. **Princess Amapola:** Princess of Spearim, elegant, fiery, and passionate.

3. **Princess Laurina**: Princess of Bruag, she loves her dragon, exploring, and is the boldest of the born princesses.

4. **Princess Zelda:** Crown Princess of Hyvil, curious, inquisitive, and will take any excuse to use her Magus tablet.

5. **Bella:** A dreamer, high in the ranks but friendly with the other girls, most of all Azalea.

6. **Dahlia:** The most competitive of the girls. She's used to winning her matches.

7. **Jonquil:** Is one of the friendliest girls, yet judgmental of the others.

8. **Lilly:** Is the youngest Chosen. She's very shy and sensitive.

9. **Kascia:** Came here out of loyalty to her family but would rather be anywhere else.

10. **Azalea:** Tries to look after the other girls like she looks after her younger siblings at home.

11. **Ericka:** Is sure she's already princess and should be treated as such.

12. **Forsythia:** Is clever, and happily aligns herself with Dahlia and Forsythia in a click nicknamed "the elite".

13. **Isla:** Is a woman of faith. She's shy and quiet with the other girls, often studying cannon.

14. **Kamala:** Is proud of her island home and sure she'll do them proud as princess.

15. **Marigold**: Loud and confidant, loves teasing her friends Kamala and Hawi.

16. **Nichol:** quiet and mysterious though she's always asking everyone else questions.

17. **Hawi:** She spends all her time with Marigold and Kamala and enjoys intimidating the others.

18. **Lark:** As her name implies, she loves music. She also loves the conservatory.

19. **Elice:** Strong and wants the power but not the rules of being princess.

20. **Florence:** Elegant as a princess and as a lawyer, the best versed in law.

The Royal Family & Staff

- **King Aster**: Is friendly and likes a good joke, but his borderline humor makes some girls nervous.

- **Queen Dalilly**: The elegant queen who plays her role faithfully. Is an anxious personality.
- **Prince Gavril**: Only son of King Aster and Queen Dalilly. He's ready to prove himself worthy of the power to help his people but his blind, over-protective parents still refuse to see it.
- **Sage**: The prince's Custod guard. Here on a six-month assignment that was up a long time ago. There are rumors about why he stays, but no one knows for sure but him and the prince.
- **Hydie**: The castle's head of staff
- **Vivian**: Kascia's head maid who keeps everything orderly. She hates the rebels for their hypocritical methods.
- **Flur**: Kascia's second maid who is rather shy. She married Kerrigan, a castle guard.
- **Ro**: Kascia's third maid who always is ready with a questionable joke. She hasn't been heard from or seen since the rebels took her during a raid.
- **Godwin**: The prince's faithful and playful valet.
- **Reinold:** The prince's new court liaison. He's Godwin's twin brother.
- **Maryum:** The queen's faithful lady-in-waiting.
- **Porteous:** The king's loyal valet.
- **Lila**: Kascia's head of security. She's a Custod.
- **Keva:** The royal etiquette teacher
- **Gentian:** Sage's father who comes to provide back up of his own volition.
- **Hydrengia:** The royal political science, economics, and history teacher
- **Grand Duke Aldgrone:** The grand duke of Purerah. Heir sec-

ond to the royal family's line of succession

Other:

- **Joy:** Prince Gavril's red husky puppy given to him by Kascia for Christmas.
- **Peodrick**: Kascia's loving father who pushes her to fulfill her Custod duty
- **Chryasinth (Chrisa)**: Kascia's loving mother who runs the theater and helps her daughter make her own choice.
- **Jake/Jacek**: Kascia's fiancé in a marriage arranged when she was young.
- **Alsmeria**: Kascia's best friend and first soloist at the theater.
- **Jashon**: The cobbler who makes Kascia's pointe shoes and a friend of Kascia's.
- **Yarrow**: Kascia's first attendant who wants to lead the cutting-edge fashion world.
- **Damian**: Kascia's new attendant with an unknown past. His skill with magic is greater than anyone expected.
- **Adam**: The impressionist the royal family trusts most.
- **Omran**: The leader of the Loyalist rebellion. He's Jake's father.
- **Nippers**: The black castle cat.

- **Marlon**: Omran's falcon that has a soft spot for Kascia.
- **Fabian**: The lead reporter for the Purerah Chronicle
- **Cuppy**: Ericka's little curly haired dog
- **Duchess Clarisse:** Head of the Purysian delegation, wife of Duke Cedree
- **Duke Cedree:** Head of the Purysian delegation, husband to Duchess Clarisse.
- **Marquise Loretta:** One of the delegates from the Alalusian delegation.
- **Grand Duchess Kira:** The head of the Japcharian delegation.
- **Princess Tsikyria:** Crown princess of Japcharia hiding some dangerous secrets.

The Rebellions:

- **Loyalists:** The oldest rebellion. The seek to put a common man of Purerah on the throne.
- **Potentates:** Almost as old as the Loyalists rebellion. They want a properly endowed Potentate to take the throne, but not the direct Purerahian royal line.
- **Custod:** The Custod rebellion seeks to have a Custod turn Potentate to rule

About the Author

Lives near Mt. Shasta in Northing California and loves the nature there (though she'd like some more snow and rain). She wrote her first 700+ book when she was eleven-year-old and published her first book when she was twenty-one.

When she's not reading and writing, she enjoys making and watching YouTube videos, gaming, hiking, swimming, and sitting outside while working on projects.

Sign Up for her newsletters for updates and exclusive content:

Sign Up

And see sneak peeks, enjoy some memes, and more on her social media platforms.:

Instagram@charitymaeauthor

YouTube@mistressoflore

Facebook@charitymaeauthor

Pinterest@charitymaeauthor

Website:charity-mae.com

Other Books by Charity Mae

See full List Here:

Complete Works of Charity Mae
Or scan the QR Code:

www.ingramcontent.com/pod-product-compliance
Lightning Source LLC
Chambersburg PA
CBHW030540310726
48979CB00010B/1974/J

* 9 7 8 1 9 5 8 7 9 7 1 8 1 *